THE DIABLO'S CURSE

THE DIABLO'S CURSE

GABE COLE NOVOA

RANDOM HOUSE · NEW YORK

Text copyright © 2024 by Gabe Cole Novoa
Jacket art copyright © 2024 by Hillary D. Wilson

All rights reserved. Published in the United States by Random House Children's Books, a division of Penguin Random House LLC, New York.

Random House and the colophon are registered trademarks of Penguin Random House LLC.

Visit us on the Web! GetUnderlined.com

Educators and librarians, for a variety of teaching tools, visit us at RHTeachersLibrarians.com

Library of Congress Cataloging-in-Publication Data
Name: Novoa, Gabe Cole, author.
Title: The diablo's curse / Gabe Cole Novoa.
Description: First edition. | New York: Random House, 2024. | Audience: Ages 12 and up. | Summary: Dami, a nonbinary former demonio, must cancel every deal they have ever made in order to tether their soul to earth and remain human, but first they must help a boy named Silas find Captain Kidd's treasure and break a family curse.
Identifiers: LCCN 2022061075 (print) | LCCN 2022061076 (ebook) | ISBN 978-0-593-37805-2 (hardcover) | ISBN 978-0-593-37807-6 (ebook)
Subjects: CYAC: Demonology—Fiction. | Blessing and cursing—Fiction. | Gender identity—Fiction. | Fantasy. | LCGFT: Fantasy fiction. | Novels.
Classification: LCC PZ7.1.N687 Di 2024 (print) | LCC PZ7.1.N687 (ebook) | DDC [Fic]—dc23

The text of this book is set in 11.5-point Adobe Jenson Pro.
Interior design by Michelle Crowe
Smoke cloud: elephotos/stock.adobe.com
Paper texture: siam4510/stock.adobe.com
Skull and crossbones: barks/stock.adobe.com

Printed in the United States of America
10 9 8 7 6 5 4 3 2 1
First Edition

Reader,
society tells so many of us we'll never get our happy ending.
Don't listen.

Prologue

······················

Once upon a time, a beautiful woman with hair like spilled ink entered her local taberna and sat next to el Diablo.

"I was told you grant wishes," the woman said.

El Diablo laughed into the muted din of conversation around them. The sound was cold, haunting, but the woman didn't flinch. She lifted her chin and held his gaze, her dark eyes meeting a stare like burning embers.

"That's a generous interpretation." El Diablo smirked. "What wish do you want me to grant?"

The woman didn't hesitate. "Love. Every man I have ever loved has left or died. I want a love that lasts for the rest of my life."

"How trite," el Diablo responded, but though his tone was bored, his gaze was anything but.

He looks at me like a wolf gazing at his next meal, the woman thought. It should have scared her, but it didn't. The gaze was all too familiar—how impossible it was to move through a man's world as a woman without encountering that hunger.

"Can you do it?" she asked, and her voice did not tremble.

"That's not the question." El Diablo leaned his back against the mosaic bar top, shifting coins jingling in his pockets. His long coat rippled even after he stilled, as if lifted by a nonexistent breeze.

The woman nodded. The same people who'd told her about the strange man who regularly appeared at the local taberna had also warned her away from him. *He'll take more than you can give*, they'd said. *Whatever he promises you, it's never worth the price.*

But for her it was the opposite: though some could endure it—relish it, even—the price of a loveless life was too high for her to bear.

"You want to know what I will give you," she said. "What would you ask for such a gift?"

El Diablo watched her in silence, appraising her with those chilling eyes. Smoke curled around the edges of his sleeves. The hum of conversation around them fell away. For a moment, it was as if el Diablo and the woman were the only two people in the taberna—the only two people in the world. The air became warm and honeyed; her breaths slowed.

Curious, whispered a voice in her ear, but el Diablo's lips didn't move.

"You ask for lifelong love," el Diablo said.

The woman nodded. "Love that lasts my natural life span."

El Diablo smiled. "You're worried I'll cut your life short if I grant you this request. I won't." He stood, towering over her small frame. "I will grant you this request. And in return, your firstborn child will be mine."

The woman blinked and covered her mouth. El Diablo smiled—and behind her hand, so did the woman. For most, such a request would be grotesque, unthinkable. But the woman had become pregnant many times— and had never brought the baby to term. The midwives had made it clear she couldn't bear a child. That reality had destroyed her first marriage, and very nearly ruined her.

Now this. She'd never imagined that her body's limitation would grant her such a gift: a wish without a price.

"Those are my terms," el Diablo said, evidently mistaking her silent stare for horror.

"It's a high price," the woman said softly.

"You ask for no simple trinket," el Diablo responded.

Slowly, she lowered her hand, her smile hidden away behind her eyes. "And if I never have children?"

The sneer that slicked over his face was poisonous. The malice of it sent a chill down her spine, but she wasn't afraid. She didn't fear twisted men and hollow threats. "Then I suppose you'll have nothing to worry about," he said. "But once a deal is made, I can't change the terms."

"I understand." She suppressed the excitement bubbling in her chest. It seemed impossible, swindling a diablo like this. She could hardly believe her fortune. But it was real. El Diablo asked only for what she would never have. By the time he realized he'd never get his end of the deal, it would be far too late.

....

3

She didn't know that her mind was an open book, with el Diablo the reader paging through her life as easily as breathing. The devil liked what he saw, and he never forgot a promise.

So the woman squared her shoulders. She allowed a warble into her voice, for effect, and said, "I accept."

El Diablo tipped his head, and when he looked up at her again, his eyes flared with a red-hot glow—a fire with fresh kindling. "So be it."

Once upon a time, a beautiful woman who couldn't bear children promised her firstborn to el Diablo in exchange for lifelong love.

Two months after her ill-fated agreement, the woman met a beautiful man and they fell for each other like a roaring river over a cliff. When she told him of her inability to bear heirs, he promised they could adopt a child if they want to start a family, and she was delighted because an adopted child would not be her firstborn. They wouldn't be born of her at all.

She was never supposed to fall pregnant.

"Es imposible," she said as her bleeding ceased.

"Es imposible," she said as summer turned to fall and her stomach grew.

"¡Es imposible!" she cried when her water broke and her labor began.

She was never supposed to carry the baby to term. But as she held the midwife's hand and birthed what never should have been, as she held the impossible child to her chest, she couldn't stop the sob that ripped through her. Because her child was beautiful, perfect in every way, and she understood then what she had given up.

She was holding a lifelong love in her arms, but she had given them away long before they'd drawn their first breath. This perfect child was hers, but they weren't.

So, after the midwife left the room to fetch the woman's husband, she wasn't surprised when the room darkened. She stared at her beautiful baby, memorizing their thick black hair, their tiny nose, their ten delicate fingers. She didn't look away, not even as the jingle of coins and heavy footsteps announced his presence, not even as el Diablo peered over her at the child and smiled.

The woman ran her finger down the baby's perfectly smooth cheek. Her voice broke when she said, "What will you do with my baby?"

"Every diablo needs demonios," el Diablo said. "I'll raise this one to be my most proficient apprentice yet."

"My husband—"

"Will believe it didn't survive childbirth. As will the midwife."

She trembled with the force of nine months of denial. Day upon day of refusing to see the impossible, refusing to believe there was a child at all. But now there was nothing to deny. Now was the time to say goodbye.

"I can't," she whispered.

"You must," el Diablo answered.

And though it broke her heart, she did.

Chapter 1

·················

JANUARY 13, 1821

T he best part of being human, Dami decides, is feeling alive.

Dami feels alive every time they eat a delicious meal, like a plateful of freshly fried maduros (their first meal as a human). They feel alive every time they kiss someone attractive, like when they kissed a boy and a girl in the same night (their first night as a human). And right now, a little over four months later, sitting in the Green Dragon Tavern with a bad poker hand, losing a rich white boy's money, Dami feels well and truly alive.

Life, Dami thinks with a smile, is dangerous.

The rich boy's name is Charles Edward Talbot III. He's seventeen, so the same age Dami has estimated for themself. Charles Edward Talbot III sounds like an ass, not that Dami would know, as they've never met him. They just observed him from afar for a day so they could copy his face, walk, mannerisms, and speech well enough to pretend to be him. It's easy, pretending to be someone else. Especially when that someone has access to a lot of money.

The real Charles Edward Talbot III is now at boarding

·········

school rubbing elbows with other white boys who were fortunate enough to be born rich. The Charles who Dami is pretending to be returned home early due to illness and will take a few weeks to recover. No one questions this because, of course, Charles is moneyed and you can do whatever you want when you're rich enough. Even Charles's father, who lives somewhere in the massive estate the Talbots call home, barely looked up from his newspaper when "Charles" announced their return.

(It's a bit rude, actually, that man's complete and utter disregard for his son. But it serves Dami well.)

The Green Dragon Tavern is full of people, as it always is. The endless music of conversation, of tinkling glasses and pouring ale, of uproarious laughter and shouts like cymbals and the guiro-like scrape of wooden chairs on squeaky floorboards—it's a symphony to Dami's ears. Even the nearby fireplace crackles in a percussive undertone. Being a part of the clamor of reality is all Dami ever wanted.

And now they have it. And they're losing this poker game. Badly.

Dami's already burned through Charles's weekly allowance, so they'll probably have to sell more of his stuff soon. Or . . .

"What if I throw in my waistcoat?" they ask the table. It's a nice waistcoat. Powder blue with silver-threaded flowers and opalescent buttons. It brings out Charles's pale eyes. One of the Talbots' staff members must know it, because Dami took it from the very front of his closet.

"You really want to walk out of here naked?" asks Saul, a bearded older man seated across from Dami. Dami has played poker with Saul nearly every night this week. Dami hasn't won once, but they think they're starting to get the hang of the game.

They haven't gotten the hang of *winning*, mind you, but that hardly matters when you're losing other people's money.

"I could think of worse things," Dami says.

"It's *snowing*," Saul reminds them with a laugh.

He has a point there.

"I do like that waistcoat," says a greasy blond boy not much older than Dami—or Charles, for that matter. The boy has mentioned his name at least six times tonight, but Dami is determined not to know it.

"I'd look good in that waistcoat," Greasy adds thoughtfully, staring at Dami's clothes with a wolfish gaze.

"Right." Dami lowers their cards. "Well, in that case, I fold."

Greasy scowls as Saul guffaws and others around the table chuckle or hide smirks behind their hands. Dami winks at the oily trust-fund boy and waltzes over to the bar top, weaving around tables pushed together and dodging drunken hand gestures.

Leaning against the bar, Dami finds the bartender. He's a young man with muscled arms and a pleasant face. *Oh, hello.* "Hot ale, please." Dami flashes their signature winning smile.

"Of course, Mr. Talbot." He slides a basket of freshly baked buns and a plate of butter over. "For your wait."

"Don't mind if I do." They wink at the bartender, who offers a hesitant smile before turning back to the liquors.

Dami slices a bun open with the provided butter knife, mouth already watering as the warm scent hits them. The bun is fluffy and soft, exactly how Dami has learned they like them best. After meticulously buttering each steaming half, Dami closes their eyes and breathes in the warm, salty scent. Like the first rays of morning light to kiss your skin.

When Dami was a demonio, they never realized how *good* food smells—even the simplest of meals. It was an aspect of living they'd never really thought about; after all, if you've never experienced smell, there isn't much to wonder about.

Life without touch, without taste, without smell was empty. Now that Dami has experienced them all, they're never returning to that hollow existence. Not even the King of Hell could drag them back to their former half life.

The first bite of bread is so airy and warm—with just a hint of sweetness—that Dami nearly groans. The second is a little drier, but when that melted butter hits their tongue, it's euphoria. The third bite drier still—almost stale. That doesn't make sense; these rolls just came out of the oven.

The fourth bite collapses, filling their mouth with a dry powder that sits like chalk on their tongue. Or sawdust. Or—

Dami gags and spits into their hand. Again. And again. But their mouth is a desert, and all they can taste is—

"Here you are," the bartender says, placing a steaming pint in front of them.

Dami grabs it and takes a huge swig. But the moment the hot liquid hits their tongue, it turns to powder—this time so much their mouth feels stuffed with it.

The bartender and Dami lock eyes. It takes every ounce of Dami's self-control to keep the powder sitting in their mouth without choking on it or retching all over the bar. Instead, Dami breathes through their nose, heart pounding, as they lower the pint back to the bar top. The liquid sloshes in the glass, mocking them.

"Are you all right?" the bartender asks with a frown. Except he isn't the handsome young man Dami was admiring just moments earlier—his face has transformed into something older, something crueler. A trim black beard accentuates his defined jaw, and as his gaze meets Dami's, his eyes glow like burning coals.

Dami gets up so quickly they knock the stool over and trip over it. They catch themself on a nearby table and beeline for the door. The pounding of their pulse drowns out the tavern's song. Their mouth tastes like death. The powder is so close to the back of their throat.

It can't be him. Something is wrong. He's dead—

"Charles!" The greasy boy from the poker game is the last human on earth Dami wants to see right now, so naturally he's the one who steps right in front of the exit, just feet away. "Do you have a moment? I was thinking—"

Dami shoves past him, slams through the front door, races around to the alleyway on the side of the building, and bends over, gagging as powder pours from their lips. They spit and cough, eyes watering as they scrape their tongue with their shirt-sleeve. It's barely enough; their mouth is pasty. But every time they spit, they clear a little more.

Catching their breath, spitting, shuddering, Dami crouches over the snowy brick, pressing their palms against their closed eyes.

El Diablo is dead, they remind themself, like they have nearly every night since they betrayed him.

"El Diablo is dead," they whisper, like they have in Charles's dark bedroom after waking from dreams full of their former keeper's laughter.

But if he's dead, why do they keep seeing him everywhere?

Slowly, Dami wipes the wet from their eyes as they take a steadying breath. The stuff from their mouth is now piled between their shoes. Painted in night, the powder is gray and fine, with a tinge of yellow. Almost like . . .

Dami runs their fingers through the pile—then yanks their hand back. The pounding in their ears crescendos in a tidal wave. They know exactly what it is, and as reality crashes into them with all the force of a hurricane, Dami can't breathe.

Piled on the ground, undeniably, are ashes.

Chapter 2

· · · · · · · · · · · · · · · · · ·

There are two sets of doors at the entrance to the Boston Athenaeum library: on the outside, intricately carved and wooden; on the inside, studded red leather. Dami supposes the former protect the latter from the elements, and they can't help but appreciate the ostentation.

Naturally, in the middle of the night, all the doors are very much closed. But this would only be a problem if Dami were there to see the books, or the statues, or even the impressive building itself. They have more pressing matters at hand.

Matters like their mouth still tasting of ash.

Dami waltzes up the two smooth steps, their boots crunching on fresh snow, and stops directly in front of the threshold. They clear their throat and say in an unwavering voice, "Juno."

For a moment nothing happens. The night is quiet and still. A cold breeze blows, carrying the faint scent of salt and winter. Dami shivers. But they stand firm, waiting until—

"*Enter.*" The voice is barely a whisper, easily mistaken for the wind. But this isn't Dami's first visit to the Diablo of Knowledge. They step forward, not even flinching as the wooden, then leather, doors ripple around them like the sea—and Dami walks *through*.

The Boston Athenaeum is intimidatingly beautiful during the day—an enormous building full of vaulted ceilings, statues, and multilevel bookshelves—so it's not really a surprise that at night it takes on the eeriness of a crypt. Each of Dami's footsteps echoes on the polished brown marble floors, breaking the hush of emptiness with an unsettling staccato.

Because, of course, no one is here. Except her.

Of course, she could be anywhere in the enormous building. It would take Dami hours to check every room and comb through the shelves, so they don't. Instead, they take a left into the reading room, their footsteps muting as they step onto the large plush rug and settle in a comfortable chair in the middle of the room, positioned across from a matching chaise. They lean back, sighing into the soft fabric, then cross their legs at the ankles and drum their fingers on the chair's arm.

They don't have to say anything. Juno knows they're here.

"Well, well. The prodigal child returns."

A tall woman with olive skin settles in the seat across from them, her silky black hair swaying down to her hips, matching the movement of her equally black dress. She peers at them with unfathomably dark eyes over spectacles she surely doesn't need, but they suit her. Silver moonlight spills in from a nearby window, washing over her and giving her the quality of a beautifully rendered statue.

"Miss me?" Dami asks.

"More like already missing the peace and quiet."

Dami tries to laugh, but it's . . . hollow. Juno's eyes narrow; they've known each other too long for her not to notice Dami's malaise. Juno was the one who explained to Dami what being a demonio meant. She taught them what they needed to survive.

What they needed to escape.

Of course, she didn't do so for free. Juno was a diablo, after all. She didn't do charity.

"I need information," Dami says. "And I have some to trade in return."

She looks at them over the frames of her glasses. "And is what you need equal in value to what you're willing to trade?"

"If it isn't, I'm sure you'll let me know."

She smirks. "Let's start with what you want."

Dami grimaces. If they start with their request, she'll get to name her price. And Dami has a sneaking suspicion her price is going to be far more expensive than, say, a juicy piece of gossip.

But what choice do they have? Bread and booze turned to ash in their mouth. It was far too reminiscent of— They can't even think it. Don't even want to entertain the idea. And yet, when it comes to unraveling magic, ignorance isn't bliss.

"Something's happening," they say at last. "With me."

"I hope I don't have to explain puberty."

"This is serious." Dami runs their hand through their hair—startling at the short curls. They'd forgotten they still looked like Charles. Dami closes their eyes, focusing on returning to themselves. With a sigh, their shoulders relax, hair turning black and long, chest reshaping as their silk shirt and breeches become a black dress that flows like water studded with shimmering silver—like the night sky. The dress sleeves stop at their elbows, showing off the smokelike tattoos spanning from elbows to wrists. When they speak again, their voice is softer. "I need your help. He's dead, but el Diablo's been

....

haunting me for months. Food turned to ash in my mouth. I don't know what's happening."

Juno regards them for a long, alarmingly silent moment. "I think you do."

Dami frowns. "What do you mean?"

"Let me ask you something, Dami. How many humans do you know who can change their appearance at will?"

Their blood goes cold. The answer to this is obvious: none, as far as they know, including people they've met whose sense of gender is as fluid as Dami's—but they've brushed off this reality as a stroke of luck. A token, for losing years of their life to being a demonio.

"I just thought . . ." Even trying to say it aloud now feels foolish. They thought what? That el Diablo would do something nice for them? That the universe would look upon them favorably? Were they really that naïve?

Not naïve, they think, *just in denial.*

Dami tries to speak again, their voice fading with every word. "Are you saying I'm not . . . actually . . . human?" They finish on a near whisper. Just saying it aloud restarts the panicked gallop of their heart, heat attacking their chest.

But if they aren't human, what are they? "I'm *not* still a demonio," Dami says, strength returning to their voice. "Everything is so different now. I can *taste* and *smell* and *feel*. I can be corporeal during the day. I would know if I were still a demonio, and I'm *not*."

Juno nods. "You're not a demonio, not entirely." She pauses. "Not yet."

They can barely breathe. "Not yet?" they croak. "You can't mean . . ."

"You can't taste anymore, can you?" she says softly.

The ash.

No. No, no, no. It can't be. It *can't* be. Anything else—they can't go back.

They won't survive it.

"That's not . . . possible," they croak out. "I had a deal. El Diablo . . ."

Juno arches an eyebrow, locking eyes with Dami. She doesn't have to say it, not really. Dami spent the entirety of their existence around el Diablo. They know all too well how he worked, how he was never—not once—up-front about what the full terms of his deals really meant.

Of course, most diablos and demonios aren't, and when Dami was a demonio, they were no exception. Otherwise humans would never promise away their souls.

"What did I miss?" Dami asks at last. "I can't go back to being a demonio. What do I need to know?"

Juno drums her perfectly manicured nails on the arm of the chair. They're painted deep red, shiny—like blood. "Your happiest memory," she says at last. "That's my price."

It doesn't surprise them. This is how Juno operates—where most diablos and demonios deal in souls, Juno derives her power from knowledge. Memories, primarily, but also skills, expertise, even rare artifacts. Dami has always been a little jealous of the demonios who work for her—amassing knowledge sure sounds less terrible than collecting souls.

Dami knows instantly which memory it'll be: their first night as a human. San Juan. They said goodbye to their friends, Mar and Bas, astonished by the notion that they could say for the first time in their life that they *had* friends. They ate their first meal at a nearby taberna and nearly died of happiness as they experienced flavor for the first time. Those maduros were *divine*—sweet and soft, freshly fried, crisp and chewy at the edges and still piping hot. A handsome boy started talking to them, and after laughing together for an hour they went to the beach together.

There, with the waves lapping at their ankles, bathed in moonlight, the boy held Dami's face in his hands and called them beautiful, so beautiful.

It felt so good to be seen. It was everything.

Dami's stomach squirms at the thought of losing that moment. That euphoria of first human contact. But if they refuse the deal, they risk losing everything. If Dami is really reverting to a demonio, back to that miserable unlife . . . the thought of it makes them cold.

"Okay," they whisper. "My happiest memory—but you'll tell me what I need to do to stay human. Everything, Juno. No details left out."

Juno nods. "Everything you need to know." She holds out her hand, black ring glistening in the moonlight. A single piece of obsidian carved into a rose, the band like woven thorny stems.

Dami stands and approaches her, holding the memory tight in their mind.

The boy's fingers are soft on their cheeks. Warm. His smile— magnetic. "I've never met a boy like you," he whispers. "You're so beautiful."

Dami's eyes sting. No one has ever called them beautiful before. Looked at them the way the boy is looking: with awe and wonder. Not a hint of hatred or anger, just pure admiration. The cool sand shifts under their toes as Dami moves closer to him—chest to chest. Hips to hips. Warmth and muscle and the softness of his gaze.

So beautiful.

Something hot splashes on Dami's hand, yanking them to the present. Their cheeks are wet. They're crying? It's just a memory—they'll make more. And it's not like he was the only one to call them beautiful over the past few months.

But he was the first. And in a mere moment Dami won't remember him.

Their throat aches. "I don't want to do this."

"I know," Juno says. "It's a treasured moment—that's what makes it a powerful deal. If it didn't mean anything to you, it wouldn't be worth it."

"You'll tell me everything." Dami meets her eyes. "If I do this—"

"You have my word." Juno pauses. "I don't do charity, Dami, but I'm not going to cheat you. You deserve better."

Dami isn't sure that they do, but they nod anyway. They don't trust many people—and even fewer diablos and demonios—but they trust Juno. She's always been honest with them, even when they didn't want honesty. She doesn't sugarcoat, but she doesn't deceive, either. She doesn't need to.

Biting their lip, Dami takes her hand. They close their eyes, savoring it one last time: *so beautiful.*

It's a mercy, in a way. They can't miss something they don't know they had.

Dami blinks, clearing away a fog in their mind. They're kneeling, holding Juno's hand, their lips on her ring. They pull away, blinking hard as a full-body shiver rolls through them.

What did they give her?

. . . .

Juno sighs and slips her hand out of Dami's fingers. "Delicious." If she can see the question in their eyes, she ignores it. Instead, she nods to the seat behind them. "Why don't you sit while you get your bearings?"

Dami stands on shaky legs, relieved when the plush seat catches them. They won't ask what they gave away. It's better this way, not to know. Not to wonder.

"As you guessed, you're reverting to your former self. A being of the dead. A demonio." Juno leans back in her seat. "Your deal with el Diablo may have freed you, but he never told you how to tether your soul. Without that, you'll return to the plane of the dead—and this time you won't be able to leave. You'll be as you were before, forever."

Dami's stomach flips. "So I need to . . . tether my soul."

Juno nods. "You can't be fully human as long as you have active demonio deals with living humans. You need to end your deals with each of them. Once that's done, you'll be fully mortal. Fully human." She pauses. "Of course, if you make any new deals with a human using magic—even one—or if you die, you'll become a demonio again immediately."

Sure. Right. End every active deal they have left. That's . . . how many? Dami takes a minute to run through their mental list. As a demonio, Dami always knew how many deals they had running and with who; it was innate knowledge, impossible to forget. That they can recall it now so easily probably should have been a warning sign on its own.

One hundred twenty-seven. One hundred twenty-seven active deals they have to end. With people all over the world.

"And . . . how long do I have, exactly?"

"A year from your first day as a human. The closer you get

· · · · · · · · · ·

19

to your deadline, the faster the reversion will be. You'll lose everything that tethers you to the plane of the living—your senses, then your corporeality—until you become fully as you were. A demonio."

Dami grimaces, staring at their palms. They became a human on September 22. It's now January, which leaves them with a little less than eight months. That would mean ending a deal every two days, give or take. As a demonio it would have been easy—they could zip around the world in a blink. But as a human? It takes days to get to another city, let alone across the world.

It's impossible. Unless . . .

Dami looks up at Juno. "Yes," she says, "you'll need to make a deal with a diablo to give yourself a chance." She must see the concern on their face because she adds, "Humans make deals with diablos and demonios all the time, so you won't revert. Only making a demonio deal with a human will untether your soul for good."

They swallow; their throat is paper-dry. "Okay," Dami rasps. "Another deal, then."

She stands, towering over them as her heels clack on the tile before stepping onto the rug. Dami resists the instinct to shrink in their seat as she runs her nail over the arm of their chair with a grating sound like a hiss. "I must admit, I'm curious about how this will turn out. I'll transport you to each person—once. In return, I'll know everything you do about how your little adventure is going. I'll have access to your memories about your journey—but I won't take them from you."

"Deal. Absolutely. Yes."

Juno chuckles softly, offering her hand once more. Dami

reaches for it, but she pulls her hand away. "Remember, only *once* each. If you lose track of them after I bring you there, you're on your own to find them again."

"I understand."

She offers her hand again. Dami takes it and kisses her ring. A burst of magic rushes through them like hot sparks running through their veins. When the sensation fades, Juno takes her hand back and turns away.

"Well, what are you waiting for? Time's ticking."

SIX MONTHS LATER

Chapter 3

· · · · · · · · · · · · · · · · · · ·

There was a time when Silas thought dying was the worst possible thing that could happen to him. Now, as he squints at the gray Boston sky, hard, wet brick beneath his damp hair, and rain spattering his face, he knows better.

Dying once would have been unfortunate. The true hell lies in dying and waking endlessly.

He rolls over and groans, wiping at the still-wet blood on his neck, warm and slippery on his fingers. The rain helps. After a few minutes of leaning his head back toward the sky and wiping his rain-slick fingers over his skin, it's mostly gone. Best he can tell anyway—blood stops wiping off on his hand when he touches his neck.

He'll add an entry to his book later, when he isn't rain-soaked. *July 14, 1821: Robbed at knifepoint. Conked on the head and stabbed in the throat.*

Or at least he *would* have been robbed if he'd had anything of value on him.

Silas isn't sure, exactly, how long it takes him to wake after dying. He estimates maybe fifteen to twenty minutes. Long

· · · · · · · · ·

enough to be presumed well and truly dead. Short enough that his spilled blood hasn't yet dried.

What time is it?

Silas blinks through the rain. The overcast sky makes it difficult to estimate the time of day, but a chill still hangs in the air. The bustle of nearby carriages, wheels splashing through puddles and axles squeaking through the steady patter of rain, is familiar in the way the brick beneath him is familiar; home.

The only problem is home doesn't sound like this early in the morning. And Silas has a meeting at nine a.m., like he has every morning for the past four months. And he's never missed a meeting.

Stumbling to his feet, Silas scrubs the blood from his shirt as best he can with his palm and the rain, which does little more than smear the edges pink a bit. The blood has already set into the fibers, which is perfect because he doesn't exactly have another shirt. That's a problem for later, though.

State Street is full of people, as he'd feared. His stomach twists, and his skin warms even in the chilling rain as he hustles down the brick road, ignoring the way people look at him with disgust—or mild horror—and step out of his way.

He imagines he looks like a boy returned from the dead, which might be amusing if it weren't true.

"Are you okay, son?" An older man has stepped out in front of him, blocking his way. Sure, Silas could step around him—judging from his perfectly cut wool peacoat and shiny boots, Silas assumes the man probably won't lower himself to run after him if he takes off—but something in the stranger's eyes stops him. It isn't wariness that has prompted this man to step into his path, but concern. A Good Samaritan, then.

Silas forces an embarrassed smile and shoves his hands into his pockets. "I apologize for worrying you, sir. I lost my balance and hit my nose and, well . . ." He gestures to the blood on his collar. "I'm heading home to get a new shirt now."

The man smiles and his shoulders lower, visibly relaxing. "Must have been quite a collision. Yes, probably for the best that you change, then—you look terribly frightening covered in blood like that. I won't delay you further."

Silas's smile thins as he steps around the man, biting back a few choice words. As if Silas doesn't know he looks awful. He's going to need a new shirt if he doesn't want to attract attention everywhere he goes.

With a sigh, Silas turns the corner to find the State House, perched proudly ahead. And at its peak is what Silas is looking for: a clock.

"Goddammit."

It's nearly ten a.m.

Silas sprints across the street and into the park, swearing under his breath the entire time. The good news is that he isn't far from where he meets Ana every day—on the northern side of the lake in the middle of the park. The bad news is that he's nearly an hour late, and it'd take a miracle for Ana to still be there.

His boots pound gravel and his lungs and legs burn as he races as fast as he can muster. Oddly enough, fewer people seem to notice him as he sprints across the park—perhaps because he's moving fast enough that most aren't getting a good look at him and his macabre wardrobe. Whatever the case, Silas is grateful for it because no one stops him.

Not that it makes a difference. Silas is fresh out of miracles, because when he arrives on the northern side of the lake, Ana is

. . . .

nowhere to be found. He groans, bending over and resting his hands on his knees as he catches his breath.

He can't blame Ana for leaving. Though originally he'd been paying her a half cent for each of her daily reports on his little sister, Maisey, he'd run out of money long ago. It's a wonder that she keeps delivering her reports at all—Silas suspects she just feels bad for him. He doesn't love that, but he isn't in any position to turn his nose up at charity.

Still, he'd been late. All right. He evidently won't get his daily report from Ana today. Which means he won't get an update on Maisey. It's not ideal, but Ana didn't have anything new to report yesterday, so in all likelihood Maisey's just fine.

Hopefully.

Silas sits at the edge of the lake, folding his arms onto his knees and flattening muddy grass beneath his dirt-spattered boots. Of all the horrible ways the Cain family curse has ruined his life, this is the worst of it. Silas could handle the repeated dying if at least Maisey knew he was alive. If he could just see her, hug her, help her like an older brother should, it wouldn't be so unbearable. Then his curse would be like a chronic sickness—horrible, yes, but something he could bear in the privacy of his home, surrounded by the love of his family.

But that's not his reality.

In reality, it was only the second time Silas died that Maisey watched it happen.

He'd drowned on the beach, in full view of the public—and his family. They'd brought him home, cold as a wagon wheel, and while his mother was crying over him, he'd choked up entire lungfuls of water.

It hadn't been the most pleasant awakening.

Silas picks up a pebble, running his thumb over the smooth edges. A warm breeze tousles his wet hair and rain drips down his nose. His mother, though relieved to see him alive, was familiar enough with the Cain family curse to know they didn't ordinarily return from the dead after their untimely ends. Consequently, she didn't greet him with a relieved sob and embrace. Instead, she stared at him in horror.

"What have you done, Silas?"

The words have haunted him every day since, because he *had* done something. If he hadn't, he would've died from flu long before the drowning ever happened. If he hadn't, Maisey wouldn't have watched as a man dragged his corpse from the drink. He would've been dead, but she'd have experienced one less trauma.

If he regrets anything, it's that Maisey witnessed that. But who's ready to die at fifteen? He certainly wasn't, and after five days of a fever that set a chill in his aching bones, and two days of being unable to keep even water down, death was imminent.

Or it had been. Until a demon with a magnetic smile and the face of a handsome boy his age promised to save him.

"*All you have to do is promise me your soul.*"

"*My soul?*" Silas asked weakly. "*Won't I be dead without a soul?*"

"*That's why I won't take it until you're ready to die for good. You can live however long you'd like.*"

Silas shook his head, wincing at the movement, which sent a fresh wave of shivers down his spine. "*My family is cursed. Even if I don't die today, I'll still die young.*"

"*Do you want to die young, Silas?*"

Silas shivered again, this time not from fever. "*I don't want to die at all.*"

And there it was—that smile. It made Silas want to smile too, which was absurd, given the circumstances. But the boy touched his cheek, and his fingers were smooth and warm, and for just a breath his body didn't hurt. The fever receded. "Let's make a deal, Silas Cain," the boy said with a honeyed voice. "Your family curse won't kill you, not until you're ready to die. And after you've lived a long, fruitful life full of adventure and promise, I'll take your soul. But not a minute before you're ready. How does that sound?"

It sounded like a miracle. It sounded impossible. And Silas was uncertain that this wasn't a dream, but this handsome boy was touching his face, and that felt real. Maybe he was feverish and hallucinating, but maybe he wasn't. Maybe this stranger with silky black hair that begged to be touched had magic that could counteract his family's curse.

Maybe this boy could save his life.

Of course he said yes. And the hunger in the stranger's eyes when he did—it would haunt him forever.

"Is that blood?"

Silas startles, turning to a small girl with chestnut-brown curls holding an umbrella. Relief washes over him like a wave. "It's—Never mind that. What are you doing here?"

Ana wrinkles her nose. "Meeting you, genius. Like every day?"

Silas's face warms. "I know that, but . . . I'm so late. I thought you left."

"I did." She shrugs and walks around him, looking at him with distaste. "You need a bath. And sitting in the rain doesn't count."

"And you need some manners." Silas laughs softly. "How is Maisey? Is everything all right?"

"Like always." Ana rolls her eyes. "You're a really overprotective brother, you know that?"

"You'd be worried too, if you had a younger sibling who you could never see."

"Maybe." She tilts her head. "She has piano today."

Silas blinks. Maisey has piano lessons every Thursday, but today is Tuesday. Unless—his stomach twists nauseatingly— how long was he unconscious?

"Ana . . . ," he says slowly, "what day is it?"

Ana wrinkles her nose. "Tuesday, of course. Maisey's lesson was just moved this week because her teacher is busy later."

"Oh." Silas lets out a relieved laugh. "Right."

"If you hustle, you might still make it before she gets there. The lesson's at eleven."

The July day is warm, and up on this rooftop Silas is sure to bake now that the rain has stopped and the sun has continued to rise, but that hardly matters. He made it before Maisey arrived at St. Mary's Cathedral across the street, where she gets her piano lessons from Sister Ruth, a nun so perpetually cranky Silas frequently forgets she's only in her thirties. She acts at least eighty.

"She does not!" Maisey said with a laugh. "She's perfectly nice if you get to know her."

"Why would I want to get to know her? She looks at me like I'm a rat."

"She's never said a bad thing about you. In fact, she always asks how you're doing, every lesson."

Silas narrowed his eyes. "I find that hard to believe."

"It's true!"

Silas shakes his head. He'd never shatter Maisey's image of

Sister Ruth, but Silas once saw her at the Boston Athenaeum after he'd been kissing Jack Anderson in the ancient history section. They've never spoken about it—and she's never mentioned it—but he suspects she saw them.

Silas's mother and Maisey were always perfectly welcoming to the boys Silas brought home, but of course, they weren't Catholic nuns. Silas was all too aware of what most of the clergy would think of his attraction to other boys, but when he'd brought his fear of damnation to his mother, she'd said, "It doesn't make sense that a God so full of love would punish his people for loving someone."

That had been enough reassurance for Silas, even if he didn't think it would convince Sister Ruth.

Now Sister Ruth thinks Silas is dead, like most of the world. Only Silas's mother knows the truth, and she's made it clear it must stay that way. If their neighbors—or worse, the church— learn he's risen from the dead, they'll accuse the whole family of devilry. Silas can't do that to his family.

So instead, he lives like this. In shadowed alleys and on rooftops, digging food out of trash and stealing from rich tourists to survive. It isn't ideal, but he's alive and, more importantly, Maisey is safe. He would move mountains to keep her safe.

The faint sound of laughter catches his ear. Silas searches the sidewalk—there! Her blond ringlets are easy to spot as she laughs at something their mother has said. They walk hand in hand, and from afar Silas is struck by how much Maisey is growing to look like their mother.

If his mother looked at him, would she see his father? He barely remembers what his father looked like—Silas was so young when he passed.

Then Maisey looks across the street. Not just across the street—she tilts her head up, up, until—

Silas gasps and drops flat on the roof, heart pounding. Has she seen him? He squeezes his eyes shut. The roof is rough and cold against his cheek. The endless Boston breeze tousles his hair. There isn't any yelling—would Maisey have yelled if she'd seen him? Surely, she would have said something and their mother would have tried to convince her otherwise. But Maisey is bright—if she got a good look at him . . .

God, how could he be so reckless?

He waits for what feels like an eternity, swearing softly under his breath as he counts down the minutes. When he's certain it's been far too long for anyone to reasonably stand and stare at an empty rooftop, he slowly, carefully, peers over the edge.

Maisey and his mother are gone.

Silas breathes a sigh of relief, pressing his face into his palms. He shouldn't be doing this. There are ways to keep tabs on Maisey without the risk of her seeing him—he's already doing as much with Ana's reports. And anyway, if he really gets desperate he can probably leave a letter for his mother. But if he's being honest with himself, there isn't any need. Maisey and his mother are safe. There isn't any danger, not so long as he stays away.

Silas rolls onto his back, staring up at the cloudy sky. Reality hurts more than any death.

"You're incredibly boring to watch, you know that?"

Silas's heart punches his chest as he jolts up, eyes wide. Standing there, just ten paces away, waits a tall person all in black, silky black hair pulled back in a bun with long strands framing their sharp jawline.

The demon who ruined his life.

Chapter 4

....

"You." Silas's expression is nothing short of murderous. His poison-green eyes narrow and his pale face reddens as he clenches his fists. "I could kill you," he growls. "I *should* kill you."

"Glad to see you're well," Dami says calmly. The cool rooftop breeze tousles their hair; it's a relief from the hot sun. "How's your sister—Maisey, was it? I take it the not-dying thing is going well if you're spying on her."

Silas barks out a laugh and stands too close to the edge. His fists are shaking. Dami figures there's a fifty-fifty chance one of those fists swings for their face. Maybe they should have spent some of the last six months brushing up on their once-honed fighting skills, now that they can't just conveniently phase in and out.

Hindsight, and all that.

"You *completely* fucked me," Silas says. His voice is acid.

"Well," Dami says, unable to help themself even as they see the metaphorical cliff rapidly approaching, "not *completely*."

Silas lunges with a roar. Dami sidesteps him—barely—and takes a few extra steps back to keep their distance.

....

Silas's chest heaves as he spins to face them again. There's a dried bloodstain on the bottom left edge of his once-white shirt, right where it's tucked into his black breeches. A second, fresher-looking bloodstain soaks the collar and spills down his chest, though it's hard to tell whether the stain is newer or if it's just sweat-soaked. Dami wonders idly if he's changed his clothes since he last died. "Do you know how many times I've died?" Silas shouts. "Go on! Have a guess!"

"Oh, I don't know if that's—"

"Fifty-nine! Fifty-nine *fucking* times!"

"Hmm," Dami says. "Sounds unpleasant."

"You were supposed to *keep* me from dying," Silas seethes, "not make it so I die over and over again!"

"Technically, your soul never leaves your body, so you haven't actually died," Dami says. Which, judging by Silas's darkening expression, is exactly the wrong thing to say.

They suppose they could have *tried* to make the deal differently. Dami never had the power to nullify a curse, though in hindsight they could have made the process painless. But demonio deals aren't supposed to be pleasant, especially not ones for immortality. Someone with true immortality without any of the unfortunate side effects of a deal would take far too long to relinquish their soul—if they ever did at all.

Silas's situation is, to say the least, unenviable. But if they had to do it again, Dami would do it all the same.

"Give me one reason why I shouldn't kill you," Silas says through gritted teeth.

Dami sighs and glances away, doing their best to appear bored. Uninterested. Like this isn't the most important deal they've ever had to make.

· · · · · · · · ·

Like Silas's refusal won't cost them their life.

They slip their hands in their pockets, hating how clammy their palms are. Dami doesn't *get* nervous. Never has. They've never had anything to lose before—after all, up until el Diablo freed them at last, they were already living their worst, unending nightmare.

But now that they've had a taste of what life could be like, of what it's like to really *live*, the thought of going back to that un-life for eternity makes their stomach twist like rope. The shift is annoying, to say the least—it's much more difficult to maintain an air of apathy if you aren't, in fact, apathetic.

Of course, Silas can't know that. Dami keeps their advantage, their cool disinterest. A refreshing breeze tinged with salt and city grime fills their lungs. They look over a sea of Boston rooftops, of brick-front buildings and horse-drawn carriages below, and keep their voice calm.

"You mean besides the fact that you literally can't?" Dami answers. "It's impossible for you to hurt me while our deal is active—part of the fine print of a demonio deal."

"It was a verbal agreement."

"I don't see why that should change anything."

"You can't have fine print in a—"

"My point still stands," Dami interrupts. "Whether you were aware of it or not, you can't hurt me until our deal is over."

If they're being entirely honest, Dami isn't *actually* sure that's still true given they're no longer a demonio. It *is* baked into every deal, sure, because otherwise it'd be too easy for unhappy deal recipients to take matters into their own hands. Still, it's hard to say what applies while Dami is in this in-between state.

Not fully human. Not fully demonio.

Too human to transport themselves at will or change their corporeality. Too demonio to eat or need food to live.

Silas certainly looks tempted to test those boundaries, though.

"At any rate," Dami says breezily, "as fun as it would be to watch you try to incinerate me with your stare, that's not why I'm here. I have a proposition for you. Well. More like an *un*-proposition, really—"

"No." Silas turns away from Dami and sits at the roof's edge, his legs dangling over the side.

"I want to set you free," Dami continues, undeterred. "End our deal early. And as a bonus, you get to keep your soul. It'll be like we never made the deal to begin with."

Silas snorts. "Do you think I have a death wish?"

Dami eyes him. "You *are* sitting on a roof's edge while cursed with fatally bad luck."

"I died this morning," Silas grumbles. "It doesn't ordinarily happen twice in a day—it's more of a once-a-week deal."

So. Probably *hasn't* changed his clothes since last dying in them, then. Dami resists the urge to grimace.

Silas shakes his head and adds a little louder, "Not that I have to explain myself to you."

"You were furious at me thirty seconds ago because of our deal. I'm offering you a way out. Why *wouldn't* you take it?"

"Oh, I don't know," Silas says dryly. "Maybe because it's the only thing keeping me alive?" He stands and turns back to Dami, arms crossed. "In any case, why do you want to cancel it? Don't promised souls make you more powerful?"

Don't show your cards. The first rule of dealmaking, of keeping the advantage. But Dami didn't have to justify their request with any of the others—they'd all just been so relieved to be released from the impulsive deals they'd come to regret.

Granted, none of the others were depending on said deal to survive.

Dami just shrugs. "I have my reasons. That's not important."

"Now *that* I don't believe. You wouldn't have come here asking me for anything if it weren't important."

"Maybe I'm just trying to be a better person."

Silas laughs. Loudly. Dami bristles—is it so hard to believe they'd want to better themself? "Is that funny?"

"It is when your way of *bettering yourself* is trying to convince me to do something that will kill me."

Okay. They suppose they deserve that.

"Tell you what." Silas sits on a wooden crate and extends his legs, crossing them at the ankles. Smirking. He looks so full of himself. That's how Dami's supposed to look during these encounters. They're not enjoying the reversal.

"Let's make a deal."

Dami scoffs. "I'm trying to get *out* of a deal. I'm not making any—"

"Not a magical deal," Silas interrupts. "Just a verbal agreement. Man to—uh, demon. Help me break the curse that keeps killing me, and I'll agree to cancel the deal."

Dami has to give Silas credit. He may not know for sure just how desperate Dami is to cancel their deal, but he knows he has something Dami wants. And though he's unaware, he's using their desperation to his advantage.

Just like Dami did to him a year ago.

They suppose they deserve this, too.

Dami sighs. If they've been counting right, they have a little over two months left before they fully revert to a demonio forever. This is the last deal they have to cancel. It'll have to be enough time.

"Let's say I agree."

Silas's mouth drops open. "Just like that?"

Dami lifts their index finger. "*First,* what would we have to do to break your curse?"

Silas stares at them, possibly in stunned silence. Evidently he wasn't prepared for the possibility that Dami would even consider agreeing.

Dami taps their foot. "Well?"

"You must really need this."

"No more than you do. So? What would we be doing?"

"Well"— Silas chuckles, perhaps nervously—"we have to return Captain Kidd's lost treasure to his body."

Chapter 5

· · · · · · · · · · · · · · · · ·

The demon laughs.

It'd be infuriating if it weren't expected. After all, seriously proposing a search for pirate treasure that most think doesn't exist is . . . well. If it weren't an impossible goal that had consumed his entire life, Silas would have laughed too.

"Find buried pirate treasure," the demon says. "*That's* your plan? You know most stories about buried treasure are just legends, right?"

Silas sighs. "This one isn't."

"Yeah, that's what every treasure hunter thinks."

"It's the only way to break the curse." Silas crosses his arms. "And if it didn't exist, I wouldn't be cursed. That treasure is the reason my family has been cursed for generations."

The demon looks at him appraisingly, like one might at a slab of meat for sale. "And why is that?"

It's not a story Silas enjoys recounting. But if he's really trying to convince a demon to help him break the curse that ruined his family—and his life—maybe it's worth the telling.

· · · · · · · · ·

Even if it does require continuing a conversation with the last being in existence he'd ever want to see.

"My great-great-grandfather was part of Captain Kidd's crew. The second mate. Before Kidd's infamous last trip to Boston, he buried his treasure hoard and made my great-great-grandfather swear a blood oath upon threat of death to find and return the treasure to him no more than two years after their voyage. Except after the crew arrived in Boston, nearly all of them were arrested. My great-great-grandfather wasn't, though. He escaped while the rest of the crew were shipped over to London to be tried and executed."

"So your great-great-grandfather went back for the treasure and took some for himself?"

"No," Silas says sharply. "He never went back for the treasure at all. And two years to the day after Captain Kidd's execution, he was struck by lightning and died."

The demon snorts. They might as well have slapped him; Silas glares. "I'm sorry," the demon says, "but death by lightning strike? That's kind of funny."

"Just as hilarious as his son dying horribly in a house fire, his grandson getting beaten to death, and my dad getting shot in the stomach."

Then something strange happens: the demon's face softens in a way that almost looks . . . human. If Silas didn't know better, he might have mistaken them for just another young person, not so different from him.

Thankfully, Silas knows better.

"Okay, so your ancestor pissed off Captain Kidd's ghost and now your family's cursed." Dami stretches their arms over their head, all gangly limbs and angles. "If the curse is untimely terrible deaths, how did that bloodline even survive four generations?"

Silas frowns. He's wondered himself. No one has ever confirmed it for him, but . . . "Well, to begin with, most of us didn't. By the time I was born, my father was the only surviving child of eight. My grandfather was the only survivor of twelve, until my father was ten years old. Maisey and I are my dad's only children."

"So if you two die, it's over."

Silas grinds his boot heel into the ground. "Yes . . . but I think the curse is intentionally leaving one person alive, so there's always a chance to break it."

The demon tilts their head. "If that's the case, why have you died—what did you say? Fifty fucking times?"

"Fifty-nine. I think if I hadn't made that deal with you, I would have died, and then it would have been up to Maisey." He frowns. "But if I don't break this curse, she'll probably die as soon as she has a child. Nearly all my father's female relatives who lived to adulthood and had children died in childbirth."

"And yet here you are. You're welcome."

Heat flashes through Silas. *You're welcome?* After everything—what a callous—

Silas closes his eyes and inhales deeply through his nose. When he opens his eyes again, the demon has a self-satisfied smirk that makes him want to punch them directly in their perfect nose.

Instead, Silas says, "So do we have a deal or not?"

"The one where I help you find Captain Kidd's lost treasure and break this generational curse on your family, and you agree to cancel our original deal?"

Silas nods.

The demon's gaze settles heavily on him. They look so deeply into Silas, with eyes like a starless night, that he resists the urge to squirm.

"A nonmagically binding deal," they say slowly. "So how do I know you won't ignore your end after I help you break the curse? It'd be a devious revenge plot."

It would be, wouldn't it? "I won't need our deal after the curse is gone."

They scoff. "Even setting the revenge angle aside, the promise of immortality is kind of a big deal to most people."

Silas lifts a shoulder. "Sure, but at the end of it, when I decided I was done, I'd end up like you."

Something flits through the demon's expression, too fast to catch. "Didn't stop you when we made our deal."

"I was dying of flu then."

"My point still stands."

"I was fifteen."

"Yes, you seem much wiser now at the ancient age of sixteen."

Silas rolls his eyes. "You haven't answered the question."

"That's true." The demon sighs heavily and kicks a stone off the rooftop, watching it clatter down into an alleyway. "Well. If you're *absolutely determined* not to accept my original generous proposal—"

"The one where I die."

"—then I suppose I have no recourse but to accept your counteroffer."

Something airy, something alive flutters in Silas's chest— a sputtering candle trying to light. If the demon will help him, then it might actually be possible. For the first time in his life, he actually has a chance—a *real* chance—to break this curse.

He could save Maisey.

"*Thank you, Dami,*" the demon says in a rough approximation of Silas's voice. "*That's really magnanimous of you. You truly are an incredible being. And underappreciated, too—*"

"That doesn't sound anything like me," Silas cuts in.

"That's true. You evidently don't know a good thing when it appears in the form of a stunningly handsome person with a way to save your life."

"You're not—"

"Please, I'm gorgeous."

"—good," Silas finishes. "You're not good. You're a demon. Nothing changes that, no matter how attractive a body you give yourself."

The demon stiffens, but just for a second. Then their face melts into a slick smile. "But you *do* find me attractive."

Heat flashes through Silas's face. He opens his mouth to deny it, but what's the point? It'd be a hollow lie that wouldn't deter them in the least.

The demon is all smiles and teeth when they mercifully give him an out. "So where do we begin, oh curse breaker?"

Silas takes a deep, cleansing breath. They better get this mission over with, fast. Silas isn't sure how much of them he can handle.

"First we're going to need a horse."

Chapter 6

· · · · · · · · · · · · · · · · ·

The first time Dami watches a man die, they're seven years old.

By seven years old, el Diablo has brought them to the making of hundreds of deals. They've watched people of all ages and genders promise away their souls for money, for love, for health, for fame. They've seen el Diablo be charming, terrifying, comforting—whatever he needed to make the mark trust him.

By seven years old, they know how to twist words without forming a lie, to hide the ugly truth while spinning rose-tinted promises. They know how to listen for the despair song, the hum and tinkle like wind chimes that bring them to a desperate mark. They know how to page through a human's mind like a book, how to lift the relevant details and skip disinterestedly through the rest. They know how to shift their appearance not only in the way that suits them best, but in the way that will be most comforting to the mark.

· · · · · · · · ·

They do not know what happens when a diablo comes to collect.

"It's time for your first Reaping, my apprentice," el Diablo says. "You know all there is to find the perfect mark and spin the perfect deal. Now you must learn how to end it."

The truth is, Dami has never liked endings. It's why they've left so many books unread. Why they've never asked what happens when a deal comes to a close. They aren't oblivious—they know the payment of a soul must happen sooner or later, but they haven't been pushing to witness it themself.

Of course, they were never going to have a say in the matter. Dami doesn't have the luxury of pretending death doesn't exist, not even as a child. It's not possible when you're a being of the dead.

So el Diablo takes them to a pueblo in Puerto Rico and Dami doesn't protest. The night is warm and thick— the air full of chirping coquíes in the otherwise quiet village. Their boots crunch on gravel and their black skirt swings idly around their ankles. El Diablo's heavy steps rattle the coins in his pockets, disturbing the quiet night with jingling footfalls as they approach the lone blue-stucco home.

At the doorstep, el Diablo turns to them. "You are here to observe. You don't speak to him, and you don't interrupt. ¿Entiendes?"

Dami swallows hard. They nod.

He knocks on the door, his knuckles booming against the wood. Dami imagines it must sound like a gunshot inside. For the first time, they consider that the mark's familia might be home. What would that mean? Would they even see el Diablo? Or would they be frozen in time, oblivious as to what's about to happen to their loved one?

The door swings open, a young man in the frame. His shoulders are broad and he's nearly as tall as el Diablo, but there's something strange about his face. Yes, his face is smooth and wrinkle-free, his hair dark without a single strand of silver. But his eyes.

They look so exhausted. Older, somehow.

Not for the first time, Dami wonders what the deal was here. But el Diablo didn't volunteer that information, and Dami knows better than to ask.

Upon seeing el Diablo, the man just nods. Then his gaze falls on Dami and his eyes widen. "¿Tienes . . . un hije?"

El Diablo laughs. "¿Eso te sorprende?"

"Sí," he admits.

His shock over el Diablo's having a child is warranted— Dami doesn't know any other demonios their age. To their understanding, the only way a child can be a demonio is in Dami's exact rare situation. Lucky them.

The man moves out of the way so el Diablo and Dami can enter. It's a small home. The entry room consists of a sort of living room with two cushioned seats. A low table between them with a mosaic top holds two saucers with two empty coffee cups. Like he'd been expecting company.

Like he'd been expecting el Diablo.

El Diablo sits on one chair as the man walks into a

different room, then returns with a metal espresso pot. He pours the dark coffee into each tiny cup—it's still so hot, steam rises into the air. El Diablo scoops the small cup into his hand, brings it up to his nose, and smiles. "You always did make the best café, Ernesto."

The man—Ernesto, presumably—sits across from him and takes his own cup. "Gracias. We're very proud of our coffee beans. I'm glad for the opportunity to share it." He frowns at Dami. "Would you like some, hije?"

Dami opens their mouth, but el Diablo speaks first. "No, they're fine."

Dami's mouth snaps closed. They bite back their jealousy. Daywalkers like el Diablo can do more than just materialize during the day. They can also smell, taste, feel. Enjoy food and drink. Experience the world.

Dami doesn't know what any of that is like, but they're desperate to find out.

Ernesto and el Diablo sit in companionable silence, drinking their cafés. The mood is so different from what Dami's observed when a deal is made. In a Making, there's an excitement in the air, so potent it sets the hairs on the back of Dami's neck on end. It's a delicate negotiation, a weaving of half-truths and searing emotions, of carefully prodded wounds and promises of respite. The Making always fills Dami with restless energy, and they haven't even made a deal of their own yet.

But this Reaping isn't like that. Both Ernesto and el Diablo know how this night will end. There's a finality to it, and a somberness. Ernesto is currently enjoying his very last café—which may be why he's drinking it so slowly. But el Diablo doesn't rush him. What's a few minutes, after all, to an immortal being?

Eventually the cup runs dry, as it must. El Diablo waits for Ernesto to place the empty cup back on the saucer, then says, "Two lifetimes."

Ernesto nods. "You've held up your end of the bargain. I've seen my grandchildren's grandchildren born. I've been here long enough."

El Diablo smiles. "Then you're ready."

"I am." He squares his shoulders as he meets el Diablo's gaze. "How is this done?"

"Dami."

They jump at their name. El Diablo is looking at them, and when they meet his eyes, he gestures for them to come over. They do, slowly, heart pounding. They're only here to watch, right? Surely el Diablo wouldn't want Dami to Reap him, not when they've never even seen it happen before. And anyway, he can't possibly want that because then Dami, not el Diablo, would get his soul.

"Taking Ernesto's soul won't be pleasant for him," el Diablo says to Dami, which seems like a mean thing to say in front of Ernesto. "But for me, and one day, for you, it's power like you've never imagined. The more souls you Reap, the more powerful you'll become. One day you could be a demonio. Or even a diablo like me." He smiles wickedly.

Dami swallows hard and just nods.

El Diablo pats their cheek, not that they feel it. "One day, but not today. Today you watch and learn." And with that, he stands and turns back to Ernesto.

·········

The man looks a shade paler than he did a few minutes ago, but to his credit, he stands tall and meets el Diablo's gaze.

"Anything you'd like to say?" el Diablo asks.

"I already told you I'm ready," Ernesto answers firmly.

El Diablo takes two steps forward, cupping Ernesto's face in his hands. And for a moment, nothing happens. Is this part of el Diablo's intimidation? Is he just dragging it out? Enjoying Ernesto's buried fear?

Wait, no, something *is* happening. Ernesto trembles, and silver begins streaking his hair. His skin takes on a grayish tinge and his face begins to age—smooth skin turns mottled and wrinkled, eyelids droop, eyebrows turn silver. Ernesto groans, shivering violently as his shoulders go frail, his hair sheds from his head.

And then he's looking at Dami with rheumy eyes. They stumble a step back. Ernesto reaches toward Dami, letting out a long, croaking groan as his face continues rapidly aging. "Look away, child," he wheezes in a pained voice.

"Do not," el Diablo says firmly. "This is your future. Embrace it."

And for the first time since this horrifying process started, Dami looks at el Diablo—and gasps. The veins in his neck, on his hands, his face are glowing bright white. His eyes are pure white with the same light, and his skin all but shines with power. He's radiant, almost difficult to look at, but now that they have, it's impossible to look away.

And then el Diablo opens his mouth and Ernesto

screams. Something wispy, almost like white smoke, pours from Ernesto's mouth into el Diablo's. It starts in a small stream but quickly multiplies, faster, more, until a bright orb forms between Ernesto's teeth, spinning and glowing brighter by the second. The orb slowly pulls from Ernesto's mouth, and the man makes a horrible groaning sound, like a wounded animal. The gray pallor of his skin intensifies, and by the time the orb has traveled to el Diablo's lips, he nearly looks dead despite the terrible crooning noise still coming from his lips.

It's terrifying to watch. But Dami doesn't look away.

Not even when the orb enters el Diablo's mouth and he swallows it. Not even when Ernesto goes limp in el Diablo's grip and he lets him fall to the ground with a muffled thump. Not even when light bursts out of el Diablo so bright that the entire room is washed in white.

Dami watches until the room returns to the warm candlelight. Until el Diablo exhales and laughs, then pats Dami's back.

And then he waltzes out of Ernesto's home, leaving his corpse on the floor. For some reason, the two empty espresso cups still on the saucers on the coffee table catch Dami's eye. Ernesto's cup is off-center.

Dami straightens it, then follows el Diablo out into the night.

Chapter 7

· · · · · · · · · · · · · · · · · ·

I t's not so much that Dami doesn't like horses as that horses don't like them. They once assumed it had to do with their general lack of corporeality, but it turns out having a body hasn't much improved the situation.

Carrot, the dark chestnut horse, regards Dami with suspicion while trotting begrudgingly along beside them, his hooves clattering on the cobblestone. No one pays them much mind—people, horses, and horse-drawn carriages move around them while Dami pretends they know what they're doing. They haven't attempted to ride Carrot yet—they didn't admit this to Silas yesterday when he'd suggested buying a horse, but they never actually learned how to ride one on account of the aforementioned not-having-a-body thing. Given the way Carrot is looking at them, they aren't entirely enthusiastic about the opportunity to acquire this skill.

"Look," Dami says to the horse trotting uneasily beside them. "This isn't going to be a perfect experience for either of us. All I ask is that you don't make a fool of me."

· · · · · · · · ·

Carrot snorts. Then he releases a huge dump on the road. Dami wrinkles their nose. This is sure to go splendidly.

"So they only had one horse," Dami tells Silas sometime later. They've met up outside a dilapidated tavern along Boston's outskirts before noon. Silas has a canvas bag presumably full of supplies at his feet, while Dami's satchel filled with food is thrown over the horse.

Silas gives Dami a withering look. "What kind of stable did you go to that only had one horse?"

Dami leans against the side of the brick-front building, examining their black-painted nails. "I got the distinct impression the stable owner didn't like me very much."

Carrot trots up to Silas and nuzzles his outstretched hand. Dami narrows their eyes at the horse.

Silas smiles at Carrot and affectionately pets his face and reddish mane. "What did you do to make him dislike you?"

Dami stiffens. Was it really that obvious? "What makes you think Carrot doesn't like me?"

He rolls his eyes. "I meant the stable owner."

Oh. Right.

"Nothing!" they say, affronted. "I showed up, asked how much it'd be to buy a horse, and you'd think he'd just sucked a lemon with the way he looked at me. It was pretty rude, actually. I'd even made an effort to cover my tattoos so he wouldn't think I was a pirate, but he stared at my nails for a solid thirty seconds while his face contorted ridiculously. I *wanted* to tell him I could get a portrait done so he'd have something to remember me by—"

Silas groans and covers his face.

"But I *didn't*. I just stood there politely while he inspected me like a rotten piece of fruit and then *finally* he said"—Dami clears their throat, dropping it a pitch—"'For *you* it'll be forty dollars for the horse and sixty dollars for the saddle and I only have one horse available to rent.' Which is *robbery*, by the way—you should be able to buy a trail horse for fifteen dollars max—"

Silas stares at them. "How did you do that?"

"Well, I didn't *mean* to be unlikable. Actually, most of the time I'm very charming, as I'm sure you can attest. Must be something wrong with that man." They frown and mutter, "Probably a bigot."

"No, not—" Silas makes a frustrated noise. "Your voice. It didn't sound like you."

Dami blinks. "Oh. That's easy—I can change how I look and mimic anyone, even their voice." They clear their throat again, grinning as they adjust the pitch and tenor of their voice again. "I can even sound like you if I'd like."

Silas stiffens. "Stop that."

"Why? You make it so fun."

"If you don't shut pan, Dami, I'll—"

"Do absolutely nothing, because you need me to break your curse?" Dami winks at him, but they let their pitch fall back to their own. "Anyway, we should get going before I get bored. Where are we going, exactly?"

Silas takes a slow breath, like he's trying to calm himself, though Dami can't imagine why. They weren't being *that* annoying. If mild teasing irritates him that much, this is going to be a more entertaining adventure than Dami has anticipated.

Silas reaches for the reins, but Dami pulls them out of reach.

"Ah-ah. Location first, and *then* if you ask *very nicely*, I'll let you steer." Dami doesn't have the faintest idea how to ride a horse, let alone steer one, but Silas doesn't need to know that.

Silas scowls. "Connecticut."

Dami snorts, but then Silas looks at them without a hint of humor in his face. They stare right back. "I must have misheard you. For a second there I thought you said the legendary Captain Kidd's treasure is buried in *Connecticut*, of all places."

"Yes," Silas deadpans. He extends his hand. "Well?"

"Really?" Dami grimaces. "Why would Captain Kidd bury his treasure in Connecticut?"

Silas sighs and drops his hand. "He stopped there on his way to his aforementioned last trip to Boston, where he was arrested and shipped overseas to London to be executed."

"Connecticut."

"Yes. Can we go now?"

"I think you're forgetting the 'ask very nicely' part."

"I'm not saying please."

Dami rolls their eyes. "Are you always this unpleasant? Or do I get special treatment?"

Silas scoffs. "*I'm* being unpleasant?"

"Very."

"Fine!" Silas throws his hands up. "You steer, then—it doesn't make a difference to me so long as we get there."

Oh. Dami looks at the leather reins in their hand. They hadn't anticipated the possibility that Silas would rather let Dami steer than actually be nice to them. That was . . . a choice. Evidently, they've underestimated just how deep Silas's hatred

....

for them runs. All over a deal that saved his life! Completely unreasonable.

Not that any of that answers the question of how to navigate on a horse.

Silas takes in Dami's hesitation with a slow shake of his head. "You don't know how to steer, do you?"

Dami's face warms, and they offer a small smile. "To be fair, I haven't had much need to learn, being able to transport myself anywhere for most of my life."

Silas tilts his head. "If you can transport yourself anywhere, why don't you transport us to Connecticut?"

Carajo, Dami, don't give the game away. They throw out the first excuse that pops into their mind. "I can't right now."

"Why not?"

Dami hands him the reins. "I hope you know how to get there. You would *not* be pleasant company to get lost with."

"You didn't answer the question."

Dami turns to Carrot, eyeing the horse, who looks at them with more skepticism than any horse should be able to convey. To be fair to the horse, Dami is skeptical too. Why people voluntarily sit on the back of a huge animal that can kill them and poops as it walks is beyond them, but they suppose that short of a carriage, this is the fastest way to travel.

Come to think of it, maybe they should have bought a carriage. Oh well, too late now.

Determined to change the subject, Dami gestures to Carrot. "So how do you . . . do this?"

"Do what?"

Dami waits. They're not going to say it aloud. This adventure is unbearable enough without humiliating themself.

"You don't even know how to get on a horse?"

Dami turns to Silas. "Catch on fast, do you? I like that about you."

"Have you ever *been* on a horse?"

They grin. "How hard can it be?"

Chapter 8

....

"I can't feel my legs."

Silas takes a slow, deep breath through his nose, fighting the urge to shove the demon off the horse. If said demon weren't absolutely vital to the success of this trip, he would have already. It's the seventh time in the last *hour* that they have complained about how uncomfortable they are, and any enjoyment Silas may have gotten from the demon's discomfort is ruined by how much more of an annoyance they're becoming by the second. They seem determined to make Silas as miserable as they are—and, well, it's working.

The demon rests their forehead against Silas's shoulder—or that's how it feels. It's been disconcerting enough having their hands around his waist all day, but the more tired the demon gets, the more comfortable they seem to be with throwing themself all over him.

If the demon were *human*, Silas might not have even minded. They aren't exactly unattractive—but they aren't human. They can look however they want. Naturally, the demon would appear in the most attractive form possible when trying to entice some-one like Silas. It's pure manipulation. Nothing else.

Silas jerks his elbow back, connecting with what feels like their ribs.

The demon jerks upright with an "Ow," but at least they aren't leaning their head on his shoulder anymore. He smiles.

"That was rude," the demon mumbles.

"I don't care," Silas responds pleasantly.

After several minutes of rare, blessed silence, the demon yawns exaggeratedly. "It's getting dark. Surely it's okay to stop now. We've been on this cursed horse all day."

"Carrot isn't cursed." Silas pats the horse's neck affection-ately. "He's been an excellent mount."

They huff. "He doesn't like me."

"Neither do I."

"That's right—and look at you. Cursed."

Silas scowls. "Ha ha," he says flatly. "You know, Carrot might like you more if you didn't call him a cursed horse."

"He didn't like me from the moment I entered that stable." A pause, then they add, "Horses and I don't seem to get along."

In lieu of a response, Silas directs Carrot off the road and into the woods. They ride in silence—actual silence!—for only the sec-ond time since the beginning of the trip. Only the crackle of snap-ping branches and the muffled steps of horseshoes on muddied leaves. Only Silas and the demon taking in the darkening night, their breath warm against his ear. It makes the hair on the back of Silas's neck stand on end. Hopefully the demon hasn't noticed.

"You know," the demon whispers, "if you're taking me into the woods to murder me, our deal will end and so will you."

"I thought you said it was physically impossible for me to hurt you."

They pause for a suspiciously long time. "It is."

"It is a tempting idea, though."

The demon laughs. Silas doesn't. Their laugh dies awkwardly in the quiet night, and they clear their throat. Silas smirks. Let them stew over whether he was joking.

They stop at the first clearing. Silas slides off Carrot with practiced ease, shaking his sore legs out. The demon just sits on the horse and stares at him.

"Well?" Silas says. "Weren't you dying to get off the horse?"

The demon opens and closes their mouth. They clear their throat again. Laugh a little, perhaps nervously. "I really can't feel my legs."

"You're jesting."

"I see why you'd think that, but no. I've been telling you for hours that my legs were hurting. What did you expect?"

"I thought you were exaggerating!"

"I've never been on a horse before!"

That was obvious. Silas sighs heavily, scowling as he nears the demon-mounted horse. As amusing as it might be to let the demon sit there all night, Silas would like to sleep tonight, and he doesn't question for a second that they would be obnoxious until daybreak if he left them there.

So, begrudgingly, he offers his hand. The demon takes it—the touch sends a jolt down Silas's arm, making him flinch. Their hand is surprisingly soft and warm. Silas hadn't noticed it before, but their fingers are long, too—piano hands, his mother would have said. If Silas didn't know better, he absolutely would have thought they were just a cute boy.

"As nice as it is to hold your hand, I'm going to need more help than that."

Silas bristles. Hold hands? Scowling deeply, he grabs the demon's waist and yanks them down. They yelp and crash into him, all elbows and legs. Silas staggers back. But then their chest is against Silas's, and he somehow hasn't fallen over, and the demon seems to be struggling to stay on their feet but at least they're off the horse.

"Thank you," Dami says breathlessly. "This is—nice. See? You must not hate me so much after all."

Silas drops them.

Sometime later, the two sit on opposite sides of a roaring fire, eating tonight's rations—bread, an apple each, a strip of dried beef, and cheese. Or at least, Silas is eating. The demon says they aren't hungry, which seems impossible given Silas hasn't seen them eat all day, but what does he know? Maybe demons don't eat.

But if demons don't eat, why have they been eyeing his food so hungrily?

It doesn't matter. Sure, Silas could ask, but then they would launch into some story that, quite frankly, Silas doesn't care about. He doesn't need to know more about them. He doesn't want to become familiar with them. All he needs is to get to the blamed treasure and return it to Captain Kidd's grave. Then they can part ways and never meet again.

The end of this adventure can't come fast enough.

A loud snap in the night breaks Silas from the pull of dreams. He blinks blearily into the darkness, squinting up at a starry night sky. It's still dark as ink, only the embers of the once-roaring flame still aglow in the firepit.

But something woke him. A stick breaking—which, if he's being rational, was probably nothing. A deer or squirrel could have easily snapped the twig that alerted him.

On the other hand, cursed the way he is, Silas doesn't exactly have the best luck when it comes to safe probable odds.

Silas sits up, rubbing the sleep from his eyes. It hadn't really occurred to him to bring weapons on this trip, and besides, Silas has never held a gun. But he does have a knife holstered at his hip, which he pulls out now just in case. Not that a knife is likely to protect him from a bear. Should he have purchased a rifle before leaving Boston? Or maybe he just shouldn't have wandered into the woods. Silas figured the woods would be safer than the road, if only to avoid any ill-intentioned travelers, but maybe he should have considered the local wildlife more carefully.

Are there wolves in New England? There aren't any in Boston proper, obviously, but Boston is a day's ride behind them. Silas has never been this far from the city. What does he know about life outside the city?

"Demon," Silas whispers, but the demon is sprawled across the grass thirty feet away, mouth agape in their sleep. Silas has intentionally not slept anywhere near them, but now he's mildly regretting that decision if only because they aren't within kicking distance.

Silas sits absolutely still, only his breath interrupting the absolute quiet of the night. If it was an animal, it probably would have revealed itself by now—or moved away from them.

But if the danger has moved on, why does Silas still feel like a taut string ready to snap?

. . . .

"Demon," Silas hisses louder. "Wake up. I think something's—"

Another snap of a broken twig. Quick muffled footsteps behind him. Silas spins around as a figure emerges from the darkness—a man swinging his fist. Silas shouts and falls backward, scrambling to his feet. The stranger throws himself at Silas—his heavy weight slams him back into hard-packed dirt. Silas screams. Then a hand is over his mouth and the cold edge of a blade presses against his neck.

"You should have put out your fire," the man hisses into Silas's ear, his breath rancid. Then pain bites deep, bright and burning across his neck. Slick, hot blood spills down Silas's front—way too much, way too fast. Blood fills his mouth in a rusty, choking wave, gathering in the back of his throat as his compressed lungs demand air and spots of darkness bloom in his vision.

Then the night comes for Silas again, an all-too-familiar friend. And as he has done every week for a year, he welcomes it.

Chapter 9

· · · · · · · · · · · · · · · ·

As far as awakenings go, screaming and the thick smell of blood isn't the option Dami would have chosen. But they wouldn't have chosen any part of this terrible scavenger hunt.

Dami is on their feet, smoke swirling around them as blood blooms bright over Silas's shirt, spilling from the waterfall carved into his neck. There's no saving him—their deal will do that—but the deal won't take care of the man cutting Carrot's reins loose or the one looming over them before they summoned the smoke.

And unlike Silas, Dami won't be fine if the strangers kill them.

Now all three men stare at them with perplexed faces. Dami smiles, relaxing into the smoke's familiar embrace. It seems obvious now, as the smoke turns opaque and their features change, that they were never fully human. What human can transform at will? And not just transform, but do it like this, thick with the breath of fire?

Dami wanted to believe they could have the best of both

worlds: humanity and the transformative ability that's integral to who they are. They should have known the universe isn't so kind. Not to the damned like them.

They were foolish to think they deserve better.

Long horns burst from their forehead as their skin turns a hellish shade of red. Their hair, black and long as always, grows to their waist as their legs and torso expand—seven feet, then eight. They add a whiplike forked tail for good measure; then the smoke falls away.

Dami towers over the three foolish thieves and grins, revealing a mouthful of knife-sharp teeth.

"Hello, boys," they say in a guttural voice, like grinding gravel.

The blood-spattered man screams first, tripping over himself to get away from Silas's corpse and their camp. The second man, holding a small canvas bag, looks ready to faint—which would be really annoying because then Dami would have to get rid of him—and the third bolts into the forest without a glance behind his shoulder.

Which leaves Dami with just one thief: the one they'd really prefer didn't faint. "Well?" Dami says, staring him down. "Are you going to run away with your friends, or am I going to eat you for breakfast?"

The man drops his bag and takes off shrieking.

Unfortunately, so does Carrot. Dami's stomach drops out from under them as they lunge after the horse, but Carrot is terrified and *fast*. And chasing after him looking like the devil incarnate isn't going to help.

Dami swears under their breath and closes their eyes, allowing the smoke to obscure them once more. They're not going to be able to catch up with Carrot—that much is obvious. They suppose the next responsible thing to do would be to hunt the thieves down so they don't hurt anyone else, but what the thieves do next isn't really Dami's concern. Instead, they relax as the warm smoke remolds them with softer features and curves, with black trousers, shining boots, and a black shirt beneath a vest embroidered with red roses. They run their fingers through their waist-length hair. Hmm. In-the-woods hair is probably best kept up, so they reshape it pulled back.

When the smoke fades, Carrot is still gone and Silas is still dead. Dami isn't sure exactly how long it takes for him to wake again. Does the time vary? Does it depend on the severity of the injury? Silas's neck is still split open like an axe bit into a log. Does he heal after waking or before?

Dami picks up the abandoned bag and rifles through its contents. The thieves don't seem to be very good—or maybe they just started for the night—because there isn't much. A few coins, a stoppered inkpot, and a single tarnished ring. Useless.

Unless . . . they glance over at Silas's corpse as an irresistible idea strikes them. They grab the inkpot and approach Silas, peering down at him with curiosity. Crouching beside his head, Dami carefully unstoppers the inkpot, dips their finger in, and traces a long, curly mustache over Silas's lips and onto his right cheek. Cackling, they do the same on the other side, then add the world's tiniest goatee onto his chin.

Satisfied, they stopper the inkpot and toss it into some nearby bushes. It takes all of half a second for the smoke to wash their hands clean of the evidence. And Silas will be none the wiser because it's not like they were carrying mirrors around.

Genius.

Snickering, they wait for Silas to wake, but it doesn't take long before they're bored again. This will be the first time Silas has seen them as a girl. Dami's sure he'll still recognize them—everyone who knows them always seems to, regardless of which version of themself they take—but they wonder nonetheless how he'll react. Will he still hate them as much when their face isn't the exact one that reminds him of their deal?

He might hate you even more after he finds out what you did to his face. Dami giggles.

Silas gasps, jolting up as his hand slaps over his neck with a gross wet *splat*. Dami wrinkles their nose. Silas stares up at them, wide-eyed, chest heaving, and when his hand drops back to his lap, his neck is smooth.

Interesting.

And then Silas says the most unexpected thing of all.

"Mother?"

"I still can't believe you thought I was your mother." Dami collapses into a chair, closes their eyes, and tilts their head back, enjoying the simple pleasure of sitting. The tavern is a flurry of movement on the floor below them—with overlapping voices, chairs scraping the worn hardwood, and heavy pint glasses sliding over tables, all barely muffled by the thin walls. If Dami gets their way, they won't be moving for *at least* an hour.

The two of them never did find Carrot, which meant they had to walk the rest of the way to Milford. What was a three-to-four-day trip on horseback became twice that on foot.

And Dami thought their legs hurt when they were on a horse all day.

·········

The fake mustache lasted about half of their trip before fading, which gave Dami a solid three days of entertainment. Silas never understood why Dami kept bursting out laughing after looking at him, and Dami never told.

The marks were gone now, but thinking of it still made them snicker.

Silas groans. "That was six days ago. Forget it already."

Dami doesn't even open their eyes, but they do smile. "Never."

"I always wake a little disoriented," Silas says. "You don't look like my mother, I was—confused."

Dami scoffs and sits up, finally opening their eyes. "I know I don't look like your mother. I'm gorgeous."

Silas's eyes narrow. "Are you insinuating—"

"Anyway, I've done what you asked." They lean forward, tapping their long, glossy black nails on their knee. "We made it to Milford—"

"Three days later than we should have," Silas mutters.

Dami ignores him. "And I got us this room to stay the night, as requested. Now what's the plan?"

The room they've booked is small and bare, with nothing but the tiny beds so near each other they might as well have been pushed together. But it's a place to sleep indoors and the food at the bar downstairs is even halfway decent.

Silas stands rigidly next to one of the small beds and looks Dami over. They can't imagine what's going on in his head as he stares at them, but there better be some gratitude in that stubborn skull. Even though they lost Carrot, they would have lost a lot more if Dami hadn't scared the bandits away. Not to mention Dami funded this entire trip using *their* money from literally selling the clothes off their back. Sure, they have essentially an infinite supply of clothing to sell, but it was still *their* doing.

Whatever mental calculation Silas makes, he must decide Dami has earned the right to know what, exactly, the plan is, because he sighs, pushes off the wall, and sits on the bed. It barely moves under him. Dami felt it earlier—the mattress feels like a stack of hay covered in a sheet. They didn't look beneath the sheets, but they suspect that may be exactly what it is.

"Well," Silas says, "the treasure isn't in Milford, exactly."

Dami stares at him. "Your next sentence better be 'But it's really close by' because I didn't walk across New England with you for fun."

"It is," Silas says quickly. "Five miles off the coast, to be precise."

Dami crosses their arms over their chest. "As in . . . in the middle of the ocean? I don't know about you, but I can't breathe underwater." They scowl. "Wait. You don't think I can turn into a fish, do you? I can't turn into animals. And even if I could—"

"No." Silas laughs a little. He better not be imagining them as a fish. "It's on an island. Legend has it Captain Kidd buried his treasure on an island off the coast of Milford. Everyone believes it's Charles Island—there's this sandbar path that appears at low tide so you can walk from the Milford beach to Charles Island if you time it correctly—but that's not where the treasure is."

"I'm confused." Dami tilts their head, their long hair spilling over their right shoulder. "Is it or is it not five miles off the coast on an island?"

"It is, but not on Charles Island. There's another island behind Charles Island, but it's hidden from the human eye with magic."

·········

They pull a face. Seriously? "Of course," they say dryly. "An invisible island."

"It's not any more absurd than a shape-shifting demon who manages to be the most annoying being in existence no matter what form they take."

Dami gasps in mock offense. "Annoying? Me?"

"Only all the time," Silas mutters under his breath.

"At least I don't snore."

Silas's face warms. "I don't snore."

"Tell that to my sleep-deprived body."

"Since when do demons need to sleep anyway? I thought demons did all their dealmaking at night," Silas asks, veering way too close to a truth Dami is *not* going to discuss with him.

"Since when do you care what my needs are?" they shoot back.

Silas scowls. Thankfully, Dami's diversion works, because he returns to the original subject. "The island is magically hidden but I know how to find it. All we need to do is row out there, reach the island, find the treasure, then return it. I've rented us a boat for tomorrow."

Dami sits on the other bed, then falls back on it. Their head hits the mattress with a thump. There's no give whatsoever—Dami's teeth clack together with the impact. They grimace, staring at the ceiling and pretending their back isn't aching already. Mortal bodies are so . . . fragile. Though Dami likes to pretend everything about being a demonio was terrible, they miss being unbreakable.

"Here's the part I don't get," they say, forcing those unwanted thoughts from their mind. "You said we have to return the treasure to Captain Kidd. To his grave."

"Yes."

"But Captain Kidd doesn't have a grave." Dami sits up, meeting his gaze. "He was executed in London; then they hung his body over the Thames for years as a warning to other pirates. He literally rotted in a cage hung over the river until there was nothing left but scraps of fabric and bone."

Silas stares at them blankly, which makes Dami think his great-whatever-grandfather forgot to mention that detail. "All right . . . then what did they do to the bones?"

Dami shrugs. "Dumped them in the River Thames, I'd assume."

"Then that's where we go."

Dami frowns. "London?"

"Do you have any better ideas?"

Dami's frown deepens. Their deadline is September 22—a day shy of two months away. Without demonio transportation, they'll need to take a ship to get there, which is roughly a six-to-eight-week trip assuming the weather is nice. "That's not going to be a quick trip."

"I'm sorry, do you have somewhere else you need to be?"

Actually, yes. But Silas doesn't need to know that.

Dami examines their black-painted nails. "I'm just saying it seems like you haven't really thought every step of this plan through."

"Let's find the treasure first, all right? None of that matters if we don't find the treasure to begin with."

They want to argue, but what's the point? It's not like Silas can change the terms of his curse. And anyway, it's still theoretically possible to find the treasure and get it to Captain Kidd's bones before their time is up . . . so long as they find the treasure in two weeks.

. . . .

71

Laughter echoes in the room, bone-chillingly familiar. Dami bolts up, twisting to look around the small room, wide-eyed. Silas stares at them warily, but no one else is here.

Relax. He isn't here.

"What is it?" Silas asks.

Dami shakes their head and lies back down. "Sorry," they say over their pounding heart. "I thought I heard something."

Chapter 10

·····················

"I can't believe you got a rowboat with just one set of oars," Dami growls.

Their shoulders burn as they row, and row, the boat bobbing precariously in the ocean. The blue water ripples with light—the sun is hot on the back of their neck, certain to burn. Sweat drips down their spine plastering their black shirt to their skin. The fabric feels like it's soaking up every ounce of the sun and painting Dami's skin with it.

In hindsight, today might have been a good day to make an exception to their almost-all-black wardrobe. But they look amazing in black, and so what if they want to look good? Not for *Silas* obviously, for themself. It'd be a waste of their transformative ability to not always look their best.

Then again, drenched in sweat isn't exactly screaming *kiss me*. Not that it matters. Silas, with his shaggy brown hair and green eyes, may actually be the last person on earth that Dami would want to kiss. He's not Dami's type, even if he is handsome.

No amount of chiseled jaw or plush lips is worth putting up with a puritanical boy who insists on calling them demon.

·········

Dami wrinkles their nose. Chiseled jaw? Plush lips? The sun and exhaustion must be getting to them.

"Why would I rent a boat with two sets of oars?" Silas says, breaking them out of their truly disturbing thoughts. "I don't want to row."

Dami levels Silas with their most cutting glare. If he notices, he doesn't show it. Instead, he peers somewhere behind Dami's shoulder, to wherever he's making them row.

"We'd get there faster if you were helping," Dami grumbles.

"That's fine," Silas says. "This pace works for me."

"Oh, does it? Well, that's a relief, I'm so glad this works for you."

"So we're both happy, then. Perfect." Silas smirks at them, crossing his arms behind his head and leaning back, perfectly relaxed. Dami has half a mind to pull one of these oars out of the sea and smack him with it.

Knowing Silas's luck, it'd probably kill him, though. And then Dami would have to row and navigate on their own, at least until Silas woke up again. Upside: Dami wouldn't have to look at his smug face while they're rowing. That alone makes the notion more tempting by the stroke.

"How much farther?" they pant.

Silas points to their right. "See that island there?"

Dami spares a glance. Off in the distance, over an expanse of shimmering water, they can just about make out a small island. They grunt in the affirmative.

"That's Charles Island."

"So?"

"Keep rowing."

Dami groans, closing their eyes as they pull on the oars

....

again, again, again. With the salt in the air and the ocean breeze tousling the strands of hair that have fallen in their face, this would almost be nice if they weren't so completely exhausted.

And if they weren't trapped on a tiny rowboat with the biggest pendejo on the planet.

Too many strokes to count later, Charles Island is still a dot in the distance and the sun has eased. Not just eased—Dami looks up at the sky, gritting their teeth against their burning muscles—the once-cloudless sky has turned to a blanket of steel-gray clouds.

"That's weird," Dami pants out.

"Hmm?" Silas looks at them, stretching his legs out and crossing them at the ankles. Absolutely relishing Dami's exhaustion while he relaxes. Definitely enjoying every second of this torment, knowing Dami will do it because they want something from him.

If he's this insufferable without knowing *why* Dami needs him to agree to end the deal, they don't want to even begin to imagine how he'd be if he found out just how vital the agreement is.

"What's weird?" Silas prompts.

"The clouds," they spit out between breaths. "They've come in. Really fast. Don't you think?"

Silas glances up and shrugs. "I suppose."

"It was sunny," Dami says. "It was burning me five minutes back."

"Welcome to New England. It's just some clouds, I'm sure the sun will come out again in a few minutes."

The sun does not, in fact, come out again in a few minutes. The farther Dami rows, the darker the sky becomes—and the more the seas rock the boat beneath them. Just as Dami opens their mouth to point out the inevitable storm, Silas bolts ramrod-straight.

"There! The fog, that's it, I'm sure of it. I can feel it."

"The storm—"

"It doesn't matter, keep going. We're almost there."

Dami peers over their shoulder, shaking with strain. Behind them is a wall of fog so thick it looks like the storm clouds above have come down to the earth in an enormous sea-to-sky curtain.

"How do you expect to navigate in that?" Dami asks.

"I don't need to see. Trust me, demon, I know where we're headed. I'm meant to go there. It's—it's pulling me."

"My *name* is Dami," they say with a scowl. "And pretty sure if anyone is pulling anything it's me pulling you in this maldito rowboat." Something wet and cold plops on Dami's nose. A raindrop. "Perfect. It's going to rain."

"Row fast enough and maybe we'll arrive before the storm hits."

Dami barks out a laugh. "I'd like to see *you* row fast enough, pendejo."

Thunder like a thousand drums rumbles through the air, so loud even Silas breaks his carefree facade and cringes. Then the sky opens up and rain hits them in a sheet. The barrage pelts their heads and shoulders, drenching them instantly.

"Really?" Dami shouts at the sky.

Silas scrambles to grab his ratty coat and holds it over his head like a makeshift shelter. Of course, he doesn't bother to cover Dami. Instead, he grimaces beneath his dripping coat and yells, "Keep rowing!"

As if Dami has any choice whatsoever, now several miles into the Atlantic in the middle of a godforsaken rainstorm. "Pinche gringo," Dami mutters, rowing harder.

"What?" Silas yells over the clatter of the downpour.

Dami just smiles at him. Silas looks at them suspiciously, but he's clearly not going to leave his makeshift shelter, and anyway, even if he did, it's not like he understands Spanish.

One bright light in an absolutely cursed situation.

The sea rises and falls beneath them in nauseating hills and valleys. The boat tilts dangerously left and right—Silas even lets go of his jacket to grab the sides of the boat and steady himself. A crack of lightning splits the sky, and the thunderclap that follows is so loud Dami jumps.

"I can see it!" Silas yells. "The island! We've almost arrived!"

Dami dares a peek behind their shoulder. The good news is Silas is right—Dami can just barely make out a strip of land in the distance, obscured by the sheeting rain. The bad news is it seems way too far, and the waves are rising beneath them at increasingly worrying heights.

Something twists in their gut, churning their stomach nauseatingly. *You're mortal*, a small voice reminds them. *If you die in this damned boat, it's over.*

"I don't think this boat can handle this storm!" Dami shouts. "We're going to tip over!"

"No, we're not! Keep going, it's far too late to turn back in any case!"

As much as Dami hates to admit it, Silas is right about that at least. They must be over four miles from the Milford shore by now. Dami isn't sure they'd have the strength to row that far even if they weren't in the middle of a terrifying storm.

Fear sings bright and hot in the center of their chest. They may not be fully human, but they aren't fully demonio, either, which means if they die, they'll be a demonio again, this time forever. The fear gives them a burst of energy the likes of which they've never felt, and somehow, they row faster.

This fragility is really inconvenient, they think bitterly. They don't want to die. They just need to make it to shore. Just keep rowing. Just keep—

"Oh no."

Dami didn't think it was possible for Silas to turn whiter than he already is, but the boy goes so pale his face looks bloodless. His eyes are wide as saucers, staring in terror at something behind Dami.

They don't want to look. They don't want to know.

But they look.

The wave building behind their shoulder looks like a giant rising out of the ocean. Enormous shoulders tower above them, ten feet, fifteen feet, twenty. Dami's heart leaps into their throat. They don't have to be an experienced sailor to know this is a ship-eating wave. And they aren't even on a ship.

Their rickety little rowboat doesn't stand a chance.

They aren't going to make it. And something about that reality numbs the fear blooming in their chest. They aren't going to make it, and they have—a minute? two?—to plan for that.

"Silas," Dami says, their voice stronger than they feel. The boy stares, paralyzed, at the wave behind them. "Silas!"

He jerks as if Dami had slapped him. He doesn't speak, but his gaze meets Dami's and that's enough.

"Can you swim?" Dami asks.

Silas nods.

"Good. This wave is going to flip us. We need to swim to shore, okay? We can make it. We're not that far."

The boat tips violently forward as the ocean swells beneath them. Silas closes his eyes, his lips moving quickly—praying, maybe. Dami drops the oars—not much point in rowing now— and grips the sides of the boat until their knuckles turn white. They need to breathe. They need to get as much air as possible before the ocean tries to drag them into the deep.

They can do this. They *must* do this. They can't die, not now.

The wave pulls them higher. Dami doesn't look back. They grip the boat harder as the angle steepens. They're practically sitting above Silas's head—and it's then that terror slams into their chest with breathtaking force. For a moment, all they hear is the crashing of their pulse in their ears as the terrifying orchestra of the ocean's storm dance falls away.

They don't want to die. They don't want to die. They don't want to die.

The boat tips back—vertical—and for a breath Dami is suspended in midair, no longer rising, not yet falling. The deluge pelts their face so hard it's near impossible to keep their eyes open.

If nothing else, they think, *this is an incredible way to die.*

And then they're falling.

Chapter 11

....

D ami topples backward, heels over head, before hitting the ocean hard. The cold water is a full-body punch. They tumble, and tumble, and tumble, the sea pulling them deeper, colder, darker. They scramble to right themself, their eyes stinging in salt water as they squint through shadow.

The surface. Where is the surface? Dami rotates in a slow somersault, heart crashing in their ears, reminding them of the very urgent need to breathe. Darkness swallows every direction but—there. In the distance, a churning, and maybe a bit of light? Not much, but the water is moving, which is more promising than the still black in every other direction.

Dami swims, kicking hard, trying to conserve their arm strength as much as possible. Once they hit the surface, they're going to have to find the shore—then swim hard. Their lungs and legs burn, and the cold makes their bones ache, but they push and—

Rain directly in their gasping mouth. The rough seas slap Dami's face, making them splutter, but they stay afloat. That's all that matters. Stay above the surface. Find the island. Swim.

....

They twist as they tread water, but it's so hard to see above the choppy ocean and through the unrelenting rain. Something large and dark bobs fifteen feet ahead of them. The boat!

Dami throws themself toward it, thanking every star in the sky that it wasn't destroyed. The boat has capsized and there isn't a chance in hell Dami will be able to flip it over in these stormy seas themself, but they're too relieved to see it in one piece to care. They clamber on top, throwing their arms up to grab the ridge in the middle of the boat and gasp for air, pressing their face against the wood. At least they can give their body a break, even if just for a few minutes. They can make it to the island on this capsized boat. They can.

Wait. Dami blinks through the rain, squinting in the darkness. They're forgetting something important.

Where is Silas?

With a groan, Dami hoists themself higher onto the upside-down boat, dragging their legs out of the water. The boat bobs threateningly beneath them, but Dami hangs on like a starfish on the side of a ship.

Pulling in a lungful of air, Dami bellows, "Silas!"

A crack of lightning arcs overhead, so loud the storm swallows their voice. Unless Silas is very nearby, Dami can't imagine he would have heard them. Assuming he's conscious.

Oh no. What if he drowned? Sure, he'll wake, so he won't really be dead, but how long will that take?

"I swear to god, Silas," Dami grits out, "if you make me drag you to shore . . ."

And that's when Dami sees him—facedown in the water and somehow still holding on to an oar, which may be the most useful he's been all day. He's much too far away for Dami to grab him without getting off the boat, which is a terrifying prospect. What if Dami leaves the boat and a wave destroys it? Or the ocean yanks it too far away for Dami to get to?

But they need Silas. If he gets lost at sea, drowning and waking and dying of dehydration and waking and starving and waking, he'll never cancel the deal. He'll curse Dami every godforsaken day, maybe even for years before he finally reaches a shoreline.

Dami isn't sure if they can survive without the boat. But they definitely can't survive without Silas.

"Pinche madre," Dami whispers to no one at all. This is the worst treasure hunt ever.

Though every bone in their body begs to stay on the boat, Dami throws themself back into the ocean. Even in the July air the ocean is cold, nothing like the warm gulf waters near their birthplace. They grit their chattering teeth as they swim toward the damned boy. Assuming they survive this, they don't know how they're going to move tomorrow. That's a problem for Tomorrow Dami, though. Today they need to get Silas. Get them both back to the boat. And row to shore. With one oar.

They will never forgive Silas for dragging them along on this absolutely cursed trip.

Fueled by bitter rage, Dami reaches Silas faster than they thought possible. They wrap their left arm around his chest, propping him against them, and grab Silas's fist holding the oar. The last thing they need is to lose the oar while pulling him from the ocean.

Swimming with one arm while dragging an unconscious boy is taxing and slow. Every stroke gets them less than half as far as they could propel themself on their own—and the ocean bobbing the boat farther away from them every other stroke isn't doing them any favors.

But eventually, with every muscle burning, and gasping for air, Dami reaches the boat, clambers on top, and drags Silas up with them. A crack of lightning lights the sky, followed by bone-shaking thunder, and Dami laughs with delirium born of exhaustion.

A capsized boat. An unconscious boy. A single oar. Rain coming down like heaven itself is punishing them. And a demonio determined to see this through. They didn't ride on the back of a lumpy horse and walk over a hundred miles just to die in the middle of the Atlantic. It'll take more than a storm to kill them.

Dami doesn't know how long it takes to drag Silas just high enough on the beach to avoid the tide. A long time. When it's done, they drop to their knees on the gritty, wet sand, then flat on their back. There isn't a muscle in their body that doesn't hurt, but the storm, inconsiderate, rages on. They went through all of that just for the rain to keep spitting in their face? Rude. But none of that matters, because they're on land, and they survived.

They survived. And yet, all they can think about as they lie, drenched, on the wet sand, the air thick with salt, is that they wouldn't have been in this nightmarish situation to begin with if Silas had simply agreed to cancel their deal like literally everyone else.

Next to them, Silas sputters, then lunges off the sand and vomits seawater. Dami lies there, blinking through the pelting rain, unmoving as Silas retches and coughs and finally, gasping for air, rolls over and pulls himself up onto his hands and knees.

"We made it?" he asks hoarsely.

And with every ounce of strength they have left, Dami kicks Silas's arms out from under him.

Chapter 12

The first time Dami Reaps a soul, they cry until they throw up. As they sit crouched over the vomit-splattered ground, they find themself thinking how unfair it is that they're not able to eat food but they're still able to vomit.

Dami presses their palms against their eyes and takes a deep breath, momentarily glad they don't have a sense of smell. Their body still trembles with the power of their first stolen soul—though was it really stolen, if it was promised away? It doesn't matter. Every time they close their eyes, they see her face.

No one told them it'd feel like that. Like their blood is singing, like they could laugh and cry at once. Like every breath is their first, and every heartbeat fills them with power. No one told them Reaping a soul would make them feel more alive than they've ever felt in their entire life.

It shouldn't feel like that. They aren't supposed to enjoy it. If they enjoy taking a human soul, what does that make them? Certainly not someone worthy of getting a second chance at life.

"I'm sorry," they whisper, but it doesn't matter. Her brown hair is spilled across the New York City sidewalk, drenched in rain. Her brown eyes stare at them, wide and unseeing. They did this. She's dead.

Because of them.

To think demonios Reap thousands of souls—even tens of thousands—to amass enough power to become a diablo. Dami shudders with revulsion, closing their eyes and breathing deeply through their nose to resist the urge to retch again.

If el Diablo finds them like this, a hysterical mess on the side of the road, he'll be furious.

They stand, taking another deep breath. They're wet, but they aren't cold—they don't get cold. After a second breath, then a third, they feel a little less like they might shiver to pieces. And the thing is, they don't have to feel good about what they just did. They just have to pretend they do.

And Dami is excellent at pretending.

So they smooth down their shirt and wipe their mouth with the back of their hand. They roll their shoulders, paint their face with a small smile, and walk. They aren't ready to face el Diablo, not yet: they need time to convince themself they're okay. They need time to settle into the persona of someone who didn't just—

No, no. Don't think about it anymore. It's done. It can't be undone. Now they have to be calm. Confident. Collected.

The city library isn't open at this time of night, but something draws Dami to its doors anyway. They run their hand over the smooth wood surface, close their eyes, releasing their hold on their body as the smoke pulls them through the door.

And then they're inside. And it's quiet. Dead silent, really. But Dami isn't alone.

"Ah," says a soft voice from the shadow. "So you're the one Reaping in my city."

And all at once, Dami's carefully constructed veneer fractures. The nausea returns in a dizzying wave as a woman steps out of the shadows, her heels clacking on the polished hardwood. Her long black hair spills over her left shoulder, and her tight-fitting dress is the color of rubies.

In the dark, it almost looks like blood.

"Just the one," Dami says, barely avoiding a stammer.

She arches an eyebrow. "You say that as if it should matter."

Warmth colors Dami's cheeks. "I just mean—I can't possibly be the only one . . ." Their voice fades as her gaze settles on them. The distaste in her expression is impossible to ignore—and makes them want to crawl into a corner and disappear. Instead, they stand rooted to the spot.

They're not confident they'd be able to move if they wanted to.

"Of course there are others in my city," she says, "but none who dare Reap here without my permission."

Dami swallows and lowers their eyes. "I'm sorry. I didn't know."

"Hmm." She circles them slowly. "I suppose the more interesting question is why a child is Reaping at all."

They don't answer. There isn't a good answer, not really. They don't really know exactly how old they are—time moves differently in the space of the Undead. Dami has seen futures and pasts and their fair share of presents. But in human years, they think they're about eleven.

"I'm el Diablo's apprentice," they finally say, meeting her gaze. They hope that explains enough.

Her face darkens at his mention. "I see. And how did you come to be his apprentice?"

Dami has pieced together the story over the years, not that there was much to tell. Their mother made a terrible bargain and Dami paid the price for it.

"My mother made a deal with him before I was born," they say, trying to keep their voice light. They've known the story long enough that it shouldn't hurt to tell it, not anymore. But being reminded that their own mother didn't think them worth holding on to stings nevertheless.

It doesn't matter that it was an accident. Why would she ever take the risk?

The woman's lips purse. She shakes her head and looks off into the shadows. "You have a cruel teacher."

Dami blinks. It's not that they don't agree—el Diablo's cruelty is brazen. He enjoys hurting people. They've just never heard someone say it aloud before. "He wants me to be like him one day," they say uncertainly.

She meets their gaze again, looking them over appraisingly. "Do you want to be like him one day?"

They hesitate. The answer is no. The answer is yes. They don't want to be like him—cruel, cold, malicious.

....

They don't want to revel in hurting people and laugh at their pain. They don't want to enjoy making deals they know will only lead to suffering.

They never want to be someone who would take someone's child. Who would steal a life from someone who never had the chance to live it.

But they don't want to be like this, either. Unable to materialize in the sunlight. Unable to taste, or smell, or feel. The numbness and unwanted invisibility are maddening. An ever-present reminder of the life they never got to have.

No, Dami doesn't want to be like el Diablo. But if they could be a Daywalker like him, maybe their life as a being of the dead wouldn't be so bad.

They just wish the price for obtaining it weren't so high.

"I want to be a Daywalker," they finally say, "but I don't want to be like him. I want to be free of him."

"Hmm." The woman nods, as if deciding something, then turns away from them. "Walk with me."

So they do. Their footsteps are silent next to the *tap tap tap* of her heels. Her skirt is slit down the sides, so the back of it trails out behind her. Dami walks quickly to keep up—each of her steps is three of theirs. The two of them walk past white marble columns into a room with evenly spaced tables, stocked with empty chairs. Golden candelabras dot the dark wood-paneled walls, built-in bookshelves filling the space between them. Dami considers reaching out to run their fingers over the books' spines, but the gesture seems guaranteed to disappoint without a sense of touch.

"Do you know how one becomes a diablo?" the woman asks.

Dami hesitates. "Taking a lot of souls."

She smiles. "That's the simplified version, but essentially, yes. To become a diablo, you must amass enough power to create other demonios—ones who work for you. But to do that, you must become a demonio first." She looks down at them. "I assume el Diablo has explained that part."

Dami nods. Souls that are Reaped are transformed into energy and gone forever, but diablos and demonios don't Reap every soul promised to them. Choosing to keep a soul is a way to build power—and notoriety as well. Most kept souls remain just that—kept, essentially ghosts unable to interact with anyone or anything. But sometimes el Diablo will choose a number of kept souls who have potential to become demonios and grant them the power of the bargain, like he did with Dami.

What they do with that power is up to them. But if they make enough bargains—and enough humans promise them their souls—they'll become powerful enough to be a demonio. Able to transport across the world at will, without el Diablo's help. To make more and more powerful deals. To change the course of someone's life.

Tonight wasn't Dami's first deal. They started small, as every Potential must—essentially harmless exchanges for an hour of a life, or a certain emotion for a day, or even an interesting trinket. But the more deals they make, the stronger they become, until they're able to do what they did tonight.

....

Dami bites their lip. As much as it makes them sick to think about it, they feel stronger already. They haven't tried to transport themself anywhere, but they suspect they could without calling on el Diablo as they've always had to. Their body feels more—solid. Formed.

And they've only taken one soul.

"Good," she says. "Now let me ask you a different question. Do you want to be a Daywalker, or do you want to become human again?"

Dami stops short. Their heart leaps in their chest, their breath stuttering in their lungs. Become human? Is that an option? "I can . . . do that?"

The woman stops and faces them, a small smile on her red-painted lips. "You can. But it won't be easy."

Dami closes the gap between them, eyes wide as they look up at her. "How?"

"There are two ways a demonio can find freedom. The first is to become a diablo. The second is to kill the diablo who took them to begin with."

Kill el Diablo? How on earth were they supposed to do that?

"I—can I even do that?"

"Hmm." She looks them over, assessing them from head to toe. "Maybe you can, maybe you can't. But you certainly can't like this. You're not even a demonio yet."

Dami's stomach sinks. And so they're back where they started. Any hope of escape requires becoming a demonio first, and doing that requires Reaping many more souls than they want to think about. Just imagining it makes them shiver with revulsion.

. . . .

They look at their boots. "I can't do it," they whisper. "That was . . . that was horrible. I hated it. I can't do that again."

The woman laughs—actually laughs. Dami stares at her as she shakes her head and crosses her arms over her chest. "Don't lie to yourself, child. The only reason you're upset about it is because you didn't *dislike* it."

Their eyes widen. How did she . . . ? They catch themself and neutralize their expression. They have to be more careful; they can't just give away their emotions like that. They bite their lip. "Does it get easier?"

"If you want it to." She shrugs. "But that doesn't matter. What matters is what you're willing to do to get what you want."

Anything. They know it immediately, know it like breathing. And it's disconcerting how sure they are, how ready they are to do even the unthinkable if it means freeing themself. They didn't ask for this life, but they'll sure as hell do whatever they can to get out of it.

Dami bites their lip, pulls their shoulders back, and nods. "Okay."

"Good." She smiles, turning away and stepping deeper into the shadow.

"Wait! What do I do?"

"You know what you have to do. Find me again when you're a demonio."

Dami's pulse pounds in their ears. Find her? "How? I don't even know your name!"

She pauses, then looks over her shoulder. "You can call me Juno."

. . . .

91

Chapter 13

....

The thing is, Dami has never needed to make a fire by hand before—and certainly not in the middle of an endless thunderstorm.

They've seen it in others' memories before—making a firepit with a circle of rocks and piles of sticks and leaves in the center, and something with twisting a stick between your palms as rapidly as possible. But the stick is just turning the wet leaves into mush, and Dami is pretty sure this method only works when everything is dry.

Which makes their attempt absolutely useless, because it was raining when they passed out in this dingy cave and later woke to the gallop of a deluge, with absolutely no indication of stopping. It's impossible for anything to dry without a fire, but a fire is impossible without dry materials.

The stick snaps in their hands and collapses into the doomed, wet firepit. Dami scowls and throws half the stick out into the wet forest. Thunder rumbles overhead, matching their dark mood.

If they weren't actively trying to rid themself of their demonio status, they'd just make Silas agree to a deal with them to create a fire with magic. But Juno was very clear about what would happen if they made any new demonio deals.

Better to be damp and miserable than dry and doomed to be a demonio for eternity.

Wait. They don't have to be damp. Dami stands, closing their eyes as warm smoke surrounds them. A clean, dry shirt, new trousers, underclothes, and boots. They even tie their long black hair up and freshen up their kohl for good measure.

Just because they feel miserable doesn't mean they have to look it.

Silas watches them emerge from the smoke, face flat. "I've never seen a girl wear trousers before," he says, evidently choosing the most slappable thought possible.

"I literally wore pants the other day," they say.

Silas's face goes pink. "I meant . . . before you."

Dami sits on the cold rock floor, leaning back against the cave wall, long legs extended in front of them, crossed at the ankles. They don't answer. It's a nonsensical thing to talk about—they'll wear whatever they damn well please, thank you very much.

Unfortunately, the silence doesn't last.

"Can all demons change their appearance at will?" Silas asks.

Dami sighs and looks at him. "No. Some can, some can't. Others have different gifts. But I've always been able to." They hesitate. "I think it's because my sense of who I am shifts all the time. Sometimes a boy, sometimes a girl, sometimes neither. Or both."

Silas nods slowly. "Is that why you became a demon? So you would have that power?"

....

Dami bristles. Why did everyone always assume they chose this life? "No."

Silas looks away. They sit quietly for a while, with only the endless patter of rain filling the silence, which is nice, but Dami has a deadline. And anyway, they're not here to change Silas's opinion about demonios.

"So where's the treasure?"

Silas glances at them, then looks into the gaping maw of the cave, which continues into the dark behind them. Just when Dami's about to press him for an answer, he says, "It's here on the island. But I don't know exactly where."

Dami stands corrected. *That* was the most slappable thing possible to say. "You can't be serious. You dragged us all the way here and you don't even know where to look? Don't you have— I don't know—a map or something?"

Silas laughs. "A map?"

"It's a treasure hunt! Treasure hunters always have maps! Or at least an old riddle, or *some* kind of clue. How could you not know?"

"I've told you all I know," Silas snaps. "My family has always said the treasure is somewhere on this island, but if we ever knew precisely where, that information never reached my generation."

"Well, *someone* in your family knew, seeing how they put it here."

Silas sighs. "Well, that family member has been dead for a very long time."

"Unbelievable," Dami seethes. "You dragged me from Boston to Connecticut, forced me to row us *five miles* through a dangerous storm to an island where you don't even know where to *begin* looking? I nearly drowned saving you!"

"You're a *demon!*" Silas shouts. "You can't possibly expect me to feel bad for you when you can't even die!"

Dami laughs. "In that case, I shouldn't feel bad for *you*, either, because you aren't any more capable of dying than I am!"

The implication that Dami can't die is, of course, not true, but they certainly aren't about to reveal their mortality to a boy who despises them.

Silas glowers at them. "I don't expect that you feel empathy at all, as that would require having a heart."

Dami rolls their eyes. "Sure, because demonios can't have feelings."

"Not any that I care about," Silas bites back.

Dami could strangle him. But that would be counterproductive and anyway, it would only buy them fifteen minutes or so of quiet. And they'd still be stuck on this island.

With a frustrated sigh, they ask, "How did you expect to find it when we got here?"

"I don't know!" Silas exclaims. "A month ago, I didn't even think it'd be possible to get this far. I apologize if I don't have every blamed detail laid out for us already."

Dami snorts. "It'd be nice if you had *any* detail laid out for us."

"At least I directed us to the right island," Silas grumbles.

"That remains to be seen." Dami shakes their head and stands, resisting the urge to kick him. "What was your plan once we got here? Surely you didn't think the treasure would be waiting for us on the shore, ready to take."

Silas grimaces. "Certainly not."

"Then?"

He sighs. "I don't know. I hadn't thought this far ahead."

Dami groans. "Perfect."

"I didn't actually believe we would make it here, all right?" Silas snaps.

They wrinkle their nose. "What, you thought we'd die before we got here?"

"No. I didn't think you'd agree to begin with. And when you did, I thought you'd clear off. I didn't think you'd actually put up with everything all the way here." Silas frowns. "Why are you even here?"

Silas can ask why Dami's so invested all he wants, but who says they have to tell him? The why doesn't matter. They're both here, trapped on this godforsaken secret island where they'll definitely never be found, because whether Silas trusts Dami or not, he needs their help.

Dami is used to the distrust. Every culture has their own version of the demonio, many of which make it quite clear that beings like Dami are agents of evil, not to be trusted. And to be honest, Dami can't say that they don't deserve the malice. They've convinced hundreds of people to give them their soul. And while they're being honest, most of their deals don't leave the mark better off. Not by the time Dami comes to collect, anyway.

Sure, outside of a Reaping, Dami has never directly killed anyone like so many diablos before them, but that doesn't mean they're blameless.

The truth is, they don't need Silas to trust them, or even like them, because they don't deserve it.

"We made a deal," Dami says. "Maybe that doesn't mean anything to you, but I always hold up my end of a bargain."

·········

Silas laughs. "Of course, because leaving me in this death loop was what we agreed."

"We agreed the curse wouldn't kill you. It hasn't. You're still very much alive and a pain in my ass."

"I'd wager you're regretting making that deal now."

"Actually? Yes. I'd be done with this ridiculous journey if you were dead."

Rain batters the cave walls, pattering incessantly around them. A crack of lightning splashes Silas's face with light. And maybe what Dami said was harsh, but it was true. They'd be human by now if they'd never made that deal with Silas. He was the only one who didn't agree to immediately cancel the deal.

He was also the only one who would die without it. But right now, Dami can't be bothered to care.

"Then why are you still here?" Silas asks again. "And don't give me that nonsense about being so *honorable* that you can't break a nonmagically binding deal. You could clear off at any time."

And here they are, back in territory Dami does *not* want to talk about. But if brushing him off isn't going to work, then they'll need a better distraction. One Silas won't be able to ignore.

"Like you did to Maisey?" they say coolly.

Silas jerks back as if Dami slapped him across the face. "Excuse me? I didn't *leave* Maisey; I *died*."

Fish. Bait. Hook. Though they'd like to smile, Dami keeps their expression flat, unaffected. Bored. "You don't look very dead to me."

"You know what I mean."

·········

"I do." They shrug. "But Maisey doesn't. Can't imagine how painful it must have been mourning the loss of her brother. Do you think she thinks about you every day and feels that loss over and over again? Or do you think she's forgotten you entirely?"

The hurt in Silas's face is so raw, they actually kind of regret pushing so hard. Maybe they went too far.

Silas stands, turns away from them, and sits at the mouth of the cave, just behind the curtain of vines. They got exactly what they wanted. Silas stopped prying about why Dami couldn't leave. They won.

So why do they feel terrible about it?

Sometime later, Dami starts exploring the cave. Dami and Silas made camp at the mouth, just a few feet from the vine-covered entrance into the torrential rain. But now, standing ten feet away from their camp, peering into the cave's throat, Dami can't see the end of it.

It certainly doesn't help that the sun is well hidden by thick, dark clouds and they still don't have a fire going.

Dami takes a few steps into the darkness, their hand dragging against the damp cave wall. Their boot bumps a rock. They pick it up and throw it as hard as they can into the shadow. For a beat there's just silence, then, somewhere way up ahead, a quiet clatter.

The cave goes deeper than Dami imagined. But there isn't a chance they'll go in there without being able to see—that'd just be asking for disaster.

Silas mutters something behind them, and Dami looks toward him. Crouched above their firepit, Silas warms his hands over a small but growing flame. Dami blinks and walks to him, half expecting a breeze to put the flame out before it can grow any further, but it doesn't. Instead, it eats the kindling Dami set for it until it becomes a respectable little campfire.

"How did you . . . ?" Dami leans closer to the flames, shoulders relaxing as the warmth paints their skin.

"The leaves and sticks you found finally dried," Silas mutters. "Also, I had a tinderbox in my trousers."

Dami could slap him. He had. A tinderbox. This entire time?! "Are you serious?"

Silas looks up at them, eyebrow raised. "Tinderboxes are useful when you live on the streets in New England."

"I can't believe this. You had a tinderbox. When I was trying to start a fire for like half an hour."

Silas shrugs. "The tinder was soaking wet—I *drowned*, remember? Everything needed to dry first."

That was . . . actually logical. Dami bites their lip and sits, scowling into the flames.

Silas may be right, but they aren't about to admit that to him.

Wait. If they have a fire, then they can explore the cave. All they'll need is—"I need to make a torch. Do you know how to do that?"

"Why?"

Dami gestures behind them. "I want to explore the cave. Maybe we'll get lucky and stumble across the treasure you don't know how to find."

If Dami's verbal jab bothers Silas, he doesn't show it. He just shrugs. "I haven't made one before, but I'm fairly confident we could figure it out. Even if your survival skills seem to be . . . lacking."

"Lacking?"

"You tried to make a fire with wet kindling."

Dami throws their arms up. "Everything is wet! If I'd had dry kindling, I would have used it."

"Can't you transform into someone holding a torch? Or a lantern?"

Dami sighs. "It doesn't work like that. If I can't wear it, I can't make it."

"That could be useful nevertheless." Silas looks out into the storm. "We're going to need two large sticks. And some strips of fabric, and maybe some twine if you can manage that."

Silas volunteers to go looking for the sticks, which is good because Dami absolutely was not getting wet again. It doesn't take long—Dami has just stripped off an awkward outfit with a baggy shirt and woven twine bracelet and changed back to their regular attire when he returns. And soon, they have two torches.

Chapter 14

· · · · · · · · · · · · · · · · · · · ·

The cave goes deep, but not so deep that Silas has anything to be concerned about. They walk for around five minutes down a long tunnel descending steadily into the earth and something odd happens. A tug, like an invisible hand reaching into Silas's chest and pulling him forward. Whatever is up ahead wants to be found. He knows it like he knows he's breathing air. This is right. This is where he's supposed to go.

Could the treasure actually be in this cave?

The path opens up into a massive cavern. Silas's jaw drops as he peers up at the huge stalactites, like teeth in an enormous mouth. And then the cave *breathes*—a whisper slips past his ears, like someone exhaling against his cheek. Silas shivers, gooseflesh spreading over his arms.

The demon mutters something in Spanish that Silas doesn't understand and wanders off in the opposite direction. Honestly, Silas isn't sure why the demon is still here. Sure, they made a deal, but it wasn't magically binding and they couldn't be off to a worse start.

· · · · · · · · ·

He supposes he can't expect to understand how a demon thinks, though.

Silas walks along the perimeter of the cavern, holding the torch up to peer at the walls. There's something peculiar about them. Something . . . wrong. The rock is dark gray, streaked with white, but something is smeared over it. Streaks of rust, hard to make out against the dark rock but . . .

Silas holds up his torch against the rock, frowning at the rusty shapes. No, not shapes—his breath catches in his chest—rust-brown letters. The letters are old, definitely dry, even flaking off in places. But along the ends of the letters are long drips. Like blood.

His stomach churns. Now that he's thought it, he's sure of it. The letters are written in blood. Someone—or something—wrote a message in blood.

Silas, someone hisses in his ear. Silas jumps and spins around, but the demon is nowhere near him. He makes out their torch, way on the other side of the cavern. Even if they'd whispered loudly, there's no way Silas would have heard it so clearly.

Silas Cain, the air whispers again, but this time it's not just one voice—his name repeats in the darkness, like hundreds of people whispering his name over each other.

"Demon," Silas calls shakily, "do you hear that?"

"Hear you refusing to use my name?"

Silas scowls and turns back to the painted wall. Now that he's heard them, the whispers are endless. He can't make out most of it—there are too many speaking at once—but hearing his name in the darkness is like icy water spilling down his back.

He tries to ignore it and focus on the strange wall in front of him. In the circle illuminated by the torch, he makes out a handful of letters:

ED ISL

"Come here," Silas says over their shoulder. "I need your torch."

The demon sighs exasperatedly, as if walking across the cave is a massive inconvenience. When they step to his right, Silas gestures at the wall. "Hold up your torch. There's something written on the walls."

They do as instructed, then go rigid next to him. "That's not paint."

Silas grimaces at the confirmation. "Keep your torch raised."

ED ISLAND

Silas frowns. "Do you think it's the island's name?"

The demon laughs. "You think this place is called *Ed Island?* And why would someone write the island's name in a cave in blood?"

Silas bristles. "I don't know. Why would anyone write anything in a cave in blood?" He moves left, holding his torch up, heart pounding in his ears.

S CURS   ISLAN

"Cursed," the demon whispers behind him with a shiver. Silas sweeps the torch farther left, and a cold wave washes over him at the full message.

A clatter and a scream very nearly rip Silas's soul out of his body. He whirls on the demon, splayed out on the floor on top of—

A skeleton. A very much human skeleton. The skull rolls and the jaw pops off, gaping up at him obscenely.

And for the first time, Silas thinks he might actually die here.

D ami grabs Silas's arm as he yanks them up. "Well, I've done enough exploring. Time to go, I think. No treasure here, clearly."

Chittering above them stops Dami cold. The two stare at each other, then, slowly, look up.

The ceiling is moving. A blanket of bats covers every inch of stone, their chittering growing louder as they wake.

Because Dami screamed.

"Run," Dami says, but Silas doesn't move. He stares, pale and wide-eyed, at the ceiling as the first few bats peel off, their veiny wings extending. "Silas!"

The boy rips his gaze from the ceiling and looks at Dami. In most circumstances, Dami might have enjoyed the utter terror in his face, but right now they need to run and Silas looks more likely to collapse on the ground in the fetal position than run.

So Dami grabs the crook of his arm and yanks him along with them.

No sooner have they started running than the chittering turns to screeching and the beating of wings fills the air. Dami and Silas race down the narrow pathway leading uphill to the cave's mouth. But the ceiling is low, and the bats aren't far behind them—the screeching of the swarm sounds close, too close—and if they don't get out of this cave now—

Something warm and velvety smacks the back of Dami's head, and it takes every ounce of their self-control to hold in the shriek that wants to bubble out of them. Instead, they run faster, yanking Silas harder, legs burning as their boots slam into the earth.

The mouth of the cave is just ahead—the campfire they left behind still paints the walls orange. They don't hesitate, don't look back. Dami barrels past the fire, still gripping Silas's arm, still panting, and as soon as they've sprinted out into the rain, they turn a sharp right.

Wet leaves slap their face. The ground, covered in drenched greenery, is slippery and soft beneath them. But Dami and Silas don't stop. The rain hasn't eased—they're racing through a warm, permeable wall—and their torches sputter out. They run through darkness, through splashing puddles and under low-hanging branches and over fallen logs, and then something beneath Dami's foot gives.

They trip, slamming into Silas, but they don't hit the ground—instead, the ground snaps up beneath them, throwing them into the air. Dami yelps as a corded material swallows them up, cinching somewhere above their head.

A net.

Wait. A net?

Silas groans and tries to push away from Dami, but they've been yanked up so abruptly that they've landed essentially on top of each other. Dami on one side of the net, Silas on the other, each of them falling onto the other. There's no way around it really, not with the way the net is shaped, and no amount of pushing against the corded fabric is doing anything. The net just stretches against Dami's hand until it pulls taut and springs back into place as soon as they stop.

And it's still pouring.

Incredible.

"This can't be happening," Silas groans. "Are we— Is this a hunter's trap?"

"Sure looks like one." Dami pokes at the net again, squinting at the fabric. It's too tightly corded to unwind, unfortunately. But if they had something sharp . . . "Do you have a knife?"

"No," Silas answers glumly.

Dami scowls at him. "A tinderbox is important to have living on the streets, but a knife isn't?"

"I *had* a knife," Silas bites back, "but it was knocked off me when the ship turned over, so it's probably at the bottom of the ocean by now with the rest of our supplies."

Dami glowers at the net. Rain runs into their eyes, and they blink hard to clear it, but it's useless. The air trembles with rumbling thunder, thick with static. This rain is never going to end.

"Transform into someone who has a knife. A hunter."

Dami rolls their eyes. "I already told you it doesn't work like that."

"Hunters wear knives! They have them strapped to their legs and in their belts!"

Dami shakes their head. "It doesn't matter. I could make a holster, for example, but I can't make the gun that goes in it."

"You're the most useless demon I've ever met," Silas grumbles.

For some reason, that stings. Not because Dami has ever prided themself on being useful, but because they've never been helpless before. *Losing magic is the price of being human*, they remind themself, but the thought is deeply uncomfortable.

"I'm the only demonio you've ever met," they say.

"Yes, but I'd wager literally any other demon would be able to get out of a net."

It's annoying because it's true. Hell, Dami of a year ago would have been able to get out of this easily. They wouldn't even need to make a deal to do it—they'd just phase right through. But unlike their transformative ability, they haven't been able to phase since giving up their demonio status.

Unless . . . Dami frowns. They *are* reverting—that's why they can't eat or drink anything. Is it possible that they may have reverted enough that they can phase again too?

Do they want that to be true?

Dami closes their eyes and bites their lip. Phasing was changing their corporeality—essentially turning off their physical body so they could pass through something, or something could pass through them. It was always about intent, all they'd have to do was *want* to be immaterial and it would just . . . happen.

But nothing is happening. And as useful as it would be right now to be able to phase out of this net, Dami can't help but be relieved. Their deadline may be fast approaching, but they aren't that far gone.

Not yet.

Chapter 15

· · · · · · · · · · · · · · · · · · · ·

When Marisol snuck onto the ship headed to America, she'd imagined suffering a few weeks of cramped quarters and stealthily stealing food from unsuspecting sailors in exchange for a new start. The opportunity to wipe the slate clean and begin again in Connecticut, where her brother, Guillermo, was going to school, this time as herself.

In America, no one knew her old name, or her parents' insistence on clinging to the past. No one knew how the Romero Lunas prided themselves on their two "sons." No one knew the strange twins who, despite appearing nearly indistinguishable, lived in entirely different worlds. No one knew, and no one had to, because in America she could finally be the daughter and sister she always had been. She could finally be Marisol.

She hadn't anticipated the shipwreck. Or the nightmarish island they ended up on. Now Marisol has exchanged dreams of glamour, dresses, and makeup for a dead boy's thick boots—a necessity, given the number of lethally venomous snakes here—rain-drenched hair in her eyes, and a freshly sharpened machete strapped to her hip. She marches through the thick vegetation, ignoring the cold slap of wet leaves and grass against her arms and legs.

It isn't her first time traipsing through the rain forest alone, but this time she can't come back empty-handed—not if she doesn't want to get assigned to night watch *again*. Many of the others don't seem to mind night watch, but *some* people need their beauty sleep.

Guillermo was already in Hartford, so he wasn't trapped on this horrible island with her, but she could imagine what he would say.

You sure do need your beauty sleep, hermanita.

The thought makes her smile as she continues forward, pausing every couple of minutes to check the animal traps she made. This is a skill she learned from others on the island. It took weeks of trial and error before Marisol caught her first capybara. Even now, six months after she started setting traps, she only has a 33 percent success rate, at best.

Still, catching dinner a third of the time is better than not catching any food at all.

After covering the tenth snare trap under a pile of leaves—which, like the others, is empty—there's just the big one left. She stands, stretching her arms over her head. Her stomach growls, but she ignores it. Though animals have set off her big trap a number of times, she's never actually caught anything in it.

Marisol rolls her shoulders back and begins walking again, pulling the machete from her belt to cut through the thick vegetation when needed. "I still have one more trap," she says to herself. "You never know, maybe you caught something."

Marisol doesn't really believe it, but still, she won't give up until she's seen the empty trap for herself.

·········

········

It's about a fifteen-minute walk to the final trap. This one is a net trap, with a hidden net set beneath leaves with a trip wire to trigger it. It's the kind of trap that could catch large game, if it ever catches anything at all.

Marisol has walked into this clearing every day for six weeks, and every day it looks the same: towering trees with palm leaves covering the sky. It's finally stopped raining, and thick green knee-length grass and an inch of leaves blanket the ground. A handful of large, bright yellow flowers dot the perimeter, which Marisol avoids on the grounds that everything on this island kills.

She has never walked into the clearing and found her net hanging in the air, cinched around a large mass.

Dios mío.

Marisol quickly closes her mouth—her jaw was hanging open. She rushes forward, then abruptly stops and squints at the net. She didn't catch one thing; she caught *two.*

Two people, that is.

"Coño," she whispers. Marisol hurries to the tree holding the net up. The rope is anchored to a groove cut into the thick trunk—she grabs it and begins working at the knot.

Chapter 16

······················

It's the sensation of falling that wakes Dami up.

For a disorienting moment they don't understand what's happening, because falling asleep was a chore and Dami doesn't remember actually dozing off. It seemed like they'd just closed their eyes.

And then their back crashes into Silas's chest, Silas groaning beneath them, and the net falls away like a thrown blanket. They blink up at the overcast sky, barely visible in the gaps between wide green leaves, their vision clearing as their body throbs with pain. Then Silas shoves them and they roll into the mud, grimacing as slick cold earth paints their forearms and front.

At least it's stopped raining.

"So," says a voice above them. "Who are you two?"

Dami blinks up at a girl, about Silas's age, with light golden-brown skin and rain-drenched black hair pulled back into a ponytail. She wears long black trousers and a loose-fitting shirt tied at the waist, and the toe of her boot is nudging Silas's head.

"You're a girl," Silas says absurdly.

The girl looks at Silas with distaste. "Did you hit your head

········

on the way down?" Then her gaze falls on Dami, and her face softens before melting into a frown.

Dami sits up, wincing at their protesting muscles. They almost run their fingers through their hair but catch themself— their hands are absolutely slick with mud. Lovely.

Silas stands, stumbling a step before catching himself. "How did you get here?" he asks. "Were you shipwrecked as well?"

"You first," the girl says. "How long have you two been on the island?"

Dami stands, stretching their stiff, sore arms above their head. "Less than a day. How about you?"

She hesitates, then says, "We were shipwrecked six months ago."

Silas blinks. "We? There are others here?"

Rather than answering, the girl frowns and mutters, "If you just arrived . . . ella va a saber."

Dami smiles—it's been months since they've heard Spanish. Coming back to it feels like embracing an old friend. "¿Quién va a saber?" they ask without missing a beat.

She looks at them wide-eyed, startled. Dami grins. "I was born in México," they add.

El Diablo told them that much about their birth after Dami hounded him about it for years. They even found their own tiny grave marker some time ago. It was a haunting experience, but at least it proved el Diablo wasn't lying about their birthplace.

The girl grins. "So was I!"

"I was born in Boston," Silas says helpfully. Dami cringes with secondhand embarrassment.

"You should come with me," the girl says. "If you want to survive on this island, there's someone you have to meet."

. . . .

Chapter 17

....

The girl leads them through the temperate forest in silence. Now that it isn't raining like the coming of a Biblical flood, and Silas isn't running for his life, he takes in their unusual surroundings.

The trees here are unlike any he's seen before, with wide leaves—some as large as his head—waxy trunks, and fruit of all kinds dotting the foliage around him. He spots bunches of bananas and what he is mostly sure are mangoes, in addition to other colorful fruits he doesn't recognize.

Silas has never been to Connecticut before, but he's fairly confident bananas and mangoes don't grow anywhere in New England.

It doesn't make sense—not the tropical trees and fruits, not the enormous pink, yellow, and white flowers growing in bushes and grass, not the humidity so thick it feels like the air itself is liquid.

On second thought, maybe that last one isn't entirely out of the question for the height of summer in New England. Still, it's

....

113

certainly not the norm, and though Silas hasn't been here long, he'd wager that the island sees a lot of this thick heat.

Is it possible that they could have somehow strayed more than five miles off the Connecticut coast? Surely it would have been impossible to get from New England to the Caribbean in a rowboat in under two hours. But Silas doesn't know how else to explain this strange island.

Eventually, the girl leads them into a clearing and Silas's jaw drops open. This isn't just a campsite on a forgotten island, this is a village.

Huts upon huts dot the perimeter of the space, followed by a second, inner row set up in a concentric circle. Past the rows of huts is a large space, at least fifty feet across, with a huge camp-fire in the center and split logs set down like benches around it. Two men sit on the log benches, stopping their conversation to glance at the newcomers warily. Another walks around the huts, his eyes narrowing into something that looks like hostility. Silas spots fewer than half a dozen people, none of them happy to see Silas and Dami's arrival.

"Chilly reception," he mutters. Neither Dami nor the girl responds, and the quiet that falls over the small village makes Silas shiver.

Directly behind the fire is a building larger than the rest—more of a small cabin than a hut. Silas presumes that whoever they must meet lives there. Questions bubble up in his mind. Are all of these huts for five people? How long has this village been here? Are the villagers indigenous to the island? The girl said she'd been shipwrecked like he and the demon had with some others, but surely she didn't mean the entire village. So how did the others come to be on this strange island?

....

114

Then again, if the entire village consisted of five people, not counting himself and Dami, maybe they *were* all shipwrecked. But then, why would they build more huts than they had people?

"Wait here," the girl says. She walks up to the cabin and knocks on the door.

Silas feels other men watching them and tries not to squirm under their scrutinizing gazes. What exactly is happening here? Silas presumes they're probably about to meet the leader of the village, but why? Is it for an introduction? If this is just how they welcome new people to their village, why are the villagers watching them so coldly?

Maybe being found isn't the godsend it seemed to be.

The cabin door opens, and Silas's eyebrows shoot into his hair. Standing in the doorway is a girl, no older than his sixteen years. Her skin is as pale as Silas's, and her hair is so blond it's practically white.

Silas can't hear what the girl who found them says, but when the pale girl's gaze snaps to Silas, he can't look away. Something about her stare demands attention. Her eyes are an uncomfortable shade of light gray—almost like the color has been drained out of her. Gooseflesh prickles up his arms and down his back; it feels as though the girl is peering directly into his soul. When she finally shifts her gaze to Dami, Silas breathes, shoulders relaxing at last. He hadn't even realized he'd been holding his breath.

She walks with the girl until she's standing just two feet in front of them, then nods to her. "Thank you, Marisol."

Marisol nods and moves over to the side, taking a seat on one of the log benches.

Then the blond girl is looking at Silas again, and his spine goes rigid.

·········

"My name is Eve," she says soothingly. "Welcome to my island. What are your names?"

They introduce themselves. The girl doesn't even glance at the demon—her gaze has settled steadily on Silas, in a way that feels unnervingly like a lioness eyeing her dinner.

And yet he can't look away. There's something magnetic about her, something beckoning him closer. He leans forward, toward her, until his heels lift off the earth before he grounds himself again.

He takes back his initial reaction to her gaze. Her eyes are . . . stunning.

"We were shipwrecked," Silas adds. "A storm turned our boat over. We rowed over from Milford, but the storm caught us by surprise and we nearly drowned." Silas isn't sure why he's sharing so much detail about their journey—he'd only meant to say they were shipwrecked, but the rest of the story just pours out of him. "We're here to—"

"Explore," the demon cuts in, staring at him incredulously. Silas's face warms. He was about to tell her they were here to look for treasure. Even now the knowledge is an itch. He has no reason to tell the girl, but for a reason he can't explain he *wants* to. Silas clamps his mouth shut and bites his tongue. What's wrong with him?

Eve just laughs. "Explore," she says dryly. "Of course you are. We're all *explorers* here, isn't that right?"

The villagers nearest them chuckle.

The demon frowns. Silas isn't sure what she's insinuating either.

"Please." She waves her hand and settles her gaze on Silas

again. "You can be honest with me. You're here to look for treasure, aren't you?"

"Yes," Silas says immediately. It's a relief, admitting the truth—his shoulders relax, his breaths come easy. Holding that in was so *difficult*, but now she knows, and it's fine. Everything is fine. For reasons he can't quite comprehend, he wants to look at the demon and smile reassuringly but he can't look away from the girl. Her stare demands his attention, and he's glad to give it.

Eve smiles. Her voice is honey-sweet when she says, "That's okay, Silas. Most of the villagers here came searching for treasure, just like you. But it's never been found for a reason. Those who know what's good for them have stopped searching, just as you will. They've come to realize the island demands a high price for her secrets."

Silas frowns. What does that mean?

"We can pay it," the demon says firmly beside him. Silas starts—he'd forgotten they were there. Their voice is grounding, pulling him back to himself. He rubs his eyes, light-headed. He hates to admit it, but the demon is right—whatever the island demands as payment, they'll have to pay it. Silas can't go on living like this—and even if he could, he must end this curse for Maisey's sake.

If he fails, Maisey will die next. If she's lucky, she might live to see two more decades, but even that is uncertain.

Eve just smirks. "You're not the first to think you can pay her price. You should know that everyone who didn't abandon their treasure-seeking has died searching for it. I won't stop you from searching, but I don't have to. The island will."

Silas isn't sure what to make of that. The girl speaks of the island like it's alive. Like it has a consciousness, like the island itself is protecting the treasure. He can't begin to imagine what that might look like.

It's not a question he gets answered, because Eve turns to Marisol and says, "We have a recently vacated hut, don't we? They can share it."

Marisol nods. "I can show them the way."

"Good." She turns and walks into her cabin, without so much as a glance back, leaving Silas with a strange sense of longing.

As soon as the two of them enter the room, the demon throws themself toward the bed, smoke enveloping them midair. They emerge wearing a completely new set of all-black clothes before dropping onto the mattress, arms crossed behind their head, sighing contentedly.

The bed is only a thin mattress on the thatch floor, covered in blankets, but it's still larger than Silas would have expected— it's just big enough for two people. It takes up the majority of the floor space in the very small hut.

And then, with a start, Silas realizes why the bed is so large: there's only one.

"Oh no," Silas says.

"Oh yes." The demon sprawls out with a grin, then pats the empty space on the mattress next to them.

"Can't we get separate huts?" Silas asks. "It's not as if there's a shortage of them."

"Do you want to explain to Eve why you're so special you need your own hut?"

Silas groans, but they have a point. Such a request would

probably look exceedingly selfish. So, reluctantly, he pulls off his mud-encrusted boots, peels off his cold, soaked jacket, and turns to the bed.

It's only then that he realizes the demon didn't just change their wardrobe; their face has become angled, jawline sharper, shoulders broadened, chest flattened. Their hair is still long, but the right side of their head is shaved. That self-satisfied grin, though . . . that's the same.

He's going to share a bed with a stunningly handsome boy-demon, then. That certainly won't be at all problematic. Still, what other choice is there? There's barely a foot of space between the side of the mattress and the wall. He could try to sleep at the foot of the bed, he supposes, but the thatch floor hardly screams *soft*.

So, despite being certain this is a terrible idea all but guaranteed to end in his humiliation, Silas steps toward the bed.

"Whoa." The demon lifts their hand. "What do you think you're doing?"

Silas's face flames. They *patted the bed*—what else could they have meant other than inviting Silas to sleep next to them?

Their nose wrinkles in disgust. "You're covered in mud. You can't get on the bed like that."

Oh. Silas looks down at himself. The demon isn't wrong—his pants are muddy and sandy up to the knees on the front, and entirely covered in the back. He can't see the back of his shirt, but he can feel the stiffness of the dried mud all over it. He's probably flaking off dirt just standing there.

"I don't have any other clothes," Silas says. "I hope you don't expect me to sleep next to you naked because— What are you doing?"

The demon has stripped off their shirt and thrown it at

Silas's feet. His gaze lands immediately on their forearms, which bear identical tattoo sleeves of smoke drifting from their elbows to wrists. The demon isn't built like someone who works out, but their waist is thin, and a trail of black hair dusts their navel down to their pants—which they're unbuttoning?

Silas spins around, his face burning. He squeezes his eyes closed and thinks of mud, and drowning in the ocean, and blood. Anything to distract himself from the heat that has bloomed uncomfortably between his legs.

"There," the demon says after a minute. "Now you have clean clothes."

Silas looks at the pile at his feet, afraid to turn around. They were thorough—they even gave him a pair of drawers. "Um," he says. "Thank you. Are you dressed?"

The demon snickers. "Have you really never seen another naked boy before?"

"I *have*, but—"

"I'm dressed. Wouldn't want to rob you of your innocence."

Silas bites his tongue and turns around. The demon is dressed, as promised, but they've done nothing to hide their smirk. "Close your eyes," Silas says, picking up the shirt and drawers.

They roll their eyes, but they fall back on the bed and wait beneath the blanket, fully covering their head. Silas begins undressing, grimacing as he unpeels the muddy fabric glued to his skin.

"So," the demon says beneath the blanket, "what the hell was that out there?"

Silas tosses his dirty shirt on the floor and grabs the one the demon gave him. "What do you mean?"

"You just *told* her we were looking for treasure. What were you thinking?"

Silas stills. The truth is he's not sure why the truth spilled out of him like an overflowing cup. It was just so difficult to lie to her—and anyway, why should he? "What difference does it make? It's not as if she didn't know—she essentially said everyone comes here looking for treasure."

"Even so, you didn't have to tell her. We don't know her or anyone else on this island. We should be careful until we know who we can trust."

Silas snorts as he changes out of his trousers into the fresh ones. "You're one to talk about *trustworthiness.*"

"Oh, I get it. Because I'm a *demonio* I'm automatically evil and can't be trusted."

Now fully dressed, Silas turns around and crosses his arms over his chest. The demon is sitting on the bed with a blanket over their head. They look absurd—laughably so.

"Incredible," he says, "you're really going to sit there and chastise me about stereotypes *after* you manipulated me into accepting a horrible, life-altering deal?"

"It was life-altering," the demon snaps, "because you'd be dead without it. So *you're welcome.*"

Silas scowls and opens his mouth, but they continue before he can speak.

"Are you done changing yet? I feel *ridiculous* arguing with you with a blanket over my head."

"No," Silas lies. "I'm not." Then, for good measure, he adds, "And you *look* ridiculous."

"Not as ridiculous as you did with that fake mustache on your face for three days."

Silas pulls a face. "Fake mustache? What on earth are you on about?"

The demon outright cackles. "When those bandits killed you, I drew a curly mustache on your face with ink." They laugh harder. "You walked around like that for *three days*."

Silas's face goes hot. Was *that* why the demon kept having inexplicable laughing fits when they were traveling to Milford? "You wouldn't dare."

Infuriatingly, this only makes them laugh harder. "Oh, but I did. You looked *absurd*."

Silas pinches the bridge of his nose. As he marches out of the hut, the demon's laughter rings in his ears.

Chapter 18

·····················

"You aren't seriously going treasure hunting, are you?" Marisol asks the next morning.

Dami watches, chin on their hand, as Marisol shares a large fruit basket with Silas. They're sitting in the grass outside Marisol's hut. A dirt path right next to Dami leads down to the campfire in the center of the village, about thirty feet away. Some men walk past them, inexplicably glaring at the three of them as they head toward the campfire, where large baskets overflowing with fruit have been laid out.

Dami isn't sure why everyone except Marisol seems to hate Silas and them, but it fills their gut with cold dread. And then a second thought hits them: besides Marisol and Eve, they haven't seen any women or girls here. Odd.

Everything looks delicious—perfectly ripe bananas, two oranges, two grapefruit, four mangoes, and a huge green coconut the size of their head. Marisol offered them some, and they had to make up some nonsense about not being a breakfast person.

They aren't sure how they're going to explain that they aren't a lunch or dinner person, either, but that's a problem for later.

·········

Maybe they'll get lucky and nobody will ask. Marisol took Dami's change in appearance in stride—after Dami mentioned a bag of their clothes that had washed up with them, she said, *You look good*, and that was the end of that.

"We are," Dami says, answering the question about treasure hunting. "You're welcome to join us, if you want." It might be useful having her around—Marisol may not have been born here, but she's survived on this island for at least six months, so she certainly knows it better than Silas and Dami do.

"No thank you," Marisol says, dashing their hopes without missing a beat.

"What did Eve mean yesterday?" Silas asks, wiping mango juice off his chin. "About the island dissuading us from looking for treasure."

"Everyone who goes looking for that treasure dies," Marisol says bluntly. "You see those men over there?" She jerks her chin at a small group of five white men sitting near the campfire.

"What about them?" Dami asks.

"They used to be two teams of a dozen each. They came here specifically looking for treasure. It hasn't gone well, as you can tell."

Dami frowns. "What's killing them?"

"The island," she says seriously. "Animal attacks, poisonous flowers, drowning, falling off cliffs, sickness, infected wounds . . . One guy was killed by a swarm of wasps."

Dami and Silas exchange a glance. Neither of them has to say it aloud: they're suddenly rather glad they're paired with someone who literally can't die. Maybe their deal with Silas will come in handy after all.

The only problem is Silas's deal doesn't protect Dami.

·········

Granted, Silas thinks they can't die because they're a demonio, but that hasn't been the case for a while. If they die, it's over. They'll be a demonio again. Forever.

This whole mortality thing is more inconvenient than they anticipated.

"We'll be all right," Silas says confidently. Then, to Dami, "Won't we?"

They start at the question, then paint on a persona of absolute confidence. "We'll be fine."

As the sun rises, the air warms and thickens. It doesn't take long for Dami to sweat through their shirt. It probably doesn't help that today's all-black attire is trousers, again, and a long-sleeved shirt, again. They miss wearing a dress—or even a skirt—but Marisol mentioned snakes and their pant legs have already snagged on thorns more than once, so clearly uncovered ankles and shins are a bad idea here.

At least their chest is flat today, so they don't have to bother with undergarments. Though maybe they should have gone with short hair. Or fully buzzed hair. They've tied it back, showing off their half-shaved head, but the heat is getting more oppressive by the moment.

After some time, the air fills with a gentle rumbling. The island itself is still—or as still as a lush forest can get—so it doesn't feel like an earthquake. But the more they walk, the louder it gets. As they continue through the trees and brush, the deepening roar suddenly clicks in their mind.

"A waterfall," they say.

Silas nods. "I think so."

They walk faster—right into a clearing around an enormous lake. And a huge waterfall feeding right into it. The impact of the water against the lake creates a band of foggy mist in the air, like a cloud hovering at the bottom of the falls, just over the surface of the lake. As the mist disperses it catches the light, glittering with a rainbow. The lake itself is perfectly clear—a sapphire blue with white sand at the bottom.

It's beautiful.

"Wow," Dami says. And then, with a grin, they strip off their shirt.

Silas stares at them—and maybe it's the heat, but his face seems pinker than usual. "Um," he says. "What are you . . . ?"

Dami strips off their pants next, leaving just their drawers, then with a wink, races into the lake. The moment the cool water hits their legs they sigh a breath of relief and let themself sink into the water. Submerged, the world is quiet, even the roar of the falls muffled underneath the surface. Dami blinks through the water. Tiny fish swim around them, some ignoring their presence while others gently nibble at their legs. They break the surface with a laugh and wave at Silas.

"C'mon!"

Silas peers suspiciously at the water. "Are you certain it's safe?"

Dami stands and turns, looking over the placid lake. "I mean, I wouldn't try to swim under the waterfall, but the lake seems fine. Just small fish in here. And anyway, the water's so clear I don't think anything could really sneak up on you."

He hesitates, then nods and peels off his shirt.

The polite thing to do would be to look away. They could easily swim around, sink underwater, anything to give him privacy as he takes his breeches off next. But Dami won't pretend they haven't wondered what Silas might look like without his shirt, and reality doesn't disappoint.

Silas looks at them, and Dami averts their eyes, leaning back to float on the water's surface. Quiet nearby splashes tell them Silas has entered the lake, but they play it cool. Like they weren't just ogling him.

Silas clears his throat, now next to them. Dami lowers their legs and faces him with a smile.

"You know," Silas says, "it's rather unfair that you're able to choose how you look. If I could change my body at will, I would . . ."

Dami tilts their head. "Change nothing, I hope. You're gorgeous." Silas's face flames red, and Dami laughs. "For what it's worth, this is how I look. My features shift a little depending on my sense of self—more feminine, or more masculine, or more androgynous—but there's a reason I'm always the same height, with black hair, and everything else. You're looking at me."

Silas frowns. "But you can look however you want, right?"

They lift a shoulder. "Sure. But why would I be anyone else when I didn't have to be? I'm incredible." They grin at him, and Dami fully expects him to roll his eyes, or groan, or deny it. But he doesn't. There's an odd look on his face, like he's seeing Dami for the first time.

Maybe he is.

Oddly, ridiculously, Dami is suddenly self-conscious. Obviously if Silas thought they were manipulating their body to be the ideal form or whatever, it means he likes what he sees. But no one has looked at them like this, so carefully, so intensely. It makes their insides squirm. It makes them want to sink under the water.

. . . .

It makes them want to stay right here, looking right back at him.

"What will you do if you break the curse?" Dami asks.

Silas blinks, as if he hadn't thought of that. "I'll . . . go home, I suppose." He laughs a little. "Honestly, I haven't really given much thought about what I'd want to do with a normal life span. But knowing Maisey will get to live out hers . . . that's enough to make all this worth it."

Dami smiles. Obviously, they knew Silas cared about his sister, but that he put her needs before his, even when imagining the future . . . they've never had that kind of familial connection, that kind of genuine love. They don't know what it's like to want good for someone else so much that it eclipses their own desires.

It's a strange relief to see that Silas understands how special that is. How special he is.

"Did you have any family before you became a demon?" Silas asks.

"I've always wanted siblings, but there is no *before*," they answer. "So no."

Silas frowns, but Dami isn't ready to bare themself to this boy they barely know, so they change the subject. "Can I ask you something personal?"

Silas's gaze snaps up to their face. "I suppose so."

"Are you . . . ?" They clear their throat, ignoring the way their heart is suddenly drumming in their ears. "Are you attracted to people of all genders? Or specific ones? Or not attracted to anyone?"

"Oh." He hesitates, then glances around like he's checking to make sure no one else is nearby. "I've never been asked that before."

"I'm attracted to all genders," Dami says, not really sure why they're volunteering information he didn't ask for. "I mean, that doesn't necessarily mean everyone, but more like gender isn't really a determining factor for me. If someone's attractive, they're attractive, you know?"

Silas hesitates and looks around again. He opens and closes his mouth soundlessly—his hesitation alone already begins to answer their question.

There are several avenues that Dami could take to persuade Silas to answer the question, but this time they don't want to take any of them. This isn't something they want to twist out of him.

"No one is going to judge you here," Dami adds, with more genuine gentleness than they realized themself capable of. "It's literally just the two of us. But if you're not comfortable—"

"I find myself mostly attracted to boys." Silas pauses, then laughs slightly. "I haven't said that aloud before, but it's true. There are some girls that have caught my eye too. And before you I hadn't met anyone who wasn't either, but . . ." He shrugs. "You're never ugly."

Dami snorts. "High praise."

Silas's face reddens again, but this time he sinks under the water, presumably to hide it. Dami smirks and swims farther out into the lake, deep enough that their feet can't touch the ground anymore. They keep an eye out for snakes or any other unexpected water dangers, but for the moment, it actually seems safe.

Dami turns over from swimming on their back to their front, and in doing so something catches their eye. Just ahead, deep at the bottom of the lake, something brown and rectangular is sitting on the white sand. The green-blue water of the lake is so clear it looks close enough to touch, but as Dami swims over it, it's obvious that's not the case. They aren't sure exactly how deep the lake is—if they can see the bottom, it can't be that deep, can it?

So Dami takes a deep breath and plunges beneath the surface.

Turns out the lake *can* be much deeper than it appeared. After swimming for a solid twenty seconds, Dami still hasn't reached the bottom, but the wooden chest—and it's clear now that it is a chest—is just ahead. Finally, they reach it. They grip the lid to try to pry it open, but it's locked—padlocked, in fact. They dig their fingers into the sand beneath the chest and try to lift it, but it's so heavy it doesn't even budge.

With a frown, they kick off the bottom of the lake and swim back to the surface. They break the surface with a gasp, and Silas yelps nearby.

"What on earth!" he shouts. "I turned around and you'd just disappeared!"

"There's a chest," Dami pants, pointing at it. "At the bottom of the lake. It's locked, and it's really heavy. I need your help."

Silas swims next to them and peers down into the water. "It looks large."

Dami nods. "Like I said, it's too heavy for me to pick up alone. But I think if we do it together, we should be able to get it to the surface. We'll just need to make sure we get a good grip and kick off from the bottom of the lake hard."

Silas takes a deep breath and nods. "All right. Let's give it a try."

The two reach the bottom quickly, but the chest is heavier than Dami anticipated. Even with Silas holding the opposite end, and even with them pushing off with the full strength of their legs, the chest barely wobbles. They swim back up to the surface, muscles aching as they regroup above the surface.

"Okay," Dami says between breaths. "I underestimated how heavy that is."

"Why don't you transform into a body builder or something of the sort?" Silas asks. "If you're very strong, you may be able to lift it yourself."

Seems dubious, but Dami figures it's worth a try. They close their eyes and let the smoke take them, body reshaping into someone larger, someone with a wide waist and arms and legs corded with thick muscle. When the smoke clears, Silas stares at them. Then laughs.

"Excuse me," Dami says, their voice deep. "This was your idea."

That only makes Silas laugh more, which for some reason makes Dami smile. "Yes, but I didn't realize how absurd it'd be to actually see you do it."

Dami smirks, fills their lungs with air, then plunges back into the lake. With their extra-muscly legs and arms they reach the bottom faster. They plant their feet in the sand, then reach their giant arms around the trunk and pull.

The chest doesn't budge. Not even an inch.

If Dami weren't underwater, they would scream in frustration. Instead, they kick it, and the pain that shoots through their foot nearly makes them choke. They swim back up empty-handed, their toes throbbing.

"How is that possible?" Silas asks. "You look strong enough to snap a tree trunk in two."

Dami laughs bitterly. "Well, if there really is curse-breaking treasure inside, it could be magic keeping it stuck down there.

Or maybe it's just full of rocks." They close their eyes, sighing as smoke surrounds them, transforming them back to their regular self. When it clears, Silas is still frowning.

"Let's go back down one more time," Silas says. "I want to take a closer look."

So they do. This time, while Silas examines it, Dami hangs back, looking at the surrounding area. It looks completely normal down here—nothing but what you'd expect at the bottom of a lake. Silver fish dart around them, largely ignoring them. Some dark rocks sticking out of the silvery sand. Some flowy green plants that look like they're dancing underwater. All in all, it's a pretty average-looking lake, save for the shockingly clear water and pure white sand.

Dami stands, digging their toes into the soft sand, and something sharp pokes the bottom of their foot. They crouch and dig out a large, sharp rock about the size of their fist.

An idea strikes them.

After surfacing one more time, Silas shakes his head. "I don't understand what's keeping it down there."

Dami lifts the rock in their hand. "What if we don't bring the whole chest up?"

Silas's face lights up. "You think you can open it down there?"

"I think I can try." They laugh a bit. "Hopefully it's not full of paper."

"Sure feels heavier than paper."

Dami takes another breath and then they're under again. They swim quickly, trying to conserve as much air as possible for the task of trying to break into the chest. Once in front of it, they plant their feet, wind back, and swing.

It feels like trying to punch through gravy. The water slows their arm, and by the time they hit the padlock, it barely has any power at all. They try again with the same result and stop. Maybe they're going about this wrong. They scooch closer to the lock, then hold the rock just a foot away and smash it against the lock. This time it hits hard enough that their arm vibrates with the impact. Dami tries two, three more times before their lungs start to burn and they kick off for the surface again.

"Any luck?" Silas asks when they resurface.

"You have to do short swings. You should come down with me—there are more rocks down there. If we time it right, we can take turns hitting it."

So down they go again, this time with Silas at their side. It doesn't take long for him to find another large rock while Dami smashes the lock over and over again. After two more trips up to the surface and back down again, Dami's shoulders are absolutely burning with strain. But they can't stop now. It can't be coincidence that they just happened to stumble upon this chest, right?

The lock gives way so abruptly that Dami accidentally smashes it a second time. Their eyes widen as Silas yanks the padlock off and opens the chest. The two peer inside, shoulder to shoulder. It's dark, but Dami can make out . . . rocks?

Seriously?

They touch the contents, picking rock after rock out of the chest. They can't believe this. When they suggested before that it might be full of rocks, they were joking. But it really is exactly that.

A chest full of rocks.

This can't be right. They didn't—they haven't gone through all of this for a chest full of pinche *rocks*.

. . . .

Silas seems to be thinking the same thing because he starts digging through the chest with a fervor. Dami's lungs are burning again, and dark spots in their vision are all the warning they need. They elbow Silas and point to the surface. He nods, and Dami kicks off again.

They break the surface with their biggest gasp yet, shuddering as they greedily drink in oxygen. That was a close call. They were so distracted by the chest, by the lack of a find, that they forgot—

Wait. Where's Silas?

Dami peers down into the lake, heart pounding, just as Silas bursts through the water. He coughs and sputters, spitting water as Dami resists the urge to hit him.

"What did you do that for? You could have drowned! Again!"

"Apologies," Silas pants. "I know—but—look!" He shoves something hard and angled at Dami's chest. A small wooden box. "It was at the bottom of the chest, beneath all the rocks."

He actually found something. Dami laughs and throws their arms around Silas—remembering only after they sink under the lake for a second that they're both treading water.

"Sorry!" Dami says with a laugh. "I can't believe you did it! We found something!"

"Let's not get too excited until we open it," Silas says, but his eyes are gleaming.

They swim to the shore, practically jittery with excitement. They actually found something—and on their first day of searching!

Dami climbs out and squeezes the water out of their hair with their hands. As Silas pulls himself out of the lake, he's holding the box so tightly his grip is shaking. He runs his free hand through his hair, slicking it back and out of his eyes.

And then they're both out of the lake. And Silas has the box. And there's nothing left to do but open it.

Silas stares at it, turning it over in his hands. It's not a very large box—about two feet long and maybe half that tall. But treasure doesn't always have to be a giant chest overflowing with gold. It could be diamonds. Or a precious relic, maybe a crown. There are so many invaluable things that could fit into a box of that size.

But when Silas looks up at Dami, the fear in his eyes is obvious. "What if this isn't it?"

In reality, the question is a boot to the stomach. But they force a smile and it's so easy to make it natural, to fake calm. They've spent their entire life acting more confident than they feel. It's essential to survival when you need to convince strangers to trust you if you don't want to fade into nothing.

So when they say, "Then we'll figure it out together," they wish the words felt as true, as easy as they sound. They want to believe they'll figure something else out, that they could shrug off walking away empty-handed. But the truth is that while they still have some time, they don't have much. And they don't have the faintest idea what to do next if this isn't what they're looking for.

Still, as they hold Silas's gaze, the air between them feels electric. Something has shifted in his face, in the way he looks at them. For the first time, the undercurrent of disgust that was always there when Silas looked at them is gone. In its place is . . . something else. Something softer.

Do you see me yet? Dami wonders. *Or am I still just a demon to you?*

Dami's promise seems to bolster Silas. He takes a deep breath and straightens his shoulders. And then he opens it.

Inside is a corked glass bottle with a rolled-up bit of paper in it. Dami stares at it, their stomach sinking. This can't possibly be it, can it? But maybe inside will be a map?

Silas grabs the bottle and drops the box in the sand with a soft thump. He uncorks it, shakes the paper out, and flattens it on his palm. Dami leans closer, his face so close to Silas's they can feel his breath against their skin.

On the paper is a message. Just one sentence.

What you seek lies in the abyss.

Chapter 19

· · · · · · · · · · · · · · · · · · ·

B reathless with laughter, Dami and Silas retrace their steps through the forest. The air is warm, but the sun is setting and the evening coolness is settling over the island. The forest is alive with sound; the rumble of the waterfall in the distance, the chirping layers of a variety of bugs and frogs, the chittering of nearby animals and the whisper of leaves dancing in a breeze. They hadn't wandered far from the village—even with Silas's endless lives they didn't want to push their luck before getting acquainted with the island—so it's not long before they make their way back to the small dirt path that leads from the village to the beach.

"What do you think it means?" Silas asks, running his thumb over the curl of paper for the umpteenth time. Dami watches him with a small smile; Silas's excitement over their find is contagious. Frankly, Dami was shocked to have found anything at all given their utter lack of direction. It almost feels fated. Like they were meant to find it.

If you believe in that sort of thing, anyway.

When Silas looks up at them, his green eyes are warm,

· · · · · · · · ·

smiling. It's an odd sort of relief to see Silas looking at them with something other than distaste. To see the warmth in his face and know it's directed at them.

Granted, it isn't *Dami* making him happy, but that hardly matters. This treasure hunt will be infinitely less terrible if Silas doesn't hate them.

"Dami?" Silas prompts.

Dami's breath catches in their chest. Silas used their name. He didn't call them demon. Something light and hopeful bubbles up in their chest. Maybe Silas is starting to see them after all.

They're still staring at him.

Dami blinks and wrenches their gaze away, shoving their hands in their pockets as they pray Silas doesn't notice the warmth coloring their cheeks. They hadn't even realized they were staring at him.

"Not sure," they say. "But we've only been here a day. I'm sure we'll figure it out."

They break through the forest and into the clearing that houses the village. Walking down the center path toward the outer ring where their hut is located, Dami ignores the double takes from some of the villagers. But they don't think it's their painted nails or kohl-lined eyes paired with their masculine body drawing attention.

Dami could be wrong, but it *kind* of seems like no one expected them to return.

"Oh!" Marisol walks over with a relieved smile. Her hair is down now and cascades just over her shoulders in loose, dark curls. "You're both still alive. Good."

Silas laughs, but Marisol doesn't, and his laughter dies away quickly. She is, apparently, serious.

·········

Dami grimaces. "Do people really die *that* quickly when they go looking for treasure?"

Marisol lifts a shoulder. "Sometimes. Anyway, Eve wanted me to give this to you." She offers Silas a slip of folded paper sealed with black wax. Dami doesn't get a good look at it, but it kind of looks like a rose is stamped into the wax.

They arch an eyebrow as Silas takes it. "What is it?" he asks.

"I don't know," Marisol says. Then, flatly, she adds, "It's sealed."

He flushes adorably. "I know that, but I thought maybe she would have told you."

"I barely know Eve. She wouldn't share that with me."

Dami tilts their head. "She apparently trusts you enough to deliver it to Silas."

Marisol's lips thin. "She would know if I didn't pass it along. Anyway, everyone here knows better than to get on her bad side. You'll last longer if you learn the same."

She doesn't elaborate before walking away, but something about her tone makes Dami's stomach twist. There's something strange about Eve, about the glassiness in Silas's eyes when she spoke to him last night. Something is off—what has Eve done that would make Marisol give them such a cryptic warning about her?

"Huh," Silas says next to them. He's unfolded the paper. Dami peers over his shoulder and scowls.

Silas,
I'd love to sit down together for a few hours and get to know you. Please join me for dinner at my cabin this Sunday.
                    Sincerely,
                    Eve

·········
139

Chapter 20

······················

Years of dealmaking taught Dami that most people would do anything for love. Love makes people desperate—the mere notion of it makes some invent entire alternate versions of their lives that were never meant to be, only to be devastated when they don't come to pass.

It was the promise of love, after all, that had damned Dami before they were born.

For a Potential looking to amass enough energy to become a demonio, however, love makes for easy pickings. Which is how Dami finds Cara Jameson.

Cara is easy to spot. Her grief rolls off her like pulsing waves, rippling through everyone in her path. Grief alone doesn't necessarily make for a good target for a demonio, but grief coupled with desperation is a powerful lure.

They find her in a church.

There's a misconception that demonios and diablos can't enter places of worship because they're sacred. What so many don't understand is that in most cases, the building doesn't make a place sacred—the people inside it do. But people are rarely holy.

Cara has come to the church late in the night, long after the service has ended, but before the doors have officially closed for the night. There are a few others here with her, some seated in the wooden pews reading the Bible or praying, some on their knees before the altar set below a crucifix.

Cara is in the third row of pews from the front, sitting on the far right edge of the row. Well out of earshot of the others. Her hands are in a gesture of prayer, pressed against the edge of the pew in front of her, her forehead resting against them. Her lips move quickly, and though her whisper is inaudible to most, it rings clearly in Dami's ears.

"Please, God. Please. Haven't I been a faithful servant? Haven't I dedicated my life to you? I don't ask for your aid often, but please, please, please bring him back to me. I can't go on like this. Please, I'm begging you. . . ."

Dami sits beside her. Though they aren't a demonio yet, they know they're close because they've been able to materialize a body at night for some time now—they just can't hold on to it for very long, and only the person they're speaking to can see it. Still, it's infinitely better than the disembodied voice they had to work with at the beginning.

Today they wear the face of a middle-aged white man, handsome enough to not seem threatening, but not distractingly handsome. Dark brown, perfectly trimmed hair speckled with gray at the temples. Wire-rimmed glasses. And—this is important—warm brown eyes and a kind smile.

Everything about them screams safe, from their buttoned, perfectly pressed shirt to their black peacoat, shined black leather shoes, and golden wedding band. For religious white American women, the affluent, kind—but married—man at church is the least-threatening form Dami can take.

When Cara realizes Dami is sitting next to her, she sits up with a gasp, quickly wiping her tearstained cheeks.

"I'm so sorry," Dami says in a soothing, deep voice. "I didn't mean to startle you. You just seemed upset and I thought perhaps some company would be comforting."

"You haven't done anything wrong," Cara whispers quickly. "I should be apologizing—look at me. In this state, in public . . ."

"No, of course not. If you can't be honest about your emotions in the house of the Lord, where can you be?"

She smiles softly and dabs at her cheeks again. Dami wishes they could grin at how good they've become at this. Taking a deep, shaky breath, she says, "I don't think I've seen you here before. Do you go to the evening services?"

"Not usually." Dami takes her in—her tired but awake eyes, her put-together night outfit. She isn't new to late-night outings. "I tend to be more of an early bird myself, most of the time."

"Ah." She laughs a little. "Then it's no wonder we haven't met. My name is Cara Jameson."

Dami smiles at their successful calculation. "Fred

Abernathy," they say, thinking of the most boring name possible.

"Oh, what a good name. My father's name is Fred."

Dami holds in a laugh. "How about that?"

It takes them all of twenty minutes to get her sobbing hysterically into their shoulder about the love of her life who doesn't love her back—by then, everyone else in the church has left. His name is Samuel, and yesterday he said he fell for another woman. Given they've only been together two months, Dami doesn't find this especially egregious, which really just makes what they're about to do more unfortunate for Samuel.

Dami rubs her back soothingly and keeps their voice low and quiet. "What if I told you I could fix this?"

Cara looks up from their shirt, her face red and splotchy, eyes swollen. "Wh-what do you mean? It can't be fixed—he left me!"

"That's true, he did. But I can get him to realize his mistake and return to you."

She hiccups. "I don't understand. How?"

"Don't worry about that," they say smoothly. "What would you give for Samuel to love and cherish you for the rest of his life? For him to see you as his sun, his heart?" Dami smiles. "His queen."

She stares at them, wide-eyed. "You can do that?"

If Samuel had left because he'd fallen in love with another man—because he could *only* fall in love with other men—Dami wouldn't have been able to offer this deal. But because he left for another *woman* . . . "I can."

Dami watches her carefully as she processes this.

. . . .

She hasn't moved away from them, not yet, which means she still feels safe. Her eyes are still leaking tears, but her breaths are slowing. The idea is taking root, hope blossoming in her eyes.

"Are you an angel?" she whispers.

At that, Dami does laugh—they can't help it. They know demonios—and a couple of diablos—who will look a mark in the eye and say they were sent from heaven. Such a bold-faced lie has always seemed tacky to Dami, though. They don't have to lie to get what they want.

"Not quite. But I do hold a certain power that allows me to help people like you."

She sits up a little, not quite pulling away, but the thought is entering her mind. This is the first part where Dami has to be careful. Religious people can go one of two ways: either they run away screaming "Demon!" or they accept Dami as a miracle they won't question. It depends on whether their desperation overrules their piety.

But if Cara is here this late, it's because she either missed the evening service or is so despondent that she's stayed for many hours past the end of the service, so Dami has a pretty confident guess which direction she'll fall in.

Slowly, she pulls out of their arms, but she doesn't move away. She's still sitting so close their legs are touching, and she doesn't seem in any hurry to get away. And then she says, "If you can really do what you claim, what would it take?" and like an expert fisherman feeling the tug on a line, Dami knows they have her.

"After you've lived a long, happy life with Samuel, after you've had children and grandchildren and great-grandchildren, your body will grow old and your time on the earth will end. Eventually, you'll die, and only then will I hold your soul."

Cara's eyes widen. "My . . . soul?"

Dami nods.

She squeezes her hands together, then flattens them on her lap. "If you . . . hold my soul, will I still go to heaven?"

This is the second danger point with religious people. The promise of an eternal afterlife in the promised land is a terrifying thing to lose. Dami doesn't know if heaven is real, but they know the lake of fire priests use to terrify their followers into obedience certainly isn't.

"I don't know," Dami says honestly. "I won't need your soul forever. Once I'm done, it's possible you'll go to heaven. All I can promise you is you won't suffer."

Cara bites her lip, then looks back down at her lap. She hasn't run away screaming. She's still considering, as Dami knew she would. After a moment, she meets their gaze again. "How do I know you can really do what you promise?"

Dami tilts their head. "If I can't, then I can't take your soul, either, so your agreement will be harmless."

Cara wrings her hands together, and when she looks at them, her brow has creased into a frown. "Your name isn't Fred, is it?"

Dami only smiles.

They sit in silence for a while, but Dami is patient.

. . . .

Watching el Diablo swindle soul after soul, they learned fast the power of silence. They lean back in the pew, their arms resting on the back of the seat. The church is so quiet now that every sound carries. The quiet whistle of wind outside. The squeak of their boot on a loose floorboard. The muffled hiss of the heel of Cara's shoe digging into the red carpet runner in the aisle. The quiet tap of Dami's fingers drumming softly on the backs of the wooden seat.

Dami isn't sure how long they sit there, but eventually, Cara turns to them again. "I want his love to be true."

An odd word to choose, *true*. "If Samuel's love were true, you wouldn't need my assistance," they say. "But I can promise it'll be genuine. He will love you like he loves no one else. You'll be the light of his life."

"And he'll be happy?" she asks.

Dami's lips twitch with a smirk. Cara's made her decision—that much is clear. Now she's just trying to justify her actions. Convince herself that there isn't anything wrong with interfering with reality. Dami's seen it before—even as they know they're doing something wrong, humans want reassurance about their guilt. It's why Catholicism works so well; first the church makes their adherents feel guilt for even the most natural of urges, then they ensure that the only way to relieve that guilt is to go to church.

Dami isn't a priest, but they know how to twist any emotion to their favor. "He will be," they say. "That I can promise you."

She nods, squaring her shoulders. "I'll do it."

They smile and offer their hand. "Shake on it, and it'll be done."

Perhaps motivated by a desire to make this a certain thing before she can change her mind, Cara doesn't hesitate. Dami has no sooner extended their hand than she takes it and shakes twice.

A rush of wind swirls around them, circling them like a cyclone. Dami closes their eyes and smiles as energy surges through them, kick-starting their heart and electrifying their veins—but this time, something shifts. The heaviness of holding on to a corporeal form lifts. Their waning energy reserves refill like an overflowing dam. The fight to maintain a body fades away, and in its place settles ease. Holding on to a form that can interact with the living is as natural as breathing.

A smile bubbles up, impossible to hide. They don't need el Diablo to know they finally did it.

After years of struggle, they're a demonio at last.

The wind settles. The church is quiet, undisturbed. Cara stares at them, wide-eyed, her hair tousled. Dami stands, clasping their hands together with a soft clap. "Well, it was wonderful to meet you, Cara. I'll see you again."

They turn and step into the aisle, but Cara grabs the sleeve of their coat. "Wait," she whispers urgently. "Is it— is it done? How long will it take? How will I know?"

Grimacing, Dami carefully slides their coat fabric out of her fingers. "It's already done. I'm sure you'll hear from Samuel soon."

"What if I don't? How do I find you?"

"You don't." The manufactured warmth in Dami's face melts away. The deal is made; they don't need to pretend anymore. "When the time comes, I'll find you."

Something like fear creeps into her face—her eyes widening, what little color she had leaching out of her pale skin. Dami sighs, facing her again. "I haven't swindled you. We've made an agreement, and I always uphold my agreements. Samuel will reach out to you soon. Go home, get some rest, and have some faith."

Her tense shoulders relax. "Okay," she whispers. "Whoever you are . . . thank you."

Dami's stomach swoops. They purse their lips and turn away, moving quickly down the carpeted aisle with muffled steps and into the night. There's nothing to thank them for; they haven't done her any favors. They've made an agreement, and like most who make deals with demonios, she'll be cursing them soon enough.

Chapter 21

· · · · · · · · · · · · · · · · · · · ·

S tanding just outside Eve's cabin, Silas hesitates with his knuckles inches from the door. He isn't certain why anxiety coils in the pit of his stomach like a garden snake. It's not as if the dinner means anything beyond what the note said—that Eve wants to get to know him. The whole thing has made Dami astoundingly grumpy; over the past four days the demon hasn't missed a single opportunity to take a jab at Eve or her invitation while they've explored the village's surrounding area together in an unsuccessful search for more clues.

Silas hasn't said it aloud, but he can't help but suspect Dami is bitter they weren't invited too.

Clearly, Silas's original theory that demons don't feel emotions was wrong, because Dami is full of them. And then, of course, there was the moment by the lake, when Dami promised to keep looking for the treasure with him . . . and Silas actually believed them.

Then we'll figure it out together.

Silas isn't certain why Dami is determined to see this through, but he can't deny that the demon genuinely seems to

· · · · · · · · ·

want to help him end the curse. Whatever Dami's motives are, Silas must admit he's grateful not to be doing this alone.

The door swings open, catching Silas awkwardly frozen midknock. Eve smiles as he drops his hand, heat creeping up his neck.

"Thanks for joining me, Silas," she says with a voice like strawberries dipped in sugar. "Come in."

"Thank you for the invitation." Silas steps inside, taking in the room as Eve closes the door behind him.

The cabin is nearly as large as his home back in Boston, which is to say not very large, but easily four times the size of the tiny hut he currently shares with Dami. Her bed—which actually has an elevated wooden frame in addition to the mattress—is twice the size of the one he and Dami share. A crackling fireplace to the right is cooking something that smells *incredible* over a spit. To the left, a closed chest and a small but beautifully carved wardrobe sit against the wall. A bearskin rug is laid over the floor—are there bears on the island?—with a small coffee table set up in the center, two pillows on the floor on either side.

"Where did you get all this furniture?" Silas asks, awestruck. "Unless—did you make it?"

Eve laughs like wind chimes in a gentle breeze. "No, but my father did." Silas's eyebrows rise in surprise, but she shakes her head. "My parents were shipwrecked here many years ago, just like you, but they were the only ones here. They built this cabin and this furniture—my father was a carpenter—all before I was born. Unfortunately, they both passed several years ago."

Silas's shoulders slump. How horrible it must have been, being trapped here alone after her parents' deaths. "My condolences. My father died when I was young, and that was hard

·········

enough. I can't imagine what it must have been like here on your own."

Eve shrugs and moves over to the fireplace, peering at the food cooking on the spit. "Losing them was difficult, but this island is my home." She pauses, glancing back at Silas with a small, contagious smile. "And anyway, I wasn't alone here for long. It was barely a month after their passing that another shipwreck brought the first inhabitants of the village we have now."

Eve grabs a thick wooden board that was leaning against the wall and pulls two fish off the spit and onto the board. Silas sits at the coffee table and a few minutes later Eve serves the fish—skinned and cut into fillets—on the wooden board.

"This is a bang-up meal." Silas grins at her. "Thank you very much."

She winks at him. "Thanks for wandering into Marisol's trap."

Silas's smile becomes awkward, and he turns to the food. The fish is soft and hot—it practically melts in his mouth—and is seasoned with herbs grown around the island, he'd wager. This may be the best meal he's eaten in over a year.

God, being here with Eve in this homey cabin, eating delicious food, sitting on a soft pillow—it all feels so *right*. Her voice is like honey, her proximity fills him with warmth. It all feels comfortingly familiar, as if he's been here before, perhaps in a dream.

"So where are you coming from?" Eve asks lightly.

Silas blinks, his mind moving like molasses. His thoughts feel muddied and warm, viscous—they slip off his tongue and disappear into the ether. "Boston," he says between mouthfuls. "This food is incredible. . . ."

. . . .

"I've never been to Boston," Eve says, then laughs a little as if she'd forgotten. "Well, I've never left the island, so I suppose I haven't been anywhere, really."

Silas grins, though he doesn't know why. Then again, why shouldn't he smile? He's with Eve. Eve is an angel. "Why haven't you ever left?"

She blinks, wide-eyed, as if the thought had never occurred to her. "Why would I leave?"

"To get supplies? See the world?"

Eve shakes her head. "Everything I need is on the island. I have no reason to leave my home. I love it here." She looks at Silas, her expression full of warmth. "The island may be difficult for strangers to understand, but it's my home. I know this land like I know myself."

Silas supposes that makes sense. Prior to meeting Dami, he'd never left Boston, and he'd never had much desire to. If it weren't for the curse, he might have been perfectly content staying there forever—it was home, after all.

This is Eve's home. Why would she ever want to leave? Why did he even ask that?

"I love hearing stories from around the world, though," she gushes, resting her chin on her hands. "I've met people from all over. A number of Englishmen, Frenchmen, and Americans have come onto my shores to try their hand at treasure hunting. You might have met some of the Americans already."

Silas hasn't really interacted with them, but he nods anyway. "They came to this island on purpose? Not Charles Island?"

"A couple have come here on purpose," she says. "Most have washed up by accident. The seas are especially rough around the island."

"We noticed," Silas says with a small laugh.

"I'm very glad you survived. So many get caught out there in the storms and never make it to the shore."

A thought like a chill washes over him: *Silas* didn't make it to the shore at all. Everything from the moment they left Milton Beach was by Dami's effort. If it weren't for them, Silas absolutely would have drowned.

He never did thank the demon, but maybe he should.

"I got lucky," Silas says at last. "I was knocked unconscious, but Dami swam us to shore."

"How fortunate. How do you like the fish?" Eve asks.

Silas sighs happily as her voice warms over the chill. "It's delicious. It's so impressive that you can do all this without a full kitchen."

She beams. "Why, thank you, Silas. I'm always happy to provide for a cute boy."

Ah, and there it is. Silas finds himself smiling, if only because he doesn't know how else to react. Eve isn't exactly unattractive, but while Silas has lost count of how many boys he's daydreamed about, he can count on one hand the number of girls who have caught his eye. And even with the sense of warm familiarity that makes him want to stay here, Eve isn't one of them.

But Dami is, a traitorous voice whispers in his mind, reintroducing the chill. Silas shoves the thought far, far away. Dami is a demon. An unfairly attractive demon, but a demon nonetheless. He won't allow himself to entertain whatever attraction he may feel for them.

Still, Eve seems amicable enough, and Silas can work with that. "I was actually wondering if you might be able to help me with something."

Eve smiles wryly. "Let me guess. You want me to help you with your treasure hunt."

Silas grins guiltily. "Am I that predictable?"

"It's what anyone who came here with purpose wants." She shakes her head and looks away, but the smile hasn't slipped off her face, so she doesn't really seem that annoyed by the request. "What do you need my help with?"

The truth flows out of him like water from a spout. "We found this . . . clue, I suppose. It says, *What you seek lies in the abyss.* Do you have any idea what that could mean?"

Eve arches an eyebrow. "Where did you find that?"

"In a chest, at the bottom of a lake. Dami is actually the one who noticed it."

"Interesting." She sighs and leans back on her arms. "I'll give you the same warning I give everyone else: if you insist on searching for the treasure, you will die. It's cursed—everyone who goes looking for it meets an untimely end. If you value your survival, you'll stop looking."

"Wouldn't be the first time," Silas says, the words sliding off his tongue like melting ice cream.

Eve arches an eyebrow. "What do you mean?"

Why did he say that? Silas frowns, blinking hard as he tries to clear his muddled thoughts. "I've . . . survived a lot."

Eve looks at him skeptically. "Well, believe me when I say you won't survive this. Don't say I didn't warn you."

Chapter 22

....

Dami isn't jealous.

Annoyed? Sure. Already tired of an absolutely doomed relationship between a cursed boy and an ominous girl? Absolutely. But *jealous?* Please, what is there to be jealous about? If anything, it's nice that they're getting some time to themself in their hut. Alone.

"God, Dami," they whisper to themself. "Get yourself together. You're embarrassing yourself."

"You never did like being alone," says a voice directly behind them.

Dami freezes, their spine ramrod-straight. Gooseflesh races down their back and their heart leaps into their throat—but he's not here. He can't be here.

El Diablo is dead, they remind themself over the pounding of their pulse. *I saw him die.*

But, god, the voice was *so clear*. Like he's standing right behind them.

Dami jumps to their feet, refusing to look back. Being alone in their hut is overrated. They're taking a walk.

....

The cool summer breeze grounds Dami when they step outside. They close their eyes and inhale deeply, taking in the fresh outdoor air, tinged with sea salt. *This*, they think as the wind tousles their hair, *this is why I'm here.*

It's such a simple thing, being in the world. But to Dami, it's everything.

They've just stepped into the center of the village, where the campfire is always roaring and people gather, when a man's voice rings out.

"Over here, beautiful!"

Dami grimaces. The catcall comes from the oldest of the six American men sitting on a log bench across the fire—a rough-looking man with unflattering muttonchops and a ruddy, sunburned face. His companions, men varying in age from their early twenties to middle-aged, all smirk or snicker as they watch. Dami can't say this is any better than the glares they were getting the day prior.

"Where were you hiding yesterday?" the man continues. "Your brother isn't nearly as cute as you."

Dami isn't sure whether he's referring to Silas or themself on a boy day, but either way . . . gross.

"Why don't you come over here, and when I find that treasure, I'll take you with me." He winks.

Dami doesn't bother disguising the revulsion on their face, but before they can say anything, someone shouts behind them.

"Dami, ¡ahí estas! ¡Te estaba buscando!" Marisol wraps her arm around Dami's waist. The winking man's smile slips off his face as she leans close to them. "Paul and his friends will lose interest if they think you only speak Spanish," she mutters under her breath.

Dami grins as Marisol whisks them around, turning back toward the huts. "Esos hombres son asquerosos."

"Disgusting *and* dangerous," Marisol agrees as they move out of earshot. "No dejes que descubran que estás buscando el tesoro."

Dami frowns and lowers their voice. "Do you think they'll hurt us if we find it?"

"I think they'll do anything for that treasure," she answers darkly. "It's the only way off the island."

It's endearing how terrible Dami is at playing dominoes. After saving them from the leering Americans, Marisol invited them to her hut. Dami spotted the mostly complete set she'd found washed up on the beach almost immediately, and so here they are, sprawled out on her hand-braided grass rug, on their fourth game.

"So how do you know the treasure is the only way off this terrible island?" Dami asks, frowning at their dominoes.

Marisol lifts a tile and runs her thumb over the indentations of the pips. "I don't know for sure, but it's what everyone says. Supposedly the treasure is cursed, which is why everyone who looks for it dies, but it's also impossible to leave the island without it."

"Have you tried?"

Marisol snorts. "Do you really think I've just been sunbathing and eating coconuts for six months?"

Dami grimaces. "Sorry, I just meant . . . how can you be sure it's impossible to leave without the treasure?"

"Because we've all tried. Every time, something ridiculous

happens to ruin the effort. We made a raft a month after the shipwreck that landed me here and lightning struck it and destroyed it. Someone else tried to swim to Charles Island and a shark attacked him—*a shark!* Everyone has a story about how they tried and failed to leave, and not all of us survived the attempt."

Dami's face darkens. "I'm sorry."

She lifts a shoulder, placing a tile into play. "I wouldn't even care about the treasure at all if I could just leave. I'm the only person here who didn't come looking for it."

Dami blinks. "Everyone else came hunting for treasure?"

Marisol nods. "I didn't know it at the time, but the ship I stowed away on was full of treasure hunters who were looking for treasure in la Nueva España before setting their sights on this island. Eve said once that the island calls to the greedy and I thought she was being dramatic, but *every* shipwreck has brought more treasure hunters here."

"That's . . . odd."

"I think it's all part of the curse. Like a siren's call."

Dami nods slowly, turning a domino tile in his fingers. "Has anyone come close? Or found any clues?"

Marisol bites her lip. "Not that I've heard. But everyone's so secretive about it. No one knows exactly how the curse works, so they all want to be the first one to find it. I suppose maybe some are worried the treasure will only grant passage off the island to a few."

Dami's following silence is unusual. Marisol looks up, studying their face more carefully. Dami is looking at their tiles but when they glance up and see her watching them, they quickly avert their gaze. Are they . . . hiding something?

"Did *you* find something?" she asks. Dami rather pointedly doesn't look at her. Marisol gasps. "You did! What did you find?"

Dami sighs and places their tile. "*What you seek lies in the abyss.* That's the only clue we have, and we have no idea what it means."

Marisol grins. "Have I mentioned I *love* puzzles?"

Dami laughs slightly. "Oh yeah? Any idea what it could mean?"

She frowns, thinking it over. She certainly hasn't come across anything on the island that might qualify as an abyss. Is the clue metaphorical? But what would that even mean?

"Not yet . . . ," she says ruefully. "But I'll let you know if I think of something."

Dami nods, then changes the subject. "So you stowed away on a ship. Where were you trying to go?"

"My twin brother, Guillermo, is going to school in Hartford. We have a cousin who lives there, and I was going to join them."

Dami frowns. "They must be worried about you."

"By now I imagine they think I'm dead." She sighs. "I just want to get off this island and see him again. Guillermo was the only one who . . ."

Marisol hesitates. The truth isn't something that's always safe to share, but she's certain Dami would understand. After all, from what Marisol has observed in her short time knowing them, Dami's appearance seems to shift with their gender.

So if it's safe to tell anyone about her truth, she imagines Dami would be the one.

Dami has looked up from the dominoes, concern etched on their face. Marisol takes a deep breath and says, "Guillermo was

· · · · · · · · ·

the only one who always saw me as his sister, rather than his brother."

Dami's eyes widen in understanding, and they smile. "Kindred spirits," they say. "I knew I liked you for a reason."

The relief of being seen feels like a leaden blanket slipped off her shoulders. For a moment they just look at each other, and the warmth in Dami's expression is so comforting Marisol can't help but relax. It's such a balm, being fully seen and accepted. Dami places a tile, still smiling. "So is that where you'll go when you get off this island? Hartford?"

"When?" Marisol grins. "Are you really that confident?"

"Well, *I'm* not staying here forever," Dami responds. "So I guess I'll just have to take you with me."

Marisol laughs. "I would love that."

Sometime later, Dami makes their way back to their hut and is startled to find Silas pacing inside.

"There you are!" he says. "Where have you been?"

The truth is Dami lost track of time with Marisol. They can't remember the last time they laughed so hard or smiled so much—their cheeks still hurt from grinning.

It was such a relief to spend time with someone who doesn't see them as a demonio.

"What has you so agitated?" they ask.

Silas shakes his head. "I was hoping I might be able to get more insight into the abyss clue with Eve, but . . . I couldn't even ask. As soon as the treasure came up, she kept saying we'll die if we look for it. But I don't know who else could possibly know."

Dami frowns. "I mentioned the abyss clue to Marisol, and

she didn't seem to have any ideas, but . . . maybe we could ask her again in the morning. We could try to come up with some ideas together."

Silas blinks. "You told Marisol?"

"She doesn't want the treasure," Dami says quickly. "At least, not for herself. Apparently everyone on the island thinks the treasure is the only way *off* the island. I don't suppose Eve said anything about that."

Silas shakes his head, his brow furrowing. "No, but . . . Eve doesn't seem at all interested in leaving the island, so I suppose that's not a surprise. But if everyone thinks the treasure is the only way to leave . . ."

"Then we're competing with the Americans here too," Dami finishes. "And they're all just as desperate as we are to find it."

Chapter 23

· · · · · · · · · · · · · · · · · · · ·

When Silas wakes in the morning, he no longer has the thin blanket he'd fallen asleep with. He peers over his shoulder and finds it instantly: wrapped around Dami, on top of the *other* thin blanket they already had.

Silas scowls and grabs the edge of his blanket and tries to yank it back, but Dami has managed to wrap themself in it entirely in a cocoon-like fashion, so they—and the blanket— barely budge. With a huff, Silas lies on his back and glares at the thatch roof. As if to spite him, a leaf dislodges from the roof and floats down on top of him, landing square on his face. Or it would have, anyway, if Silas hadn't batted it out of the way and rolled off the bed onto the thatch floor with a muffled grunt.

Side throbbing, Silas sits up, ready for the day to be over. Dami doesn't seem to have noticed his rude awakening—or else they're pretending not to, because they still seem to be fast asleep.

What do demons dream of?

Before this misadventure, Silas hadn't realized demons sleep

· · · · · · · · ·

at all. The new question blooms in his mind, unbidden. *I don't care*, he reminds himself.

Dami would say, *You wouldn't have to remind yourself if you really didn't care*—and Silas isn't sure why he's supplying answers from Dami, but he doesn't like it. Rubbing his eyes, he inhales deeply through his nose and pushes the unwanted thoughts from his mind.

A knock at the door makes him jump. Silas frowns—what time is it? He doesn't *think* he slept late, but then again, he has no way to tell the time, especially since he can't see the sun from inside the hut.

Dami grumbles, *Five more minutes*, so Silas forces himself to his feet and crosses the small space to the door.

"Oh, great!" Marisol says when he opens the door. "I hope I didn't wake you."

"I was already awake," Silas says.

"Perfect. Can I come in?"

Silas shrugs and steps out of the way. When he turns around, Dami is sitting upright on the bed, fully dressed. Black trousers and an expertly tailored black shirt threaded with silver at the cuffs. Their hair is long and tied up in a knot, their jaw angled, their eyes framed with smoky kohl, and their lips glossy.

Silas is sure Dami was asleep fifteen seconds ago, but here they are, making Silas the least put-together person in the room.

"Buenos días, Marisol," Dami says.

Marisol smiles. "Buenos días. So I was thinking about that clue all night and"—her smile widens into a grin—"I think I know where we should look next." Without further ado, she pulls a folded piece of parchment out of her pocket, unfolds it, and carefully flattens it against the bed.

·········

A map of the island. Or at least, Silas is mostly sure it's a map of the island. He blinks at it disbelievingly before turning to Marisol. "Does everyone else know you have a map of the island?"

Marisol lifts a shoulder. "I don't think so, but even if they do, it doesn't matter. My map doesn't mark treasure, it's just the areas of the island I've been to."

Silas's mouth nearly falls open. "Wait, *you* drew this?"

She smiles sheepishly. "I did. My father is a cartographer, and he taught me the trade. . . . Anyway, it's not complete, but here." She points to a spot on the western coast, which is colored dark on the map, labeled Black Rock Cove. "This area here is a really rocky coast—and the rock is pure black, like obsidian or granite. It has a lot of shallow pools that look endlessly deep because of how black the rock is, like—"

"An abyss," Silas finishes softly.

"Exactly." Marisol grins. "At the very least I think it's worth exploring."

"Sounds cool even if there isn't treasure there," Dami says, stretching their arms over their head. "I'm in."

Marisol looks at Silas expectantly.

He hesitates. "Why are you helping us?"

"Do you think I enjoy being trapped on this island?" Marisol arches an eyebrow. "The way I see it, the sooner we find the treasure, the sooner I can leave this godforsaken place. Because if I help you two find it, you'll take me with you on your way out. Deal?"

Silas looks at Dami, who shrugs and says, "Sounds fair to me."

He has to agree. So, pulling his shoulders back, Silas extends his hand to her. "Marisol, you have yourself a deal."

. . . .

• • • • • • • •

When Dami suggested working with Marisol to find the treasure, they'd forgotten the risk that Marisol might see Silas die, which could be a problem. Still, Silas died the day they arrived on the island. He'd told Dami before that he usually only dies once a week, and today is their eighth day on the island . . . but what are the odds, really, that it'll happen today?

Hopefully they won't have to find out.

As they traipse through the forest, the air smells fresh—like water and, well, *green*. The chirp and squawk of birds and the rustle of small animals darting through the undergrowth are so unlike anything Dami has ever experienced, it feels otherworldly.

They've only been walking for ten minutes or so, but the heat is intense—and so humid Dami can practically feel the still air against their face. It's like a warm, wet, unwanted blanket. They wish once again that they could wear a skirt— or even a dress—to try to mitigate the heat, but at least their linen blouse is airy and tying their hair up into a bun has kept their neck cool.

For the most part, Dami is used to it—though they stayed a couple of months in Boston, they'd spent a considerable amount of time in the Caribbean before that—just not in the rain forest. Still, the weather here is unnervingly similar, which again makes no sense whatsoever.

How on earth is it rain-forest levels of humid in Connecticut?

Silas, on the other hand, does not seem at all prepared for this climate. His shirt is already soaked through, sticking to him like a second skin. Long strands of brown hair are plastered to his face, and his skin shines with sweat. It probably doesn't help that he's carrying their only shovel—courtesy of a reluctant Eve—over his shoulder.

"It feels like August," Silas pants. "A really horrible August."

"I suspect it's like this year-round." Marisol lifts her shoulder. "In the six months I've been here, there haven't been any season changes besides rainy and really rainy."

"I don't get it," Dami says. "Nothing about this island fits with where it's located. If I didn't know better, I'd think we were in the tropics."

Silas shakes his head. "It's an island hidden by magic. Did you actually expect it to follow New England rules?"

That's . . . possibly a fair point.

In the last ten minutes, neither of them has been in any mood for talking. Silas has drunk probably half of his glass water bottle already, and Dami's calves are burning. Truth be told, though they've done plenty of walking during their time in a human body, they haven't done that much walking on uneven ground.

Turns out walking over fallen logs and under low-hanging branches and around rocks and up steep hills and down mud-slick declines is a little more difficult than walking along a city road.

"Ow!" Silas yelps, and collapses, clutching his ankle.

Dami grimaces and steps up to him, offering their arm. "Roll your ankle?"

"Something bit me!"

Marisol's eyes widen. Dami frowns and crouches next to Silas. With him holding his leg like that, it's impossible for them to see anything. Not to mention that whatever bit him—if something did indeed bite him—must be small, because Dami certainly didn't see anything.

"Are you sure? Let me see."

"Of course I'm sure!" Silas snaps. "I felt teeth in my leg!"

And that's when they spot it—a glint of color slithering away. Reddish-brown scales, so dark on top it's nearly black, with a pale snout.

"Oh no," Marisol says.

A snake. Bright colors usually mean venomous, right? But this snake isn't brightly colored—does that mean it isn't dangerous? Something in the back of Dami's brain tells them there are similar varieties of snakes, some venomous, some harmless— and the color doesn't always correspond to how dangerous it is. But Dami sure as sin can't identify what type of snake that was.

"Do you know if that kind of snake is venomous?" Dami asks her.

Marisol shakes her head. "I'm not familiar with the individual snakes on this island, but people *have* died of snakebites here so at least *some* of them are."

"Let me see," Dami says to Silas again, more urgently.

Silas winces but pulls his hand away. Dami carefully rucks up his trouser leg. Three pairs of two small red dots right above the end of Silas's boot. The wound is bleeding, but not much. Dami grabs a black handkerchief from their pocket and hands it to Silas. "Press that against it until the bleeding stops."

To Dami's surprise, he does as instructed without comment.

"We should head back," Marisol says. "Eve would know if that snake was venomous."

They nod. "I agree."

"No!" Silas says quickly. "We're nearly there. And in any case, there aren't any venomous snakes in Connecticut." He frowns. "I think."

Dami arches an eyebrow. "Even if that's true, I thought we just agreed this island doesn't play by New England rules?"

Silas waves them off. "I'll be fine. It hurts, but I'm sure I can still walk. I've had worse, believe me."

"But—"

"What's the worst that could happen? It kills me?" Silas looks at them, his gaze heavy with implication.

Another fair point, they suppose.

"Um," Marisol says, "dying seems like a bad worst-case scenario."

They haven't told her about Silas's curse. Dami looks at Silas questioningly, but he shakes his head.

Dami sighs and stands. "Fine, but if you die, I'm not carrying you back to the cabin."

"I'm not going to die." Silas ties the handkerchief around his leg and stands. He cringes as he puts weight on his foot, but he doesn't collapse, and Dami supposes that's good enough. "I can make it. We're nearly there."

Marisol looks at the two of them incredulously. "Are you really going to keep going? He could be poisoned!"

"I want to carry on," Silas says stubbornly.

Marisol mutters something unkind in Spanish, but they move forward.

Dami isn't sure how long they walk before they notice how oddly quiet Silas has been. They turn around and find him lagging fifteen feet behind. His steps are uneven as he drags the shovel alongside him. He's sweating and sickly pale.

"Are you okay?"

Silas waves them off. "I'm fine," he says breathlessly. "Just a little nauseous—the heat may be affecting me."

Marisol rolls her eyes.

Dami's frown deepens. "The heat or the snakebite?"

"I just need a quick break," Silas says. Then adds, "Please."

So he's definitely ill, then.

Marisol and Dami meet him halfway in a small clearing. Silas sticks the end of the shovel into the dirt with a wince, then lowers himself to the ground while leaning against a tree. Dami frowns at him until Silas catches on and stares back at Dami with an arched eyebrow, as if to say, *What?*

They turn away with a roll of their eyes after that.

I only care because I don't want to drag him all the way back to the cabin, they tell themself. If Silas dies, Dami isn't sure how long it'll take for him to wake, and they don't want to be stuck waiting around for him here on the beach.

Sure.

They sigh, wiping sweat off their brow with the back of their hand. Finding this treasure is proving to be more difficult than they'd hoped. They still have seven weeks before their deadline, and though they might be cutting it close with the whole getting-to-England part, it's still possible.

Dami allows themself to imagine what it might be like if they actually pull this off. Silas could be free of his curse, and Dami could finally be human. Really human. They'll never have to live a half life again.

But what if I can't transform anymore? The thought shudders through them, twisting their stomach. Being stuck in a static body while their sense of who they are shifts day to day would be . . . difficult. Dami has never had to experience not fitting into their body, because their body has always shifted to fit them. But it's entirely possible—probable, even—that

• • • • • • • • •

169

when they fully become human they won't be able to do that anymore.

The thought is terrifying. But the only thing that scares them more is the prospect of an eternity as a demonio. They can't go back to that half life, not now that they've tasted incredible food, felt the warm touch of another, smelled the fresh salt of sea air. Even the cold rain on their skin, the stench of garbage, the sting of a cut—even the bad reminds them they're alive. They're here, grounded, real.

They can't go back. They can't. They won't survive it.

Dami turns back to Silas, who seems determined to look casual even though he's paler than usual—and a bit flushed. His forehead is beaded with sweat, though in all fairness that could very well be from the sticky heat.

"I still think we should go back," Marisol says. "You look ill, Silas."

Silas shakes his head. "I just need a few more minutes. I'll be fine." He leans his head back against the tree trunk and closes his eyes. "Eve did warn me searching for the treasure is dangerous."

Dami snorts. "Of course she did."

Silas opens his eyes, narrowing his gaze at them. "What do you mean by that?"

"There's something off about her. Don't you think it's odd how suspiciously callous she is about all the death happening here?"

Silas's frown deepens and he shakes his head, wiping sweat from his brow. "If you grew up on an island where people were dying all the time, you'd probably be more casual about death too."

"Absolutely not."

"How would you know?"

Dami opens their mouth and then, spotting Marisol looking at the two of them like squabbling children, snaps it shut. Dami *would* know; they may not have grown up on this island, but they *were* surrounded by death. They've watched more people die than they care to think about. But they can't say that without revealing their upbringing to Marisol.

"Death should never get easier," they say instead. "No matter how many times you've seen it happen. But Eve seems to *like* throwing the threat of death around."

"Eve doesn't have any reason to want the people who come here to die."

Dami snorts. "Doesn't she? If people find the treasure, they'll get to leave—then she won't be the leader of her own de facto village."

But Silas just shakes his head. "If everyone dies, she won't have a village to lead either. And anyway, I don't think that's in her character."

Dami laughs incredulously. "Based on what? You've spoken to her, what, twice?"

"I suppose I don't immediately think the worst of people," he says coolly.

The words are a slap in the face. Dami has always thought the expression *seeing red* was an exaggeration, but for a moment their anger is so clear, so intense, that their vision narrows on the boy as their pulse throbs in their temples.

"No," they manage to say, a tremble in their voice. "Apparently you just save that honor for me."

Silas has the audacity to laugh. "You're a demon. What else am I supposed to believe?"

Dami freezes, their spine a column of ice. Did he really just *say* that, aloud, in front of Marisol? They dare a glance at her out of the corner of their eye, but to their relief she isn't looking at Dami with horror but frowning softly at Silas.

Maybe she thinks it's a figure of speech? Or that Silas is just being mean?

Unexpectedly, Dami's anger fizzles away, leaving them exhausted. They made a deal with a dying boy with horrifying consequences, and they walked away, never thinking of it again until they had to cancel it. As much as Dami would like to believe otherwise, they can't say they deserve anyone assuming the best of them.

So they don't yell. They don't bite back at Silas; they don't argue. Instead, they stand, trying not to wither under Marisol's confused gaze.

"If it helps," she says uncertainly as she stands, "I do think being wary of Eve is warranted."

Dami looks at Silas pointedly and offers him their hand. "We should head back. We can look for the treasure again tomorrow."

Silas looks at Dami's hand suspiciously, like it might be some kind of trap. They could probably find something bitterly witty to say about that, but they're tired of arguing with him. They just want to lie down in the shelter of their hut and pray Marisol assumed Silas was calling them a demon figuratively.

Whatever trickery Silas thinks Dami might have in store for him, he apparently decides the risk is worth it, because he takes Dami's hand. They pull him up—

Silas shouts and collapses to the ground again, practically pulling Dami's arm out of his shoulder in the process. Marisol gasps. Silas groans and clutches at his leg, swearing softly under his breath.

"Um," Dami says. "What was that?"

"I—I can't." Silas's voice trembles. "I can't put my weight on it. It's too painful."

Marisol throws her arms up. "Claro que sí."

So much for the snakebite not being a big deal.

"Let me see." Dami crouches next to him, gently touching his arm. "Move your hands out of the way."

Silas's eyes are wide, and he doesn't move his hands. His skin shines with sweat—Dami had assumed it was from the heat, but now they're not so sure. "I haven't been honest with you. While we've been walking, I haven't been feeling great."

"No shit," Dami says. "Let me look at it."

"I don't want to see it."

"Then don't look. Move your hands."

Silas groans but finally pulls his hands away. Dami gingerly rolls his pant leg up, and cringes. The six puncture wounds just above Silas's boot are puffy, red, and oozing. More terrifying is the enormous dark bruise the size of Dami's hand covering the area and spreading up Silas's leg. The veins around the bruise are stark red, streaking up and down his leg. Dami isn't a poison expert, nor are they a doctor, but this is very clearly beyond a mild garden snakebite.

"I think that snake was venomous," Silas says, stating the obvious.

"No kidding," Dami says. "This looks bad, Silas. We should get you back to the village."

"If he can make it back," Marisol says behind Dami. They

glance at her; she's watching them with pursed lips, shaking her head. "I've seen that before. I *told* you I've seen people die of snakebites here."

Silas grimaces. "She's right. I can't make it back to the village in this condition. It took us half an hour to walk here."

"I'll help you. We can do it—"

"There isn't any *we*—I'm the one in pain! And I'm telling you I can't do it."

Dami lets Silas's pant leg drop, crossing their arms. "Well, I'm not just leaving you here."

"Certainly not. You must kill me."

The silence that falls over the three of them is tangible. Marisol shakes her head and walks away, moving far down the clearing before sitting on a fallen trunk and staring into the trees. Dami stares at Silas, trying to process what he just said. Because Dami is quite sure that as much as they've fantasized about doing just that in the past, they definitely don't have it in them to actually murder someone.

"Counterpoint," Dami hisses under their breath, "no."

Silas rolls his eyes and whispers, "You can't possibly be squeamish about this. You're a *demon*, for Christ's sake—"

"You sure have a lot of preconceived notions about what it means to be a demonio—"

"Are you actually telling me you've never killed anyone?"

Dami hesitates. They've certainly made a good number of deals that have inadvertently led to someone's death—and of course, there were the Reapings. Shortly after becoming mostly human, they were briefly involved in a battle and were armed with a gun, but if they hit anyone, they didn't see it happen. Still, by that count, it wouldn't be accurate to say they've never killed anyone. But . . .

"Not like this," they finally say. "And I'm not interested in changing that."

Silas closes his eyes and shudders. Dami's stomach twists—he must be in a lot of pain. Which is probably why he's making the request to begin with.

"Dami," Silas breathes out, opening his eyes again. "You're worried over nothing. You won't even be killing me, not really—because of our deal, remember? I can't die. But when I die and wake up, my body heals, and that's what I need."

"I don't even have a knife on me!" Dami protests. "I don't know how you expect me to kill you, but if you think I have the physical or mental strength to strangle you, you're wrong."

In hindsight, it was probably foolish to venture out into the forest without a knife. Noted for next time, though a part of Dami is relieved they don't have one, if only because it gives them one less way to kill Silas.

"Use the shovel," Silas says without hesitation.

Dami blanches. "You want me to beat you to death with a shovel?"

"If you aim right you can kill me with one blow. Or at least knock me out with the first blow and kill me after."

"Coño, I'm not murdering you with a shovel! Do you know how horrible that sounds? I just told you I'm not even that strong—"

"Then transform into someone who is!"

"Not to mention the blood and—no. Absolutely not." Dami slides their arm beneath Silas's, wrapping it around his back. "Marisol!" they call across the clearing.

"What are you doing?" Silas asks.

Marisol looks over at them. Dami waves her over. "We're returning to the village! I need help holding Silas up!"

She nods and stands, rubbing dirt off her legs.

Dami turns to Silas. "I'm not killing you. Maybe Eve will know how to treat this."

Silas groans as Dami forces them both onto their feet again. Silas leans hard against Dami, putting his full weight on his right foot, and throws up. Dami cringes.

Silas wipes his mouth with the back of his hand and shivers. This close, it's obvious he's feverish—heat radiates off him like a campfire. "Weren't you trying to convince me five minutes ago that Eve is trying to murder us?"

"And weren't you trying to convince me not to think the worst of her?" Dami snaps.

That shuts him up.

Dami isn't sure how long they've hobbled along before it occurs to them that everything looks the same. But not in a vaguely familiar we-saw-this-an-hour-ago way, more of a have-we-made-any-progress-at-all way. It feels as though they're walking forward and the forest is moving along with them.

Are they even headed in the right direction? They thought they were walking west—it was, essentially, a straight line back to the village, but when every tree looks like the last one and there aren't any landmarks to distinguish their progress, it's all too easy to get disoriented.

And as much as Dami hates to admit it, they're disoriented.

They glance at Silas, who is looking sicklier by the minute. His skin has gone a sallow pale, and he's completely sweated through his clothes. His gaze looks distant, like he isn't really seeing the forest ahead of them. Something like guilt twists like a knife in their chest.

Their inability to kill Silas, even temporarily, is making him suffer. It may not be their fault that a venomous snake bit him, but it is their fault that he's still in this state, worsening by the moment. If they just had the nerve to get it over with, Silas could heal. But is it so unreasonable that they don't have it in them to kill? Especially not in such a raw and violent way?

This would be so much easier if they hadn't started caring about the stubborn boy. Dami isn't used to being invested in someone else's well-being beyond what they can do for them.

They aren't sure they like this new development.

Dami clears their throat. "I hate to say it, but I'm not sure we're walking in the right direction."

Marisol frowns. "We should be headed west . . . I think."

Dami peers up at the sky. Or tries to, anyway. The leaf coverage is so thick they can barely make out the blue between them. Where is the sun?

Maybe they can . . . climb up? No, that's a terrible idea. They aren't an experienced climber, and these trees are giants—the shortest one they can spot is at least forty feet tall. They'll certainly lose their footing and come crashing down to their death.

"What are you looking for?" Silas asks.

"The sun. It's useless, though, I can't see anything through the foliage." They sigh. "We'll just have to keep going."

They take a couple of steps and Silas sags, dragging on Dami's right side. Dami and Marisol grunt under his weight, staggering to a halt. "Silas . . ."

"I really can't," he pants. "I'm sorry—the pain . . ."

Carajo. Dami sighs and stops trying to move forward. Maybe

they can find materials to make some kind of stretcher, then they can drag him back. There are plenty of sticks around—Dami is fairly confident they'll be able to find some long, thick branches. They don't have the cloth to make a stretcher on hand, but maybe they create a long and flowy dress. . . .

"Dami," Silas says softly. "While I appreciate you trying to figure this out, this isn't working. If you kill me—"

"I already told you I can't—"

"Please. I'm begging you. I don't want to die slowly of poisoning."

"Eve might have—"

"Eve isn't going to have a magic antidote, Dami!" Silas closes his eyes and shudders. "She isn't a medic—she's just a girl."

"A girl who knows this island literally better than anyone," Dami says. "If anyone knows how to make an antidote for a snakebite, it'll be her."

Marisol meets Dami's gaze with a furrowed brow. She doesn't say it, but they imagine she must be thinking that Eve didn't save whoever else she saw die of a snakebite.

Silas just groans. "You're so stubborn."

"I'd argue in this situation it's a good thing."

Silas opens his mouth—but then a whoosh past Dami's face makes them flinch as a muffled, wet *thunk* sounds far too close to their ear. Warmth splatters against their cheek. Silas drops to the ground, the back of his head bleeding. Not just bleeding, absolutely drenched in blood. Dami goes cold as they stare at him. Marisol covers her mouth and staggers back, eyes wide.

What just—

How did—

Eve steps around them, peering at Silas's corpse facedown in the mud. She spins a bloody shovel in her hand as she crouches next to him, nods, then stands again. "Well, that's that." She turns to Dami, arching an eyebrow at their stricken face. "You're never going to survive here if you're squeamish about hard decisions."

And without another word, she marches off into the forest, shovel tossed over her shoulder. As she disappears into the foliage, blood still drips off the blade.

· · · · · · · · ·

Chapter 24

....

Dami's fingers are slick with cooling blood. They're holding Silas's torso while Marisol carries Silas's legs as they follow Eve out of the rain forest. Marisol hasn't stopped crying since Eve killed him something like ten minutes ago. Anger simmers in their chest like a pot about to boil over. Dami is severely regretting every decision they made today, including allowing her to come along. It's true Silas will be okay, but they're not sure Marisol will be.

And yet Eve seems completely unbothered that, to her knowledge, she just murdered Silas in front of them as carelessly as swatting a fly.

With the edge of the forest just ahead, Dami stops. "What is *wrong* with you?"

Eve pauses and glances over her shoulder. "Who, me?"

They bark out an incredulous laugh. "Yes, you! Silas needed help, and your response was to try to kill him!"

She tilts her head and turns to face them. "I didn't *try* to kill him. He's dead."

"He'll wake up."

Eve looks at Dami for a long moment; then her gaze drops to Silas before settling back on them again. "He'll wake up," she echoes. Dami isn't sure if it's a statement or a question.

Marisol sniffles. "What do you mean, he'll wake up?"

"He's cursed," Dami answers. "He can't die—not permanently, anyway. He'll wake up and heal . . . at some point."

It's mostly true. Granted, Silas's curse isn't what's keeping him from dying—quite the opposite—but they don't need to know that.

Marisol's nose scrunches up. "That's not possible."

"Neither is a tropical island off the coast of Connecticut."

She frowns.

Eve arches an eyebrow. "Interesting."

Dami stares at her. She's still acting like it's no big deal at all, like it's perfectly normal that her instinct wasn't to help a poisoned boy, but to kill him.

Who the hell is she?

Eve sighs impatiently. "You just told me he's going to—what did you say? Wake up and heal? If that's the case, I don't see why you're upset at all. He'll be fine."

Dami laughs incredulously. "You don't see why I'd be upset that you were okay with murdering my friend?"

"Is that what you are? Friends?" She smirks. "Does he know that?"

"Don't change the topic. You murdered him."

Her smile drops. "I put him out of his misery. He was clearly poisoned and in excruciating pain. But you insisted on dragging him all over the island while his condition deteriorated. He was begging you to kill him." She crosses her arms. "Some friend you are."

"I was trying to save his life!"

"Which would have been futile even if he were a regular mortal boy. But instead, you knew he would wake up if he did die, and you insisted on prolonging the inevitable anyway. And you act like *I'm* the cruel one."

Dami laughs. The thing is, they've been trained in the art of manipulation since they could speak. It's an essential skill as a demonio, to know which strings to pull and buttons to press to make people feel however the demonio wants.

To make people agree to deals that are certainly not in their best interests.

It's not a skill they're proud of, but it does mean they recognize another manipulator when they see one.

"Bullshit."

Eve's eyes narrow. "Excuse me?"

"You really think you can convince me that *not* wanting to murder someone makes me a bad person? That's completely absurd, and you know it. Maybe others on this island swallow your every word, but I won't be so easily manipulated."

The venom in Eve's expression is so clear, Dami wouldn't be surprised if she came after them with the shovel next. Instead, she shakes her head. "I told you everyone who has gone out there has died. I warned all of you that no one has found the treasure, and everyone who has tried is dead. But you three insisted on going out there anyway. So don't come crying to me when your friend suffers needlessly over it."

"She's right."

It takes Dami a second to register that it isn't Eve or Marisol who said that, but Silas, now shifting in their arms.

Dami knew Silas was okay. They knew he'd wake up. That was never a question—why would it be? They've witnessed his revival twice already, and they know all too well that their deal is still active.

Nevertheless, seeing him breathing again brings a lightness to their chest; a bubbling over that makes them feel as though they could float. Relief. He's okay.

Marisol, on the other hand, shrieks and drops Silas's legs. "You were—but—"

"Cursed," Dami reminds her as Silas gets his legs under him and pushes off them to stand.

He rolls his shoulders and runs his hand through his hair, then stops at the bloody matted mess at the back of his head. Silas yanks his hand away, grimacing at his blood-smeared hand. "Disgusting . . ." He wipes his hand on his trousers and nods at Eve, his eyes suspiciously glassy. "Thank you."

Dami's mouth nearly falls open at the audacity. Eve smiles at him—*smiles!* "You're welcome." Then she walks through the trees into the village.

"Eve thought she was murdering you," Dami says, their voice shaking, "and you *thank* her?"

When Silas faces them, the strangeness in his gaze is undeniable. His pupils are dilated, and his eyes shine like he's holding back tears—but as far as Dami can tell, that doesn't seem to be the case. What's wrong with him?

"She did what you refused to," Silas says, even as his pupils slowly begin to shrink back to a normal size. "Now I'm not in agony thanks to her, so yes, I'm grateful."

Dami shakes their head. "She thought you were *dead.* For *good.*"

Silas shrugs. "She knew there wasn't any saving me, so she did me a favor."

"She didn't even *try* to help you!"

"Putting me out of my misery *was* helping me!"

"Unbelievable." Dami laughs, though nothing about this is funny. "Jesus, Silas, how did she get you wrapped around her finger so quickly?"

Silas rolls his eyes. "Oh, because I don't think the worst of her, she's somehow manipulated me, is that it? You know, Dami, I hope I never end up as jaded as you."

Dami can barely believe what they're hearing. Eve tried to murder him and somehow *they're* the bad guy? "Pinche chupamedias."

Silas's eyes narrow. "What does that mean?"

"It means you're a bootlicker, Silas. Eve literally *murdered* you, and here you are acting like she's some kind of saint."

Silas's face reddens. "I'd rather be a *bootlicker* than a *demon*." And with that, he turns on his heel and follows Eve's path out to the village.

Dami doesn't realize they're shaking until Marisol gently touches their shoulder. They don't realize they're crying until she touches their cheek with her thumb and it comes away wet. They don't realize how fragile they are until she wraps her arms around them and they break.

D ami expects her to ask.

Silas has called them a demon in front of her twice now, and she knows about Silas's curse. It must have occurred to her by this point that Silas might not be insulting them metaphorically, but if so, she doesn't bring it up once during their walk back to Dami's hut.

"Are you sure you don't want to stay the night with me?" she asks when they reach their hut.

The truth is, they're sure they want to. The thought of seeing Silas right now makes their stomach flip nauseatingly. But the longer they put off facing Silas, the harder it'll be.

"I'm sure," they answer hoarsely. "Thank you again. I'm sorry today was so awful."

Marisol shakes her head. "You couldn't have known what would happen, and even if you did, I volunteered. You have nothing to apologize for."

They smile weakly, wishing they could believe that. Turning toward the door, they pause. "Um, about Silas . . ."

"I won't tell anyone," Marisol says. "Lo prometo. Your secret's safe with me."

The relief is overwhelming. "Thank you," they breathe. Their shoulders relax. Something about the smile in her eyes and the warmth in her voice makes them want to tell her everything. Marisol must see the question in their gaze, because she tilts her head and asks, "Is there more?"

And standing there with Marisol in the cooling night air, with only the crackle of the distant campfire and the murmur of conversations too far to hear, Dami doesn't want to keep secrets anymore. Not from her. They're so tired of carrying the extraordinary weight of it all alone. Marisol is here, and she's giving them the chance to bare their soul. She's offering to listen.

So, in Spanish, Dami tells her. About Silas's curse, about why he calls them a demon, about the magically binding deal they made over a year ago and the verbal one they made that brought them to this island.

They even tell her why finding the treasure is so important to them. Why they aren't as indestructible as Silas thinks. Why they don't want Silas to know.

Dami expected coming clean to be terrifying, but instead, the moment Marisol looks at them and the warmth in her eyes is still there, it feels like a weight lifts off their chest.

"Wow," she says softly.

Then Marisol wraps her arms around them and squeezes tight. Dami's skin prickles with warmth as they relax into her arms. For a moment, as they close their eyes and try to memorize this feeling of being held, they believe everything will be okay. Dami returns the embrace and buries their face in her hair. She smells sweet, almost a little flowery, and they never want to let go.

But eventually, they do. They pull away, heart in their throat, eyes shimmering with unshed tears. But this time when they smile softly, it's genuine.

"Thank you for trusting me with that," Marisol says.

Dami smiles softly.

After a pause, Marisol lowers her voice and asks in Spanish, "Do you think Silas's curse has anything to do with why he's so spellbound by Eve?"

Dami blinks. "You've noticed it too," they whisper.

Marisol nods. "His eyes look . . . strange around her. Unnaturally so. I wasn't sure what to make of it before, but after what you've told me . . . maybe there's some kind of magical influence?"

Dami frowns. "You think Eve can do magic?"

She shakes her head. "I don't know."

Dami isn't sure what to think either. Before meeting Silas and coming to this island, they'd assumed they could sense all types of magic, but Silas taught them that curses were out of their purview. Maybe there are other types of magic they can't sense either? It would help explain Silas's seemingly blind loyalty to a girl he barely knows.

Dami sighs. "It's been a long day. I'm too exhausted to figure this out—let's just keep an eye on him for now."

After the two say their goodbyes, Dami watches Marisol leave, then, running their hand through their hair, enter the dark hut. It takes a moment for their eyes to adjust, but then they're able to make out Silas's form in bed, already asleep. They change into sleeping clothes quickly before slipping into the other side of the bed, their back to him. Silas's breaths are slow and steady and, absurdly, that brings a wave of fresh tears to Dami's eyes.

So they close their eyes, pull the blanket up to their shoulders, and imagine Marisol holding them through the night.

Chapter 25

· · · · · · · · · · · · · · · · · · · ·

I t takes most of the morning to trek through the jungle to
Black Rock Cove. When Silas steps out of the tree line onto
the shiny dark rock, he closes his eyes and breathes in the sea
air. The thunder of waves crashing against the rocks makes him
smile. It'd oddly soothing, and the cool, salty air feels good after
such a long trek.

"Wow," Dami says, peering across the cove. The jet-black
rock stretches down for close to a quarter mile, jutting out into
the ocean. At the far end, right up against the water, the rock
towers high in a natural monolith. Silas must admit it *is* rather
impressive to look at. Even if the treasure isn't here, he's glad they
made the trip.

"Be careful as you walk," Marisol says. "The rock is smooth
and slippery when wet, and it's uneven. You don't want to roll
your ankle here."

Together, the three of them walk carefully over the bumpy
ground. Marisol wasn't jesting about the slickness of the rock—
Silas almost immediately slips, but luckily he lands on his ass.

Marisol stares at him wide-eyed while Dami laughs and Silas grimaces at his throbbing hip bones.

"Be *careful*," Marisol hisses.

"I'm not dragging you through the rain forest *again*," Dami says.

"Apologies," Silas mumbles to Marisol, his face flushing.

The demon doesn't get an apology.

By the time they reach the monolith, Silas can feel the cool sea spray on his face. The seas are rough, and the tide seems high. This side of the monolith is far enough from the waves, but peeking around it confirms what he suspected: the back side is only about a foot away from the cliff's edge, and the entire area is soaked.

But between the crashing waves there's something else, too. A sigh, directly in his ears. Someone whispering against his cheek . . .

"All right," Marisol says. "We need to stay on this side of the monolith. The seas are rough today—we could easily get swept into the ocean if we get too close."

"Noted. I've done enough swimming for a lifetime," Dami says.

Silas presses his hand against the rock, frowning. If he closes his eyes, he can almost make out—

"Silas, are you all right?" Marisol asks.

He nods, opening his eyes. "I thought I heard . . . Never mind."

"So what now?" Dami asks. "We're here. The rocks are . . . abyss-like." They look at Silas. "Any ideas?"

Silas continues examining the monolith in silence. He has nothing to say to Dami—and anyway, even if he *weren't* angry with them, he doesn't have any ideas. Just a strange inkling that he should look more closely at the other side of the monolith.

"How did you find the first clue?" Marisol asks behind him.

Silas presses his ear against the cool rock and closes his eyes again. Dami is saying something—responding to Marisol's question, probably—but Silas forces his focus onto something else. The hiss inside the rock as if—

Silassss . . .

Silas jerks back, heart pounding as he stares at the monolith. The pitch-black rock is so shiny he can make out bits of his reflection, but the surface is so uneven it breaks his image up into oddly shaped ridges and planes.

He presses his ear against the rock again and closes his eyes once more. *Silasss*, the rock whispers. *Look . . .*

Opening his eyes, Silas frowns at the monolith. Look at what? He runs his hands over the surface, examining every inch of the six-foot-wide surface in front of him. The crevices and ridges in the rock are almost reminiscent of petrified tree bark, but that's the only remarkable thing about it.

You haven't checked the other side, though.

Marisol told him to stay on this side of the monolith, and he understands why. But something inside him is sure if he braves it, he'll find what he's looking for. There's something here, calling him. If he's careful . . .

Silas steps to the leftmost edge of the monolith and glances back at Marisol and Dami. The two are deep in conversation. Maybe he if moves quickly enough they won't even notice if he checks the other side of the monolith. He could scoot back there, take a quick look around, then return.

Before he can talk himself out of it, Silas presses himself flat against the monolith, chest sliding against the rough rock, and holds on the best he can as he slips around the corner.

Unfortunately, Marisol notices.

"Silas!" she screams. "We have to stay on this side of the monolith—it's too dangerous!"

Silas meets her gaze. "There's something back there—I can hear it!"

Dami frowns and says something, but their voice is lost in the waves smashing against the rock behind him. He slips completely behind the rock, his heart thrumming in his throat. Cold water splashes him. The ground and the rock are so slick it's as if he were walking on ice. Silas moves slowly, the whispers growing louder with every step.

Silasss . . .

Look . . .

And then he finds it: a hole in the monolith, about the size of his fist, but deep. Too deep to see what's inside.

Silas hesitates. What if there's a snake or something else venomous in there? He's already gone through that once, and he'd rather not repeat the experience, especially so soon. But what choice does he have? If he doesn't find the treasure, he'll be cursed to live this awful life forever—and Maisey will certainly die. He must do everything possible to save them both. He can't fail her.

So even though every instinct tells him he's making a terrible mistake, Silas takes a deep breath and plunges his hand into the hole. His pulse is pounding so loudly in his ears he can barely hear the roaring waves behind him. The inside of the rock feels the same as the outside except wetter, perhaps—some seawater has pooled at the bottom.

....

Then his hand bumps against something hard and smooth, something that clinks against the rock when moved. Silas bites his lip and carefully wraps his fingers around it, then pulls it out.

A small, corked bottle with a rolled piece of paper inside. Just like what they found in the chest.

Silas grins and whoops.

"Silas!" Dami calls. "Are you dead?"

"I found something!" he yells, momentarily forgetting he's not supposed to be talking to the demon. "I'm coming back!"

Sliding against the rock, Silas carefully makes his way to the edge of the monolith, then around the corner. Marisol is on the other side of the rock, reaching toward him. Silas hands her the small bottle, takes another step—

Cold water slams against his back with breathtaking force, smashing his face against the monolith. Silas yelps as his boots lose purchase. The water pulls back and he's falling.

And, painted in night, the unforgiving ground comes up to meet him.

Chapter 26

....

With Dami's help, Marisol managed to pull Silas to the dry side of the monolith before the ocean took him. In a way, she's glad the rock is as dark as it is because it helps hide the pool of blood that has formed around his head. Marisol and Dami have sat several feet away from Silas's body, but the shiny glint of spreading blood makes her shiver.

Dami doesn't seem that bothered by the turn of events, but seeing Silas like that makes her stomach churn. *He'll be okay,* she reminds herself. *He'll wake up, just like last time.*

She forces her gaze away from Silas. "Does this happen often?"

Dami frowns. "That's the odd thing. Silas told me he usually dies about once a week. But he died the day I caught up with him, then again on our way to Milford, then he drowned when we were trying to get to the island, then the snakebite, and now this. And that was all in, what? Around three weeks?"

Marisol grimaces. "Five times in three weeks is a lot more than once a week."

"That's what I'm worried about. It's almost like once he decided we'd be coming to the island, the curse has been working overtime to try to kill him."

"Sounds like the curse doesn't want to be broken," she answers softly.

Dami sighs and lies back on the rock, arms crossed behind their head. "Guess not."

"Then we need to find the treasure quickly. For Silas's sake."

For a few minutes neither of them speaks. The hiss and sigh of the crashing waves fill the space between them. The sea breeze throws her hair, weightless, into the wind. The rock is cool and slick beneath her. And Marisol does her very best not to look at Silas.

"What did Silas give you?"

Marisol blinks at the question. Then, in a rush, it comes back to her. The bottle. He gave her a small bottle and she tucked it into her pocket. She pulls it out, laughing slightly. "I completely forgot. . . ."

Dami's eyes widen. "Wait, we found one of those in the chest at the bottom of the lake. That's where the abyss clue was."

Excitement buzzes in her chest. She turns the small bottle in her hand. "Do you think Silas would mind if we opened it?"

"He gave it to you, didn't he?"

True. Marisol supposes it probably doesn't matter *who* opens it, so long as someone does. They can catch Silas up once he's awake.

Satisfied with that justification, Marisol grabs the tiny cork and wiggles it side to side until it finally gives with a pop. She turns the bottle over, but the rolled paper gets caught in the narrow neck of the bottle, and the opening is too small for Marisol to even fit her pinky.

So much for doing this delicately, then.

Holding the narrow neck of the bottle, Marisol smashes it against the rock next to her. The glass shatters and she carefully picks the paper out of the pile of shards. She unfurls the paper against her leg. Dami leans over to look at the paper, their face suddenly close to hers. Ignoring the warmth of their body pressed against her arm and their slightly smoky scent, Marisol clears her throat and reads the message aloud.

Among the oldest trees, I fashioned a boat. Now I'll bring it to the island's core. If I fail, she will kill us all.

"Oh, good," Dami says. "Promising. Who do you think *she* is?"

"This letter looks too old for it to be Eve," Marisol murmurs, "so I'm not sure, but . . ." She reads it again, smoothing the paper's curled edges against her leg. "The oldest trees . . . ," she murmurs, then with a gasp she sits up and turns to Dami so quickly they nearly hit foreheads. "I know where that is!"

Dami blinks at her rapidly, startled. "Where what is?"

"The oldest trees on the island! There's no guarantee anything will be there, of course, but if we can retrace this person's steps—"

"Maybe we can find another clue." Dami grins. "Have I mentioned how glad I am you joined us?"

Marisol's cheeks warm. "Well, I'm glad you're here." She frowns. "Is that terrible to say?"

Dami laughs. "Maybe a little, but I know what you mean. Meeting you has been the only good thing to come out of this godforsaken place."

"Agreed," Silas says, wiping blood from his face as he approaches them. "Now please tell me the bottle I died for is actually helpful."

Chapter 27

·····················

As it turns out, the island's tallest trees aren't far from Black Rock Cove, so the three of them agree to clear off right away. After an hour of hiking buzzing with excited energy, Silas spots a tree trunk as thick as he is tall. He slows, mouth falling open as he approaches the tree and cranes his neck back, trying to peer up to the top.

The tree is a giant. Taller than any building Silas has ever seen, its branches create a shaded canopy that blends into the canopy of the equally enormous tree next to it. Looking around, Silas spots many more gigantic trees scattered ahead of him. Even the smaller trees here would be impressive in any other location.

"Amazing, isn't it?" Marisol asks.

"I've never seen anything like it," he breathes.

"I have," Dami says nonchalantly.

Silas rolls his eyes. "Curse someone to a terrible life there, too?"

Dami scowls. "I don't *curse* people."

"Same difference."

·········

"Okay!" Marisol interrupts. "What we're *not* going to do is waste time bickering. Should we look around?"

Walking among the towering trees makes Silas feel like an ant. He wanders with his eyes on the canopy, so far above that the leaves scrape the sky. It's breathtaking, walking among the roots of such ancient life.

Something catches his foot and Silas pitches forward, throwing his hands out to break his fall. His hand conks against a tree trunk before he hits the ground.

"Silas!" Marisol runs over, Dami on her heels. "Are you all right? Did you get injured?"

"Not seriously, unexpectedly enough." The back of Silas's left hand is burning and bleeding—he scraped it raw on that tree—but that seems to be the worst of it. Silas stands, brushing the dirt off his palms. "The island's going to have to try harder than that to kill me twice in one day." He grins, but neither Marisol nor Dami matches his smile.

"Don't give it ideas," Dami says. Then, as an afterthought, "Glad we don't have to wait for you to wake up again."

Silas back on his feet, they continue exploring—though this time he watches where he steps. They walk in relative quiet with just the crunch of the underbrush beneath their boots and the chirp of birds somewhere high above.

Silas Cain.

The whisper is so sudden Silas jerks to a stop.

"Whoa," Dami says. "Are you—"

"Shh!" Silas closes his eyes. Then he hears it again, his name, overlapping again and again, beckoning him forward. He opens his eyes and keeps walking, more quickly this time—then, just ahead, he spots a large tree stump.

"There!" Silas rushes toward the stump, heart pounding. Carved into the rings of the wood is another message:

THEY WHISPER WHISPER WHISPER WHERE ARE MY ANCESTORS TAKING ME?

Silas runs his fingers over the carved letters, his roaring pulse drowning out the rest of the world. Someone else has been here—someone else who was experiencing the same thing he is. The whispers—are they . . . his ancestors? What would that even mean?

Something cold and wet lands on the scraped back of his left hand. Silas moves to wipe it off and freezes. He'd assumed it was just a drop of water from the canopy above, but it is most decidedly not. Sitting on the back of his hand, no larger than a wax seal, is a bright yellow frog with black toes. It stares at him with shiny black eyes.

"Oh no," Marisol whispers, taking a step back.

Dami swears softly. Silas's scrape tingles worryingly—is it from anxiety, or is something happening? The frog blinks at Silas, then hops off him, disappearing into the underbrush. Silas's entire hand is tingling now, like it's falling asleep. The wound on the back of his hand glistens with something slick.

"That was poisonous, wasn't it?" Silas says, a little light-headed.

"I think so," Marisol says grimly at the same time Dami says, "Oh, definitely."

In truth, Silas didn't really need to ask—the tingles have

already traveled up his arm and his fingers are twitching. He sits against the tree stump with a groan and wipes the back of his hand on the grass, but it's clearly too late for that. Black spots swim in his vision, and Dami crouches in front of him. They're saying something, but Silas struggles to focus on their words— his breaths come in quick, short pants and his chest feels like someone is sitting on his sternum.

Dami's lips are moving. "Don't . . . okay. We'll . . . here."

Silas tries to open his mouth to speak but he can't. No matter how much he tries, his mouth won't move. He tries to reach for his face, but his arms are so heavy he can barely lift them more than a few inches. He can't move. He can barely breathe. He blinks and blinks, trying to clear the black spots from his vision, and his chest *hurts*.

And then Dami is holding his shoulder and their touch is grounding. He can feel that. Their face is oddly close to his and they're saying something. Their lips are moving. The same movement, over and over and over again.

It'll be okay.

Silas isn't so sure, but the reminder that he isn't alone is a comfort he needs before the pressure on his chest pushes him into darkness.

Chapter 28

·····················

Between waiting for Silas to wake and walking all the way back to the village, by the time the three of them reach the clearing, night has fallen, bathing the earth in a deep ink wash. When the hazy orange glow of the village's ever-burning bonfire breaks through the trees, Marisol breathes a sigh of relief. Moving through the rain forest in the middle of the night is always a bad idea, but doing so with a boy cursed to die seemed like an especially ill-fated choice.

Feet aching, she looks back at Dami and Silas with a small smile. "I don't know about you two, but I'm ready for bed."

Dami groans, wiping sweat-slick hair out of their eyes. "I've been ready for bed since before we left those giant trees."

"Oddly," Silas says, "I'm still full of energy."

"Oh, good," Dami says. "You can carry me the rest of the way." They reach toward Silas, who shoves them away.

"Absolutely not."

"Why not? If you're so full of energy—"

Marisol's steps slow as they approach the village entrance. Standing there, arms crossed, are Paul and his five friends. And

·········

judging by the sour look on their faces, the men aren't particularly happy to see the three of them.

"Well, well, well," Paul says. "So you *do* speak English."

Marisol grimaces as she stops several feet away from them. She supposes it was a matter of time before Paul discovered she's bilingual. In truth, it's impressive that she managed to keep up the charade for as long as she did.

"What do you want, Paul?" she asks coolly. Dami and Silas flank her, frowning. She hadn't expected how reassuring it is to have the two of them at her side; even though they're still outnumbered, their presence infuses her voice with steel.

"I heard a rumor you three children are looking for the treasure. But that couldn't possibly be right, because it would be *ridiculous* if you actually believed three *children* could find it when no one else could."

"Good thing you have nothing to worry about, then," Marisol says. "Now if you'll excuse us, we've had a long day."

Neither Paul nor his friends move out of the way.

"We also heard a rumor," Paul says, "that you actually managed to find something."

"And that you have a treasure map," a blond, middle-aged man adds.

Dami laughs. "A treasure map? You think we have an actual *treasure map*, but *we're* the children?"

"Give us what you have," Paul snaps. "Now."

Marisol glowers. "Or what? You'll stand there all night?" She recognizes her mistake as soon as the words are out of her mouth. Paul lifts his eyebrows.

"So you *do* have something. Well, I'll make this simple." He pulls out a pistol, gleaming silver in the moonlight. "Give us *everything* you've found, or I'll shoot you in the stomach. Let you die real slow so you can watch while I kill your two friends."

Marisol's breath catches in her chest, her heart thundering in her ears. Paul might be a blustering fool, but she doesn't doubt for a second that he would actually shoot them. She clenches her fists, fighting the tremble in her bones. She didn't survive this long on this damned island just to get shot by some American pendejo.

At this, the blond man frowns. "But that won't be necessary because you'll cooperate. Just do what he asks, and no one has to get hurt."

Dami rolls their eyes. "What is this? Good cop, bad cop?"

Marisol doesn't know what that means, but she understands the bright malice in Paul's eyes well enough. Slowly, she raises her hands in surrender, nodding at Silas and Dami, who do the same.

"We didn't find much," she says honestly. "Just some vague reference to a boat." She reaches into her pocket and pulls out the scrap of paper from the bottle at Black Rock Cove. "And I do have a map, but it's not a treasure map. It's a map I drew of the island as I've explored it. There isn't anything special about it."

Paul nods to his blond friend. "Get it."

The second man crosses the distance between them and extends his hand. Marisol gives him the paper, then reluctantly pulls the folded map out of her pocket as well and hands it over. The man smiles softly at her, almost apologetically. He passes the map to Paul.

"*Among the oldest trees, I fashioned a boat,*" Paul reads off the paper. "*Now I'll bring it to the island's core. If I fail, she will kill us all.* What is this crap? This is useless!"

"We tried to tell you," Dami says flatly. "We don't know what it means."

Paul's face has gone red. "This can't be everything!" he splutters. "Search them! Now!"

His accomplice grimaces, but Marisol doesn't move as he returns to her and searches her pockets. He does the same to Silas, who just stands stiffly with his arms crossed, but when he approaches Dami, they take a step back and scowl.

"Dami," Marisol says quickly. "Just let him. Then they'll see we have nothing and leave us alone. Por favor."

Dami purses their lips, looking physically pained, but when the man approaches them again this time, they don't move. "If you get handsy," they hiss, "I will murder you in your sleep."

The blond man blanches, but when Dami doesn't protest any further, he searches their pockets as well. Finally, he turns back to Paul with a shrug. "They don't have anything else."

Paul swears, throws the map on the ground, and stomps on it repeatedly. Marisol cringes as the paper tears under the heel of his boot, grinding into the damp, muddy dirt. Paul turns back to them, shoulders heaving, eyes wide. "No one gets that treasure or escapes this island without me," he seethes. "Do you understand? *No one.* The treasure is *mine.*"

"We understand," Marisol says flatly.

Shaking with fury, Paul shoves his gun back into the holster and turns away, stalking into the village, his accomplices trailing behind him. The three stand in silence until Paul has disappeared around a row of huts.

·········

With a heaving sigh, Dami lets their head fall back as they groan. "I hate this place."

Marisol grimaces and crouches over the ruined map. She picks up a soggy scrap and shakes her head, dropping it into the mud again. "You and me both."

Chapter 29

·····················

As Dami watches the starlit forest, they find themself thinking, again, how exhausting it is to try to keep someone alive who is cursed to die. It's been six days since that adorable tiny frog killed Silas and Paul threatened them, and in that time, he's still managed to die once a day despite their best efforts to protect him.

They suspect it would have been a near-impossible task even if they weren't stuck on an extremely deadly island. Maybe if they stayed in the village it would be easier to keep Silas in a protective bubble, but that's not an option. Since finding the last two clues, they've run dry. Marisol doesn't know of any other areas in the island that might qualify as an abyss, and Silas insists he hasn't heard any whispers since the frog incident.

Which leaves them with an entire island to explore and less than a week left to do it. Dami's deadline may not be until September 22, but Silas needs to bring Captain Kidd's treasure to London to break the curse. Unless they can find a friendly demonio to transport them to England, at minimum, they need to be on a ship to England by August 11, less than a week away.

·········

Then there's the whole awkwardness with Silas. Dami isn't really sure where they stand—neither of them really apologized after the argument about Eve, or their bickering thereafter, but Dami felt pulled to comfort Silas as the frog's poison took hold. They held on to Silas, wishing they could do more, until he started seizing.

Out of all of Silas's deaths that Dami has witnessed, that one was easily the most haunting. They'd never felt so helpless as they had watching him convulse until his heart finally stopped. Then half an hour later he woke up, and neither of them spoke about what had just happened.

The uncomfortable ambiguity between them made it easy to say yes when Eve asked Dami to take the night watch this week. The night watch is easy, and boring—it's mostly a lookout for wild animals as all of the island's human inhabitants live in the village. At least this way by the time they finally go to bed, Silas has passed out.

Dami groans and rests their chin on the palm of their hand. The night watch is on a small platform built into a tree in the northeast corner of the village. From here, Dami can see deep into the forest, and if they turn around, they can see the entire village, too. They've avoided that view, though, if only to avoid accidentally finding Silas. They don't want to know where he is, what he's doing, who he's with. They don't want to imagine the terrible things he might be telling people about them.

They don't want to hear him spitting out the word *demon* like a rancid piece of meat.

"Well, you *are* a demonio," a voice says beside them.

Dami bites their lip hard, staring intently ahead of them into the still forest, ignoring the dark shape in their peripheral vision.

·········

"You aren't here," they say firmly.

El Diablo chuckles. "You keep saying that." His gaze prickles the side of Dami's face. Their heart thrums loudly in their ears as they lean their forearms on the small platform's banister. El Diablo leans casually against it next to them, coins shifting in his pockets. If Dami moves even an inch, they'll knock into him. The thought paralyzes them; it seems impossible that el Diablo would have a physical form—after all, he has to be a figment of Dami's imagination, right? But if he is actually corporeal, that would mean he's really here and that knowledge might just break them.

They would rather not know. They'd rather assume he isn't real. El Diablo returning from the dead might be the only thing that could possibly make their current situation worse.

Still, the specter of their old boss—because they *refuse* to call the man who stole them away at birth their father—has been haunting them since the day they betrayed him. Dami thought they could just ignore him—maybe forever, if needed—but they're exhausted.

So finally, they face him.

He looks exactly the way he did on the day he died: trim black beard, short-cropped wavy dark hair, a shirt the color of red wine tailored to fit his broad torso perfectly.

"I liked you better with your face melted off," Dami says flatly.

El Diablo laughs—the chilling sound makes them flinch. "I missed you too, mije."

"I'm not your kid," they answer sharply. "I never was."

El Diablo shrugs, like the fact of their abduction is inconsequential, pushes off the banister, and stands. "Come with me."

Dami doesn't move. "Why should I?"

"You want to know why I've been visiting you all these months, don't you?" He doesn't wait to see if Dami will follow; he just walks to the edge of the platform and steps off, plummeting soundlessly to the ground below.

Which leaves Dami with a decision. They could stay—they *should* stay, as no one is permitted to leave watch until someone comes to relieve them, and it's not exactly safe walking out of the village at night. But if they stay, el Diablo is sure to keep haunting them. Or they could end this. Follow el Diablo wherever he may lead them and confront him at last.

They've been ignoring him for nearly a year. Enough is enough.

Dami climbs down the rope ladder to the ground. They aren't surprised to find el Diablo still there, waiting for them. With a smile Dami had hoped never to see again, el Diablo turns toward the forest and disappears into the trees.

This time, Dami doesn't hesitate to follow.

Silas groans into his hands as Marisol clears away the dominoes with a grin. It's a victorious grin, as it should be after she's beaten him over half a dozen times in a row. The campfire roars behind her, spewing smoke into the dusky purple-and-orange sky. "You should play with Dami," she says. "They're not very good either."

Silas's smile fades. "I'm not convinced Dami will want to play anything with me for a while." *Or ever*, he thinks. "I don't know where we stand, exactly."

"About that . . ." Marisol sighs as she scoops the last of the dominoes into a small canvas drawstring pouch. "Have you considered maybe . . . apologizing?"

Silas bristles. "For what? They should be apologizing to *me* for making me suffer."

Two men walk past them, laughing as they settle on a log bench on the other side of the campfire. Marisol lowers her voice. "You know they weren't trying to make you suffer."

"Intended or not, that was the result," Silas grumbles.

Marisol grimaces.

"Regardless," Silas says, "I don't think Dami has a problem with watching me suffer."

She frowns. "Why would you say that?"

Silas pulls a blade of grass out of the ground, slowly, careful not to rip it. That Dami enjoys watching him suffer is the only explanation he can think of for why the demon has stuck around on this cursed mission for as long as they have. Part of him feels perfectly justified telling Marisol exactly what Dami has done to him. But even though he's called Dami a demon in front of her several times, he doesn't think she knows the truth. Perhaps she deserves to know. Perhaps it would be right to tell her that her new friend is a demon.

But right or not, it doesn't feel like Silas's revelation to share. So he doesn't say anything at all.

"To be clear," Marisol says, "you're angry at Dami for *not* killing you."

Silas grimaces. "They weren't really going to kill me. I would've woken up."

Marisol leans back on her hands, legs outstretched in front of her. The gesture is unnervingly like Dami, except they would've rested on their forearms instead of their hands.

Silas isn't sure he likes that he knows that.

"And you gave them a shovel," Marisol says, "to kill you with." Silas might be imagining it, but her tone sounds . . . disapproving. "Have you ever killed anyone?"

Silas blinks at the question. "No."

Marisol nods. "Have you ever seen anyone die?"

Silas frowns, then slowly shakes his head.

"Right," she says. "Well, I haven't killed, but I *have* seen someone draw their last breath. I mean it when I say I will genuinely never forget it. It's one of the worst things I've ever experienced. So maybe reconsider begrudging them for being unable to go through with murder."

Silas opens his mouth, but Marisol lifts a finger. "Even if it was temporary, it still would have been a horrifying experience. Especially since Dami cares about you." She drills him with a look, daring him to disagree.

Silas sighs, shoulders slumping. "I suppose you have a point. But they haven't exactly been dying to speak to me, either."

"Well," Marisol says, "you might be put off too, if after trying to save their life Dami defended the person who killed them."

Silas supposes that's a fair point as well. "Damn."

"Mm-hmm," Marisol agrees.

"I suppose I could apologize," he mutters.

Marisol arches an eyebrow at him.

"I'll go apologize," he amends.

"Por *fin*," she groans.

Silas doesn't need to ask for a translation to have a guess as to what that means. He stands, brushing dirt off his trousers as he turns to find the watchtower in the northwest corner of the village.

·········

A bloodcurdling scream makes Silas jump. More screams overlap the first as Marisol rises to her feet and Silas faces the direction of the shouts. Two men run toward them—whatever is causing the panic seems to be coming from the outer ring of huts. A terrifying sound like a cross between a scream and a roar chills Silas to the bone.

"What was that?" he asks, his voice shaking.

Marisol doesn't get the chance to answer, but she doesn't need to. No sooner has Silas asked the question than something leaps between two huts in the inner ring and lands just fifteen feet from Silas, licking blood off its snout.

A jaguar.

Chapter 30

....

D ami really should have brought a torch.

It was just past dusk when they walked into the forest, but the sun is setting rapidly and the thick foliage overhead blocks out most of what little light is left. They stumble after el Diablo, tripping over thick roots and rocks as they try to keep up. El Diablo *is* holding a torch, at least, though Dami isn't counting on that lasting half as long as they need.

They should turn back before they go in too deep, before they get lost or happen upon a dangerous animal. But they don't. It's as if el Diablo has reached into them and is pulling them forward by the spine. And then they burst through a thicket of trees to a clearing around a large lake backed by a roaring waterfall and Dami knows exactly where they are. This is where they found that chest with the cryptic message, where they swam and laughed with Silas. Where they believed, if only for a moment, that Silas might not hate them anymore.

That was a nice day. But that fantasy is over.

El Diablo stands at the lake's edge, peering down into the glassy water, his back to them. Dami approaches cautiously, stepping beside him. El Diablo doesn't look up. Dami glances at their reflection in the lake's surface, rippling with the gentle movement of the water. With a start like a punch to the stomach, they realize el Diablo doesn't have a reflection.

Because he's not here, they remind themself. *He's dead.*

But can you really kill what wasn't living? Dami is starting to have their doubts.

"What do you see?" el Diablo asks.

Dami peers down at their face looking back at them. Their features are soft today, stubble shading their cheeks and chin, thick kohl lining their eyes, shoulder-length hair loose and swaying in the gentle evening breeze.

"Me," they say flatly, glancing up at him.

"Look again."

They do and their breath catches in their chest. Dami's reflection is still them, but a much younger version. Their reflection is fourteen, and they're standing in el Diablo's hall, where they've stood hundreds of times before.

"¡Mije!" el Diablo exclaims with outstretched arms and a proud smile.

Dami shifts uncomfortably, but they force themself to smile. The room around them is warmly candlelit; the dancing flames shimmer over the polished hardwood. Red-painted walls, deep, like wine—or blood—surround them. At the far end of the room is a large desk, beautifully carved in obsidian. Long, thin legs with clawlike feet hold up the perfectly smooth surface.

They don't touch it, but they know it'll be cold.

Pulling their shoulders back, they walk down the long side of the room, past white marble statues of cowering people, past a pile of carved white stone skulls, the one on top wearing an ivory crown. Gold-framed paintings on the wall, every one of the same man in different forms: a noble, a merchant, a black market collector, a Spanish captain, a king.

El Diablo watches them approach with a smile, leaning on the desk behind him. "I'm so proud of you," he says. "Ready for a promotion already. How do you feel?"

"Good," they admit. They're so close to demonio status that they can almost taste it. "I'm ready."

El Diablo laughs. "You certainly are. Ven aquí, mije."

Dami walks up to him, as instructed, and takes his outstretched hands.

"Close your eyes."

They do. For a long moment nothing happens. They worry their lip, breathing evenly, resisting the urge to peek. And then something strange happens. A tingle begins at the back of their neck, where their spine meets the base of their skull. As soon as Dami notices the odd sensation, it bursts from their neck to the rest of their body. Then, like a kick in the chest, power slams through them, freezing the air in their lungs and making them go rigid. White flashes behind their eyes as their head snaps back.

Then inside their head, el Diablo's voice says, *Bienvenido, hije. Hazme sentir orgulloso.*

El Diablo releases their hands, and just like that, it's over. The voice, the light, the energy, it all stops like flipping a switch, leaving them breathless.

"Wow," Dami breathes.

They did it. They actually did it. They're a demonio. Now they can find Juno and learn how to escape this unending nightmare. They can reclaim their life and be free of this monster at last.

El Diablo smiles. And so does Dami.

Chapter 31

· · · · · · · · · · · · · · · · · · · ·

S taring into the pale yellow eyes of a jaguar, it occurs to
Silas that he's probably moments away from experiencing
his most horrific death yet. "Mauled by a jaguar" isn't a
fate he would wish upon his worst enemy, but despite the fresh
blood still dripping off the animal's pink-stained snout, it's eyeing him like he's its next meal.

Marisol whimpers a foot or so behind him, somewhere off
to his right. The jaguar's gaze snaps to her—Silas's stomach
drops.

"No!" He waves his arms, and the jaguar looks at him again.
Silas slowly steps to the left, away from Marisol, both relieved
and terrified as the predator's gaze follows him. Silas's head is
light, his bones vibrating with fear.

A gunshot rips through the air. Silas jumps, heart thundering as the jaguar snarls. It spins around to the source of the blast,
but as far as Silas can tell, it doesn't seem injured.

Whoever fired missed.

Facing down the jaguar now is one of the Americans, a young
man with a thick mustache, holding a long rifle. The jaguar

· · · · · · · · ·

stalks toward him, black-tipped tail whipping side to side like a snake.

Marisol grabs Silas's arm and yanks him back. "Let's go," she hisses. "Before it decides you're easier prey."

Silas doesn't need to be told twice. The two of them race around the campfire, to get away from the animal. Another gunshot and a raw, pained scream tells Silas all he needs to know about the young American's fate. They've just crossed over to the north side of the village when Eve's cabin door bursts open. She steps out, lips pursed, and frowns at the carnage behind them. Then, with a sigh, she walks past the two of them without so much as a glance in their direction, toward the roaring jaguar, gunfire, and screaming men.

Silas has the ridiculous urge to warn her, even though she's better placed to see everything. He skids to a stop, watching openmouthed as she calmly walks down the path to where the jaguar stands over two corpses, slashing at the remaining three men who attack it with machetes.

"Enough." Eve doesn't shout, but somehow her voice carries clearly over the chaos.

More incredibly, the jaguar stops. And so do the men.

Eve walks up to the animal and pets its bloody snout. "That's enough," she says tenderly. "Back to the forest with you."

And with that, the jaguar turns around and races into the trees.

Silas stares, hardly processing what he just witnessed. How did she do that? It was already clear to him that Eve was special, but this was another level entirely.

Eve looks down at her feet, which sink into the blood-saturated earth, with a grimace. Then she looks up. "Who was on watch tonight?"

•••••••

D ami wakes on cold, slippery mud. They sit up, shuddering at the unsettling sensation of cool, slick earth that is painted from their hair all the way down to their heels. Revolting.

After changing into fresh, mud-free clothes, they rotate slowly in place, trying to get their bearings. The roar of the waterfall overpowers most other sound, save for the chirp of frogs. So they're still at the lake. El Diablo brought them here; then they passed out. How long have they been lying here? The sky is still dark, but there's just a hint of light in what must be the east. Which means they've been here nearly all night.

Fantastic.

By the time they near the village, that hint of sunrise is undeniable, streaks of orange and red bleeding through the dawn. They've been gone for way too long—their watch shift was supposed to end just before sunrise, so there's no chance their absence hasn't been noticed. With any luck they'll get a lenient penalty for a first offense.

Then they spot a destroyed hut and any thoughts of leniency drain away. The hut has half collapsed because of a massive hole in the back wall and a heavily damaged side wall. Blood is smeared along the interior, the bed is torn to shreds and stained crimson brown, and now that they're closer they spot the missing front door, too.

Dami steps cautiously around the devastated hut, cringing at a long smear of blood across the grass, like something—or someone—was dragged across the ground while gravely injured.

"¿Qué coño pasó aquí?" they mutter under their breath.

Rounding the corner to the path leading to the campfire in

the center of the village, they find more blood, this time so much the dirt is still damp in places. The pit in their stomach grows heavier. Whatever they missed last night, it was clearly serious. They just hope Silas and Marisol are okay.

They move down the center path as if in a trance. The dread constricts their lungs in a vise. When they reach the campfire, to their relief Silas and Marisol are there, along with a couple of other villagers they only vaguely recognize at best, and Eve. Dami's friends—if they can call them that—look unharmed, thankfully.

Dami can't say the same for all of Paul's friends.

Upon seeing Dami, Silas's shoulders visibly relax and Marisol jumps to her feet and races over to them, wrapping her arms around them. Dami closes their eyes, taking in the embrace and returning it. For just a minute they can forget the deep shit they're probably in.

"I'm so glad you're all right," Marisol says into their shoulder.

"So am I," they answer. "What happened?"

Eve clears her throat. Marisol pulls back with a grimace. "Everything will be okay," she says softly.

Oddly, the reassurance only makes Dami more anxious.

"Dami," Eve says stiffly. "You left your post."

In hindsight, they probably should have taken some time to come up with an excuse that isn't "I followed a dead man into the forest and passed out." Instead, they only have a half-truth they suspect won't win them any favors.

"I did," they say. "I'm sorry, it was only supposed to be for a few minutes but I—I passed out." They grimace at their verbal stumble. Sloppy.

Eve looks at them with a piercing gaze. "Three people are dead because of you."

Dami cringes. "What happened?"

"Maybe Marisol would be willing to tell you, since you're such good friends."

Marisol glances at Eve and says, "A jaguar attacked us."

Dami's eyes widen. Sure, they'd been keeping an eye out for animals, but a *jaguar*? There are jaguars on the island? Suddenly, the stench of blood, the wreckage, it all paints a horrifying picture. "Dios . . . ," they say. "And if I *had* stayed at my post, how was I supposed to stop a jaguar?"

"You could have warned us!" Paul's blond friend shouts. "Then Eve could have stopped it before it ever entered the village!"

That seems like a leap, but saying that isn't likely to help their case, so they stay quiet.

Eve nods. "Leaving your post unattended is a betrayal to us all, with grave consequences. You must leave this village immediately. You're no longer welcome here."

Marisol gasps. Dami can hardly believe their ears. Banishment? For not being there to stop a jaguar they never would have been able to stop? "Are you serious?" they ask. "The village is the only safe place on this island. How am I supposed to survive out there alone?"

"Because of you, the village was not safe for the three innocents who died," Eve says coldly. "Your sentence is decided. Don't make me tell you to leave a second time."

Marisol covers her mouth, eyes wide, and Silas . . . Silas just stares at Eve with that strange shine in his eyes, and an expression like adoration. Dami looks at him imploringly—surely, he could at least *try* to change Eve's mind—but it's like he doesn't even notice them.

So, with nothing left to do, Dami turns around and walks back over the blood-soaked earth and toward the woods once more.

Chapter 32

· · · · · · · · · · · · · · · · · · · ·

An elbow jabbing Silas's ribs shatters the lull in his mind.

"Ow," he hisses, yanking his gaze from Eve to glare at Marisol as he rubs the aching spot on his side. Marisol doesn't look remotely apologetic—she meets Silas's heated stare with her own.

"Dami is *leaving*," she whispers sharply. "*Alone*. We have to do something!"

Silas blinks. Dami is leaving? They'd been standing just feet from him before. When did they move? Why doesn't he remember? Dami said they'd passed out, then Eve was speaking and . . .

The warmth of her presence washes over him like a steaming hot spring in the dead of winter. His whole body relaxes at her honeyed voice. What is it about her that makes him feel so at ease? His shoulders relax as he melts into a smile. He's safe here, with Eve. Everything will be okay.

Her words grow distant, unintelligible, like sinking into a bath and melting into warmth. It makes him want to close his eyes and float away.

Then Marisol elbowed him in the ribs and now Dami

· · · · · · · · ·

is leaving and a sinking feeling in his gut tells him he missed something important.

"Where are they going?" Silas whispers.

Marisol stares at him for a beat, then shakes her head. "Eve is blaming them for the jaguar attack. She just banished them. How did you miss that?"

Silas's breath catches in his chest. Banished? Dami may not be able to die out there, being a demon, but they would certainly suffer. And he supposes the time he's spent with Dami has softened him, because he doesn't want Dami to suffer.

Sure, they're often obnoxious and even infuriating at times, but they also care more than they pretend to. Dami *held* him while the frog's poison took over. They carried him through the jungle after Eve had killed him. They dragged him out of the ocean and scared away bandits.

Dami might pretend not to care, but their actions said otherwise.

Silas spins around, spotting Dami at the edge of the village, headed toward the jungle. Just a few seconds more and they'll step beyond the tree line and disappear.

"Wait!" Silas shouts, a note of panic creeping into his voice. "Dami, hold on!"

He turns back to Eve, who is watching him with a stormy expression that churns his gut.

"Dami had a serious lapse in judgment," Silas says quickly, forcing the words out before the dread gathering inside him chokes out his voice. "But from what I gathered, I don't believe they'd intended to be gone for more than a few minutes. If they fainted—"

"Silas," Eve interrupts coldly. "You don't really believe that they *fainted*, do you? It's fairly obvious that's an excuse because the consequences of their slacking off are more severe than they expected."

Could that be true? Silas frowns. "I haven't known Dami to be a liar." Sure, they've been deceptive, particularly with their demon deals, but Silas is nearly sure Dami has never outright lied to him.

Then again, they *are* a demon.

"Fear makes liars of us all." She shrugs and Marisol scoffs beside him.

"Still," Silas presses, "it's the first time they've done something like this. Don't you think sentencing them to suffer and possibly die in the forest is a bit harsh?"

"Three people are dead," Eve says flatly. "Those people won't get a second chance, why should Dami? No, I don't think it would be fair to lighten their sentence. This is the only way to honor the dead's lives."

Silas shivers under her penetrating gaze. He hadn't intended to upset her—the curling in his gut is reminiscent of the disappointment of upsetting his mother. Eve's dissatisfaction hits him so viscerally it makes him dizzy. Still, he can't just abandon Dami to the mercy of the island. . . .

"But—"

"I've made my decision. The answer is no."

The disapproval in her voice is a kick to the chest—Silas finds himself reeling, his fingers shaking. But why? Why does her distaste feel so gut-wrenchingly awful?

Dami's voice comes back to him. *Jesus, Silas, how did she get you wrapped around her finger so quickly?*

Was Dami right? Silas hasn't thought much of his instant connection with Eve, but what if there's more to it?

Silas pushes through the nausea gathering in the back of his throat. "You can't banish Dami."

Eve laughs loudly, sending a shiver down Silas's spine. "Can't I? Perhaps you've forgotten, but this is *my village* on *my island.* You're lucky I haven't banished them from the entire island and left them to drown in the ocean."

Marisol gasps. "Esta maldita," she hisses.

Silas doesn't know what that means, but he has a guess.

"You know," Eve says smoothly, "I *do* understand Spanish."

"If you banish Dami, you banish me, too," Silas says, pulling his shoulders back. "I won't leave them to suffer out there alone."

Eve goes rigid. "Excuse me?"

"I'm going too," Marisol says. "If you banish Dami, you banish us both."

It takes a moment for Silas to place the bark of laughter that breaks the tense quiet. Paul has dragged a mutilated corpse toward the village center, and though Paul is covered in gore, as far as Silas can tell he unfortunately doesn't seem injured.

And yet the man is laughing. "Survived a jaguar just to martyr yourselves—guess I won't have to worry about you three finding the treasure after all."

Silas scowls, but right now Paul's opinion doesn't matter—it's Eve who has him trembling.

She clenches her fists, and the fury in her stare is so intense Silas feels as though he might collapse under the weight of it. But he forces himself to meet her gaze, her anger, to choke back the fear threatening to paralyze him. He won't leave Dami to face the dangers of the island alone. Not after everything they've done for him.

"Fine," Eve spits. "But if you leave, you can't return. Ever. I will *kill* you if you step foot in this village again."

The venom in her voice hurts more than it should, but Silas won't back down, not now. Dami was right—there's something strange about her hold on him, and he can't succumb to it anymore.

So even while something inside him screams at him to apologize, to beg for forgiveness, to turn her rejection around, Silas forces himself to turn away. He meets Dami's gaze. They've been watching, wide-eyed, and something in their eyes calls to Silas. Every step closer to Dami is easier than the last, and soon he and Marisol are standing at their side.

"You don't have to do this," Dami says quietly.

"Yes," Silas says, taking their hand in his. "We do."

Chapter 33

· · · · · · · · · · · · · · · · · · · ·

Being trapped in a highly dangerous rain forest on an extremely cursed island would have been bad enough. Being trapped in a highly dangerous rain forest on an extremely cursed island with el Diablo stubbornly haunting them is exponentially worse.

"It's cute that you think you still have a chance," el Diablo sneers. "It's August seventh. That leaves you with, what, five days before it'll be too late to get to London before your deadline? And that's assuming the weather conditions are perfect for six weeks." He laughs.

Dami sits at the lake's edge, wishing the waterfall would at least do them the courtesy of drowning out el Diablo's endless taunting. Marisol has gone looking for firewood nearby while Silas somewhat futilely tries to catch fish with his hands. Dami dips their toes in the water and closes their eyes, relishing the cool water lapping at their feet.

"It's for the best, really," el Diablo says, apparently unbothered that Dami has been ignoring him all morning. "You didn't really think you deserved to be human, did you? After everything you've done?"

The accusation cuts deep because the truth is they don't. How many lives did they ruin in pursuit of a better life for themself? Too many. They should feel lucky they even had the chance to *taste* a full life.

Part of them wonders if it would have been less painful to never know what they were losing, though.

"How long do you think it'll be until you start losing the rest of your senses? I wonder which will go first. Smell? Touch?"

"Will you *shut up?*" they snap, finally turning to face him.

Silas straightens and frowns at them. "I didn't say anything."

Dami's face warms. "Sorry. I was talking to . . . Forget it."

El Diablo's laughter lingers, but no one is there.

Dami sighs and stands. Then they look at Silas and smile. At least this time they aren't alone. A small part of them had hoped that maybe *someone* would go looking for them, but they certainly hadn't imagined that both Silas and Marisol would banish themselves in solidarity with them.

Dami doesn't deserve their loyalty, but they're grateful for it nonetheless.

As Silas abandons his laughable attempt to catch fish, Marisol steps through the brush, her arms full of branches and a bunch of bananas. "I found some food."

Dami catches Silas's eye. They've never directly told Silas they can't eat, but certainly by now he must have noticed that Dami hasn't eaten once in their journey together, and as they aren't starving to death, has probably come to his own conclusion.

Marisol must see the look on Dami's face, because her smile fades. "Is something wrong?"

Dami sighs. "I, uh. Can't eat. Demonio thing."

Marisol's eyes widen.

"Sorry," they add, "I should've mentioned it earlier. You two enjoy."

She frowns, but when Silas grabs a banana and starts setting up the campfire, Dami plasters a soft smile on their face. She looks at them hesitantly, then picks up a banana and begins peeling it.

"So," Marisol says, ripping a piece of banana off with her fingers. "I know how important finding the treasure is for the two of you, and I think I know how we'll get off this island."

Silas pauses, lowering the banana from his mouth. "You . . . do?"

"I told Marisol everything last week," Dami says. "Sorry, I would have mentioned it, but we weren't really speaking."

Silas's brow furrows, but he nods and takes another bite of the fruit as he steps back from the fire he made. "All right. Then let's hear it—how do we escape?"

"I've been thinking about the last note we found—the one that mentioned the boat. I think it must be hidden on the island somewhere."

Dami blinks. "You think the boat is still here?"

She nods. "I know it would have happened before Eve's time, but I really do believe this place is so deadly no one has ever left."

Silas's eyes brighten. "We'll need a way off the island once we get the treasure in any case. So if we find it—"

"Then we have our way out once we find the treasure," Dami finishes. "But how do we find the boat?"

Marisol smiles. "I was thinking about that, too. If someone left clues, that means they wanted someone *else* to find them and figure out where the treasure is, right? Because otherwise why hide clues at all?"

They hadn't thought of that. "So . . . you think whoever left the clues . . ."

"Wasn't actually looking for the treasure. I think they left them for someone else. And I think the boat was meant as a means to escape. And if *that's* true, then the boat is probably with the treasure."

Silas's eyes widen. "So if we find the treasure—"

"We find the boat." Marisol grins. Then, slowly, her grin slides to a softer smile. "Well. If I'm right, anyway. It's just a theory."

Dami is positively vibrating with excited energy. "Silas, what if it was your great-great-grandfather who left the clues? The one who hid the treasure here to begin with?"

Silas, who had turned away from them, looks back with a frown. "Maybe," he says. "Does neither of you smell that? It smells like smoke."

"You're sitting in front of the campfire *that you just made*," Marisol says dryly.

Silas blinks and looks at the fire, as if just noticing it for the first time. But instead of an embarrassed smile, his frown deepens. "Yes, but . . . it's too strong for that."

"I don't smell anything," Dami says, which is . . . odd. They hadn't thought anything of it, but Marisol is right—there is a fire going, so it makes sense to smell a little smoke. They walk closer to the campfire. The warmth of the flames radiates on their face, and the crackle of burning wood is thick in the air. The fire is definitely there.

. . . .

So why don't they smell anything? Unless . . .

"Actually," Marisol says, "now I smell it too."

Someone gasps—Silas. Dami's head whips up to find him. He's pointing to the west, where a large plume of black smoke darkens the sky. That's not smoke from a normal campfire. "That's . . . a lot of smoke."

Their stomach all but drops out from under them. It's hard to see through the dense trees, but it sure looks like a forest fire. And it's not that far away.

"That doesn't make sense," Dami says, "it's been raining on and off since we got here. Everything is still damp—how could a forest fire . . . ?"

Silas just looks at them, and their words die away. He doesn't have to say it—nothing on this island has made any sense at all. The strangely tropical weather and plants. The poisonous snake. Even the monsoon-like weather of their arrival was unusual.

So, no, it doesn't make sense that there's a fire, but this island doesn't play by the rules of reality. It doesn't exist, as far as any map knows. And the flames don't care whether Dami thinks their presence is illogical. The fire's here, and if the haze starting to creep into the air is any indication, it's moving quickly.

And that's when two men, one holding a pistol and one holding a rifle, step through the trees into the clearing: Paul and his blond friend.

"Hello again, children," Paul says, gesturing with the pistol. "Let's have a chat."

Chapter 34

· · · · · · · · · · · · · · · · · · ·

N obody moves.

Had this been a year ago, Dami would have been able to fight them fearlessly—after all, shooting a demonio is about as effective as punching smoke. Now they could make themself look monstrous and try to scare them off, but Dami strongly suspects the Americans' first instinct is going to be to shoot, not run. And Dami currently has a body very much capable of dying.

It's hard to maintain the carefree aura they once reveled in now that they have something to lose. Still, Dami can, at least, feign confidence they don't have.

"Do you not see the approaching forest fire?" they ask coolly. "We *all* need to get out of here."

"And we will," Paul says, "after you take us to the treasure."

Dami resists the urge to roll their eyes.

"We don't know where it is," Marisol says, her voice steady. She crosses her arms over her chest. "If you'd eavesdropped any longer, you would know that."

"Liar!" the man holding the rifle says. "I heard you kids discussing grabbing the treasure and leaving the island. You must know where it is."

"We honestly don't," Silas says. Smoke wafts into the clearing, stinging Dami's eyes. They blink hard, shivering with anticipation. The fire is getting close—they all need to leave, *now*. "You're wasting time, and we're running out of it. We need to clear off away from this fire before it's too late."

"Tell us the truth and we can do just that," Paul says. He nods at his partner, who levels the rifle on Dami.

Dami's heart skips a beat. *Don't panic*, they remind themself. *Worst-case scenario you become a demonio again, which at this rate is probably going to happen anyway.*

Somehow, that thought isn't as comforting as they intended.

"We *are* telling you the truth," Dami grumbles out, watching the weapon pointed at them warily. "It's not our fault if you don't want to hear it."

"This rifle is loaded," says the man holding it. "Don't make us ask again."

"We're telling the truth!" Marisol answers. "We haven't found the treasure yet, and we're not sure where to look. Maybe we'll find it eventually, but right now we don't know!"

Bang! Dami jumps, heart in their throat as the firing rifle kicks up leaves near their foot. Marisol screams, and even Silas is wide-eyed and pale.

That's nice, Dami thinks. *He actually cares if I die.*

"I'll give you one more chance," the man holding the rifle says. "Next time the bullet's going into his chest."

Dami's stomach churns nauseatingly. There must be some way to stop them. To save themself. To convince these men of the truth: that they really don't know where the treasure is. But the grim determination on the American men's faces is chillingly familiar.

They'll kill me. It's not a question; it's clear in their eyes, in the steady grip of the rifle. A year ago, Dami would have phased behind the man and taken the rifle for themselves. Or even let him shoot them. It would have been easy, *fun* even, to watch the men realize how little power they really had over Dami. But now they're human, and they're helpless. *This is what you wanted. This is what being human means.*

Dami has been a lot of things over the course of their life, but they've never been helpless. They hate it. And all they can think is that they could have prevented this if they hadn't insisted on being human.

The smoke is getting thicker, and Marisol's face is streaming with tears. Even Dami's eyes are starting to sting. "Please!" Marisol says. "We're telling the truth! We don't know where it is!"

The crackle of flames sounds far too close. Paul coughs and pulls his bloodstained shirt up over his nose.

Dami stands perfectly still, but their hands are shaking in their trouser pockets. *Breathe,* they remind themself. *You may not be a demonio anymore, but you still know people.*

They have two options: lie and make up some place on the island where the treasure supposedly is, or lean into rational truth. The risk with the first option is that the men will probably want Dami to take them there, so that's unlikely to get them out of danger. The risk with the second is that the men might not believe them.

If Paul were here alone, the first option might have been best. But the man holding the rifle looks uncertain. His gaze keeps darting between his partner and the three of them. If Dami pushes a little harder, they might be able to get him on their side.

"Would you like me to lie to you?" Dami says. "Make up some place on the island and say it's there? Even if I did, the island is literally *on fire* right now. What do you expect me to do?"

"Now, hold on, Paul," Rifle Man says. "I think the boy may be telling the truth. Maybe we should—"

The gunshot makes Dami's heart kick hard against their chest. Rifle Man staggers back, then falls to the ground. Their ears are ringing, or maybe it's Marisol's screaming. That stranger stepped between them and a pistol. He literally took a bullet for them.

Why would he do that?

Paul swears and crouches in front of the dying man. There's blood. So much blood. It's spilling down the stranger's shirt and bubbling out of his mouth.

Even from where they're standing, Dami can see it. The life draining from his gaze.

A hand grips Dami's arm. Silas. "We need to clear off, *now*."

"The beach," Marisol says quickly. "Run!"

The heat of the flames is undeniable, and through the rapidly thickening smoke, orange flames dance between the trees. The air is burning Dami's eyes, their throat, their lungs. They have to get to fresher air—fast, while Paul is distracted.

And so they run.

Together they rip through underbrush, slap dry palm fronds out of their faces, and trample over crunching fallen leaves. Dami runs as their legs ache and their lungs burn. The hazy air makes their eyes sting and it hurts to breathe, like liquid fire gathering in their chest. But it doesn't smell like burning. It doesn't smell like anything at all.

That should terrify them, but they don't have time to think.

A crack like a thunderclap rips through the crackling flames just as Silas trips and crashes to the ground. Dami spots it immediately: a fire-engulfed tree groaning as it pitches forward—directly toward where Silas has fallen.

For a moment everything slows. Marisol gasps next to Dami. Silas hasn't seen the tree. Flames are raging around them—so hot that Dami's skin feels as though it's cooking. The tree is tipping more steeply. It's going to fall. Right on top of Silas.

It's going to kill him.

Dami can't imagine a worse death than being pinned down by a flaming tree, slowly being crushed and burned to death.

They turn on their heel, skidding to a stop and racing for Silas. Marisol screams somewhere behind them. The tree is in the corner of their eye, the forest is an inferno, and Silas is starting to get up, but too slowly. He doesn't know. He doesn't know.

"Silas!" they yell as they slam into him, grabbing him tight as they roll out of the way. The tree crashes to the ground behind them, so close the flames breathe on the backs of their necks. But they're alive, both of them, and Silas isn't pinned under the tree.

He's pinned under Dami. Staring up at them, wide-eyed.

Dami actually smiles and laughs, somewhat deliriously. They stagger to their feet, careful not to step on Silas in the process, and offer him their hand. They make eye contact, and Silas nods. There's an odd glint in his eye, almost like he's saying thank you.

Almost like he might not hate them.

No time to think. Marisol races around the tree, letting out a relieved breath when she sees them both alive. Dami grabs Silas's arm and pulls him forward, and then the three of them are running again. Panting through burning coughs. Squinting through gray air. Pushing through trees and bushes and praying they don't get crushed by any collapsing trees.

They run until Dami's cheeks are streaked with tears, until they feel as though they might collapse if they take another step. But they take another step, and another. Their body screams for them to stop, but if they stop they die, and they're not ready. They haven't survived all of this to die on this cursed island. They haven't made it this far just to end up where they were again.

So they run.

And all at once, they burst through foliage into open air and sand. Dami, Marisol, and Silas stagger out onto the beach, ten, fifteen, twenty feet from the forest. And then, finally, Dami sinks to their hands and knees, gasping for air.

On the beach, the air is clearer. The breeze stronger. Dami's skin has gone gray with soot, and when they look at Silas and Marisol, they find it's the same for them. Head to toe, covered in ash and gray smoke, save for the streaks of clean from their tearing eyes.

"Are we . . . safe?" Silas pants.

"I think so," Dami says. "Worst case we wade into the water until it burns itself out."

Marisol nods, her expression vacant, even as tears keep

streaming down her cheeks. Slowly, she lies back in the sand, closes her eyes, and takes a deep breath. It's then, with the adrenaline fading, that exhaustion hits them. They lie down next to Marisol, groaning as their aching body settles in the cooling sand. To their surprise, Silas does the same next to them.

Together, they stare up at a darkening sky for a little while.

Chapter 35

·······················

The flames never reach the beach.

The fire rips through the forest in a sweeping wave, and the sky is clouded with smoke. But eventually, inexplicably, the fire goes out. All at once, like putting out a lantern. Completely unnatural, and yet Dami finds they aren't surprised. Not after everything.

Once they have the energy to stand, Dami gets up. "Come on." They extend their hands to Marisol and Silas. Marisol takes their hand immediately, and miraculously, so does Silas. His hand is warm in Dami's, slightly sweaty. And soft. So soft.

Together, they walk down to the shore. Dami kicks off their boots, and Marisol and Silas do the same. Marisol throws herself into the water with a laugh while Dami and Silas let the water lap at their toes. The coolness is such a relief after racing through an inferno. It's exactly what they need.

Dami crouches and discreetly presses their nose against their sweaty, sooty shirt. It should smell like smoke and sweat. It should smell like something, but it doesn't. They don't smell anything at all.

·········

Water laps at their toes and a shiver of ice rumbles through them. "Silas?" they ask, so softly the rush of the ocean almost drowns them out.

Silas looks at them, face dripping with the ocean water he's just splashed onto his skin. "Hmm?"

Dami takes a deep, shaky breath. "I know this is an odd question, but bear with me. What does it smell like?"

Silas frowns at them. "What does what smell like?"

"The beach. The air. Here. What do you smell?"

Silas shrugs. "The smoke in the air and in my clothes. The salty sea breeze. The ocean." He glances down at his gray-tinged shirt and wrinkles his nose. "Sweat."

It shouldn't surprise them, not really. In many ways, it's exactly what they expected, exactly what prompted them to ask to begin with. The absence that hinted something might be wrong.

Something *is* wrong—and they know exactly what. Their deadline is fast approaching. First, they lost the ability to taste—or eat at all, for that matter—and now the other senses grounding them to this world are fading too.

Silas may have all the time in the world to find this treasure, but Dami doesn't. And the reminder is so stark they feel as though they might be sick.

But when Silas says, "Why do you ask?" Dami doesn't break down. Instead, they take a deep breath, square their shoulders, and paint on a smile. "No reason."

"Hey!" Marisol shouts from waist-deep water. "You two are filthy. Come in here!"

Despite their somber mood, Dami laughs. "Suppose she's right," they say to Silas before throwing themself into an oncoming wave. As the cool water surrounds them, Dami stretches

. . . .

their arms out above their head, surrendering themself to the ocean's embrace, just for a little while.

D ami lies back in the cool sand, arms crossed behind their head, staring up at the dark gray night sky. The stars are completely obscured by the smoke. As they stare at the starless sky, they wonder what it looks like off the island. Could others see the smoke? Do they see it now, blotting out the stars as it disperses? Or is the smoke, too, hidden by the magical fog that renders this island invisible?

Dami supposes it's probably the latter. If this island doesn't want to be found—and it seems like it doesn't—then it wouldn't make sense for it to become a beacon of fire in the middle of the night. Not if others could see it and follow it to Eve's shores.

The crashing of the waves is oddly soothing. If it weren't such a cool night, they could close their eyes and picture themself back in la Nueva España, the land of their birth. Granted, they weren't exactly raised there given the whole diablo thing, but they still spent a good amount of time in Central America and the Caribbean. Being there always felt like getting a glimpse at what their life might have been like, even if only in fragments.

Marisol has gone to sleep, maybe a hundred feet away—she'd be visible during the day, but the darkness provides some privacy. Up until now Silas has been tending to the nearby campfire he made, but now he's standing over them.

"Why did you save me?"

Dami stills. Even their breath freezes in their chest until, slowly, they release it, then swallow their thundering heart. They bite their lip, forcing their gaze to stay on the abyss above.

Why does the question make them so nervous? Is it because they don't know the answer? Or is it because they do?

In the moment, all Dami could see was Silas suffering. The agony of burning, of being crushed. Of dying in such an excruciating way, and yes, he would have come back again, but Dami would have had to leave him. The flames were closing in fast, and if they'd stayed, trying to free him from the fallen tree, they would have burned too.

They would have had to leave him behind while he screamed.

The thought is so revolting Dami shudders. They close their eyes. It's a simple question, really. Why did they save him?

Because I wanted to.

Because I couldn't leave you behind.

Because I couldn't hear you scream.

"Would've been a pain to get that tree off you," they say.

They don't look at Silas. They don't want to see whatever may be written on his face. Relief? Disappointment? Irritation? They stare at the endless deep of the starless sky and imagine it sucking the emotions out of them. These confusing thoughts and—god forbid—feelings.

They didn't come here to have feelings about a boy who still calls them *demon.*

Silas sits next to them; then he does the worst thing possible: he lies down next to them. Not so close that they're touching, but close enough for Dami to hear him breathing. They still don't look at him. They don't move at all.

"The why doesn't matter, I suppose," Silas says. His voice is a little hoarse from the smoke. He sounds exhausted. But he's alive, and he didn't burn, and he's lying on the beach next to them, and that's enough.

That's enough.

"I haven't . . . thanked you at all," Silas says.

Dami stares and stares and stares at the sky. They swallow their words and breathe steadily, keeping their face blank. They don't know what's going on—maybe the oxygen deprivation has made Silas go soft. But they don't want to break the spell.

But then Silas doesn't say anything more, and Dami isn't ready for the moment to end. So finally, they say, "That's true. You haven't."

Silas laughs softly, and a thrill rushes through Dami— followed by their stomach dropping to their toes.

Oh no.

No no no, Silas's laugh can't do that to them. Stop it. *Stop it.*

"I've been so angry about the deal we made. I always assumed you orchestrated the deal in the worst way possible out of some sadistic delight in hurting people, but . . ." Silas looks at Dami— they can feel the weight of his gaze on the side of their face. "You don't . . . seem like that."

Dami hesitates. How much do they want to tell him? How much is safe to share?

How much would Silas actually care to hear?

"I can't undo curses," they say. "I was—am—a demonio. Not a diablo. They have a lot more power—they can do magic like you can't even imagine. But you didn't get a diablo. You got me. And our deal . . ."

They almost said it was the best they could do, but was it? They aren't sure. Theoretically they could have made it pain-less at least, maybe, but the truth is they hadn't put that much thought into it.

Dami sighs. "It was careless. I wasn't trying to hurt you, but

I wasn't going out of my way to make it easy, either. You were so desperate I . . ." They cringe, their voice softening. "I didn't need to."

And there it is. Manipulating Silas was laughably easy. El Diablo had taught Dami how to play the desperate like puppets, and they'd forced themself not to think about the consequences. But now they know Silas better than they've ever known any of their marks. They've seen firsthand, again and again, what their manipulation has wrought, and, *yes*, the deal has saved his life but it didn't have to be like this.

El Diablo raised them to think of humans as pawns, not people. But Dami doesn't want to be like the monster that raised them, so it's up to them to mend the damage.

"For what it's worth," they whisper, "I really am sorry. I never should have taken advantage of your desperation—or anyone's for that matter. You deserved better."

They close their eyes. Will Silas move away? There are two ways this will likely go: either Silas will find them disgusting (and Dami can't say they don't deserve the charge) or Dami's confession may make them more interesting. After all, some people are attracted to those who aren't good for them.

Dami has been a lot of things, but they've never been good.

Silas doesn't move away. They lie in the sand together, silently staring up at the inklike sky for minutes upon minutes, breaths upon breaths. Something like static charges the air between them. Dami is a taut string, waiting for Silas to walk away and never look at them the same way again, and that idea hurts deeply. Their eyes sting and it's ridiculous, it's *ridiculous* that the thought of some boy who has never liked them to begin with, who has *hated* them from the very first day, who might decide Dami really isn't worth his time, would bring them to tears.

It shouldn't hurt. But it does. And the longer the silence lasts, the louder their thoughts become. Is this what it's like to care about someone? To want their approval so deeply it aches in your chest, somewhere between your lungs, even when you don't deserve it? To wish more than anything else that you could take back all the ways you've hurt them?

When Dami wondered what it would be like to want the best for someone else, they didn't realize how much it would hurt.

Silas is the one who breaks the quiet.

"Why did you become a demon?"

The question is so absurd Dami laughs. Why. As if they'd had a choice. As if it'd been a conscious decision to surrender their life. As if anyone had ever given them the opportunity to hold on to a normal life, a human life.

But Silas doesn't know they never had a say in the matter. He doesn't know the workings of demonios and diablos, and truth be told, even if he did, he'd probably still think it was something Dami decided to do. After all, a number of people who promise their souls to diablos end up demonios eventually.

It's not common for people to actually give up their children. They suppose they're just lucky like that.

But Silas frowns at Dami's laugh as confusion flits through his expression. He opens his mouth, but Dami lifts their hand.

"Sorry, it's not your fault," they say. "I just forget sometimes that people think I chose this life."

Silas's eyes slowly widen. "You once mentioned there wasn't a *before*. . . . Do you mean . . . ?"

"My mother promised the soul of her firstborn to el Diablo."

Dami focuses on a single point in the deep sky, forcing their voice to stay light. Casual. Like it isn't excruciating to be reminded that your own mother gave you up. "To be fair to her, she thought she couldn't have children. She'd tried for years without success, so she thought it was impossible." Dami laughs darkly. "Surprise."

The quiet that follows has a weight, like the air itself has become heavy. Silas whispers, "That's horrible," and Dami clenches their jaw. They aren't going to cry over this. Not again. Not ever again.

"It is what it is." They sit up, busying themself with brushing sand off their shirt. "Point is I didn't choose. I didn't decide. El Diablo took me just minutes after I was born. I've spent my entire 'life' a demonio until recently."

Silas frowns, then slowly pushes himself up. "What do you mean, *until recently?*"

Dami isn't sure when they decided to tell Silas everything. They don't know why it seems safe—or at least, not actively dangerous—to tell him the truth now. But the night is warm, and Silas is so close next to them, and the malice that was in his voice for so long is gone.

So they tell him.

They tell him they haven't been a demonio for nearly a year. They tell him how they made a deal with el Diablo to free themself, but el Diablo didn't tell them what they needed to do to keep their humanity. They tell him what it's like to be a creature of the dead, a ghost during the day and unable to experience life at any time. They tell him how demonios have to make deals to survive, to plant a foot in the plane of reality, to be seen or heard in the living world at all.

When they're done, they flop back into the sand, feeling

· · · · · · · · ·

lighter. Their cards are on the table, and Silas may very well use them to hurt Dami, but for some reason they aren't as afraid about that as they once were. Maybe it's because the reversion has already started. Maybe it's because they're running out of time . . . and running out of hope.

Maybe it's because they want to believe they can trust him.

"My apologies," Silas finally says. "I didn't realize . . ."

Dami lifts a shoulder. "You couldn't have. And anyway, you weren't entirely wrong. I've ruined people's lives to try to live mine."

Silas grimaces. He hesitates and then, lowering himself back into the sand, asks, "How much time do you have left?"

Dami laughs coolly, turning their face back up to the sky. "Not enough." When they look back at Silas, he looks . . . odd. Almost like—"Don't tell me you're actually starting to feel bad for me."

Silas laughs, but the sound is hollow. "I was more thinking everything makes more sense now."

Dami tilts their head. "What do you mean?"

"This whole time I kept asking myself why. Why you ever agreed to do this to begin with. Why you wanted to cancel the deal even though keeping it would have meant getting my soul at the end. Why you've stayed, even after the bandits killed me, and I drowned, and the snake, and the frog—there have been so many times you could have cleared off but you didn't. I was starting to think you just liked watching me suffer."

Dami frowns. "I hope you know that I don't."

Silas smiles softly. "I do now."

Dami nods. "Technically, I'm just as stuck on this island as you are. So there weren't really any opportunities to leave once we got here."

"Sure, but I didn't know that. I thought you were still a demon who could disappear themself like you did before."

Ah. Dami grimaces, tracing the wispy edges of their tattoo at their wrist. "Yeah, that was pretty convenient. Suppose that's an upside if this doesn't work out." They try to say it lightly, jokingly, but even the thought of it makes their stomach churn.

"How much time?" Silas asks again.

Dami sighs, pressing their hands into the cool, soft sand. "Just over six weeks."

Silas nods slowly. Then he rolls to his side, facing Dami. They find themself suddenly aware of just how close Silas is, his face no more than a foot from the side of Dami's head. The realization makes their skin prickle.

"All right," Silas says.

Dami looks at him with an arched eyebrow, playing it cool even as their face warms at their proximity. "All right?"

"So we find the treasure in six weeks. Now we have a plan."

Dami laughs and rolls to their side, facing Silas. They've shifted even closer—six inches apart at most. "That's not a plan—that's an aspiration."

Silas smiles, and his breath warms their face as he speaks. "Fine. An aspiration, then."

They shake their head, but they can't help but smile at his optimism. They don't mention it to Silas, but after today it won't be possible anymore to get to London without magic. Still . . . maybe they can find another way. Maybe, as long as they can find the treasure on time, they can use someone else's magic to get there before it's too late.

Silas's gaze locks on Dami's, and their thoughts fall away. It's just the two of them, lying on the beach, the hiss and sigh of the ocean muffling all other sound. They're so close. At the beginning of this trip, the proximity would have been awkward, but now . . . now Dami doesn't want Silas to move away. It's comforting to have him here in a way they don't want to examine.

And then Silas reaches out, his fingers brushing Dami's cheek, making them shiver. His hand is so warm, his fingers soft. And it's *nice*. It's so nice to feel him against their skin.

How did they ever survive without touch?

"Thank you for saving me," Silas breathes. "You didn't have to."

"I did," Dami says, surprising themself. "I couldn't watch you get hurt again."

They don't know when they decided they couldn't let anything bad happen to Silas, when something shifted that made it intolerable to see him hurt. But something has changed, and they can't go back to not caring.

Strangely, they don't want to.

And then they move—or maybe Silas does—and their lips are on Silas's. He holds Dami's face in both of his hands, and Dami wraps their arms around him, pulling him close. His lips are soft and dry, and when he deepens the kiss, Dami can't taste him, but fireworks are scattering over their skin nevertheless.

God, it feels so good to be held. To be kissed. To be wanted, even if just for the moment.

Then kisses turn to touches and touches turn to sighs and Silas's mouth is on Dami's neck and they've never taken their shirt off faster in their life. Dami rolls onto their back, pulling Silas with them, the cool sand soft against their skin as Silas settles over them. Silas shrugs his shirt off, and the skin of his chest against Dami's is hot. They blend into each other,

. . . .

skin to skin, mouth to mouth, holding each other so tightly that Dami can feel every one of Silas's subtle movements.

As sparks bloom across their body, Dami could cry at how good it is to *feel*. Soon the two of them shed the rest of their clothes, and when they move together—it's bliss. The thudding of Dami's heart against their chest, the warmth of tangled limbs and breath against skin, the comfort of Silas's face pressed against the crook of his neck—this deep, grounding connection makes them feel alive in ways they've never been able to experience before.

And it's good. Because for a time, Dami is just a person holding a boy, kissing a boy, having sex with a boy. For a time, they're two stars colliding, about to bloom into a supernova. For a time, nothing matters but holding Silas close and feeling him.

For a time, Dami closes their eyes and lets the world fall away.

Chapter 36

· · · · · · · · · · · · · · · · · · · ·

It's the ticking of a clock that reaches Dami first. The steady *tick tick tick* of seconds slipping away, escaping between their fingers like shifting sand, impossible to hold. The red-painted room around them brings a shiver of horrifying familiarity.

They stand before a desk. Behind the desk, a chair, facing away from them. The chair is built like a throne, with ornate arms and padded red leather on black wood, studded with gold. The sight of it makes Dami's stomach seize with nausea. The faint smell of smoke in the air is so familiar it should feel like home, but instead it makes them want to turn and run.

Except they can't.

Dami doesn't remember how they got there, or when they started walking, but the heels of their boots clack against the floor as they move forward. Closer to the desk. Down the morbidly decorated hall.

They shouldn't be here. This room should be destroyed, along with its owner. They should never have to stand here, not again, but though every bone in their body pleads with them to

· · · · · · · · · ·

turn around and leave this place as quickly as possible, their legs carry them forward. As if they aren't in control of themself.

Finally, their feet come to a stop, exactly where Dami knew they would—just two feet from the desk, where they always stood. This was the place where they learned what it meant to be a demonio. Where they reported their successes and failures.

Where they looked el Diablo in the face and lied.

The chair swivels around silently, and Dami is left facing him again.

"Hola, Dami." He smiles. "I've missed seeing you."

And maybe they should be afraid, but instead they're exhausted. They were supposed to be done with this, they were supposed to never have to look at this monster again, but though he may be dead, he seems to be alive and well in their mind.

They settle back into the familiar, the safe, the air of apathy and boredom. They peer at their nails, running their thumb over the smooth black gloss. "Strange," they say, pleased at the strength in their voice. "I barely thought of you at all."

His smile widens, but Dami avoids meeting his glowing red-hot-coal gaze. As usual, he's dressed in the finest garments money can buy, today with a white silk shirt beneath a red vest embroidered in gold and a black tailcoat.

Dami would like to say they learned their sense of style from observing humans, but the truth is el Diablo always knew how to impress. It was part of the charismatic appeal used to lure the unsuspecting desperate.

"Now, hije," el Diablo says, "you should know better than to lie to me. I know you far too well for that."

Dami flinches at the term of endearment, *hije*. It's true that el Diablo raised them, but he is anything but a father. He stole from them their only chance at happiness. The opportunity to have a normal life, one they'd done absolutely nothing to lose.

Of course, that didn't matter. Children pay the debts of their parents, after all.

"What is this, anyway?" Dami turns away from the desk, unable to bear another moment with his gaze analyzing their face. They run their fingers against the cool red walls—the chalky texture of paint over drywall. The cool air caressing their cheeks. The ever-present scent of smoke—

They stop, midstep. Wait. They can smell it?

"Ah," el Diablo says, "there it is."

Dami frowns. "Why can I smell the smoke?"

"Why am I alive?" el Diablo counters. He leans back in his seat, lacing his fingers together and resting them over his chest. "For someone who hates me so much they spent years developing a plan to betray me, you sure seem determined to keep me living in your mind."

Determined to keep him alive? Dami almost laughs. "You think I *want* you haunting me from the grave?"

El Diablo shrugs nonchalantly. "This is *your* mind."

The *tick tick tick* of the clock fills the room again. El Diablo leans forward, hands steepled on the desk. The smile in his eyes makes Dami shudder.

"It won't be long now. I hope you enjoyed your brief taste of humanity, because it won't last." He pauses, then laughs. "Although I suspect your taste has already left you, hasn't it?"

Dami goes stiff, their breath caught in their chest. They still have time. Maybe not a reasonable amount of it, but there's room for hope. It's all Dami has, and they'll hold on to it until it disappears entirely.

"I still have time," they say softly.

El Diablo laughs. The sound echoes around them, again and again, cascading into a booming crescendo of laugh upon laugh upon laugh, so loud they can feel it in their chest. They crouch, pressing their palms against their ears as they squeeze their eyes closed and try to wrench themself from this awful nightmare.

Wake up.

The room vibrates with the thundering echo of laughter.

Wake up!

Silence. Dami doesn't move at first, still crouched as they are. Slowly, they dare open their eyes just enough to peer at the floor. Polished hardwood still. But the laughter has faded—it's only the drumming of their pulse in their ears now—so they slowly look up.

El Diablo is crouched right in front of them. Dami gasps and falls back, scrambling backward.

El Diablo only smiles. "I'll see you soon, Dami."

Dami screams, jolting up so abruptly they ram into Silas, knocking heads. Silas yelps and clasps his hand over his forehead, and Marisol screams before clapping a hand over her mouth. Silas grimaces as he squints at Dami. They're sitting up on a cool bed of leaves. Silas was evidently leaning over them, because he's now kneeling next to them.

Awake. They're awake.

Dami groans and presses their face into their hands. Maybe they'd be better off never sleeping again.

"Are you all right?" Silas asks. "You were shaking in your sleep. We thought—I don't know— Are you all right?"

Dami finally looks up at him, forcing deep, slow breaths to calm their racing heart. "I'm sorry," they say. "Nightmare, I guess." They hesitate, but Silas knows all there is to know, so they add, "I've never had one before."

"Some nightmare," Marisol says softly.

Silas lowers his hand, and Dami cringes at the red spot above his right eye. He leans closer to them, frowning, and reaches out to gently brush his finger against Dami's forehead. Presumably where Dami smacked their head against his. "Does this hurt?"

"No," they say, because it doesn't. That's odd, isn't it? If they hit their head against Silas's so hard that it left a welt on his head, then it should hurt. But they don't feel anything. Not warm or cold, not the pulsing of a forming bruise, not even—

Dami stills. Silas is running his thumb over the skin above Dami's eyebrow—they can see it out of the corner of their eye. But they can't feel it.

They can't feel it.

Nausea rips through them so suddenly they nearly vomit. Instead, they close their eyes, take a deep breath through their nose, and wait for the wave to ebb.

When it feels safe, they open their eyes, ignoring the way they're trembling all over. Silas is holding their face now, his palms on their cheeks, his fingers in their hair. And though they feel nothing, this hurts worse than any physical pain they've ever experienced.

It's a knife to the heart, not feeling his soft skin, his warmth— and before they can stop it, tears blur their vision and spill over.

Silas's eyes widen. "What's wrong? What was the dream about?"

But it doesn't matter what the dream was about; what matters is that it was right. El Diablo was right.

They're nearly out of time.

·········

Chapter 37

....

In the morning light, the forest is lush and green. The trees are unburned, the ground moist and packed with fallen leaves. The air is thick and warming quickly, though a cool breeze occasionally tousles Silas's hair as he paces along the entrance of the cave.

It's as if the island reset overnight. As if the fire never occurred.

None of them comment on it. They don't have to state the obvious—there's something unnatural about this place. Silas is getting the sense that the island's purpose is to kill everyone on it—except Eve, interestingly. In any case, the sooner they find the treasure and clear off this blamed island, the better.

He stops pacing and turns to Marisol and Dami at the tree line where the forest meets the beach. "I'm starting to believe finding this treasure would be impossible without the deal we made."

Dami smiles wryly. "Are you saying you're grateful for our deal?"

Silas snorts. "No. You're still a bastard."

For some reason, that makes Dami smile.

"But I suppose, perhaps there's a silver lining. Perhaps I'm meant to be the one to break the curse." Silas wants it to be true. With every bone in his body, he wants to end this horrible curse. The alternative—the one where he continues dying and waking and dying and waking until he can't take it anymore and eventually Maisey dies too—is just too unbearable to consider.

He must find the treasure. He can't leave this place empty-handed. It can't have been all for nothing.

"I hope so," Dami says, "but we don't have any leads. Even if the village survived, I'm not convinced it's safe for any of us to go there, not after what happened."

Marisol sits against a palm tree, her head tilted back as she closes her eyes.

Silas sighs. "You really believe someone else will attack us if we return to the village?"

"They know we're looking for treasure," Marisol says softly. "Even if they don't attack us right away, if we *do* find the treasure . . ."

Silas frowns. "Fine, but . . . how do we find it?"

"You tell me." Dami turns to him, their gaze boring into his. "This is your curse. Your mission. Your family are literally the only people who could know where the treasure is. You said you think the curse always leaves someone alive so there's a chance for it to be broken, so doesn't it stand to reason that it would leave you some way to find it?"

Silas frowns, then sits next to them. His knee brushes

against Dami's leg and his insides jolt. "That would make sense, but . . . the story passed down about our curse didn't specify where on the island to find it. I suppose I'd assumed I would . . . know somehow."

"We'll find it," Dami says. "One way or the other."

"You sure better," Marisol grumbles. "I'm not dying on this godforsaken island." Then she suddenly straightens and looks at Silas. "What about the whispers?"

The whispers? He blinks and his brow furrows. "I don't hear any at the moment."

"But you have when we've been near a clue, right?" she presses. "Is there anywhere on the island that we haven't investigated where you heard the whispers?"

Silas starts shaking his head—but wait. "Actually . . ." He turns to Dami. "Do you remember that cave we stumbled upon when we first arrived?"

Dami grimaces. "You mean the creepy cave with the blood message and the skeleton I tripped over? Sure, it wasn't traumatic at all."

Silas laughs slightly. "I heard whispers there, too, but I didn't know what it meant at the time."

"Perfect." Marisol grins. "Does either of you know where it is?"

Dami bites their lip. "Well, we arrived on the northwest side of the island. I don't think we walked for long—I was totally exhausted. And then when we left, we got caught in your trap, which wasn't far from the cave."

Marisol's eyes light up. "Oh! I think I know what cave you're talking about." She hops to her feet. "Well, what are we waiting for?"

• • • • • • • •

After they trek through the forest for what feels like hours, they find the cave. A ring of stones near the cave's mouth catches Silas's eye—within the ring is a pile of burned leaves and sticks. A small campfire, long since abandoned. The cave looks different in the afternoon light; larger and more open than he remembers.

"Cozy," Marisol says, glancing around. "Why did you leave?"

"Bats," Dami says. "There's a cavern down that tunnel full of them. *Someone* foolishly woke them up."

"Rather sure that someone was you," Silas mutters, moving deeper into the cave. He can *almost* hear it.

"Where are you going?" Dami asks. "I don't actually want to re-create the bat run."

"Shh." Silas closes his eyes and steps farther into the tunnel.

Silas. The whisper is so faint he almost mistakes it for a hiss of a passing breeze. It's not the whisper of one voice, but many— overlapping and repeating his name.

He opens his eyes. "This way."

"Are we really going *toward* the bats?" Dami asks, but Silas ignores them. With every step the whispers become louder, until he's standing in the cavern, light streaming from small cracks in the ceiling he didn't notice the first time they were here.

Silas Cain, the voices whisper. *Look.*

The whispers draw him closer to the wall with the foreboding message written in blood. Somewhere behind him, Marisol gasps, probably spotting the warning for the first time.

"Silas . . . ," she says nervously.

Silassss.

Approaching the wall, Silas spots a crevice running down it.

• • • • • • • • •

The fissure is just wide enough for a person to step through, so long as they shimmy in sideways, but it's too deep for him to see what's on the other side.

"This wasn't here before." Silas runs his fingers down the crevice. "I'm certain it wasn't. I would have noticed."

Dami frowns. "I don't recognize it either."

Silas closes his eyes and turns his ear to the crack. The whispers are so loud inside it almost sounds like wind. "The whispers. Do you hear it?"

Marisol shakes her head, but her eyes are bright.

Dami hesitates. "No, but . . . I can feel it." They frown. "Some kind of magic."

Silas's eyes widen. "Magic?"

Dami glances at him with a wry smile. "Well, you don't think it's the rocks whispering to you, do you?"

Silas's face reddens. He turns back to the crevice and mumbles, "Clearly not."

"You know," Dami says, "you're incredibly cute when you blush."

His face flames redder. Dami laughs as Silas scowls and shoves them lightly. "The whispers are louder in the crevice. We should be able to fit."

Marisol cringes. "We're going in *there*?"

"Do you have any better ideas?"

She bites her lip. Dami's face softens. "You don't have to go in," they say. "You can wait for us out here if you want."

Marisol laughs. "If I let you two go in there alone, I might never see you again, and then how am I supposed to get off this island?" She squares her shoulders. "Are we doing this or not?"

"Into the creepy narrow crevice in the black cave that leads to

....

god knows where? Absolutely." Dami grins and steps toward it, but Silas grabs their arm.

"Let me go first. If there's something dangerous at the other end . . . well. At least it won't kill me."

Dami frowns and opens their mouth as if to protest, but whatever they were going to argue dies on their lips, because they close their mouth and step aside. Silas slips into the crevice first, angling himself sideways, sliding his right arm in first and squeezing in between the two rock walls.

Rock scrapes against his back and chest as he scoots forward. It's dark in the crevice, unsurprisingly, but the walls are wetter than Silas expected. It occurs to him, as the three of them slip ever deeper into this space hardly wide enough to let them pass, that if any kind of dangerous insect lives between these walls none of them have any way to avoid it. Or snake. Oh no, do snakes live in caves?

If he never encounters another snake again, it'll be too soon.

Light up ahead catches his gaze. "I think I see the end," he whispers. "Not much farther."

Silas slips forward a little faster, and then he's out of the crevice. He shivers as he takes a deep breath and rolls his shoulders. It's warmer here than he expected, and the air feels damp. Dami and Marisol stumble out after him. Marisol looks back at the crevice with a ferocious glare, like it personally offended her.

The fissure has opened into a small circular cavern. It'd be impossibly dark if not for the lack of a ceiling. Silas peers up the walls, probably fifty feet to the forest surface. It's somewhat of a miracle that there isn't a ceiling, really, because directly in front of them, maybe three feet away, is a massive hole. The three of them are standing on a narrow ledge that goes all the way around, because in addition to this space not having a ceiling, it doesn't have a floor, either.

Silas shudders to think what might have happened if they hadn't been able to see.

Chapter 38

·····················

Inside the cavern, the call of magic is so strong Dami shudders. They've felt this only a handful of times before—the most recent of which found them the person who had enough magic to kill el Diablo. The pull is hypnotic, relentless, like a string connected to the center of their chest pulling them forward. Pulling them down.

They need to get down there.

"You really don't hear that?" Silas asks.

Dami looks at him. "I don't hear anything, but I can feel the magic. There's definitely something down there."

"What does it sound like?" Marisol asks.

"Voices," Silas says softly. "Whispering, but like hundreds of people all at once. I can't make out what they're saying anymore. There's too many of them, all speaking over each other." He shakes his head. "This has never happened before. It must be the treasure, right? The note—*What you seek lies in the abyss.* This must be it."

"Only one way to find out." Dami pulls off their shirt.

Marisol arches an eyebrow. Silas stares at them. "What are you . . . doing?"

"Being gorgeous, of course." Dami winks at him.

Marisol rolls her eyes, but Silas's face reddens again. "I—but—why is removing your shirt necessary?"

Dami laughs. "How do you think we're getting down there? Unless you happened to bring a rope you forgot to tell me about."

Silas frowns, but Marisol says, "*Oh*," then smiles. "Smart."

It takes several repetitions of Dami stripping off their shirt and pants and transforming again with a new set of clothes while Silas and Marisol tie them tightly together to begin creating a rope. It takes longer still to create one hypothetically long enough to get to the bottom, not that any of them can really tell where, exactly, the bottom is.

"Do you think that's long enough?" Marisol asks, peering into the darkness.

"That had to be at least thirty feet," Dami said. "Do you think it won't be long enough?"

She shakes her head. "I have no idea. I can't see the bottom."

Dami picks up a rock and drops it into the hole. They count two seconds before a quiet splash echoes through the room. "Two seconds," they say.

"What does that mean?" Silas asks. "How deep is it?"

"No idea." Dami smiles sheepishly. And then another thought hits them. "Wait, there was water at the bottom."

Silas nods slowly. "Yes, but if we jump from here—"

"Oh, no, that will definitely kill us. But if there's water at the bottom, we can feed the rope down and pull it back up until we see that the end of the rope is wet."

Silas and Marisol agree that this is a great idea—because it *is* a great idea, thank you very much—and so Silas holds the end of the rope while Dami shoves the rest of it into the pit. They wait about five seconds for it to settle before pulling it back up.

Dry.

Damn.

They aren't sure exactly how long they spend creating more clothes—it's a little dizzying to be transforming this often in such a short span of time—but eventually they've added another ten-ish feet to the rope.

Toss it in. Pull it back out.

Dry.

"Jesus Christ," Silas says. "How deep is this pit?"

Dami groans and kicks another rock into the abyss.

"I guess we're doing it again." Marisol looks at Dami. "One more time."

Some time later they've added yet another twenty feet of rope. "If this isn't enough, I swear to god . . . ," Dami mutters as they push the rope over the edge again.

They hold their breath as they pull it back up.

"It's wet!" Marisol says with a relieved laugh.

"Great!" Silas says. "Now what do we tie it to?"

Ah. Dami peers around the cavern. There aren't any roots or anything from the forest above. There are a couple of stalagmites, but none of the ones near them are tall enough—or thick enough—that Dami would trust it to bear their weight.

There is one on the other side of the room, though. It's nearly as tall as Dami is and probably a foot thick. That should do it.

It's just a matter of getting the rope over there without falling into the pit.

· · · · · · · · ·

"Anyone know how to lasso?" Dami asks.

Marisol and Silas stare at them blankly.

"I'll take that as a no." They grab the end of the rope, then tie off a large loop—theoretically large enough to fit far down the stalagmite they're eyeing. Dami has absolutely no experience with herding, so they don't really know what they're doing either, but that won't stop them from trying.

Pulling their shoulders back, they near the edge, leaving about a step between them and the cliff. "Okay. One of you hold the end of the rope so I don't accidentally lose it over the edge."

After Marisol grabs it and nods at them, Dami turns back to the stalagmite. They try to swing the rope over their head in a circle to gain momentum like they think they're supposed to, but the rope is heavy and lumpy with knots, so it just falls on their head. They try a few more times, each with increasing force, but the longest they get it to stay in their air is for one revolution before it bumps into their head and falls again.

So throwing it over there isn't going to be an option, then.

"Really, Dami?" Silas asks with a groan.

"It's harder than it looks—the rope is too heavy," Dami protests. "You try it if you think it's so easy."

Silas shrugs and walks over, taking the rope from them. After several failed attempts to lasso the stalagmite like Dami, he frowns and tries throwing it, but it doesn't come anywhere close to reaching their target.

"It's too heavy," Silas says begrudgingly.

"Sorry, what was that?" Dami says. "I didn't hear you."

Silas grumbles. "The rope is too heavy."

"Mm-hmm." Dami takes the rope back, shaking their head.

"If only someone else had said that before you made a fool of yourself."

Marisol snickers as Silas rolls his eyes.

Satisfied, Dami turns back to the pit, rope in hand. They bite their lip. "Okay, I have an idea." They tie the rope around their waist, knotting it tight.

Silas looks at them warily. "Which is what, exactly?"

"Both of you hold on to the far end of the rope. Wrap it around your hands or something, make sure it's a good grip."

If anything, this only seems to worry Silas more. Even Marisol is giving them a side eye. "Tell me what you're doing first," he says.

Dami gestures to the thick stalagmite on the other side of the pit. "We can tie the rope to that, then climb down from there."

Marisol looks at Dami, the stalagmite, Silas, then the rope. "And we're supposed to hold it in case you fall."

"Exactly."

Silas shakes his head. "Shouldn't I be the one doing the more dangerous job of getting over there?"

Dami snorts. "With your luck you will *absolutely* fall into the pit, and I don't trust myself not to fall in with you if you slip. And anyway, can't let you have all the fun." They grin at him. Silas doesn't look amused, but he doesn't argue, either, as he wraps the rope around his hands.

"To be clear," he says, "this is a terrible idea."

"A horrible idea," Marisol agrees.

"Well, unless you have a better one—"

"If you die it isn't our fault," Silas says.

Dami laughs. "I'll be sure to remember that while becoming your personal poltergeist." They rub their hands together and take a deep breath, walking carefully closer to the edge. When they look back, Silas and Marisol have positioned themselves behind two stalagmites close to each other. Neither stalagmite is thick enough to bear the weight of the rope, but it'll probably help keep Silas and Marisol out of the pit if Dami does fall.

Theoretically.

At least falling to their death in a strange, magical pit in a creepy cave on a cursed island is a cool way to go. And probably fast? After the falling part, anyway.

Dami presses their back against the cavern wall and slides sideways around the edge of the hole. They press themself so hard against the wall they imagine that if they weren't pretty much numb, their back would probably hurt. Maybe an upside? At least the ledge is wide enough to hold the entire length of their feet, with a few extra inches.

Slide left foot. Slide right foot. They ignore the racing of their pulse in their ears as they do it again. Again. Their hands are clammy against the rock and they try not to stare down into the terrifying pit. Instead, they keep their eyes on the stalagmite. They started probably thirty feet away. Now they're fifteen.

This is fine. Definitely not the most terrifying thing they've ever done. Definitely glad they insisted on doing this instead of sending Silas, too.

"You're almost there!" Marisol says.

Dami nods tightly. Forces themself to keep breathing evenly. "Everything is fine," they whisper to themself. "Almost there. Just keep going."

They're so close now, they can almost reach out and touch it. The stalagmite is so thick that it takes up the entire ledge— the only way to get around it would be to straddle the thing

....

269

while dangling yourself over the edge, which Dami is *not* doing. They don't have to get to the other side.

And then they're there. The stalagmite is right ahead of them; they can't go any farther. So now it's just a matter of tying the rope to it. Which, now that they're here, might be a little more challenging than they first thought.

They could try to reach across it, but it's large—that's the whole reason they chose it to begin with. They can't really reach all the way around. Maybe if they hold the end of the rope, they can toss it over the tip and then tie it down? It's pretty tall, too—at least three feet over Dami's head, so probably over nine feet tall. Another good reason to use it as an anchor, but it does make this part trickier.

And there's the minor detail of having to untie themself, too.

Dami takes a deep, shuddering breath. Their fingers shake as they start unknotting their lifeline. The cavern has gone so quiet that Dami swears they can hear Silas breathing. Finally, the knot gives and Dami nearly drops it in surprise.

They hold the end of the rope and grab another section of it, with about four feet of slack in between. It should be enough slack that they can throw it over the top and cinch it together.

Dami's foot knocks a rock, and it skitters off the edge and into the abyss. The lapse of time between accidentally kicking the rock off the edge and hearing it splash into the water below is truly terrifying now that Dami is so close to the edge.

It's fine, it's fine. They're okay. No need to panic. Worst case they fall off the edge, Silas and Marisol can't save them, and they're a demonio again forever. Not ideal. Definitely not ideal, but it's not like they'll be *dead* dead.

And yet the thought doesn't make them feel any better.

·········

"Dami, this is torturous to watch," Silas says. "Throw the blamed rope."

"You throw the pinche rope," Dami mutters under their breath. But Silas is right. The longer they stand here, the longer they'll be in this terrifying precarious position, so they might as well get it over with.

They take a deep breath, brace their side against the wall, and throw it, holding tight to the end in their right hand while allowing the rope to slide in their grip in their left. It soars up, smacks against the tip, and falls back down.

Okay.

Carefully, Dami pulls the rope off their boots. They just need to toss it a little higher. They take another shaky breath, then throw it again. It flies up almost silently, slaps the side of the stalagmite, and falls on their feet again.

"Puta madre," Dami hisses.

"Jesus Christ, Dami," Silas says as Marisol groans. "Throw it higher!"

"I know that!" Dami snaps. "I'm trying! Throwing this thing high enough without losing my balance is hard, okay?"

They don't catch what Silas says in response, but judging by the fact that he's muttering it, that's probably for the best. Dami takes another slow, calming breath. They can do this. Just one more throw. They can do this. They *have* to do this.

So they pick up the rope. Grip it again, ignoring the sweat on their palms. Throw. The rope flies up, up, up—

Snags on the very tip—

Then slips over the edge, sliding down the far side of the stalagmite. Dami's face blooms with a grin. "Yes!"

"Great!" Silas calls. "Now tie it and come back."

....

Dami shakes their head. "Once I tie it, you two should swing over here and start climbing down. I can climb down after you."

Dami carefully ties the knot, then adds an extra one for good measure. It occurs to them that their rope is dependent not just on this knot, but on every single knot that ties the random pieces of clothing together. They're pretty confident in the hold of their knots, and they're sure Silas and Marisol wouldn't have half-assed it either, but still. Those are a lot of chances for failure.

And they're climbing into a pit with someone cursed with fatally bad luck. Probably now isn't the best time to ask Silas if his curse has ever killed someone outside of the family, though.

Chapter 39

· · · · · · · · · · · · · · · · · · · ·

Before Dami can give the parameters of the Cain family curse any further thought, Marisol and Silas are swinging toward them across the void. Marisol screams. They hit the wall near Dami's feet hard, grunting with impact.

"Ow," Silas says.

"You know, you're supposed to catch yourself with your feet."

Silas glares at him. "I tried— Forget it. I'm climbing down."

Dami smirks and watches as he carefully disentangles himself from Marisol and climbs down into the pit. Marisol follows, and they grab the rope and lower themself.

At least Silas is below you, they think. If the rope was going to snap it would have already.

Unless it's Dami's extra weight that makes it snap. But there's a time and a place for catastrophizing, and this isn't either. So they think about literally anything else. The strangeness of not feeling the wall against their boots, which only makes them even more insecure on the rope. The way their fingers are gripping the rope so tightly their knuckles are white, but they don't feel the pain. That they're holding on with every fiber of

· · · · · · · · ·

their strength because they can't actually tell how tight their grip is on the rope.

That this numbness is so much more dangerous now that they have a mortal body.

It isn't long before they're ten feet down. Then deeper. The ledge above them looks so far away. Come to think of it, Dami isn't sure they'll have the strength to climb back up this way. Hopefully they'll find another way out.

Hopefully they aren't climbing down into a well or some other dead end.

"Doing okay?" Dami asks, mostly to distract themself from their doom-filled thoughts.

"Sure," Silas says, his voice trembling. "I'm climbing into an incredibly deep pit in a terrifying cave on a terrible island. I'm fantastic."

"At least if you fall, you won't die," Dami says helpfully.

Silas makes a noise that sounds like he tried to laugh but coughed instead. Marisol glares up at them. "And what about me? *I'll* die if I fall."

Dami grins down at her. "At least you're not cursed with fatally bad luck."

They keep climbing. Dami may not be able to feel the pain in their quickly exhausting muscles, but the tremble in their arms is clear enough. Sweat drips down their temples and their back. The deeper they climb, the darker it becomes, until they can't even see the rope in their hands. Their breaths come heavy and they desperately want to be done with this terrifying trip.

Maybe if they fall now they're close enough to the bottom that they won't die?

"How much more?" Dami asks, their voice strained.

. . . .

"How should I know?" Silas snaps.

They groan and look up. The light coming from the forest floor looks so far away. They must have climbed over twenty feet by now. Maybe thirty? The ledge they climbed down from looks so small from here. It's hard to tell exactly how far down they are, they're not sure they'd really be able to differentiate between twenty or thirty feet, even if they weren't hanging off a rope made of clothes.

"Oh!" Silas exclaims just before a splash.

Dami stops climbing and clings to the rope. "Silas?" They peer down. It's so dark down here they can barely see Marisol just below them. Maybe they should have brought a torch, but how on earth would they have transported it without setting the rope on fire? Or lit it down here?

"I'm all right!" Silas calls up. His voice sounds close, probably just several feet below them. "You can let go—you're not far from the bottom."

Marisol does first. After a splash and some sputtering below, she calls up, "All clear!"

So they let go. The water envelops them like a dark blanket. They surface with a gasp, treading water in pure shadow. "Silas? Marisol?"

"Right here." Silas's voice is so close Dami jumps. "Let's try to find the end of this pool."

Dami hesitates. "I think one of us should stay with the rope. We don't know how big this is, or if there's an exit at all. We should keep track of the rope so we have something to hold on to if we get too tired."

"That's a good idea. Marisol and I will go, then. We'll yell if we find something."

·········

"Okay," Dami says. They hate how small their voice sounds down here. The pit was relatively large at the top, and the walls went down for a while, but for all they know the wall they climbed down could have been longer than the rest. They could be in a cavern. Or they could be in a well. It's impossible to say in darkness so thick it's almost suffocating.

The soft sounds of moving water and breathing are all Dami hears for a while. They grip the rope tightly, wrapping it around their wrist, then unwrapping it again, over and over, just for something to do. Their legs are already getting tired.

If they never swim again, it'll be too soon.

"Dami! Silas!" Marisol's voice echoes in the room, giving them the impression they are not, in fact, in a well. The cavern seems more likely by the second. "I found a ledge! I think this might be the mouth of a tunnel. Just swim toward my voice."

Dami takes a deep, steadying breath. For some reason, leaving the rope feels like leaving safety—not that the rope was really a good long-term solution, seeing how they'd get just as tired from holding themself up as they would treading water endlessly. Still, once they leave, they suspect it'll be incredibly difficult—if not impossible—to find it again.

But Silas's and Marisol's voices are somewhere to their left, and they can swim toward them. So, after squeezing the rope one last time, they let go and swim.

Dami says, "Keep talking. Don't stop until I get there."

"Uh," Silas says, "great weather we're having."

"Really?" Marisol says. "That's the best you have?"

Dami snorts. "Sure hope you're never in a position where you have to small-talk to save your life."

"Forget that, I would be the first volunteer to die."

Dami smiles. His voice sounds nearby now, it shouldn't be much longer before—

Their hand touches something hard in front of them. A ledge. They push their arms on top and, with a groan, heave themself out of the water, rolling onto their back with a sigh. They made it. They aren't going to drown in the dark.

God, that would've been a terrible way to die.

"Dami?"

"I think I'm at your feet." They poke what they're pretty sure is Silas's boot.

"Oh! Perfect. Hi."

Dami stands, brushing the wet from their arms, as smoke envelops them, replacing their clothes with an identical dry set. "So what now?"

"I think the only thing we can do is follow the tunnel," Marisol says.

"We can't see anything," Dami counters.

Silas sighs. "We'll have to move slowly."

Dami frowns. They don't like this. At all. What if there's an animal of some kind down here? Or what if the floor ends somewhere? Or there's another pit? Not being able to see in some mile-deep caves on a cursed island seems like an exceedingly bad situation.

On the other hand, what other option is there? It's not like any of them can conjure fire. They don't have torches. And even if they tried to turn around now, there's little chance they'd be able to find the rope, let alone have the strength to climb back up to the top.

So forward it is.

"For the record," Dami says, "I hate everything about this."

"Afraid of the dark?" Silas teases.

"Afraid of what might be in the dark, more like it," they say.

Silas's fingers thread with theirs on their right, and Marisol takes their left. It feels strange—distant—like they're holding a handful of packed cotton. "To keep track of each other," Silas says quickly. "So we don't lose each other in the tunnel."

Dami smirks. "Are you saying you'd only want to hold my hand if our lives depended on it?"

The silence that follows makes Dami laugh. They may not be able to see Silas blushing in the darkness, but they can sure as hell imagine it. Silas just grumbles something Dami can't hear and pulls them forward, slowly, as they carefully slide their feet over the uneven ground.

"To be clear," Marisol says, "I'm perfectly happy holding your hand whenever."

Dami grins. "See, Silas? It's not so hard to be pleasant."

"I've got my hand on the wall," he says, ignoring them. "We'll just . . . walk slowly."

Dami opts not to think of all the ways this could go wrong. There's a constant quiet scraping as they walk—the sound of Silas's hand sliding against the wall—and their footsteps echo a little. Otherwise, the cavern is deadly quiet.

Dami imagines, if it were guaranteed to be safe, this would be the perfect place to fall asleep, if they had a bed with them. The darkness is so complete it's disorienting. They're moving forward, but they can't see any evidence of their progress. They could have walked twenty feet or a mile.

How many treasure seekers found their way down here and died in the darkness? Dami suspects it's probably a nonzero number. They just hope they don't trip over any bones like they did their first day here.

They walk for a while in silence, hand in hand. Silas's and Marisol's breathing sounds unusually loud, mostly because of how utterly quiet it is otherwise. After they've been walking for some time, something strange happens: up ahead, the end of the tunnel looks a little gray. They keep walking and Dami blinks rapidly as the gray dot at the end of the tunnel turns white—it's light. There's literally light at the end of the tunnel.

As the light grows bright enough to illuminate the tunnel, Silas finds himself shaking—but not from the coolness of the underground. There's no guarantee that the treasure is waiting for them at the end of the tunnel, but it *could* be. The whispers are louder down here, his name repeated endlessly, voices speaking over each other.

Silasss . . .

Look. Silasss . . .

Hidden this deep under the island? With strange whispers beckoning him forward? It would be sensible for the treasure to be here. Could this be it?

The rock around the three of them is utterly black, like obsidian. At the end of it are what look like torches, but instead of the orangey glow of fire, the flames are pure white. Strange. The torches are on either side of an opening to a room, with a closed wooden door built into the opening. Light spills out around the edges of the door, which looks absolutely ancient. It's for the best that the door is so old; theoretically, it shouldn't be difficult to break it down, if needed.

Assuming there isn't something magical about the door.

"Do you hear the whispers?" Silas asks quietly.

Dami glances at him. "No."

"Me neither," Marisol says softly.

Silas purses his lips.

"That doesn't mean it isn't real," Dami adds. "I can't hear whispering, but I can tell there's definitely some sort of magic down here."

Silas's shoulders relax at the reassurance, just a little, and he nods. If Dami senses something down here, that's certainly promising. "It must be behind the door, right? We've gone this far, and the magic . . ."

"I hope so," Dami answers, evidently unwilling to commit to a more confident response. "I don't think we would have been drawn down here for no reason, though."

Silas nods a little faster. "This must be it," he says again. "It must be."

Dami squeezes his hand.

And then they've reached the end of the tunnel. The dancing white light of the unnatural flames gives the tunnel a ghostly hue, painting the three of them in grayish, pale light. The wooden door doesn't perfectly fit the opening in the rock wall, so more strange light leaks out around its edges. Silas isn't sure exactly what he expected, but the utter plainness of the door feels almost out of place between the strange torches. The hinges bolted into the rock are rusty. The brass knob is dented.

Silas stands stock-still, his breath caught in his chest. A

lifetime of fear, a year of suffering, generations of death, it's all led up to this moment. But now that he's here, the possibility of failure is paralyzing.

Dami must notice his hesitation, because they squeeze his hand again and smile softly at him. "I think you should open it. Marisol and I will be right here. Nothing to worry about."

Silas shivers in the cool air. With a long, shaky breath, he nods. Then, before he can talk himself out of it, he grabs the doorknob, twists, and pulls. The door opens with a long, eerie creak. He releases Dami's hand and walks into the room.

It's small. Same black rock as the tunnel, with a white torch in every corner. Smashed crates litter the ground—wood chips are scattered everywhere like dead leaves in autumn. And knocked over against the far side of the room is a large chest.

The lid is open.

And it's entirely empty.

Chapter 40

· · · · · · · · · · · · · · · · · · · ·

Dami sits at a small, polished wooden table, positively vibrating with nervous energy. The wood-paneled walls are the same auburn shade as the table, and the built-in bookshelf to their left is pristinely packed. The moonlight pouring in from a nearby window paints the room in silver. Dami's hands practically look like porcelain in the light.

The wall candelabra placed above the chair opposite them comes to life, bathing them in warm candlelight. Dami's heart pounds a little harder as they examine the light reflecting off their perfectly painted black nails. When the chair across from them slides back, squeaking slightly on the polished hardwood, and Juno sits down, Dami looks up casually.

"This is cute," she says, gesturing to them. "You've been practicing that devil-may-care facade, I see."

Dami frowns, and she smiles. "I'm the Diablo of Knowledge, Dami. I know when you're masking. Or lying, for that matter."

· · · · · · · · ·

That's . . . annoying. Dami sighs and sits up in their seat, putting on a genuine smile this time. "I did it. I'm a demonio."

"So you are." She looks at them for an uncomfortably long time, her gaze settled steadily on theirs. Dami resists the urge to squirm in their seat or look away. Finally, she says, "I'll be frank with you, Dami. You won't be able to kill el Diablo alone. He's too powerful."

Dami feels as though the floor has dropped out from under them. They stare at Juno. "But . . . you said if I became a demonio, you'd tell me how to kill him."

"And I am. I'm not saying your task is impossible, I'm saying you'll need help."

"From who?" they all but gasp out. "No other demonio or diablo is going to help me. If I can't do it alone, who am I supposed to go to?"

"What you need," she says calmly, "is a human with powerful magia."

Dami's brow furrows. "There are humans with magia?"

"Not many, but yes." She pauses. "You'll find a higher concentration of them in the Caribbean. There's an island there hidden by magia to other humans and demonios alike, but every so often someone leaves and their magia passes to their descendants."

Dami bites their lip, pushing the panic crawling up their throat back down again. "And how am I supposed to find these people?"

"You'll know when you find them. As a demonio, you can sense magia the same way you sense other demonios or diablos." She stands.

"Okay," Dami says quickly. "So, say I find someone with magia. Then what? I'm a demonio; they're not going to want to help me out of the kindness of their heart."

Juno smirks, and when she turns away, the candles snuff out, plunging them into shadow. "You're a demonio. Make a deal."

Chapter 41

······················

Silas drops to his knees, making a low noise like a wounded animal. "No . . ." He presses his face into his hands, trembling from head to toe, and Dami doesn't know what to say. How to fix this. If they can.

"Oh no," Marisol whispers, covering her mouth with her hand.

The room looks absolutely ransacked. The chest, upon closer inspection, clearly once had a lock on it—it only takes a quick look around to find it lying a few feet away. It doesn't seem likely that it'd have some kind of false bottom, but Dami checks anyway, pressing their hand against the wood and knocking lightly. But the design isn't that clever. It's just a chest.

An empty one.

When Dami turns around, Marisol is looking at them hopefully, but they just shake their head. Silas is full-on sobbing into his hands, and something about that breaks them. Seeing him like this is devastating—their own eyes sting with oncoming tears but they hold them back. They have to do something. Anything.

·········

But whatever treasure was in this room is clearly gone, and Dami can't change that.

They crouch next to Silas and pull him into a hug. He melts against them, his face pressed against the crook of their neck, shaking like a leaf in a storm. Dami holds him tightly, rubbing his back, and this time they can't stop their own tears. So they don't. They blink them away and let them fall silently while holding a broken boy against them.

The unfairness of it all is infuriating. How is Silas supposed to break this curse if someone else already got to the treasure? Is he supposed to figure out who took it and track down all the pieces? Dami wouldn't even know where to begin.

But the curse has to be breakable, doesn't it? Unless there was a window of opportunity that has long since closed. Like Dami's own rapidly closing window.

Their thoughts are a hurricane, but the answers are elusive. Just the possibility that there may never be a way to save Silas, to save his sister, that he may be stuck like this—dying and waking and dying again—until he can't take it anymore. . . .

They can't accept that. They can't. And not just because it would guarantee their becoming a demonio again.

Dami isn't sure how long they hold Silas, but when he finally quiets, they still don't have any ideas. They stay there, in the hopeless silence, for some time. Silas doesn't move away, and Dami doesn't push him to. Part of them doesn't want to stop holding him, even while they wish it were in different circumstances.

They wish they could feel Silas pressed against them, though.

Then Silas whispers against their skin, "I should cancel our deal."

Dami goes rigid, then pulls back, forcing Silas to look at them. "What do you mean?"

He meets their gaze, eyes puffy and red, face shiny with tears and snot. "There isn't any reason to keep it now, is there? The treasure is gone. I can't break the curse. And I don't want to live like this forever. It's torture."

Dami's heart is in their throat. Here it is, exactly what they wanted from the very beginning: Silas is ready to cancel the deal. But if they cancel now, Silas will die. There isn't any question in their mind—they doubt he'll last even a few days, especially if they remain trapped on this godforsaken island.

If they cancel now, Dami will have done what they needed. Their task will be over. They'll be human.

The cruelty of the situation makes them nauseous. It's supremely unfair that the only way Dami can get a chance to live is to doom Silas to die. But refusing to cancel the deal will almost certainly mean they'll run out of time. Silas might live—maybe—and Dami will be a demonio again. Forever.

Dami closes their eyes, pressing their fist to their mouth. They want to curse this island, this magic, this goddamned horrible ultimatum that they can't win. Because how could they live with themself knowing that they traded away someone else's life for theirs? *Silas's* life for theirs?

When Dami opens their eyes again, Silas is frowning at them. "What's the matter?" he asks. "Isn't this what you wanted? I'll cancel the deal, and you can reclaim your life."

"And you'll lose yours." Dami's voice cracks. They press their lips together and shake their head. "No. I don't accept. Deal not canceled."

Silas pushes away from them. "Why not? Do you want to be a demon for eternity?"

"Obviously not." Hot bile rises up their throat, sitting in the back of their mouth. They swallow hard. "But you can't seriously expect me to be okay with murdering you so I can have a life. You really think I'd be able to sleep at night, knowing what it cost? I won't do it. I can't."

Silas laughs, but the sound is empty. "So now that I'm finally ready to do what you want, you won't do it."

"This isn't what I want," Dami insists. "This isn't what we agreed." They take a deep breath and stand, offering Silas their hand. "Either we both leave this island with what we want, or neither of us does. I won't do this without you."

Something in Silas's eyes catches them: pain. They don't get it. Why would Silas be upset about their refusal to kill him? Shouldn't he be happy that Dami hasn't given up?

"We can do this," they say. "I'm not giving up. Not yet."

"Why not?" Silas's voice is exhausted. "Look around you, Dami. There's nothing here. We failed. Someone else found it and cleared off with it."

Dami doesn't have an answer to that. Silas just shakes his head and looks away. Dami swears under their breath and runs their hand through their hair. They spot Marisol sitting in the opposite corner of the room, her face splotchy and wet with tears. With a sigh, they cross the room and sit next to her, holding back their discomfort with the outpouring of emotions everywhere.

Marisol leans her head against their shoulder. Dami looks at her, unsure of what to say.

What they don't expect is for her to say, "Why do you keep sabotaging yourself?"

Dami blinks. "What?"

She sits up straight, wiping her face with the back of her hand. "First was the night watch—you knew how important it was to stay, but you just . . . walked away."

Dami may not be able to feel the flush creeping into their cheeks, but the indignation is there all the same. "I didn't just *walk away*. I saw el Diablo and I *followed* him."

Marisol frowns. "Who?"

Oh. Right. Dami shakes their head. "It's . . . not important."

"Okay . . . but even so, why did you follow him?" Marisol looks at him without judgment, like the question is a mere curiosity.

Their voice falters. It's a valid question; they didn't *have* to follow him. At the time, the potential consequences of leaving their post just hadn't seemed that serious.

"And now," she continues, "Silas is offering you a way out and you're refusing."

"Because it would *kill* him," they counter.

"Silas knows exactly what he's offering."

"Well, I don't accept that. I won't let him throw his life away for mine. I'm not—" Their voice catches in their throat as their vision blurs. No, no. They will *not*. Dami furiously scrubs their face with their palms, rubbing away the tears gathering in their eyes.

"Not what?" Marisol presses.

They don't answer at first, stubbornly staring at the mud on their boots instead.

"I don't deserve it," they finally say. "There. Happy? I don't deserve a second chance, especially not at someone else's expense." The words burn as they force them out bitterly.

Marisol frowns. "Why do you think that?"

. . . .

They laugh hollowly. "Why do you think? I'm a demonio. The things I've done— Did you just roll your eyes?"

"Dami. I'm sorry, but get over yourself. We've all hurt people over the course of our lives. What you had to do to survive doesn't disqualify you from deserving a chance to live. You deserve it just as much as Silas does."

"She's right," Silas says from across the room. "I was wrong before. You're not a bad person, Dami. You deserve better than what you were handed."

Tears spill over their cheeks, unstoppable now. "Well, that's just not fair," they say, wiping at their cheeks, "ganging up on me like that."

"We wouldn't be good friends if we didn't knock some sense into you," Marisol says with a soft smile. "Now, are we all done with the fatalism? Because I'd like to get out of this room."

Silas sighs. "I don't know where to go from here. If someone took the treasure already, how are we supposed to find it?"

But something about that doesn't sit right with them—and then it hits them. Dami blinks. "Wait. I don't think anyone took the treasure—or at least, they didn't get far. When we first arrived at the village, Eve said no one had found it, remember?"

"So she lied. Or she was wrong." Silas gestures to the room. "Someone was clearly here."

Marisol frowns. "I don't know. She's very possessive about everything. . . ." Marisol trails off, looking with Dami more carefully around the small room.

If Eve wasn't lying or wrong—and Dami is fairly confident she wasn't—that leaves two possibilities. Either someone did find this place and ransacked the room but left empty-handed (and maybe destroyed the crates that were here in their rage?)

or the room was made to look like someone already got the treasure.

"What if there was never anything in this room?" Marisol asks, evidently wondering the same as Dami. "What if this is just made to look like a dead end? Imagine it—treasure seekers barely survive the horrors of the island, find their way down here, likely almost dying in the process, then finally arrive only to find that someone already took the treasure—"

"I don't have to imagine it," Silas cuts in flatly. "That's what happened."

"I'm not done," Marisol says, speaking quickly as her eyes light up with excitement. "So all of that happens, then what? They're distraught. They think there isn't any treasure to be found because someone else already took it. So they give up and leave empty-handed."

Silas goes quiet, slowly looking around the room, maybe catching on at last. Finally, Dami says, "It's a setup."

Marisol nods. "One last way to discourage anyone who makes their way down here—which likely isn't many people to begin with given how good the island is at killing people."

"All right . . ." Silas stands, fingers trailing up the wall. "Then . . . where is it actually?"

Marisol frowns. "I . . . haven't figured that part out."

Ah. Dami mulls that over, considering what they know. After a pause, they look at Silas. "Are you still hearing the whispers?"

Silas nods. "It's been louder since we came down here."

"Then it's nearby, probably," Dami says. "I'd think the perfect place to hide treasure would be exactly where people think it isn't."

Marisol wrinkles her nose. "Like a trapdoor?"

Hmm. The ghostly hue of the strange torches catches Dami's eye again. They walk up to the nearest torch, hung to the right of the door. The wood—if it is wood—is bone white, but it's too woodlike to actually be bone. Unless it's bone carved to look like wood? Dami gingerly touches the very bottom of the torch—no, too rough. Even carved bone would be smooth between the divots.

So, weird white wood holding weird white flame. "How long do you think these have been burning?" Dami asks.

Silas shrugs. "Who knows? They were already lit when we got down here. I didn't see anyone else ahead of us."

"The wood isn't burning." Dami's face is so close to the flame, they'd probably feel the heat on their skin if they could feel. "There isn't any smoke. I'm not even sure it's fire at all."

Silas walks over and pulls Dami's shoulder back. "You're going to burn your face."

Dami smiles at him. "It's cute that you care."

Silas's face reddens again. He bites his lip and turns to the flame, but he can't hide the smile trying to creep onto his lips. "That's strange."

"Which part? The part where the fire is white or that it isn't actually burning anything or that it's possibly been lit like this for years?"

Silas rolls his eyes. "The part where there isn't any heat coming from the flame."

Oh. Now, *that's* interesting. "Really?" They reach for the flame, and Silas grabs their hand.

"What are you doing?" he hisses. "Just because it isn't hot doesn't mean it can't burn you."

Dami arches an eyebrow. "You don't think heat is required to burn?"

Silas hesitates, his eyes darting to the flame and back to them.

"Anyway, it's not burning the wood." Dami pulls their hand out of Silas's grip. "I don't see why it should leave the wood unburned but burn me."

"The wood might be enchanted as well—you don't know."

"*Enchanted?*"

Silas groans and waves haphazardly. "Whatever this is. The wood might not be any more normal than the fire is. You said yourself it looks odd."

That was possibly a good point. They shrug and turn back to the fire. Oh well, you only live once.

Unless you're Silas. Or a demonio. So maybe that doesn't actually apply to either of them.

"I'm going to touch it," Dami says, and then, before Silas can stop them, they thrust their hand into the flame. Marisol gasps. It occurs to them, only then, with strange white flames dancing around their fingers, that if the fire *is* burning them, they probably won't feel it. Still, they leave their hand there for a few seconds before pulling it back and examining it in the light.

Completely unscathed. Huh.

"Jesus, Dami." Silas shoves them lightly. "You could have hurt yourself!"

"I could have," they admit. "But I didn't." They squint at the ghostly flames. "So, if it looks like fire, but it's not the color of fire, and doesn't burn like fire, and isn't hot like fire . . . is it still fire?"

"This is a terrible riddle," Silas says.

"I don't think this is fire," they announce.

Marisol frowns, looking more closely at the not-fire. Silas doesn't look impressed. "What does it matter if it is or isn't? That doesn't help us."

"Doesn't it?" Dami grabs the bottom of the torch, wriggling it in the brass ring holding it to the wall. "Why go through the trouble of creating not-fire when you could much more easily create normal fire? It can't just be to light the room."

"Regular fire burns out," Silas says flatly. "If this fire doesn't actually burn, then it could stay lit forever. As far as we know, someone lit it hundreds of years ago and it's remained like that since."

Dami wrenches the torch free and grins. "Sure, but why? If you're hiding treasure—"

"Why would you light the room up permanently and make it easier to find?" Marisol finishes thoughtfully.

"Exactly!"

This makes Silas pause. "Even with the light it wasn't easy to find."

"No, but it made it easier. We knew there was something to move toward when we spotted the light." Dami knows they have him there because he just frowns.

Of course, the next question is, if the fire isn't there to light the room, then why is it there? Dami holds the flame up to the wall, circling the room slowly. There isn't much to see on the rock—it's black and shiny, but unpolished and uneven. The walls look almost like a frozen black ocean in the middle of a storm, minus a few especially large waves.

But there aren't any markings and holding the torch to the rock doesn't seem to do much. Still, there must be *something*.

"What are these?"

Marisol is crouched in the corner of the room, looking at a black cup carved out of the same rock as the walls, sitting on the floor in front of her. They crouch next to her and try to pick it up, but it seems to be carved out of the wall, part of the room itself. It doesn't budge.

Interesting.

The cup is small enough to fit in Dami's palm—or it would be if they could lift it. Once again there aren't any markings, and the inside of the cup is perfectly smooth, like the inside of an egg. Peering across the room, they spot another identical cup in the opposite corner.

"There's one in every corner of the room," Marisol says. "I saw them earlier, and I didn't think anything of it, but . . ."

Four corners. Four cups. Four torches.

"What are you two looking at?" Silas walks over, then presumably spotting the cup in the corner in front of them, asks, "What do you think that's for?"

"There's one in every corner," Dami says. "And there are four torches. I think . . ." They lower the flame end of the torch into the cup, and it catches instantly. Dami pulls back with a grin as the white flame settles in the cup, burning absolutely nothing but remaining all the same.

And then the cup begins to glow. Not the entire thing—white markings spread around the middle of the cup, so bright they look like they've been drawn on with light.

Marisol grins. Silas gasps. "What is that?"

They don't know, but they don't think that's the most important question right now. Dami jumps up. "Grab another torch!"

Silas and Marisol rush to different corners of the room, where torches are hung. Dami returns their torch to its spot to the right of the door, then grabs the one hung on the left and goes to the next corner.

That cup lights in the same way. Something flutters in Dami's chest, something light and exciting and bursting with energy. They feel ready to run laps around the room. They could swim across the ocean, hyped like this. This has to be something; it has to.

By the time Dami crosses the room, Silas has already lit one cup and Marisol is crouched in front of the last one. She looks up at Dami, torch shaking a little in her hand. "What do you think will happen when we light this one?"

Dami smiles. "Only one way to find out."

Marisol turns back to the cup. Then, with a deep breath, she lowers the torch into the small bowl. For a second nothing happens, and then the cup lights up like the other three.

And the flames in all four corners leap out of the cups and onto the ground. Dami, Silas, and Marisol jump out of the way with a yelp—it's only afterward that Dami remembers this fire doesn't burn. The fire spreads from each corner in perfectly straight lines to the center of the room, where the lines meet with a roar and flare into a giant white circle of flames.

Silas stares, slack-jawed, and Dami laughs. "Now, *that*," they say, "is magic."

Then all at once the flames in the center of the room die down, burning quietly maybe an inch high in a perfect circle on the ground, roughly five feet across. But it's what's in the circle that interests them.

"Is that"—Silas squints—"stairs?"

They step up to the circle, peering down into it. Spiral, obsidian steps lead deep underground. Dami can't see where they lead—the stairs seem to go on forever—but little white flames on the walls light the way.

"Stairs?" Marisol asks. "To what?"

"Don't know," Dami answers. "But I can't wait to find out."

Chapter 42

· · · · · · · · · · · · · · · · · · · ·

A boy, a girl, and a demonio descend into darkness.

The staircase follows a tight, dizzying spiral, surrounded by obsidian walls. *Like an entrance to the island's throat,* Dami thinks. Silas insists on descending first—in case there are traps—and Marisol goes down second, leaving Dami to reluctantly enter last, trailing their hand against the slick walls for balance. As soon as they've gone deep enough for their head to clear the entrance, a grinding sound stops them.

They all look up as black stone closes over the entrance. Dami swears and reaches above their head, but the stone is firm and rapidly blocking the portal. They barely have time to panic before the entrance—and their only exit—is closed off.

Marisol stares at them, wide-eyed. "Should we be . . . worried about that?"

Should they be worried that they don't have a way out of this strange staircase leading them deep into the island's underground? Probably. The notion that they have no escape, no way back to the surface, makes Dami's chest hurt. Thinking about it too much feels suffocating.

· · · · · · · · ·

So instead, they take a deep breath and paint on a smile. "Suppose the only way out is through." They don't feel it, but they sound confident. And that's enough, because Silas and Marisol nod and continue down the stairwell.

Their boot heels against the stone echo quietly with every step. The only light showing their way comes from the weird ghostly fires that are spaced out evenly as they descend, each burning in a little alcove in the wall.

"How deep do you think this goes?" Silas asks.

Dami just shakes their head. "Couldn't tell you. Seeing how we climbed down a pit to get here, I'd guess we're at least a mile under the island by now."

Silas shivers. "Let's find the treasure and clear out of here as soon as possible."

Dami doesn't argue with that.

After over a hundred steps (Dami counts), they finally hit ground level. The room, if they can call it a room, is large. Three walls—one behind them and two on either side—are all the same dark rock as everything else. But there isn't a fourth wall. Instead, ahead is fog.

It has to be magic, because there's no way fog would've naturally formed this deep under the earth. The fog is thick—too thick to see anything beyond the wall of clouded air. At the end of the right wall is a single white torch hung on the wall the same way as in the room at the top of the stairs. And below the torch is a small table with a piece of parchment on it.

The trio approaches the table warily. The parchment has been written on in reddish ink—Dami is going to pretend it's ink and not consider the other possibility—with a message on the center of the page:

....

BEGIN THE TRIALS TO FIND
WHAT YOU SEEK

TRUE DEATH WILL COME TO
THOSE WHO ARE WEAK

"Well," Dami says, "that isn't ominous at all."

Silas stares at the parchment, then turns to the fog, his shoulders shaking. For a startling moment Dami thinks he's started crying, but then he laughs.

"Of course," Silas says. "Of course there's a blamed *trial* to get through to find this damned treasure. Because surviving this horrible island and finding our way down here and through the trick room, none of that was enough."

Dami frowns. "Your ancestor sure seemed determined to keep it hidden."

Silas shakes his head and kicks a rock into the fog. Dami doesn't say it, but it kind of seems like maybe whoever hid this treasure never intended for anyone to find it. Like maybe Captain Kidd—who, at this point, Dami can only assume had magic—actually wanted to curse Silas's family, not keep his treasure safe. Why else would you go through such elaborate measures that would almost certainly kill anyone trying to get to it?

Unless Silas's ancestor knew the way through, but if he did, he apparently didn't bother passing that knowledge on to his children.

Marisol looks worriedly at Dami. They sigh and nudge Silas with their elbow. "Might as well keep going."

"And if we lose?" Silas looks at them, the despair clear in

his eyes. "It said *true death*. It sounds as though we could actually die down here. For good."

Dami shivers. While they've spent several months *believing* they were mortal, they were never in danger—at least, not after el Diablo was dead. But this is different. Forget becoming a demonio again, true death sounds like they'd actually die.

They've never given much thought to what it would mean to no longer exist. The possibility leaves them cold.

Marisol crosses her arms over her chest. "What other option do we have? The way back is literally blocked off."

Dami grimaces.

Silas closes his eyes and takes a slow, deep breath. When he opens them again, he sets his shoulders, walks over to the wall, and grabs a torch. "All right," he says. "Let's begin the trials."

Chapter 43

·····················

The first few feet into the fog are disorienting. For a moment, Silas isn't confident the path leads to anything at all, if only because he can't see anything in any direction even with the torch. The fog leaves his skin covered in a thin sheen of misty droplets. The light of the torch flame makes the mist look thick, illuminating just a couple of feet of the ground ahead of them.

And it's so, so quiet.

As the three of them continue forward, the tension in the air is as thick as the fog.

Silas Cain.

A chill washes over him—the whispers are so loud down here it feels like someone is hissing directly in his ear.

Silas turns back to them, frowning. "I still hear the whispering."

A slow smile slips over Dami's lips. "The whispering is what got us here. We should listen to it."

They continue forward. An impossibly tall black wall looms ahead of them, made of the same dark rock as everything else

··········

down here. The torchlight spills onto a black iron door set into it.

Silas approaches the wall, beside the door, and runs his hand over it. His hand moves frictionlessly over the cold surface. Polished. Even shiny—his own reflection stares back at him through the dark stone, the torch's flame dancing on the surface with Dami's and Marisol's faces on either side of him.

The whispers are louder here. But an uneasiness in his gut makes him not want to open the door.

"What are you hearing?" Marisol asks softly.

"We must enter," Silas says. "But I have no idea what to expect in there."

Dami nods. "Well, guess we won't know until we go in." They grab the doorknob and pull.

To Silas's surprise, it swings open easily—and silently. The room floods with light so bright Silas covers his eyes with his free hand. Then his eyes adjust, and the three of them step inside.

The room is nothing like the rest of the cave. The floors, walls, and ceiling are all made of the same strange white wood as the torches. And here, the air is clear. The door swings closed behind them with a resounding *thunk*, and the grinding sound of a lock sliding into place tells Marisol all she needs to know: the only way out is through.

That seems to be a recurring theme down here.

In the center of the room is a table so long it could seat several dozen, also made of the light-colored wood. It looks like a dining room table for a king—except each of the legs is carved in a different way. One is carved to look like human skulls stacked on

....

303

top of each other; another like the table leg is wrapped in chains. The third leg is intricately carved with—Marisol squints—roses and thorns, and the last leg is made to look like a thick liquid is pouring down the leg and puddling on the floor.

Marisol grimaces. Thick like blood.

On the table are six goblets, each a different shape, color, and size—each of them made of different materials. Marisol spots wood, gold, silver, marble, and more. The three of them exchange a glance. Marisol isn't sure what she was expecting when they entered the room, but not . . . this.

The three walk up to the table, where a new piece of parchment is laid on the center. A quick glance tells her the script is written in the same eerie reddish ink. Dami picks it up and reads the message aloud in their most theatrical voice.

Each must drink to pass this test. Choose wisely and continue with aid; choose poorly and perish.

Three goblets are full of poison. Not all poisons are deadly, but two of them are.
The least-appetizing drink is harmless.
Two goblets contain opposite fortunes, one shimmering, one still.
The wooden goblet isn't deadly today.
The most valuable goblets contain poison.
The mildest poison is less harmful than one poison-free goblet.
The largest vessel is not deadly.

Dami stares at it for a moment longer, then puts the parchment back down on the table and pinches the bridge of their nose. "Incredible. It's a riddle."

Marisol shakes her head and picks up the paper, reading it over again. "So, we have to . . . drink one of them?"

"Each of us." Dami peers into the nearest goblet and grimaces. "And we'll have to pick three—one for each of us. There's just enough for one sip in here." They look at Silas. "I think your ancestor was a sadist."

Silas grimaces. "I suspect he wasn't the one to set this up."

Marisol eyes the goblets again. That each one is unique must be to help them figure out which of the goblets corresponds to which line of the riddle. The riddle makes it clear that most of them are poison, so guessing incorrectly could have severe consequences.

Silas says, "You two should drink whichever two we're the most certain about."

Marisol shakes her head. "What difference does it make? The note before we started the trials said we could *all* die here."

Silas frowns. "Yes, but . . . neither of you would be down here if it weren't for me."

"Better idea," Dami says. "We make sure we're confident about three of them."

"Does either of you have a quill?" Marisol asks.

Silas frowns. "Why would we be walking around with quills?"

Marisol pulls a face and looks at the goblets again. Her eyes widen, and she steps closer to the table, picking up a blank sheet of parchment, inkpot, and quill. "This . . . wasn't here before, was it?"

"No," Dami and Silas say in unison.

Marisol laughs a little nervously and glances around the room. "Well . . . thank you, room?" She shakes her head, then dips the pen into the inkpot and draws a six-by-six grid on the parchment, noting a *P* in three of the spaces.

"*P* for *poison?*" Dami asks.

Marisol nods. "And I've drawn the deadly poisons. If we determine more about the effects we can label more of them, but I think figuring out what won't kill us is the most important. Read me the clues again?"

Silas does.

"Okay," Marisol says. "Let's start with the direct clues. Which drink is the least appetizing?"

Dami and Marisol both step up to the table, peering into each of the goblets. There's a bright orange liquid, a pure black liquid that looks like ink, two goblets with what looks like water (one carbonated), one liquid that looks like pure gold, and . . .

"Oh. Gross." Dami wrinkles their nose at the last goblet—an intricately carved but tarnished pewter goblet with a greenish-brown liquid that looks like mud. "This is definitely it."

"Great," Marisol says, noting that on the parchment. "Put that one aside. That one is safe."

"I hope you're not expecting me to drink that," Dami mutters.

No one answers.

Marisol pauses to examine the diagram she's drawn on the parchment.

As Dami peers curiously over her shoulder at the combination of letters and symbols, their brow furrows in confusion.

"The *H* is the harmless liquid," she explains. "This will help us figure out what's in the other goblets through process of elimination."

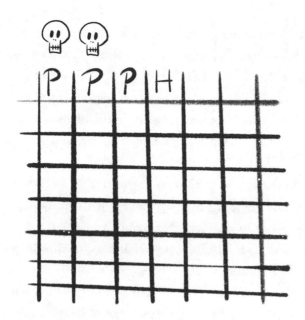

"All right," Silas says. "What's the next one?"

"How about *the most valuable goblets contain poison?*" Marisol suggests. "That could help us sort them into poison and not-poison."

Silas and Dami start grabbing goblets. Dami pulls aside a giant unpolished white marble goblet and a gold jewel-encrusted goblet. Silas grabs a silver goblet with frosted blue glass.

"Three valuable goblets, three poisons," Dami says, eyeing the remaining three: a plain wooden goblet, a bone goblet with tiny skulls carved into the cup and a vertebrae stem, and the pewter goblet with sludge they already separated from the group.

"Perfect," Marisol says, writing furiously. "Then we know the other three *don't* have poison."

"Great," Silas says. "Then we drink those three."

Marisol shakes her head. "*The mildest poison is less harmful than one poison-free goblet,* remember? One of those three has something worse than poison."

Silas's face falls. Then he peers into the remaining goblets. "Wasn't there a clue about shimmering and still liquids?"

Marisol nods. "*Two goblets contain opposite fortunes, one shimmering, one still.*"

Dami's eyes widen. "The sparkling water!"

Silas nods, grabbing the two goblets with the water—the wooden and the bone. "Oh, this makes sense! I think we all know how serious *bad luck* can be—that must be the not-poison that is worse than the mildest poison."

Marisol doesn't look up from her graph. "What about *the largest vessel is not deadly?* Can we pull that aside from the other poisons?"

"That has to be the giant marble one with orange liquid," Dami says. "That thing is basically a chalice."

Silas pulls it aside.

"That means the other two poison goblets *must* be deadly," Marisol says. "So we can eliminate those."

Dami moves the goblets out of the way, arching an eyebrow at one goblet's contents and tipping the cup toward Marisol: one of the deadly poisons looks like melted gold. "Definitely can't judge these by how they look . . . ," they mutter.

Marisol hums in agreement. "That means the marble chalice with the orange liquid is the mildest poison."

"Great," Silas says. "I'll drink that. Now we need to determine the fortune thing and we'll have three goblets."

The three of them stare silently at the clues for several minutes. Marisol reads them so many times the words stop looking like words. This whole exercise has been so mentally exhausting, but she's so close to having an answer. The line about the wooden goblet keeps nagging at her, like an itch in the back of her skull.

Marisol mutters, "The wooden goblet isn't deadly . . . today." She looks up at the two goblets they've set aside for the fortune riddle: the plain wooden and the bone. Then it clicks. With a nod, she stands and grabs the skull goblet. "I think this is the good-fortune drink. Bad luck isn't deadly every day, but it *can* be deadly. I think that's what this clue is saying."

Dami nods slowly. "That makes sense—good luck isn't typically deadly at all."

"Exactly!" Marisol grins, then, hesitantly, she offers Dami the goblet. "You can have it if you want."

"And make you drink mud?" Dami laughs, even though Marisol is sure they would very much like anyone else to drink the sludge. "You figured it out. You should have it."

She frowns. "Are you sure?"

"Very." They grab the pewter goblet, refusing to look at its contents.

"Then we're settled. Dami drinks the harmless goblet, Marisol drinks the lucky goblet, and I'll drink the mildest poison." Silas picks up the giant marble goblet with the bright orange liquid, takes a deep breath, and says, "Please don't be deadly."

He throws back his head and tosses the liquid in his mouth. He purses his lips tightly and shudders, but he doesn't drop dead, so that's promising.

"Well?" Dami says.

"It was very sour," Silas says with a slight laugh. "Similar to lemon juice, but worse. And without the benefit of the citrus flavor." He shakes his head and sighs. "Well, I'm still breathing, and I don't feel violently ill. Who's next?"

"I can go," Marisol says. She peers into her skull-covered mug, her thumb running over the vertebrae stem. "It just looks like water."

"Maybe it is," Dami says hopefully.

Marisol smiles nervously, then, with a deep breath, brings the goblet to her mouth and drinks. After a pause, she shrugs and puts the goblet back on the table. "Tasted like water."

"Do you feel luckier?" Silas asks.

Marisol laughs slightly. "What does luckier feel like?"

No one has an answer for that.

"Well, that leaves you," Silas says, looking at Dami. "Bottoms up."

D ami grimaces down at their goblet, swirling the liquid in the cup. It moves sluggishly—oh, god, it's *thick*. They're not even going to be able to taste this, but their stomach twists anyway. Even if by some miracle it doesn't taste horrible on its own, it's probably going to turn to ash in their mouth and this time they won't even have water to wash it out.

Just close your eyes and do it, you big baby.

"This might actually be the worst thing I've ever done," they say.

Silas rolls his eyes. "You are so overdramatic. Drink it so we can move on."

"Excuse me, *you* didn't have to drink sludge."

"At least we know your sludge is safe." Silas raises their

eyebrows. "Unless you'd prefer to choose a nicer-looking poison goblet?"

"Pendejo," Dami mutters into the cup. Marisol giggles.

Silas wrinkles his nose. "What was that?"

In lieu of an answer, they bring the goblet to their lips and drink. The liquid moves slowly, viscously over their tongue—and to their horror, it doesn't turn to ash. Instead, the tasteless sludge slowly moves to the back of their throat, where they have to suppress every instinct demanding they spit this horrible substance out, and—through violent shudders—swallow it.

Their stomach lurches, and Dami slaps their hand over their mouth, closing their eyes and breathing through their mouth as they swallow again, and again, and again, until it's finally gone.

Absolutely the worst thing they've ever done.

What's worse is when they turn to Silas, he's clearly trying—and failing—to hold back a smile. His shoulders are even shaking a little—he's laughing, the asshole. At least Marisol has the decency to look disgusted on their behalf.

"I feel ill," Dami says, then to Silas, "and you're the worst."

Silas and Marisol laugh. A grinding sound behind them makes Dami jump, and they spin to the wall. Another iron door has appeared and swung open on its own.

Marisol gasps and Silas whoops. "We did it!"

Dami would like to be excited, but the door doesn't seem to be leading to a room with the treasure. They walk around the table and near the door with a frown.

More fog.

They sigh. "Don't forget the torch. We're going to need it."

Chapter 44

· · · · · · · · · · · · · · · · · · ·

They've taken all of ten steps into the fog before Silas stops in his tracks.

"Shit."

"What, did you forget something?" Dami jokes, but Silas just shakes his head.

"I know what the poison did. I can't hear the whispers."

The three of them stand there silently, processing that development. The whispers were what got them here to begin with. Dami can only hope they won't need their guidance again.

"I don't suppose either of your drinks made it so one of you can hear them?" Silas asks hopefully.

"No," Dami answers flatly.

"Me neither," Marisol says with a grimace.

"We're not the ones who are supposed to find this treasure— you are," Dami adds. "It wouldn't make sense for the magic to call to one of us." Dami runs their hand through their hair and turns in a slow circle. The iron door that was behind them is gone now. When they turn around again, there's a new door, this one made of gray stone with a tiny window covered by black iron bars. Almost like what Dami might expect to see in a dungeon.

"Looks inviting," they say. "Think there's a feast waiting for us inside?"

"I hope not," Marisol mutters. "It'd probably all be poison."

A fair point. Dami nods to Silas, who grabs the door handle—a large black iron ring—and pulls. It opens with a low grinding noise that sets Dami's teeth on edge. Silas enters, followed by Marisol.

Dami's just stepped inside when the door closes behind them with a resounding thud. Dami doesn't have to look back to know the door has disappeared, but they take a glance just to confirm.

This room is enormous. Unlike everything else in this underground complex, the walls, floor, and ceiling are all made of gray stone. Hanging on the ceiling are rows of black iron chandeliers, holding black candles dripping with melted wax. The room is completely bare—no tables this time—but a giant circle at least thirty feet across is drawn on the floor in the center of the room in red.

The three of them peer at it curiously. Silas starts moving forward, but Dami throws their arm out in front of his chest, stopping him. "Don't step into it."

Silas looks at them questioningly. "Why not?"

"I don't know. Just a feeling." They look around the room, analyzing it slowly. There's no door for them to exit through, so there must be something they need to do.

"What's that?" Marisol points to the wall on the opposite side of the room, where a small piece of parchment is tacked to the wall. They walk over, careful to avoid the circle. The parchment, like every other, has a message in that same strange red ink.

·········

One to enter the ring and fight
Two to watch a duel to true death

"That's it?" Dami frowns at the message.

"How did it know there would be three of us?" Marisol asks.

Dami's brow furrows more deeply. "I . . . don't know."

Silas bites his lip, then nods and turns back to the circle. "I should do it. This is my task—I'm the one who dragged you two here."

"Absolutely not." Dami grabs his arm. "You're *literally* cursed with bad luck. There's no way you'd survive a fight to the death."

Silas hesitates; then his shoulders sink.

Dami shakes their head. "I'll handle this one. I know how to fight—and I've had experience in actual battles. I can do this."

They don't mention that their "battle" experience is exactly one battle, which was mostly spent shooting at people from behind a barrier while a more powerful friend took on el Diablo. But Silas doesn't need to know that. And anyway, the first part is true—even if they're a little out of practice, they do know how to fight. They've spent more than a couple of nights in underground fighting rings searching for marks—and fighting them to gain their trust. It was surprisingly effective.

"Are you sure?" Marisol asks. "If you die—"

"Then I'll die. The risk is the same for all of us."

Before Silas or Marisol can try to talk them out of it or do something equally thickheaded, Dami rolls up their sleeves and enters the ring. As soon as their boot crosses the line, the room begins rumbling. Dami crouches a bit to keep their balance, eyeing the chandeliers warily, but they barely move. Nothing falls from the ceiling or off the walls. The rumbling is low, vibrating so deeply Dami can feel it in their bones, like the room is growling.

Then, across the room, a massive iron door appears and swings open. And in walks their opponent.

What walks in looks more like a troll from a fairy tale than a human. Nine feet tall, hairless, with skin so pale it almost looks gray, and black veins visible beneath the surface like poisoned spiderwebs. Its arms are as thick as marble columns, its chest wider than a doorway. Its left arm drags a heavy mace along the ground, the spikes grinding against the ground like nails on a chalkboard. It wears just a black loincloth, and when it opens its mouth, Dami spots needle-sharp teeth.

"Puta madre," they say.

They back up a step, but something hard behind them stops them in their tracks. They look—nothing is there, but they're up against the edge of the circle. Dami reaches their hand out and hits an invisible barrier. It's not like glass—their hand doesn't leave a smudge, and there isn't any reflection. It's like the air has decided not to let them through.

Marisol and Silas are staring at them, wide-eyed and pale. "How are you supposed to kill that?" Marisol squeaks.

An excellent question. Dami turns back to the troll-thing, taking a quick inventory of what they have on them. It doesn't take long because they're completely unarmed. They lost just about everything when they washed up on the island, and the villagers haven't exactly provided them with weapons. They don't even have a knife on them.

Not that a knife would help them against a mace.

They could transform into someone larger, someone stronger, but there's no human on the planet that could outmuscle

....

315

that, and their *scary devil* persona isn't exactly jacked. In any case, transforming into someone larger would just make them a bigger target. They aren't going to win this with strength—but maybe they can outmaneuver it.

Or they'll die a horrible death with a mace to the stomach and that'll be the end of that.

If they lose, will Marisol and Silas be permitted to continue?

The troll-thing tilts its head back to the ceiling and lets out a roar so deafening Dami can feel the vibrations in their chest. It pounds its right fist against its chest like a gorilla, and then advances toward Dami. Every step thuds against the ground so heavily the room shakes, but its steps are lumbering, slow. Dami probably couldn't outrun it because it has three feet over them, but they can probably dodge it.

The monster raises the mace as easily as one might pick up a stick and swings. Dami yelps and dives between its legs. Really graceful stuff. Their chest slams against the ground, and they scrabble to get their legs out of harm's way as they race behind the creature. The troll's momentum proves to be too much; it slams against the invisible barrier. Silas yells and dives out of the way unnecessarily on the other side of the barrier, and Marisol cringes.

So Dami isn't the only one trapped in this terrible arena. And the monster doesn't seem to be any more capable of breaking through the barrier than Dami is. Good to know.

The troll turns around, growling furiously. Dami backs up to the center of the arena, pulse drumming steadily in their ears. Saliva drips down the troll's chin as it contorts its mouth into something that resembles a grin. A grin full of razors for teeth.

....

It swings the mace side to side like a lethal pendulum. Then it lunges toward them again.

Dami waits one, two, three steps before turning around and taking off for the opposite side of the arena. The troll's heavy footsteps are far too close, but Dami doesn't dare look back. Instead, they run as fast as their burning legs will take them; then, just before they hit the barrier, they dive to the side. The troll slams against the barrier at full speed, staggers backward, and stands there, wobbling woozily.

They don't wait for it to regain its bearings. Dami jumps to their feet and runs back to the center of the arena again. They're shaking with adrenaline, the world bright with panic. But this is working. If they can just get it to keep slamming itself against the barrier, maybe it'll knock itself out. Maybe that will be enough.

The troll lets out another bone-jarring roar and turns around, facing Dami with absolute fury in its glare. Dami supposes it might have thought the first time was clever, but it's not impressed anymore. It just wants to rip them limb from limb.

That would be a terrible way to die. Top-five worst ways, probably. So they better make sure it never catches up to them.

The troll roars again, then leaps toward them with speed Dami didn't realize it had. They blink, and it's already crossed a quarter of the distance between them. They swear and turn on their heel, racing for the opposite side of the arena, but even without looking back, they know it's far too close for comfort.

"Dami!" Marisol screams. "It's gaining on you!"

Something blooms inside them, hot and bright, a burst of desperate energy pushing them faster. They know better, but they do it anyway: they glance back. The troll is no more than ten feet behind them—which is problematic considering its several-foot arm span. They turn forward again, swallowing their panic—

And run right into the barrier.

It's like hitting a wall. Even without the pain, the sudden stop is so jarring their teeth clack together and their bones vibrate with impact. Dami groans and twists around. The troll is on top of them. The mace swings back—

Smoke envelops them, ripping them out of the air and depositing them behind the creature. The troll slams into the barrier again. Dami stares, slack-jawed. They just phased. They phased out of the way, like when they were a demonio.

The troll staggers back clumsily and trips over its own feet, plummeting backward. Right on top of Dami. Or it would have, but the smoke plucks them out of the air once again and moves them several feet to the right. The troll hits the ground with a room-shaking crash, just feet from them.

The mace rolls clunkily toward Dami. They move without thinking—grabbing it with strength they didn't know they had and swinging it at the troll's skull. It collides with a wet, nauseating crunch. Black blood splatters on their hands and up their arm, and for once Dami is grateful they can't feel it. A puddle of inklike blood blooms beneath the troll's head, quickly spreading out and touching the soles of their boots. Dami drops the mace, grimaces, and takes a couple of steps back, moving out of reach.

"Is it . . . over?" Silas asks from somewhere behind them.

Dami turns away from the massive corpse, forcing themself not to look back. They approach the edge of the circle, then step out. No barrier stops them.

They sigh a breath of relief. "Looks like it."

Marisol still has her hands over her mouth. "Are you okay?"

"No," Dami says. "My boots are ruined." They crouch, frowning at the black leather spattered with troll blood. "I'll never get this blood out."

Silas laughs slightly. "Your boots are black."

"So?"

"The blood is black."

Dami looks up at them, eyes narrowing. "If you're suggesting I shouldn't care there's troll blood on my boots forever because I can't see it—"

"Is it really a stain if it's invisible? No one's going to know there's blood on them."

"I'll know!" They stand with a scowl, crossing their arms over their chest. "You'd seriously be okay with wearing clothes drenched in troll blood?"

Silas lifts a shoulder. "If I couldn't see it after it dried? Perhaps."

"You're disgusting."

Silas laughs, and even Marisol smiles a little. "How did you do that?" she asks. "With the smoke. I thought you aren't a demonio anymore."

Dami grimaces. "I'm not . . . completely. But I guess I've reverted enough that I can do that again."

Marisol's face falls, and Silas looks like he wants to say something, but what is there to say? All there is to do is move forward and hope they manage the impossible.

Marisol's eyes widen. "A door!"

They cross the room to where the exit has appeared, once again an iron door mirroring the entrance. Dami pulls it open, and they step out in the fog again.

Chapter 45

······················

They don't walk for long. Barely twenty feet from the last door is a new one, this one a polished cherry-tinted wood with a gold handle. Silas bites his lip, resting his hand on the smooth wood. How many trials will they have to survive before they finally reach the end?

"You okay?" Dami asks behind him.

Silas glances back at them with a low laugh. "Are any of us *okay* at the moment?"

"Thank you," Marisol mutters at the same time Dami says, "Fair."

Turning back to the door, Silas rolls his shoulders and grasps the cold metal of the door handle. *Here we go again*, he thinks as he pulls it open.

Silas blinks hard, his eyes adjusting to the light as Dami and Marisol enter behind him. Polished cherrywood floors gleam in the light, meeting walls painted a deep green color, like pine. The room is entirely bare except for a table small enough to be a nightstand and an enormous hanging . . . contraption.

Five huge wooden cylinders, each probably at least four

·········

feet tall and wide, are skewered on a long copper pole that spans the width of the room. The cylinders aren't really cylinders—the widest part that would ordinarily be smooth is cut with flat panels, each with a symbol carved into the panel painted in gold. The blocks are spinning very slowly, so Silas catches some of the symbols: a key, a heart, a star, a knife, a key again—

"What *is* that?" Marisol asks, squinting at it.

Silas shakes his head, frowning at the strange machinery. Each of the wooden blocks has the same symbols, and all are spinning in sync. If this is a trial, Silas can't begin to fathom what any of them is supposed to do.

"Twenty sides each," Dami mutters, then, "Oh! It's like slots!"

Both Silas and Marisol stare at them.

"Slots?" Silas asks.

"Yeah, you know, like the gambling . . . oh." They frown, then scratch the back of their head. "Never mind. What do the directions say?" Before either Marisol or Silas can question them further, Dami waltzes over to the small table, beckoning the two of them to follow.

Silas approaches them as Dami snatches a small sheet of parchment off the table and clears their throat, facing them. In an unnecessarily dramatic voice, they read it aloud:

All but one of you have been tested
This trial is for him
A test of luck: step on the panel beneath each block to stop it.
Three keys are required to continue forward. Failure to uncover
   the keys will return you to the surface. But beware the skulls:
   five of them will kill you all.

·········

Dami's voice trails off at the last sentence. They frown. "Well, that doesn't seem very fair."

Silas's heart thrums loudly in his ears. *This trial is for him.*

Does that mean . . . ?

It must mean him. He didn't fight the troll-thing, and even if there was any ambiguity about who solved the poison cups trial—which there wasn't, if he was being honest—Marisol isn't a *him*.

"How does it know who has already done the trials?" Marisol asks with a frown. "It's like these trials were made to test *us* specifically."

"There *is* good news," Dami says. "I've been watching the blocks. There's only one skull on each of them, and there's twenty sides. The odds of hitting the skulls five times are less than one percent, so as long as Silas hits literally any other combination we'll be fine."

"But I need to hit the keys *three times* in order to get to the treasure." Silas shakes his head. "Are we really going to be *fine* if we end up deposited back to the surface of the island empty-handed?"

The silence that follows answers that question well enough.

"Wish we'd given Silas the luck potion," Marisol mutters.

Silas isn't confident that would have worked on him, but he supposes it really doesn't matter. The fact is they only have two options: refuse to participate and eventually die of dehydration in this room—repeatedly, in his case—or give it a try on the extremely slim chance that fortune will smile on him.

It isn't really a choice.

Silas sighs. "I suppose there isn't much point in waiting here."

"Look at it this way," Dami says, "you have much better odds of hitting three keys than you do five skulls. There are four keys on every block—that's a twenty percent chance per block!"

"And they're spinning slowly—that'll help," Marisol adds.

With his luck, Silas isn't so sure.

Nevertheless, he steps toward the blocks—and five glowing squares appear in the polished floor ahead. The panels. They're set up several feet in front of the blocks, so when Silas is standing on one, he'll still be able to see the rotating blocks overhead.

But with his first step, something else changes too: the blocks start moving faster and faster until they look like spinning wheels on an out-of-control carriage, each rotating at a slightly different speed.

Dami actually has the audacity to laugh. Marisol groans.

It's essentially impossible to make out the symbols now, so Silas doesn't bother looking at the spinning block ahead. Instead, he steps right up to the first panel, his pulse thrumming so loudly in his ears he can't make out anything else. His palms grow cold and clammy.

Just one at a time, he tells himself.

"You can do this, Silas!" Marisol cheers.

You must *do this.*

Biting his lip, Silas steps onto the panel. It flashes white beneath him, and he looks up, worrying his lip as the block slows. As it crawls to a stop, it rolls to a key and Silas's heart leaps in his chest—

But it keeps rolling.

To a skull.

The skull symbol glows white, and a resounding *thunk* echoes in the room. The block has stopped on the only symbol Silas *didn't* want.

"Okay," Dami says somewhere behind him. "Not a great start, but like I said, the odds of you hitting that one every time are ridiculously small."

Ignoring the twisting of his gut, Silas steps onto the next panel. This time he doesn't watch as the block slows, and when it stops with a *clunk*, he forces himself to look up.

Skull.

Dami and Marisol are whispering behind him. Silas can't make it out, but judging by the tone, he's relatively sure Dami is swearing in Spanish.

There are only three blocks left, which means Silas has to hit the key on every one for them to have a chance to move forward. A cavern yawns wide in the space between Silas's lungs. The task seems utterly impossible. At this rate he'll consider himself lucky if he doesn't get them all killed.

"I'm sorry," Silas says, turning back to Dami and Marisol. "It's like this trial was made to be specifically impossible for me. I don't know how—" His voice cracks and he presses his fist to his mouth, furious at himself as the room blurs with tears.

Then all at once he's enveloped in Dami's and Marisol's arms. Their warmth is comforting. The press of Marisol's face against the back of his shoulder, and Dami's chest against his— Silas's shoulders relax as he closes his eyes.

"Whatever happens," Dami says into his hair, "it's okay. It's not your fault."

"If I die here, Maisey will never escape this curse," Silas croaks, the pain of that reality blooming fresh and hot. "I'm supposed to protect her."

Behind him, Marisol sighs. "Silas, you traveled all the way to a cursed island and found your way to a hidden underground chamber full of extraordinarily difficult tasks. I think it's safe to say you've done absolutely everything you can to protect her."

He bites his lip. "If you two die . . ."

"You'll save me from an eternity of being a demonio," Dami says without missing a beat.

"And I've probably been doomed to die here since I got on that ship," Marisol says.

"Plus, you have to admit," Dami adds, "dying in a secret magical chamber on a secret magically hidden island is kind of an amazing way to go."

The suggestion that there might be an "amazing" way to die is so absurd Silas actually laughs. With a sigh, he wipes his face with his hands and straightens his shoulders. "I suppose I might as well have a go at it."

"Seriously," Dami says. "The suspense is *killing* me."

Marisol and Silas groan while Dami cackles.

"Just run across the last three," Marisol says. "Finish it all at once."

Silas nods, takes a shaky breath, and steps up to the left side of the third panel. Facing the last three glowing squares, he says, "Thank you both for trying to help me."

Dami scoffs. "*Trying?*"

Silas rolls his eyes. "For *helping* me."

"That's what I thought."

Silas shakes his head, but he's smiling despite himself. Before he can talk himself out of it, he takes a deep breath and runs.

Chapter 46

....

Dami spends a solid thirty seconds crouching on the floor, cringing with their arms protecting their head, before they feel ridiculous. They look up to find Marisol arching an eyebrow at them while Silas stares at the five glowing skulls carved into the blocks above his head.

They stand, brushing wrinkles out of their shirt. "Silas no necesita saber sobre eso," they mutter to Marisol. She just snickers.

"Well," they say loudly, "we're not dead."

Silas finally faces them, frowning deeply. "I don't understand. It said we'd all die if I hit five skulls."

Marisol gasps and Dami jumps. She points past Silas to—

Written in dripping, deep red pigment is a message splashed across the far wall:

WELCOME SILAS CAIN

Silas's mouth drops open as something clicks in Dami's mind. "Oh!"

....

Silas and Marisol look at them.

Dami grins. "The trial said it was testing your luck. It didn't say it was testing *good* luck!"

Marisol's eyes widen, but Silas's brow furrows. "If it wasn't testing good luck . . ."

"What's the one test *only* a Cain could pass?" they ask, their excitement bubbling over. "A bad-luck test! I told you the odds of hitting five skulls were astronomically small, but someone cursed with fatally bad luck—"

"Would be guaranteed to hit it." A smile blooms over Silas's face. "Wait, so you think—"

He spins around just as a door appears beneath the dripping letters. Silas whoops, Marisol cheers, and Dami grabs Silas and kisses his cheek—hard.

"You unlucky bastard," they say with a laugh, "you did it!"

The door has just closed behind the three of them when they realize what's different this time: the way forward doesn't lead to another door. Dami frowns.

Marisol's breath catches. "Wait . . . does this mean? . . . Did we reach the end?"

Still, Dami doesn't dare hope. After all, you can't be disappointed if you don't expect anything to begin with.

So the trio walk hesitantly forward. After twenty steps into the thickest fog yet, the air clears. They've reached an enormous cavern. The walls are made of the same obsidian they've grown used to, but torches are hung every couple of feet, lighting the stadium-sized room. It's mostly bare, mostly empty, save for a river cutting through the room on the opposite side of the cavern, with a small rowboat tied to a rock bobbing in the quiet current. The rowboat mentioned in the clue they found—it's actually here.

And then there's the matter of the pedestal in the center of the room.

And on the pedestal, a gold-engraved chest, still shiny. It looks new—the wood freshly oiled and dark, the gold shimmering as if just polished. But the trunk isn't really what grabs Dami's attention; it's what's standing behind it that makes their blood run cold.

A man with a trim black beard, a black tailcoat with gold buttons, edged with smoke, and a smile like a curved blade. He looks exactly the way he did before their friend killed him.

El Diablo.

Chapter 47

·····················

Dami isn't sure whether to laugh, cry, or throw up. All three feel appropriate as they stare at a dead man.

"Who is that?" Marisol frowns, looking directly at el Diablo. Even Silas looks confused, his gaze sliding from el Diablo to Dami and back.

Dami's jaw nearly drops open in shock. "You two can see him?"

Marisol's brow furrows further. "Why wouldn't we be able to? He's right there."

"Wait," Silas says. "Is that the diablo you told me about? I thought he was dead."

El Diablo laughs. "Aw, you told your friends about me. How quaint."

Dami's mind is reeling. If Silas and Marisol can see him, then it isn't all in their head. Which means what, exactly? Dami saw him die, watched as he burned away into charred bones, then ash. So how is he here if he's not in their head?

"You know," el Diablo says, "my heart broke when I realized you betrayed me. How could a child do such a thing to their parent? But I suppose what they say about parenting is true: all children will eventually break their parents' hearts."

"You're not my parent," Dami snaps. "I was never your kid—you abducted me."

El Diablo smiles. "You've always fought so hard to deny who you are. It's sad to watch."

"I know who I am," they grit out.

"Poor Dami," he mocks. "Sad little demonio, so full of self-loathing, so unloved and alone. Pathetic."

Dami shakes, fighting to keep their expression unaffected. They want so badly to laugh off the charge and let it roll off their shoulders, but they can't. El Diablo knows them better than anyone, and he's *right*. They're a demonio. They don't deserve loyalty or love. They don't deserve a full life. They'll always be a demonio.

"Dami isn't unloved." Marisol steps next to them, sliding her hand in theirs.

Silas takes their other hand. "And they aren't alone."

Dami blinks, clearing tears they hadn't realized were forming. Marisol and Silas are facing el Diablo with fierce determination in their eyes.

What you had to do to survive doesn't disqualify you from deserving a chance to live. Marisol's words come back to them with new clarity.

You're not a bad person, Dami. You deserve better than what you were handed.

Silas and Marisol were right before, and they're right now. Their support fills Dami with a renewed strength. They aren't alone.

"I'm not alone," they say softly, then with more confidence,

"I know who I am. I may be a demonio, but I'm not alone. Not anymore."

El Diablo rolls his eyes. "Child, please. You really think your new friends would stick with you, even if by some miracle they do survive my island? You're—"

"*My* island?" Dami interrupts. "This isn't your island. And since when do you call me *child*?"

He bristles. "I've always called you child."

"Not in English, you haven't," they retort. "Hije, sure, but never *child*."

El Diablo freezes. In that hesitation, it all pieces together. Dami knows exactly one person who calls this island *theirs*, and it isn't el Diablo.

"You're not el Diablo," Dami says with a laugh.

Then it must hit Silas, because his mouth drops open. "It can't be."

For a moment el Diablo looks like he might deny it. Then his shoulders relax and the smile that slithers over his face is unsettlingly familiar.

Dami blinks and el Diablo is gone. And in his place is Eve.

Chapter 48

· · · · · · · · · · · · · · · · · · ·

"I have to admit," Eve says, "I'm impressed. No one has made it to the trials in a very long time." Her voice echoes in the large cavern, giving the impression that it's coming from all directions at once. For Silas, it's dizzying, blending with the whispers that haven't stopped since the three of them entered the cavern. It's an endless background hiss, like rapidly running water.

Silassss Cain.

Run. Run.

Silassss.

But Eve is here, and her presence is a draw he can't resist. *Like a spider and her web,* a whisper hisses in his ear.

Yes, he thinks. *Like a loving spider tugging on a string of her web.*

Eve looks at Marisol and her smile widens. "And I certainly didn't expect to see *you* here. It's too bad you'll have to die down here with these two. You had potential."

Marisol glowers at her, her fists clenched at her sides.

Dami crosses their arms and moves in front of him, blocking

his view of Eve. Silas blinks, his head light, his body off-kilter. The ground rocks beneath him, and he staggers a step sideways before righting himself. No one seems to notice.

With Dami blocking his view of Eve, Silas's thoughts come more clearly. Aboveground Silas had thought her magnetic, but this is something else entirely. Something about her makes it difficult to think. What is she doing to him? And how?

"Who are you?" Dami asks.

Eve tilts her head, her smile unnervingly steady. "Is that the question you really want to ask?"

"I don't understand," Silas interrupts, sidestepping Dami. "How did you get down here?" As soon as his gaze falls on Eve, her pull slams into him—but this time he's braced for it, and it dissipates like a wave against a cliff. The warmth of her presence calls to him, but he focuses instead on the whispers.

Silassss . . .

Focussss . . .

Eve stretches her arms over her head, appearing bored by Silas's question. "Doesn't matter."

"You said no one had found the treasure," he presses, sweating under the strain of resisting the impulse drawing him closer to her. "If you knew where it was the whole time . . ."

And there it is. Silas looks at Dami, who just arches an eyebrow at him. Now, in the company of his friends, with the whispers grounding him, it all seems so obvious. She's been playing him this whole time, using some kind of magic to cloud his mind and make her irresistible.

This time, when Silas looks at Eve, he anchors his feet to the ground and clenches his fists. She's still smiling at him, now sitting on the chest, propping her chin up on the palm of her hand. This must all be entertainment to her, watching as three strangers she toyed with figure out just how deeply they've been betrayed.

"What are you?" he finally asks.

"Ah." Her smile widens. "Now you're asking the right question."

"And you still aren't answering."

"Hmm." She stands and walks toward them. Silas braces himself, but though the waves of her influence wash over him in pulses, with every breath they become easier to ignore. She clearly can't be a normal teenage girl—this magic she wields is powerful, and at any rate she never would've survived on the island long enough. But what is she?

Eve steps right past Dami and Marisol and touches Silas's shoulder while she steps around him, as if appraising him. Her touch makes him shudder from head to toe, waves of powerful vibration in his bones that make his teeth clatter. He doesn't move.

"Silas, how much do you know about your family curse?"

Silas's brow furrows. "How did you . . . ?"

"Please." She laughs. "I know a Cain when I see one. You're not the first in your family to make their way here, you know."

This is news to Silas. His eyes widen. "I'm not?"

She laughs again. "Of course not. Though I suppose it makes sense that you wouldn't know. None of them made it *off* the island. I made sure of that."

Silas stares. "What?"

Her words sink into him one at a time. She made sure his ancestors never broke the curse? That doesn't make sense. She may be powerful, but she can't be older than sixteen. She wouldn't have been alive when Silas's ancestors arrived here, seeking the treasure.

. . . Right?

Eve walks past him, back over to the treasure, circling it like a vulture around a dying animal. "No one leaves my island. Especially not with the treasure."

"It's not your treasure!" Silas exclaims, exasperated. "This isn't even your island! Just because you were born here—"

"This is my purpose," she interrupts. "The reason I exist. I'm the Keeper of this treasure and this island. I was created to protect them both from mankind's greed. And I do not fail."

Created. Her choice of words isn't accidental. Slowly, the pieces in Silas's mind begin to snap together. He watches her move, her barefoot steps on the rock entirely silent. There's always been something ethereal about her, something not quite . . . human.

And then Silas's breath catches in his chest. "It's you." He shakes his head and laughs. All this time. He'd been running around the island trying to free himself, free Maisey, and she was right there.

Marisol shakes her head, confused. "What's her?"

"You're the curse," Silas says, looking Eve in the eye. "That's how you could transform. How you controlled the jaguar. How you influenced me. And that's why you hated Dami so much. They were keeping me alive even as the curse was trying to kill me—but you couldn't kill them yourself because—"

"I'm not cursed," Dami finishes for him.

"Wait," Marisol says, "but she's killed plenty of people. The number of dead villagers . . ."

Silas shakes his head. "But did she kill any of them directly?

There was the jaguar, fires, poisonous snakes, but did Eve ever kill anyone herself besides me?"

Slowly, Marisol shakes her head.

"Bravo." Eve sits on the chest, crossing her arms and smirking at them both. "So, how would you like to die? Fire? Flooding? Earthquake? Or maybe I'll send you back to the trials to go through endlessly until you've gone completely mad—"

"If you're the Cain family curse," Dami interrupts, "then you can't stop Silas from taking the treasure because he doesn't want it for himself. It's not greed—he's literally here to break the curse. He's doing what was intended for the treasure to begin with."

Silas pauses. Could Dami be right?

Eve stops. Stands. "None of you are leaving."

Dami nods at Silas. "Go ahead. Open the chest—she can't stop you."

Eve laughs, shrill. "Oh, please, you really believe that?"

"Don't listen to her," Dami says. "I know magic, and I know manipulators. Her purpose is to protect the treasure from those who want it for themselves—that's why the curse is there. But you're not here to take it for yourself. She has to let you take it, or she'd be going against her explicit purpose." Dami smiles at Eve. "Isn't that right?"

Eve's face has gone so red she looks like she might burst into flames. She wouldn't be this upset if it weren't true.

Silas steps toward her—then, when she doesn't move, begins closing the distance between them. Eve glowers at him as he nears, but when he reaches for the chest with trembling fingers—

She moves out of the way.

·········

"None of you will get off this island," she hisses. "I swear it."
Then she disappears.

Dami, Marisol, and Silas exchange grins. "Go ahead," Dami says. "Open it."

He turns back to the chest, hands shaking. The moment he rests his hands on the lid, the whispers quiet. His ears ring in the silence. He runs his palms over the smooth surface. It's real. Solid. And after all they've gone through, this must be it. It must.

Silas opens the chest.

Gold. Doubloons and gems, even jewelry and the edge of something that looks like a crown. A glimmering sea filling the chest to the brim. Silas picks up a doubloon and turns it over in his hand, laughing quietly.

"Wow," Marisol whispers. "I almost didn't believe there *was* a treasure, but . . ."

"We did it," Silas says, his eyes brimming with tears. "We actually—we found it."

Dami grins. "Now we just have to figure out how to get it to England."

Silas looks up at them as the ground begins to shake. A sound like the island itself is growling rumbles through the cavern as rocks shower from the ceiling. Dami and Marisol freeze as the rumbling grows louder. Eve said she wouldn't let them leave the island. And she doesn't seem to be wasting any time.

"The river!" Dami yells. "Quick, let's get the chest to the rowboat."

Silas tosses the doubloon back into the chest and slams the lid closed. Dami grabs the left side while Silas grabs the right, and Marisol helps in the middle. When they lift, Silas's end tips up easily while Marisol and Dami don't budge.

Dami gapes at him. "How are you doing that?"

Silas frowns. "I don't understand—it's a lot lighter than I expected. Why can't you lift it?"

Marisol's eyes widen, and she releases the chest. "Dami, let go."

Dami frowns; then their eyebrows shoot up. "Oh!" They release the chest, and Silas lifts it easily.

Marisol grins. "Looks like another job only a Cain can do."

They don't have time to appreciate the victory. Rocks larger than Silas's head drop from the ceiling like overripe fruit from a tree, and he doesn't want to imagine what might happen if any of them gets hit. The trek to the other side of the cavern, where the rowboat is waiting, is treacherous, but they manage it all the same, and he places the chest in the boat.

Dami unties the boat from the rock it's moored to and tosses the rope to Silas. "Quick, use that to tie the chest closed. Last thing we need is it opening if we get knocked over."

Silas gets in the boat and begins tying as Dami clambers in after Marisol and grabs the oars. Part of Silas twinges with guilt at Dami rowing yet another boat in less than two weeks, but then a chunk of the ceiling as big as his head crashes into the ground right where Dami was standing a minute ago.

So he doesn't argue when Dami rows. The river's current begins slowly, but it pulls them nevertheless. Then the river slopes down and the peaceful current becomes rapids.

Dami yelps and pulls the oars in, gripping the sides of the boat and gritting their teeth as the current rips them down the slope. Silas clings to the chest in a way that in any other circumstance would be comical, save for the part where his life depends on not losing it. The tunnels down here aren't lit—it's so dark that the only reason Silas can see anything at all is because of the torch Marisol is still holding.

Then the boat races around a corner, tilting sideways. They even out again, hitting the river with a splash that extinguishes the torch.

Silas might laugh if he weren't utterly terrified. The boat hasn't slowed at all, and it's all he can do to hold on to the treasure and pray he doesn't get thrown out as wind whips past his face. Someone's fingers close around his arm in the dark, holding tightly. Dami? Marisol? He can't tell, and it doesn't matter.

The low rumbling has become outright roaring, as if the caves are alive—and angry. An explosive crash behind them suggests that the tunnel they're zipping through may be caving in. Silas swears softly under his breath, his voice barely audible above the growling caves and the hissing of the winding river. Then, inexplicably, Dami laughs.

"How can you be laughing?" Silas exclaims, his voice tight.

"I've never heard that prayer before," they answer. "What's it called?"

Marisol groans.

"I hate you," Silas answers.

"Odd name for a prayer."

Silas has a retort ready, but then light flickers over his face. He twists around to the source—the end of the tunnel they're racing toward.

Dami lets out a relieved sigh. "We're almost out!" But as light fills the tunnel, something much more alarming catches his attention. The river they're riding on is rising rapidly—the top of Dami's head is less than a foot from the ceiling of the tunnel.

And the end of the tunnel is still at least a hundred feet away.

"Carajo," Dami swears. "Marisol! Grab an oar!"

She blinks. "What do you—"

"The river is rising too quickly!" Silas says. "If we don't row, the river will smash us against the ceiling before we make it out of the tunnel."

The water keeps rising. The top of Dami's head brushes the ceiling, and they cringe, ducking. "Hurry!"

Dami and Marisol row as hard as they can, throwing their entire body weight into every stroke. Silas clings to the treasure with a white-knuckle grip. They hurtle toward the opening, but it's still so far. In front of Silas, the cave wall scrapes against the top of Dami's head and they duck down farther.

The water is rising, and their opening is closing. Silas imagines they're close enough now that even if they crash against the wall they'll be able to swim under, but the treasure will probably be gone. And the water is moving so quickly that not drowning will be a feat.

"C'mon . . . ," he grits out.

Dami ducks as low as they can while still rowing, the opening so close—

The water bobs up beneath them and the three of them flatten themselves into the boat as it shoots out beneath the opening, scraping against the ceiling on the way out. Once free, Dami throws their arms up in celebration.

"We made—"

Their voice—and excitement—dies as they take in the island around them. Or what's left of it.

Everything is underwater. The river whipping them past trees and down slopes is overflowing its banks—everything Silas can see is under at least six inches of water, and it's only worsening. The rumbling that was deafening in the cave isn't any quieter out here—trees have fallen and cliffsides are crumbling.

The island is sinking.

"Oh no," Silas says. "She's sinking the whole island."

Dami lets out a nervous laugh. "Guess she's kind of pissed about losing the treasure."

Marisol isn't laughing. "We need to get out of here. If we're too close when the island sinks into the ocean, it'll suck us down with it."

"Let's just make sure to stay on the river," Silas adds. "That should be the fastest way to the ocean."

The river's overflowing power is working in their favor, at least—they're moving so quickly the trees whip past them in a blur. Dami still rows, mostly to make sure they stay on the river's path, especially as the water around them continues deepening, but the raging current beneath them does most of the work.

Then, all at once, the trees disappear and the beach appears— if only briefly, as the coast continues eating up the island's edges. Silas takes over for Marisol, and he and Dami row in earnest now, pulling themselves farther out to sea, but the current isn't working in their favor anymore. As the island sinks into the ocean, the water floods toward it, dragging them back to its center.

More than anything, Silas wishes they had more than a single set of oars. He rows with shaking arms, sweat dripping down his temples and plastering his shirt to his back. He's breathing so quickly he's getting light-headed, but he doesn't stop.

Together, they're still moving forward. Away from the island. Out to sea. But their progress is so painfully slow.

"Silas," Marisol grits out, warning in her voice. The boat is desperate to move backward, to sink back toward the island, but he won't let it. He won't. Silas rows faster, pouring every ounce of strength into the oars, and all at once—

They surge forward. Breaking free of the island's pull, moving away from that cursed place at last. Rowing toward kinder shores.

Chapter 49

·····················

Dami and Silas collapse on the Milford beach, lungs heaving as they lie on their backs in the sand. Marisol climbs out of the boat on shaking limbs, smiling softly at the two of them in the sand.

"I never," Silas gasps, "want to row. A boat. Ever. Again."

Dami laughs breathily. The sun is sinking overhead, and they're on a beach with a boat full of treasure. They did it.

They actually did it.

Except it's not over. Because now they have to figure out the part that always seemed impossible, the part they kept putting off because it wasn't worth the energy trying to solve without the treasure. But the time is now, before someone sees them. Before anyone knows what they've discovered.

So, with a groan, Dami forces themself to sit up. "Okay," they say. "You two need to hide with that chest."

Silas grimaces and rolls onto his stomach. "Where?"

Dami glances around. There's no way Silas and Marisol will make it through Milford unseen lugging a literal treasure chest.

But not far from where they're sitting begins a forest. It's as good a place as any.

"Right there." They point to the edge of the woods. "Stay right on the edge there, and I'll find you. I won't take long."

Marisol hesitates. "I don't think I really want to go in there."

"It's not the island," Dami reminds her. "We're in normal, boring Connecticut now."

Silas is looking at the woods like it might reach out and eat him. Dami rolls their eyes. "We just survived a murderous spirit literally sinking an island just to kill us. You two can survive an hour in the woods."

Marisol's eyes widen. "An *hour?*"

"Tops." Dami stands and brushes the sand off their pants. "I promise I won't take long." They start toward the town, but Silas grabs their hand.

"Where are you going?"

Dami smiles.

The Milford Public Library isn't as ornate as the Boston Athanaeum, but that doesn't matter. It isn't riches, or architecture, or beauty that pulls Juno to the building.

It's knowledge.

Dami's steps echo against the polished hardwood, breaking the silence of the empty library. Like before, they don't try to find her among the shelves. Instead, after whispering her name at the entrance, they find a nook beside an unlit fireplace with two comfortable chairs set out for reading. Dami throws themself in one and groans at the plushness. It's so soft. They haven't sat in anything this soft in weeks.

God, they can't wait to con a new rich boy out of his money and sleep in his cloudlike bed.

You won't be able to do that if you're a demonio again, a voice in their mind reminds them. *Without your shape-shifting, you won't be able to as a human, either. And you're nearly out of time if you can phase again. You'll never break Silas's curse in time.*

They pinch the bridge of their nose and take a long, calming breath, forcing the thoughts to the darkest corner of their mind. They don't know how to solve their shape-shifting conundrum— they're not even sure there *is* a way to solve it. But there's still hope for escaping a hollow life. There's exactly one way they can get to England before their time is up.

They just can't do it alone.

"Well, well." Juno's voice cuts through the darkness, and the fireplace beside them springs to life. "Is that *mud* on your boot? And *blood* on your shirt? That island sure has done a number on you."

Dami looks down at their clothes, startled, and wrinkles their nose in distaste. "So it has."

"You look exhausted." She smiles, not unkindly, and sits in the chair opposite them. "But you're alive. Congratulations— watching your memories unfold, I wasn't always certain you'd escape that island."

"I barely did." They run their hand through their hair and let out a shaky breath. "The Cain family curse was . . . not what I expected."

Juno just smiles.

"One thing I don't understand." Dami sits up. "El Diablo's been haunting me for nearly a year, so it couldn't have been Eve the whole time."

"No," Juno confirms. "But after everything you've been through with him, are you so surprised it's been difficult to disentangle yourself completely?"

Dami sighs. "No." They frown. "But I still don't know how Eve knew what el Diablo looked like."

Juno pauses. "I suppose it was before your time, though I'm surprised you didn't recognize el Diablo's handiwork."

Dami blinks. "Wait. *El Diablo* created Eve?"

Juno nods. "He made a deal with Captain Kidd and a certain Cain ancestor. Captain Kidd wanted to protect his claim on the treasure and I imagine Cain would have been rewarded in some way had he seen the deal through, but they were shortsighted. The deal didn't protect Kidd's life."

Now, *that* sounds like el Diablo. Using loopholes in his deals to apply the worst possible interpretation of the bargain was his specialty. Shaking their head, Dami changes the subject. "That's not why I'm here, though."

"No," she says, "it isn't."

"I'm nearly out of time."

"So you are." Her gaze rolls over them appraisingly. "But you haven't completed your task yet. You've very nearly reverted already."

"Pretty sure the only thing I can't do at this point is transport myself and make deals," they grumble.

"Well," Juno says, "you *can* make deals. It'll just complete the reversion process, as I'm sure you're aware."

Too aware. Dami sighs and meets her gaze. "We need to take Captain Kidd's treasure to his corpse—which I'm relatively sure is at the bottom of the Thames."

"That's a long journey."

"It is." They hold her gaze, but she doesn't volunteer anything, so they add, "I can't do it in time without magic."

"That's true."

Dami's stomach sinks. Juno isn't dull—she knows what they're getting at. But if she isn't offering . . .

"Oh, Dami. The disappointment in your face is heartbreaking." She shakes her head and leans back in her seat, drumming her painted nails against the armrest. "Surely you didn't expect me to offer to get you there without a price."

Expected, no. Hoped? They should have known better.

"I don't do charity," she reminds them. "Not even for you."

They know that. They *knew* that. But how else are they supposed to get to London in under six weeks? "Name your price," they say wearily, already dreading what it will cost them. Their happiest memories? All new knowledge for the next year?

"No."

Dami blinks. "What do you . . . ? No?"

"I don't have a price you'll accept—and don't bother trying to argue otherwise. I know you. And I know I can't help you, not this time."

Dami's pulse drums in their ears. "But I can't make it there without magic." Their voice cracks. Their throat burns. They won't cry, won't beg, not in front of Juno, not if they want to retain a modicum of her respect.

"No," she says, "you can't. I've already given you your answer— it's just not one you like."

Dami opens their mouth to argue, then closes it. She has given her answer, but they don't think she means her refusal to help.

She stands, turning away from them. "You should return to your friends before someone finds them. I'll see you again, Dami."

And she steps into the darkness, taking Dami's hope with her.

Chapter 50

·····················

One complication of being a demonio: Dami hates death. The finality of it. The decay. The stillness. It's almost embarrassing, really, given that just about all of their acquaintances who aren't marks are demonios or diablos— who are all technically dead. But it isn't the after that scares Dami—they know how a soul moves on or not. It's the dying part that makes them want to turn and run.

So it's strange, really, that Dami was pulled to Silas at all, because Dami didn't typically target the dying. Sure, many of them were the definition of desperate, but Dami couldn't stand looking into their eyes and watching the specter of death loom ever closer.

It's part of why they hate Reaping so much, as essential as it is.

They can't explain why, but this time the sorrow song hits them like a punch to the stomach. It grabs them by the ribs and doesn't let go, pulling them deeper into Boston's snow-slick streets. They move as smoke, weaving between people and around buildings, through carriages and street stalls, past docks and over bridges until they slip through a nondescript wall, unseen, and materialize in the shadow.

The bedroom is small, lit only by the bright moonlight spilling through the single window, cracked open half an inch. The room seems warm enough—not that Dami can really tell—but the boy on the bed is under a mountain of blankets. And still, he's shivering. Violently.

Dami steps soundlessly closer. The boy's back is to them; he's facing the wall the bed is pressed against. His dark hair is matted with sweat, and his skin is pale, but flushed. Definitely very ill.

Definitely very desperate.

The sorrow song is a crescendo in Dami's ears, drowning out everything else. The song often grows louder as they near their next mark, but never like this. Never so demanding.

What makes you so special?

Dami gently touches his bed and the song falls silent. Finally, they can hear it. Hear him.

"Please," he's whispering. "I'm not ready. I promised Father I would take care of Maisey. I can't die, not yet. Please, please, please . . ."

They tilt their head. "You should be careful with prayers. You never know who might be listening."

The boy gasps and twists around, wincing with the movement and shuddering. He's young, Dami's age probably. Even in the darkness they can make out the green of his eyes. Light freckles speckle over his nose and cheeks. And he's staring at them like one might a ghost.

....

355

Which is fair, really.

"Where did you come from?" he asks through chattering teeth. "Who are you?"

"My name is Dami." They pause, allowing themself to settle into the Making. The boy's mind is feverish and strange, but it only takes a gentle prod for his life to spread out in front of them like a buffet. It takes seconds to find what they're looking for. "And yours is Silas Cain."

Silas blinks at them, his brow slowly sliding into a frown. "Did Mother send you? Are you a doctor?" His frown deepens. "You seem too young to be a doctor."

Dami snorts. "I'm not a doctor. And I've never spoken to your mother. She doesn't know I'm here."

Silas's gaze darts to the bedroom door, still closed, then back to Dami. Almost like he's making sure the exit is still there, still available. Which is adorable, really, because Silas couldn't outrun Dami even if he weren't dying of flu.

Ah. So that's why he's so desperate. "I'm not a danger to you," Dami adds. "I've no interest in hurting you."

Silas hesitates. "Then what do you want?"

Dami sits at the end of Silas's bed, stretching their long legs out in front of them with a sigh. "The question, my sickly new friend, is what do *you* want?"

"I don't understand."

"You're dying. You prayed for salvation." Dami spreads their arms out. "Voilà."

Silas stares at him for a beat. Two. Then he says, "You don't look like an angel."

Dami laughs. "Thank you."

·········

"Are you going to cure me?"

"Of flu? I could."

Silas shakes his head. "It's more than flu that sickens me."

Dami sifts through his mind. There's always so much to look at—too much to look at—so it's easy to get distracted. But something dark and strange twists around Silas's mind, poisoning the memories with fear. Almost like—

Oh. Now, *that's* interesting.

Dami's never tried to counteract a curse before, but they're certain that's diablo territory—and in any case, Silas's curse is no child's play. Generational and deadly.

"Well," Dami says, "I can't break a curse. I don't have that kind of power."

Silas scowls. "What kind of angel can't break a curse?"

Dami wrinkles their nose. "I never said I was an angel."

At this, Silas stills. He looks at them for a long, silent moment. Will he guess the truth? Dami hasn't really let on the extent of their power yet, so it's entirely possible he won't get it right away, which might be for the best. If Silas's first guess was an angel, then he's probably religiously inclined. In Boston that means likely Christian, which doesn't look too kindly on demonios.

Still, they suppose it doesn't really matter if Silas figures it out now or later. There's no way they'll get through an entire deal without him figuring out the truth, seeing how he has to, you know, agree to the deal.

Silas is still staring at them, so Dami helps him along.

....

"I may not be able to break your curse, but I can help you get around it. What if I told you I could make it so you'd still be cursed but you couldn't die?"

Silas's eyes light up. "You can do that?"

"I can." Dami smiles. "We just need to come to an agreement."

Silas frowns, excitement leaking from his expression. "What . . . kind of agreement?"

They slide off the bed and cross the room, hands clasped behind their back. "I'll make it so you can't die before you want to. Then, after you've lived a long life and you're ready, you'll give me your soul."

The boy's eyes widen—he gets it now. Dami frequently has mixed feelings about this part—the part where the mark realizes they need them, but also processes their disgust, their fear, their revulsion. Sometimes this is the part where Dami loses them, where the mark starts screaming or throwing things at them or runs away. Granted, Silas can't run away, and he probably doesn't have the energy to throw anything at them. But he certainly looks like he's regretting every second of this conversation.

And yet he doesn't tell Dami to leave. Dami soaks in the careful silence for a while as Silas processes—as he considers. They can be patient. Now is the time to let the mark feel like they have control. Like they can shut down this process at any moment—which they can. They just won't get what they want.

And in Silas's case, what he wants is not to die.

"You're a demon," Silas says at last.

....

"We have many names." Dami shrugs. "None of them change the power I have to help." Help perhaps is a stretch—help is freely given. What Dami is ready to propose is an exchange. And though Silas is clearly not thrilled by the revelation of who, exactly, Dami is, he seems to be genuinely considering their offer, which is as good a sign as any.

"What will happen to me?" Silas asks. "At the end. If I . . . agree to give you my soul." He winces a little at saying it aloud.

"Depends on what I need then," Dami says. "But probably you'll be a ghost. And maybe if you're lucky you'll one day be on the other end of this conversation." They smile. "Or you'll cease to exist."

Silas stares up at the ceiling, so still that if Dami didn't know better they might think him dead. "But only when I'm ready?"

They nod. "After you've lived a full lifetime, when you're ready to move on. Not a day before."

"How can I trust you?" He looks at them. "You're a demon. Demons lie."

Dami makes an affronted noise. "Humans lie too. That doesn't mean you can't trust any human at all."

"That's not the same thing. Humans aren't evil."

"Some are," they shoot back.

Silas grimaces. "That's not—that's not what I mean."

"I know what you mean." Dami rolls their eyes. "This may be hard to believe, but not every demonio—or demon—is the same, just like not every human is the same. And anyway, you don't have to trust me. You just have to trust the magic. I'm held to whatever deal we make. Once we have an agreement, I can't go back on it any more than you can."

Annoyingly, this seems to soothe him. Dami supposes they shouldn't be surprised. Religious upbringing and all.

"Fine," Silas says. "If you can make it so this curse doesn't kill me—and this flu doesn't kill me—then I agree to give you my soul at the end of my natural lifetime. When I'm ready."

Dami grins and steps up to his bed. "Excellent. Then we have a deal: you won't die until you're ready to, not even from your curse. In exchange you promise me your soul at the end of your lifetime."

"When I'm ready."

"When you're ready," they agree. Dami offers their hand.

Silas eyes it warily. He's hesitating. They just need to prod him a little more, and they know exactly how to do it.

"This way you can protect Maisey," they say. "Like you promised."

Silas's eyes widen. "You heard that?"

Dami only smiles.

With a sigh, Silas's gaze falls back to Dami's outstretched hand. "Once I shake your hand it's agreed?"

"That's right."

"How will I know it worked?"

Dami laughs. "You'll know."

And that answer must be reassuring enough for him

because Silas takes their hand and shakes it. Wind whips about them, and Dami closes their eyes with a smile as the magic of the deal howls around them. Power ripples through them, making them shiver as their pulse races. They've done this hundreds of times now, so the heady sensation is familiar. But even with the layered power of promises and Reaped souls, it isn't enough.

They aren't anywhere near powerful enough to kill el Diablo. And that reality makes it difficult to fully enjoy the process, as good as it feels.

So when the wind dies away they aren't really smiling. Silas is staring at them, slack-jawed, and he laughs a little. "I suppose you're right. That was . . . impossible to miss."

Dami plasters on a smile and pulls their hand back, turning away with a flourish. "I'll see you again, Silas Cain," they say, and with that they surrender to the smoke.

But they'll see Silas sooner than they think.

Chapter 51

· ·

After relieving herself in some bushes, Marisol pauses a moment to take in the woods of her new surroundings. The trees are different here; the bark thicker and the leaves smaller—the largest only about the size of her hand, in contrast to the enormous fronds of the island's rain forest. It's still hot—it's August, after all—but the air is lighter, less sticky. A small red bird with a tuft of feathers sticking up on its head and a ring of black around its red beak chirps at her. She smiles softly, allowing herself to relax for the first time in months.

She actually did it. She made it to America, to Connecticut. Now all she has to do is get to Hartford, where Guillermo is studying. She can't wait to see him again.

After taking some time to compose herself, Marisol retraces her steps through the woods back to the tree line. Silas's voice carries through the air, and Marisol frowns. Who is he talking to, and so loudly? She'd wandered off to find privacy after helping Silas hide the treasure in a large raspberry bush near the edge of the forest after Dami had left. It hadn't taken more than a couple of minutes. Surely they weren't back already?

"I don't know where Dami took the treasure," Silas is saying. "They're hiding it somewhere, but they'll be back."

Marisol's frown deepens. Dami doesn't have the treasure, and Silas knows that. Who is he talking to? She crouches low to the ground and carefully nears the tree line, peering around a bush into the clearing where Silas is standing, his hands held up defensively. Directly behind him stands—Marisol covers her mouth to stifle her gasp—the American man, Paul, who accidentally shot his friend. Instead of a rifle, this time he's holding a knife against Silas's ribs, and he seems to be alone.

It's supremely annoying that *he*, of all people, survived the sinking of the island.

"What about the girl?" Paul barks. "I know you were in cahoots with more than one person."

"Dead," Silas says flatly. "Dami and I barely made it off the island ourselves."

Marisol melts back into the woods, pulse pounding in her ears. She has to find Dami and warn them before it's too late.

D ami walks through the town of Milford like they're wading through molasses. A small part of them had known they might end up here, out of options and out of hope, but it'd been a possibility they'd refused to really consider. But now they're here, their nightmare scenario come true. It all just seems impossibly unfair.

At least you'll still be able to transform at will, they think. It's a small comfort, but it doesn't lessen the pain. They know what they have to do, and it's killing them.

Dami kicks a stone down the dirt road running through Milford's center. Their shirt is getting damp with sweat, which is the only way Dami knows it's hot. Already they've become so disconnected to the world, to reality. If they're being honest, the only difference between their current situation and being a demonio is they can keep a solid form during the day and can't teleport.

"Dami!"

Their head jerks up at the sound of their name. Townsfolk continue moving around them, minding their own business, and it takes them a moment to spot Marisol running up the road toward them.

They frown. "Marisol?"

She races up to them and stops just a foot ahead of them, bending over with her hands on her knees as she catches her breath.

"Are you okay?" Dami asks. "What's wrong?"

"It's Silas," Marisol pants. "The American. Paul. The one who tried to shoot you. He's here. He thinks you have the treasure."

Dami's eyes widen. "Why does he think I have the treasure?"

She looks up at them, her face flushed and blotchy. "That's what Silas told him, I think to delay him. We hid the treasure. I don't think Paul knows how close he is to it." She stands, shaking. "Dami, he has a knife."

"Okay. Are you okay?"

Marisol nods. "He didn't see me. Silas told him I'm dead, so he doesn't know I'm here."

"Okay. Good. That's good." Dami runs their hand through their hair, thinking. If Paul doesn't know Marisol is here, they can use that to their advantage. They can work with this.

"Okay," they say again, nodding as it comes together in their mind. "I have an idea."

Chapter 52

······················

Silas isn't sure how long he stands there, hands in the air, watching Paul anxiously tap his foot as he holds the knife steady against Silas's side. The knife tip digs against his skin—any increase of pressure will push it beneath the surface. So he doesn't move. He barely breathes.

Eventually, Dami crests the nearby hill, their steps slowing as they meet Silas's eyes, then Paul's. They don't seem terribly surprised, so Silas can only assume Marisol ran off and told them. But then, where is she?

His attacker wastes no time. "Where's the treasure?" he barks at Dami. "Tell me or I'll kill your friend. I'll do it! You know I will!"

Dami continues approaching down the hill, their steps slow, cautious. "Then what?"

Paul hesitates. "What?"

"Let's say you kill Silas," Dami says calmly. "Okay, then what? You kill *me*? Then you'll *really* never know where the treasure is. So what's the plan here?"

Paul stands in stunned silence, evidently not prepared for the possibility that Dami would let him kill Silas. Admittedly, Silas isn't thrilled about this line of reasoning either, but Dami has a point. Paul killing him isn't that much of a threat when they all know Silas will wake up again.

Still, it'd be nice not to die again.

"It just seems like you haven't really thought this through," Dami says. "If you kill us, we can't tell you where the treasure is, so it seems like a counterintuitive threat if you ask me."

"I only need one of you alive," Paul growls out.

Dami shrugs. "That's true, but if you kill Silas, I can promise you I'll never tell you where I hid the treasure."

Paul opens his mouth, but Dami lifts their index finger. "Before you say you'll torture me into telling you, you should know that I have a rare medical disorder where I can't feel pain. So that plan won't be very effective either."

Paul snorts. "You really expect me to believe that?"

"It's true," Silas says. "They really can't feel pain."

"I'll prove it, if you'd like." Dami extends their hand and takes another step closer to them. "Slice my palm—I won't even flinch. Go ahead."

Paul hesitates, eyeing Dami's hand. And that's when Marisol smashes his elbow with a fist-sized rock.

Paul screams, dropping the knife. Silas rips himself out of Paul's grip, kicks the knife out of reach, and throws himself forward. Paul staggers back, clutching his arm—which is bent at an unnatural angle—as Marisol steps out of the way. Then he trips and falls, his head smashing against a rock sticking out of the ground.

Silas gapes as Marisol stands next to Paul, stunned, watching as a corona of blood soaks into the sandy dirt around his head. How on earth did that just happen from Marisol hitting his *elbow?*

"Huh," Dami says, tilting their head. "I guess that goblet really *was* lucky."

Chapter 53

·····················

They retreat to the woods, and Silas and Marisol show Dami where the treasure is safely hidden. A nearby fallen tree provides a decent bench that the three of them settle on as the adrenaline of the standoff fades.

"So you two are going to England, I suppose," Marisol says. Dami flinches at the reminder and nods quickly to hide it.

"You can join us if you'd like," Silas says.

Marisol smiles weakly. "Thanks for the offer, but I still want to go to Hartford. After everything we've gone through, I just want to rest and be with my family."

"Are you sure?" Dami asks. "We'd love to have you with us."

Her smile softens and she stands. "Thank you. I'm sure, though. I miss my brother."

"I understand." Dami stands to hug her, holding her close one last time and wishing they could feel her arms around them. "Thank you for everything, Marisol. We wouldn't have made it off that island without you."

"I don't know about that," Marisol says with a slight laugh, releasing Dami.

·········

"I do," Silas says. "We would have drunk poison for sure."

That does make Marisol laugh, fully this time. After she and Silas embrace, she says, "You both must visit me."

"I think I can manage that," Silas says with a smile. "You should come to Boston, too. You could bring Guillermo, even."

"I think I just might." Marisol's smile slowly fades as a quiet settles over them. Then, pulling her shoulders back, she says, "I should go. I want to find a place to stay overnight before it gets dark."

"Won't you need some money?" Silas asks. "Dami might be able to make you some clothes you can sell, or—"

"I think I'm all right, actually. I'm feeling lucky." With a wink, she walks out of the woods.

D ami sinks back onto the tree trunk, their stomach churning with dread. With the danger gone, and Marisol taking her own path, that leaves them with just one task left.

Silas sits next to them, biting his lip. "You don't look like you have good news."

Juno said no, they want to say. *I needed her help, but she refused.*

But the truth is, they aren't really surprised. Juno has been very clear from the first time they met her that she doesn't do anything for free. Perhaps they didn't expect her to refuse to make a deal with them at all, but it isn't the first time she's refused to waste time bartering with them when she knew how it would end.

That's the trouble with trying to make a deal with the Diablo of Knowledge. She knows when it's not worth taking her time to consider it.

Still, the lack of surprise doesn't make it hurt less. The refusal feels deeply personal, even though it isn't, not to Juno anyway. Just because she likes them doesn't mean she'll do things just to be nice.

"My plan . . . didn't work the way I'd hoped." They stare down at their lap.

Juno did give them a solution—or rather, she reminded them of the solution they've had all along. They just didn't want to consider it because of what it would mean for them. After all, they've spent the last eight months using every waking moment to undo their deals so they could tether their soul to their body at last. Become human. Become mortal.

Are they ready to throw that all away?

Silas presses his lips together, searching Dami's face. "Perhaps we can find a way to get on a ship that's already headed to England. We could try . . . disguising the treasure somehow. We could put it in a crate?"

Dami laughs weakly, but their heart isn't in it. "And don't you think they'll want to know what, exactly, is in our mysterious crate?"

"We could throw linen on top."

"That chest is a lot heavier than a crate of linen would be."

"Well, I don't see you suggesting any better ideas," Silas snaps.

Dami keeps staring at their lap. The words are right behind their lips, but once they speak them, they can't take them back. Saying them aloud will be admitting defeat. It'll be accepting the very thing they've been fighting this whole time.

The thing that filled them with raw panic at just the thought of it. But oddly, now that they have to really consider it, really

....

accept it as a possibility, they just feel numb. Maybe this is the way it was always supposed to be. Maybe being human isn't for them after all.

The (very) good: they'll be able to keep shifting their body to their will.

The (very) bad: everything else.

But they're out of options, so Dami pulls their shoulders back and looks up, meeting Silas's gaze at last. "I can get us to wherever Captain Kidd's remains are. We just have to make a deal."

Silas frowns. "I thought you said you couldn't make deals because then you'd fully revert to a demonio."

They try not to flinch. "I did."

"So you were lying?"

I wish I were. They shake their head. "No."

It takes a moment for Silas to fully process what this means. Dami watches as understanding washes over his face, as his eyes widen and he starts shaking his head. "But—then—"

"It's too late for me." They force the words out, even as it hurts them to say it. "I have less than six weeks left. There's no way for us to get to England in under six weeks. So either we go by ship and I turn back to a demonio on the way there, or I get us there instantly and also turn back to a demonio. At least this way we can end your curse faster and I'm not waiting around, counting the hours until it's over."

Silas paces in front of them, still shaking his head. "No, there's still a way around this." He stops, then nods, as if deciding something, and turns back to them. "I'll cancel our deal. Now. Is that not what you need? Once our deal is canceled, you'll be human again."

Something like hope tries to bloom in their chest, but Dami squashes it. "No. If you cancel our deal now, next time you die you'll be dead."

Silas lifts a shoulder, but the motion is stiff. "Then I won't die before we get there."

They snort. "How often were you dying before we went to the island?"

Silas presses his lips together and looks away.

"How often?" they press.

"Once a week," he mutters.

"That's what I thought. Do you know how many ways you can die on a ship? There isn't a chance in hell you'd survive the journey." They cross their arms over their chest. "Making a deal is the only way. I'll get us there, you break the curse, and it's over. You'll be free."

"But you won't!" Silas turns on them so fiercely Dami almost steps back. His face is red and—is he crying? "This isn't fair," he says, and now he's definitely crying. "We were both supposed to get this. I'm free from my curse, and you're free from yours. That's how this was supposed to end."

Dami grabs Silas and pulls him into a tight hug. Silas presses his face against Dami's shoulder, and they wish so desperately they could feel him. They can see him crying against their neck, wrapping his arms around them, but they don't feel anything at all. It's like watching it happen from outside their body, and it hurts; it hurts to know it's always going to be this way.

But it's a hurt they can bear, and their load will be lighter knowing Silas is free.

They wondered, once, what it would be like to want good for someone else more than their own happiness. Now they know—and even through the hurt, it feels right. They're better for it.

Dami squeezes their eyes closed and holds Silas tightly, fighting the tears gathering in their stinging eyes. "Not everyone gets a happy ending," they say softly. "It's okay, Silas. I want you to be free more than I want to become human. I can only have one, and I'm choosing you." They pull back, just a little, so Silas can look at them. "I'm choosing you. I want to do this."

Silas's eyes are bloodshot and glassy; his face red and splotchy. It'd be touching how upset Silas is for them if it weren't so damn awful seeing how upset he is. So they do what they do best: they throw a smile on over the pain and lie. "I'm going to be just fine. I'm actually excellent at being a demonio, believe it or not."

The doubt in Silas's eyes is obvious enough, so Dami doesn't give him the chance to think it over too deeply. Instead, they say, "I'll bring you to the site of Captain Kidd's grave. In return, you'll give me your coat."

Silas blinks. "My . . . coat?"

Dami nods. "Unless there's something else you'd rather give me."

Silas hesitates, then shrugs off his coat.

Dami extends their hand. "Do we have a deal?"

Silas stares at their hand for a long moment. It's all Dami can do to keep their hand from shaking, to keep the veneer of calm plastered over the storm raging inside them. In moments it will be over. They'll be a demonio again, and this time they won't be able to escape. The thought is absolutely nauseating, but the alternative of watching Silas die—for good—is so much worse.

So they pretend. They pretend this is perfectly fine. They pretend nothing about this arrangement bothers them. They pretend it's not a big deal at all, because if they don't pretend, Silas will refuse. Silas will die. And Dami won't let that happen.

Silas takes their hand, squeezes tightly, and shakes it. For just a second nothing happens. Silas is searching Dami's gaze, and they don't let the mask falter. They can do this. They can pretend, for Silas. They can save him.

Then smoke erupts around them, engulfing them both.

Chapter 54

······················

The banks of the River Thames are muddy. Dami tries not to slide in the sludge as they find a grassy spot to stand on. The chest has sunk half an inch into the mud, but they're here. Half a world away, bathed in night.

Silas stands, openmouthed, and Dami takes his distraction as a moment to gather themself. Every time they canceled a deal it hurt, but this one was the worst of all. Their bones ache, their chest pulsing bright with pain. When the smoke surrounded them, it felt like something was ripping out of them. Like someone lit their bones on fire. Like they were moments from crumbling to ash.

But then the smoke cleared, and they were here. Their body still holds the echo of pain, and a part of them wants to hold on to it. It aches, knowing pain is the very last thing they will ever feel.

Then that, too, fades, leaving them empty.

Silas turns to him with an ear-to-ear grin. "You did it!"

Dami brushes imaginary dirt from their shirt. "Obviously."

Silas's smile fades. "Does that mean you're . . . ?" His gaze catches on Dami's hand, which, like the rest of their body, lightly trails smoke at their edges.

Dami lifts their chin and nods at the treasure chest. "You going to do the honors?" Silas's gaze darts to the treasure, then the riverbank, then back to Dami. They arch their eyebrows at him and nod at the chest again, doing everything they can not to think about what just happened.

It'll be worth it when he's free, they remind themself. This had better work.

Silas walks up to the chest and pushes it with a grunt. It slips a bit in the mud, but not nearly enough, so he lifts the chest and slides carefully to the edge of the riverbank before lowering it. There's about a four-foot drop into the river itself, which is an unappealing shade of brown. If there are any bones left down there, Dami certainly can't see them, but this is where the deal brought them, so it has to be right.

"Ready?" Dami asks.

"Ready."

With a grunt, he shoves the chest over the edge. It tumbles over the embankment and hits the water with a splash, sinking quickly beneath the murky surface. Dami watches Silas. They aren't sure what to expect, not really, but with a curse like that there must be some kind of signal. A curse that powerful doesn't break silently.

Silas keeps peering over the edge, chewing on his lip. "Do you think this is the right spot?" he asks.

"Probably should've asked that before we tossed it in," Dami says with a smirk.

Silas's gaze whips up to meet theirs, eyes wide. "Are you jesting? Is this the—"

·········

Light explodes from his mouth, so bright Dami throws their arms over their face. Silas gasps and quickly closes his mouth, slapping his hand over his lips, as if that would stop it. The light spills from his eyes like windows into the night, then Silas's hands slide off his face and his head tilts back as light pours out of him.

Acrid black smoke twists out of his mouth and rises into the air, gathering in a writhing black mass a foot above his face. It twists and rolls like a snake, moving fluidly until the last of it pulls from Silas's lips. Then it shoots off into the air and the light stops all at once, plunging them into night again.

It takes Dami a few seconds to readjust to the sudden darkness. When their light-burned retinas blink away colors and the world shifts back to normal, Silas is standing right in front of them.

"Oh," Dami says. "Hello. Didn't see you there."

Then Silas cups their face gently, so gently, and he's kissing them. This kiss, this embrace, it should be liquid euphoria. It should be a celebration, relief, and disbelieving joy that they actually did this. They broke the curse. It's over.

Which isn't to say the relief isn't there; it is. Even happiness, too. But it's buried beneath pain because Silas is holding their face, Silas is kissing them, and they can't feel it.

They can't feel him.

When Silas pulls away, his grin melts away like wax on a lit candle. He touches Dami's cheek and pulls his hand away—the moonlight just catches the wet on his thumb. "What's the matter?" he asks. "Why are you crying?"

Are they crying? They couldn't tell. Dami forces a small laugh and quickly wipes their cheeks. "Sorry, sorry, I'm just—" They can't tell him. They can't ruin this for him. They're happy, they *are*, but, god, it's hard to focus on that when so much of this hurts. "I'm just happy," they finish. "I'm so happy, Silas. You're free."

Silas laughs, and then he's crying too, and they hold each other tight. They squeeze their eyes shut as they hold him, as Silas cries into their shoulder.

This time when their tears fall, they don't wipe them away.

Chapter 55

· ·

Silas's boot shifts back and forth on the cobblestone street as the smoke that enveloped them both dissipates. Dami leans against the brick side of someone's home while Silas peers across the street at his own, blinking in the sudden light.

His home. The one he hasn't lived in for well over a year.

The sun is bright and very much up, so though Silas can see Dami, no one else can. They aren't even really leaning against the building as much as not phasing through the brick wall. Silas keeps glancing at them, and people keep glancing at him because to all the rest of the world, Silas is *very* interested in a brick wall.

In truth, he's mostly interested in stalling.

"I don't know what you're waiting for," Dami says. "Go see your mother and sister. You've been waiting for this moment since—"

"That's the problem!" Silas says, then, remembering that no one else can see Dami, lowers his voice. "That's the problem. I've built this moment up and now it's terrifying. What if Maisey panics? Or Mother faints? Or—"

"Why would your mother faint? *She* knows you're not dead."

"I don't know!" Silas exclaims. "I don't know what to expect! They could react badly and—"

"Silas," Dami interrupts. "Your anxiety is adorable but entirely unfounded. They're not going to react badly. They love you. They're going to be ecstatic." They nod to the quiet brick-front home. "Go on. This is going to be amazing."

Silas meets their gaze, his eyes glassy. "I wish I could introduce you to them. They'd love you too."

Dami scoffs. "How would that go? Hello, Mother, sister, this is the demon whose deal tortured me for a year—"

"You saved my life." Silas looks at them intensely. "Don't you realize that? You saved me, and you sacrificed something precious to you to do it. I'll never—" His voice cracks. "I'll never be able to repay you."

They shake their head. "You don't owe me anything. I did it because I wanted to. Now go make it all worth it and see your family."

Silas smiles softly, then takes a deep breath and straightens his shoulders. "All right, but don't leave. I don't want you to disappear."

Dami smirks. "Please, if you think I'm not going to haunt you for the rest of your life, you don't know me."

A s soon as Silas has reached his home's front door, a voice to Dami's left says, "You wouldn't have been happy in a single form."

Dami nearly jumps out of their skin as they turn to face—Juno?

"What?" they sputter. "How are you . . . ? We're not in a place of knowledge."

Juno snorts. "You didn't really think I was restricted to libraries, did you? I'm a diablo. I go where I please." She steps around Dami, her heels clacking against the brick street. She, unlike Dami, can have an actual body in daylight.

Dami tries not to be jealous as they peer back across the street. Silas is hugging a woman and a little girl with long blond ringlets. Everyone seems to be crying, so in a way it's a good thing they couldn't be introduced, so they could avoid that whole mess.

"I was willing to give up transforming for a chance to live," they say at last. "It wouldn't have been perfect, but since I had to choose between the two—"

"And if you didn't have to?"

Dami glances up at her. She's peering at him over her spectacles, smirking softly. It's impossible to be around Juno for long without feeling she knows more than you do—because she does—but something in that smile is more immediate.

"That would . . . be nice," they say. "Obviously if I could be human and also shift my body at will, I would do both. But that was never an option."

"No," she says, "that wasn't an option, but that wasn't what I asked."

Dami's brow furrows. "Then . . . ?" She doesn't answer, but she looks at them expectantly. Dami reviews what they just said. *I was willing to give up transforming for a chance to live. . . .*

When they meet her gaze again, she says, "You don't have to be human for a chance to live. In fact, I don't think you ever wanted to be human at all. I think you just wanted to experience what this world could offer."

"I don't . . ."

"Did you really want to grow old and die?" She laughs. "You?"

"Well, no, but I was going to get plenty of years in before I had to think about that."

"Dami," she says, in the same exasperated tone a parent might use with a stubborn child, "you don't want to be human. You want to be a Daywalker."

Oh.

Oh.

"Only diablos can be Daywalkers," Dami says slowly. "I don't want to put myself through—I know what it takes to become a diablo. I can't pay that price."

Juno shakes her head. "That's not entirely correct. All diablos are Daywalkers, it's true, but diablos also have the power to grant that status to a demonio if they so choose." She lifts a shoulder. "Most diablos just don't choose to do so."

Dami's breath catches in their throat. Is she implying . . . ?

Juno smiles. "I'd be willing to grant you Daywalker status if you agree to work for me."

Yes. The word nearly bubbles out of them, but they catch it on the tip of their tongue, yanking the word back into their throat. Being a Daywalker would be everything they wanted without the sacrifice of their transformative ability. It'd be perfect—but then, "working" for el Diablo had been an unending waking nightmare. Dami can't imagine that being one of Juno's demonios would be anywhere near as terrible, but they know better than to agree to a deal without knowing the terms.

Even if they really, *really* want to agree.

"I assume," they say, working to keep their voice level, "that working for you would mean dealing with knowledge, but not souls. Am I wrong?"

Her smile widens. "You're not wrong. My demonios make deals with humans, of course, but the only souls I deal with are the ones who explicitly want to work for me—and I do those deals myself. You'll never have to Reap a soul again. Those who work for me trade in knowledge: memories, secrets, skills, rare texts and the like."

It's all so overwhelming, so impossibly perfect that Dami feels light-headed. But there has to be a catch. There's *always* a catch.

"You don't do charity," they force themself to say. "So why are you offering me this?"

Juno arches an eyebrow. "Collecting talent for my team is hardly charity. You've always been an exceptional demonio, Dami, but I couldn't offer this until you were free from your prior obligations. Now that you are, I'd prefer to see your skills working for my advantage."

"Hmm," Dami says, holding in a smile. "I suppose I *am* a catch."

Juno's eyes twinkle with laughter. "Do we have a deal?"

S tepping around the corner, sun-warmed skin bright in the daylight, Dami catches the scent of baking bread. Warm, rising flour and butter, mixed with the Boston breeze of summer air. They don't try to hold back the grin spreading across their face as they tilt their face to the sun and close their eyes.

....

It's such a simple pleasure, feeling the heat of the sun on your skin.

They practically skip across the street, and Silas looks up at them with a raised eyebrow as they near. He can see them—of course he can, he could see them all day—but he doesn't know, not yet.

Then Maisey turns around and gives them a curious smile. "Who are you?"

Silas's mouth drops open. "You can see them?"

Maisey wrinkles her nose at Silas. "Of course I can. Why wouldn't I?"

"Sorry I'm late," Dami says with a grin. "My old friend Juno held me up."

Silas's eyes widen as his mother gives them a warm smile. "Silas didn't tell me he was bringing a friend by."

"I—I was about to mention it," he stammers.

"My name is Dami. It's a pleasure to meet all of you."

D ami's legs dangle off the rooftop next to Silas's. They sit hip to hip, on the very same rooftop where Dami found Silas a month ago.

It feels like a lifetime ago.

"So, you're still a demon," Silas says after they finish recapping their deal with Juno. "But you have all your senses."

"I get the best of both worlds," they tell him with a grin. "I can still transform and phase and teleport—all the things I liked about being a demonio—but I can enjoy this world too. I always thought the only way to be a Daywalker is to become a diablo, which requires Reaping *thousands* of souls, but I never have to

....

Reap a soul ever again! I didn't think it was possible, but . . ." They laugh. "It's even better than what I'd hoped for."

Silas grins. "I don't believe I've ever seen you so happy."

"We did what we wanted. You're free from your curse and I'm free from mine."

"What's the first thing you want to do now that you can experience the senses again?"

They know the answer instantly. "Hmm," they say, pretending to think. "This."

This time, when they kiss him, Silas's mouth is warm on theirs. His breath is hot against their skin, his fingers tangling in their hair, his skin so soft in their hands. His lips smile against theirs, and his happiness fills Dami's chest with light. With a calm contentedness carrying them away like a leaf in a warm breeze.

And as they kiss Silas on a rooftop in Boston, they know this is right. This is what they were searching for, what they dreamed of having every dark and hopeless night.

Right now, right here, Dami has never felt more alive.

Acknowledgments

·····························

While I wrote the words that make up the story of *The Diablo's Curse*, this book would not have come together without the support of some truly amazing people, including but not limited to:

Jenna, it was an incredible relief to find that you were just as excited about a Dami book as I was; even better, you understood the story I was trying to tell and helped me bring it to the surface. For every phone call, email, and MS Word comment—thank you.

Louise, can you believe this is the fifth book you've helped me bring into the world? A lot has changed since that first book we worked on together, but your passion for my work, your invaluable expertise, and your infectious excitement have not. Thank you, and the rest of your team, for always having my back.

To the Random House Children's team, including Caroline, Jasmine, Barbara, Denise, and Rebecca, thank you for your help in bringing this story to the page. To Angela and Michelle, I'm always in awe of the details that come together to make the inside and outside of a book beautiful—thank you for making *The Diablo's Curse* shine. And to Josh and Kim, I can't thank you enough for your essential work to help get my books in front of readers. Seriously, thank you, all of you.

Hilary, you should know my jaw dropped the first time I saw the color draft of the cover. I cannot thank you enough for the way you brought the spirit of Dami, Silas, and Marisol's story into a truly badass (and beautiful!) cover. I'm honestly obsessed.

Laura and Alice, I have thrown a *lot* of books at you in recent years, and you have both come through every time with feedback I could not have done without. Mark, Mey, and Shenwei, I can't emphasize enough how valuable your insight was. Thank you all for helping me bring the best version of this book to light.

Bear, you will never know I put you in these acknowledgments, because you can't read, but you *were* adamant about making your mark on this book. I don't know how you managed to insert random letters *and* delete parts of words *throughout the entire manuscript* by stepping on my keyboard *one time* while insisting I stop revising and pet you instead, but you sure did that. I was finding those errors for weeks, but I suppose I'll accept that as the cost of having a floofy lap warmer.

Jay, I can never thank you enough for the many ways you take care of me all the time, but especially when I'm on deadline. Your support, encouragement, and affection mean the world to me. I'm so happy that by the time this book is published, I'll be able to call you my husband. Thank you, my love. I feel so lucky to be yours.

And finally, to you, the reader: Without your support, my dream of becoming a published author would be short-lived. Thank you for giving this book a chance.

About the Author

....

Gabe Cole Novoa (he/him) is a Latinx transmasculine author who writes speculative fiction featuring marginalized characters grappling with identity. Now leveled up with an MFA in writing for children, when he isn't being nerdy at his day job or buried under his TBR pile, you'll likely find him making heart eyes at beautiful yarn or knitting or crocheting something cozy. Gabe is the author of *The Wicked Bargain*, as well as the Beyond the Red trilogy, which was written under a former pseudonym.

GabeColeNovoa.com

▶ @bookishpixie

◎ 𝕏 @thegabecole